LINDSAY BUROKER

STAR KINGDOM
LAYERS OF FORCE
BOOK EIGHT

Layers of Force

Star Kingdom, Book 8

by Lindsay Buroker

Copyright © Lindsay Buroker 2020

No part of this book may be reproduced, scanned, or distributed in any printed or electronic form without permission. Please do not participate in or encourage piracy of copyrighted materials in violation of the author's rights. Thank you for respecting the hard work of this author.

This is a work of fiction. Names, characters, places, and incidents either are the product of the author's imagination or are used fictitiously, and any resemblance to locales, events, business establishments, or actual persons—living or dead—is entirely coincidental.

FOREWORD

THANK YOU FOR PICKING UP LAYERS OF FORCE, the final installment in my Star Kingdom series. I admit that I fell in love with these characters over the course of writing these eight books, and I may return to this universe to tell more stories about them one day, but this wraps up the arc that started way back in Shockwave.

I appreciate you following along with the series, and I hope you have a lot of fun with the last book. It nudged out Book 6 (Planet Killer) to take its place as the longest Star Kingdom novel. Hey, there were a lot of happily ever afters to get worked out!

I would also like to thank my beta readers (Rue Silver, Cindy Wilkinson, and Sarah Engelke) for sticking with me throughout the series, as well as my editor, Shelley Holloway, who barely even grimaces when I thunk down a 150,000-word novel onto her desk (we're all digital these days, so there's not much actual thunking). Also, thank you to Jeff Brown for the fabulous spaceship cover art for this series. Lastly, thanks to Fred Berman and Podium Publishing for all the work on the Star Kingdom audiobooks.

CHAPTER 1

THE LIGHTS CAME ON BRIGHTLY AND ABRUPTLY.

Casmir flinched, banging his head on the wall of his cell. At five-foot-seven, he was far from a big man, but the hard shelf that his guards optimistically called a bunk had clearly been designed to hold potted plants, not a person. *Small* potted plants.

Footsteps sounded in the corridor beyond the translucent forcefield of the cell. Casmir sat up, sneezed, and his left eye blinked twice.

The air of the warship didn't smell like it was full of pollen, dust, or other allergens, but his eyes had been watering for the entire week he'd been cooped up in here, leaving him miserable for more reasons than his possibly impending death. Longing and nostalgia filled him for the cozy guest cabin he'd had on Bonita's *Stellar Dragon*, where the freighter's vacuums also kept everything spotless, even in the ventilation ducts.

He sneezed again.

Perhaps this was a stress response. Or a response to his complete lack of human—or crusher—companionship. The guards rarely spoke to him, and he couldn't access a network to reach out to his friends or family. His tools had been taken, so he couldn't even work on any projects.

He shook his head and decided he would never make it long-term in solitary confinement. Maybe it didn't matter. If King Jager truly believed that Casmir had killed his son, his odds of surviving long-term—or short-term—beyond the interrogation were slim.

The interrogation that was, judging by the two soldiers and the doctor with a medical kit who walked into view, about to happen.

King Jager strode in behind them. Casmir resisted the urge to groan. He debated on flinging himself to his knees and dropping his head, as he had at their first meeting, which had also involved Casmir in a cell and Jager on the other side looking in. He'd gotten out of that predicament. Was there any chance he could do so again?

Jager stopped and faced Casmir through the forcefield, his hands clasped behind his back. He wore a black Fleet galaxy suit and, in lieu of any rank, a purple silver-fur-trimmed cloak. Casmir imagined the gravity going out and the man's head being hopelessly tangled up in the flowing fabric.

Jager's flinty gray-blue eyes narrowed as if he could read these irreverent thoughts.

Casmir pushed himself to his feet and bowed deeply, though he doubted there was any point in trying to ingratiate himself now. He used the gesture to surreptitiously wipe his watering eyes. The last thing he wanted was for the king to believe he was in here weeping. Jager wouldn't be sympathetic to weakness. Instead, Casmir would project competence, confidence, and maybe even gravitas.

"Greetings, Your Majesty. Noble guards. Doctor Interrogator." Unfortunately, his nose rebelled against gravitas, and he sneezed three times and was forced to wipe his eyes again. "There seem to be allergens floating out of the vents here. If you want to let me out for an exercise period, and return my tools, I could take a look at your environmental control unit and give you a tune-up."

The king's cold, craggy expression didn't change.

"That's what you call exercise?" the doctor asked.

"Keeps my hands in shape." Casmir held up his fingers, realized he'd gnawed off his nails during his incarceration, and lowered them. "And I like to be useful."

"Useful." Jager grunted. "Is that what you were doing when you helped that traitor kill my son?"

Helped? Did Jager no longer believe Casmir had done it? That had been his accusation at the beginning of the week.

It might not matter either way. Judging by his icy tone, Jager didn't feel Casmir was any less responsible.

"Which traitor would that be?" he asked, figuring he shouldn't volunteer information.

Jager waved for the guards to leave the area. Maybe this chat was about to become top secret.

They hesitated, but all it took was another narrowing of Jager's eyes, and they scurried out of sight.

"Tenebris Rache," a familiar voice said from off to the side. Lieutenant Meister of Military Intelligence stepped into view with a tablet in hand. "Also known as David Lichtenberg. Also known as your clone brother."

"Ah, *that* traitor. Nice to see you here, Lieutenant. But is Captain Ishii no longer in need of your services on the *Osprey*?"

"You're my new special project," Meister said.

"How delightful for me. And I'm sure it's delighting you as well."

"I want you to ask him everything about Rache and how much they've been working together," Jager told Meister. "And see if he knows where Rache is now."

Casmir would rather have answered questions about himself. He couldn't betray any of his friends—like Kim—if he only spoke about himself. "Does this mean you've realized that I wasn't responsible for Prince Jorg's death and did indeed try to arrive in time to stop it?"

"You're responsible for a great many crimes," Jager said, "including giving that computer virus to Rache so he could render my son's ship defenseless."

Casmir stared bleakly at him. How was it that he had *some* of the details right but not all of them? Such as that the virus had been used on *Dubashi's* ships, not Jorg's?

"That's not what happened, Your Majesty."

"We'll see," Jager said. "Though I care little at this point. You've been a thorn in my side—in the entire Kingdom's side—for months. You will hang for your crimes."

"I guess that means your offer of Princess Oku's hand in marriage is off the table." Casmir dearly wished he'd had an opportunity to say more to her, to at least send a goodbye.

"It has occurred to me that it would be a simple matter to execute you *now*." Jager eyed his doctor's medical kit.

Meister's eyebrows lifted, but he didn't look like he would object.

Casmir scrambled for something he could say to save himself. Ask for one more chance? To—his mind gagged on the word as surely as his throat would—*prove* himself?

"But it's also occurred to me that he might try to rescue you if the word were put out that there will be a public execution." Jager's eyes narrowed thoughtfully.

Casmir didn't have to ask who *he* was. "We're not that close."

"The fact that you keep showing up in his orbit, and vice versa, suggests otherwise."

Casmir wouldn't point out that *Kim* was the only reason Rache kept showing up next to him. Meister ought to know that—he'd figured out *something* back on the *Osprey*—but if he hadn't drawn attention to Kim's possible relationship with Rache to the king... Casmir would do his best to keep it that way. Besides, if Jager wanted a public execution, that would give Casmir more time to possibly come up with something.

"If we did it on the planet," Jager mused, gripping his chin, "he wouldn't be able to skulk in with his camouflaged ship to attack. Not when he knows he could be trapped down there, because his ship would need the launch loop—*my* launch loop—to once again leave Odin's gravity. If we set it up right, Rache would have to come on foot with only the weapons he could carry. On our home turf, our people would have no trouble outmaneuvering him, even if he brought along his entire crew of scruffy mercenaries."

"You could kill Dabrowski today, Sire," Meister said, "not tell anyone, and claim there will be a public execution later."

Casmir gave him a puzzled look, wondering what he'd done to irk the lieutenant so. Was it because of his association with Rache? Or the fact that he'd used his crushers to keep Meister from questioning Kim? Admittedly, during their last encounter, Casmir and his crushers *had* fought a bunch of Kingdom troops and forced their way off the *Osprey*.

Meister shrugged, as if apologetic. His eyes didn't gleam with malicious intent. Maybe this efficiency was his way of sucking up to the king, and he was willing to toss Casmir under the rocket thrusters to do it.

"True. There's time yet to contemplate it. Our escort, speed, and slydar detector should continue to ensure that if Rache is following us, he won't risk bothering us while we're in space. Rache or any of Dabrowski's *other* friends." Jager pinned Casmir with his glare. "It didn't escape my notice that their dilapidated freighter, not to mention that entire fleet of ships that other governments sent, were very reluctant to leave our system. Numerous captains commed us personally to ask where you'd gone, Dabrowski. Were you gathering a fleet for some ambitious *personal* purpose?"

LAYERS OF FORCE

"Just to help the Kingdom with the blockade." Casmir doubted Jager would believe him.

"An act that shouldn't have required suborning two of my knights. Per Baron Farley's suggestion, and my hearty approval, Sirs William and Bjarke Asger have been removed from the knighthood and exiled from the Kingdom."

"They were only trying to help the Kingdom, Your Majesty." Even though Casmir saw there was no point in arguing on his behalf, he hated that he was taking his friends down with him. "And they were crucial in defeating Dubashi and capturing those Drucker ships for the Kingdom's use."

"For *your* use, you mean."

"I wasn't even there for that operation." Casmir kept himself from asking where Asger and Bjarke were now or what had happened to Bonita, Kim, Tristan, Qin, and all of Qin's sisters. And all of his crushers. Had they all been forced to leave the system?

Casmir feared there was nobody around to rescue him from this proposed public execution. Maybe it was for the best. If not for him, then for all of them.

Jager flicked two fingers toward the doctor. "Proceed with the interrogation. I want his version of everything. As I said, I especially want to know what his relationship is with Rache—and if there's a way to use that to get him too."

Casmir closed his eyes and leaned against the wall, hoping he could outsmart the drug enough to keep from babbling about Kim's involvement with Rache. His own story would likely doom him, but he couldn't stomach the idea of taking her down with him.

"I'm ready." The doctor held up an injector, a dubious orange liquid visible inside the capsule.

"I trust that's a drug I'm not allergic to?" If Casmir went into anaphylactic shock, he wouldn't be able to spill everything he knew about Rache, but since they weren't in sickbay, he would prefer that not happen. And since Jager seemed on the fence about delaying his execution, he would rather not make the decision easy for him.

"It's the one we successfully used on you the *last* time we interrogated you," Jager said, as if to remind Casmir of his past miscreant ways.

The forcefield dropped, and Meister and the doctor walked in. There was nowhere for Casmir to run, no way to avoid his fate.

The injector pressed against his neck, bit briefly into his skin, and Casmir slowly lost his will to hide the truth.

The greenhouse looked more like a tornado-swept office than a place for nurturing plants. It wasn't because of the bombing earlier in the month—despite the damage to the rest of the city, neither the castle nor its grounds had been struck—but due to Princess Oku's current obsession.

Her usual seedlings and various botany projects were around, but stacks of already-perused papers competed for space on the workbenches with graphs, spreadsheets, and reports she hadn't yet finished reading.

A woof came from the doorway, where Chasca lay sprawled in a morning sunbeam that stretched across the packed earth floor. Her head lifted, and she perked her gray ears as she looked outside.

"Who's coming?" Oku considered trying to hide the reports, since numerous headers of TOP SECRET were in clear view, but she doubted she had time. "Friend or foe?"

After his collusion with the underground party that had kidnapped—dog-napped—Chasca, Finn had been shipped up to one of the orbital bases to help the Fleet, so Oku wasn't worried about it being her brother, but there could be other people in the castle who wished her ill.

Chasca woofed again, but it was a mild noncommittal woof. Had something as nefarious as a squirrel or groundhog been spying on the greenhouse, she would have bayed like the hound she was.

"There's something blocking the doorway," a woman said from outside, a shadow falling across the dog.

Oku recognized the voice. She wouldn't consider Chief Van Dijk of Royal Intelligence a staunch supporter or faithful ally, but they had reached an understanding and were sharing information now.

"That's my backup bodyguard," Oku said, suspecting Maddie was still outside.

Van Dijk bent and patted Chasca's side. The dog promptly rolled onto her back, all four legs crooked in the air, her gray furry belly available for petting.

"She's very fierce," Van Dijk said.

"Her main method of defending me is by acting as an impediment to foot traffic."

"Somewhat effective." After a few more pats, Van Dijk stepped around the dog and joined Oku at the workbench.

After making a protesting noise, Chasca flopped back over on her side.

Van Dijk opened her mouth to speak but stopped when she noticed the papers. "You printed them *out*?"

"Yes."

"Those are highly confidential. Only three people in my office have access to them. There are more than four hundred people living and working in the castle." Van Dijk waved toward the sprawling stone structure looming to the south of the lawn and greenhouse.

"But only one in here." Oku pointed to her chest.

"There's not a lock on the door. Anyone with access to the grounds could come in anytime."

"Did you forget my traffic impediment?" Oku extended a hand toward Chasca.

Van Dijk, a lean fifty-something woman who'd scraped and clawed her way up the ranks and into her position, did stern and forbidding with effortless ease.

Oku lowered her hand. "I'm a tactile person. I retain things best when I can hold them and highlight and make notes." She waved to Princess Tambora's report. Those three pages had been read more than anything else, as evinced by the dirt smudges all over the corners and margins.

"I trust you'll sufficiently shred or preferably incinerate the papers when you're done fondling them."

"Even better." Oku pointed to her compost tumbler in the corner. "By this time next month, they'll have joined forces with the kitchen scraps to encourage my seedlings to get off to a robust start in life."

"If your father names you as heir, I may have to retire."

"He won't, but I am saddened by your statement. Would you have willingly worked for Jorg?" Oku knew she shouldn't malign her dead brother, especially when they hadn't even had his funeral yet, but Van Dijk's statement had put her on the defensive. She hadn't the training or the interest to rule the Kingdom, but the idea that she was worse than Jorg made her bristle.

"No. I was also going to retire if he came to power."

"What about Finn?"

"Retire and move to a different star system. In three more years, I'll have enough saved for a condo on the beach in Tlaloc's Balneario del Mar."

Oku lifted her eyebrows. "Is that truly your goal?"

"Just a contingency plan." Van Dijk pointed to Tambora's report, the one that detailed everything that had been going on during the time she'd been trapped in System Stymphalia as an invited guest for multinational inter-system gate talks on Stardust Palace Station. She'd sent a neutral third-party report on everything that Casmir Dabrowski and his friends had done there to stop the deceased war instigator Prince Dubashi. Her point of view was refreshingly different from those of the various Kingdom spies and warship commanders. "Have you had any more reports from her?"

"Just a note asking if it would be safe for us to meet and resume our work on the bee project now that the blockade is down. I told her it's probably not safe here yet and that I can't leave until…" Until she figured out a way to get Casmir off her father's warship and help him clear his name. The latest reports said he was locked in the brig and being interrogated and transported back to Odin. "Things are settled," Oku finished.

"Good. I've recommended to your mother that you not be allowed to leave the castle for now. We still haven't nailed down Finn's dubious allies—those who were trying to use him to get rid of you. They may strike again."

"Mother only suggested to me that I shouldn't plan travel out of the system right now."

"Or travel out the front door."

"So I'm a prisoner?" How was Oku supposed to help Casmir if she was grounded like a rebellious teenager?

"You're being protected for your own good. Temporarily. I'm willing to share one more report with you, from Captain Ishii on the *Osprey*, but you must agree to have your new chip tagged so we can once again track you. Again, for your own good."

Oku winced. She'd been using that as a bargaining chip, to get Van Dijk to give her all the information related to Casmir's space adventures of the last few months. Her father thought Casmir had been working at odds with the Kingdom, trying to gain allies in the other systems, and perhaps control of that ancient gate for himself. Oku hadn't believed that, but she had to know the truth.

And Van Dijk *had* given her the reports. Even though they had confirmed that Casmir wasn't obediently doing as her father had requested—even Tambora's report seemed to suggest that—he had *helped* the Kingdom on numerous occasions. Several unbiased reports said he'd been responsible for keeping Prince Dubashi from enlarging his fleet to truly threaten the Kingdom, and he had ultimately been responsible for the prince's death. Surely, Casmir's assistance in thwarting him trumped some independent thinking in regard to the gate project.

"Oku?" Van Dijk prompted. "Were you serious when you said you would consider it, or were you prevaricating with me?"

"No. I was serious. I'll allow it. I was just concerned you would stop giving me information once the procedure was done."

"I won't. You're one of your father's heirs. You *have* the clearance to see this stuff. In the past, you hadn't shown any interest."

"I know."

"I'm pretending your current interest is due to an awakened passion for understanding the political, societal, and interstellar-relations concerns to the Kingdom rather than a crush on a boy."

"It's not a crush." Heat warmed Oku's cheeks. "I just don't want to see him imprisoned or *executed* when he's been acting for the good of our people."

"Your father believes he was responsible for Jorg's death."

"He wasn't."

"Ambassador Romano's report says otherwise."

"He didn't do it. He's not a murderer."

"Has he told you that?"

"No. He hasn't messaged me since our forces returned to System Lion. I assume he's not *able* to message me right now." Oku hoped that was due to network-muffling technology in the brig, not a forced removal of his chip.

"Likely not."

"What would he have gained from even assisting someone to kill Jorg?"

"Putting you as next-in-line for your father's throne."

If Oku had been sitting on her stool, she would have fallen off. "I'm positive that's not a goal of his. It's certainly not a goal of mine. Even if it were, the Senate would never agree to me as heir to the Kingdom. Father will adjust his will and figure something out when he gets back, something that has nothing to do with me."

"We'll see." Van Dijk touched Oku's temple, where her new chip was embedded, sans monitoring capability. "Do you want Captain Ishii's report?"

"You know I do." Even if it said derogatory things about Casmir, or simply backed up everything the ambassador had said, Oku wanted it. She'd been making charts as she pieced together all the reports—finding the commonalities even from those with starkly different viewpoints.

"Then you'll let our doctor modify your chip?"

"Now?"

"Yes."

Oku slumped against the workbench. She knew this not only meant that Royal Intelligence would be able to track her; it meant that they would be able to monitor all of her messages again, even those that were encrypted. If Casmir ever were to escape and contact her… they would know about it.

"I think you'll want to read it," Van Dijk said quietly. "It's in opposition to most of what Romano sent in his."

Oku knew she was being manipulated, but she wanted the report. Especially if it might shine a different light on what had happened with Jorg's death.

And, if she ever had to, she ought to be able to take her chip offline to avoid being tracked. Nobody, including Casmir, would be able to message her then, but at least it was an option.

"Very well," she said.

Captain Ishii's report arrived, the alert popping up on Oku's contact.

Before she could start reading, Van Dijk called, "She's ready," out the door.

A familiar doctor from Royal Intelligence leaned inside with a medical bag in hand. He walked around Chasca, whose eyes were closed as she basked in the sun. Some backup bodyguard.

"Have you had any contact with Scholar Kim Sato?" Van Dijk asked, moving papers aside so the doctor had space for his tools.

"Not for some time." Oku had almost forgotten about Kim. She would have guessed that her father had taken her into custody, too, but few of the reports had mentioned her.

LAYERS OF FORCE

"There are rumors that she and our disgraced knights, the Asgers, didn't leave the system on their friend's freighter." Van Dijk raised her eyebrows. "Your father wants to make sure nobody is going to attempt to *rescue* Dabrowski."

That information made Oku want to contact Kim promptly to see if there was any hope that she and Casmir's friends *did* plan to rescue him. But if she did, it would have to be soon. In the next two minutes. As soon as the doctor installed the monitoring software on her chip, Oku wouldn't dare contact anyone who might be thinking of committing a crime.

"It wouldn't be wise," Van Dijk said softly. "The king's warship is now outfitted with a slydar detector, so no ship would be able to sneak up on it."

Oku couldn't keep her mouth from twisting with bitterness. She'd read a few reports on the new slydar detectors, enough to learn that Casmir had been the one to replicate the schematics and send them along to the Kingdom so they could start making their own. Another reason he should not be a prisoner, but rather a hero of the Kingdom. Unfair if the detectors were the reason his friends couldn't now rescue him.

"Almost ready," the doctor said, pulling out not a medical device but a wireless chip adjustment tool.

If Oku planned to contact Kim, she needed to do it now. But there wouldn't be time to compose much of a message.

An idea burst into her mind. Possibly a very bad idea.

As the doctor leaned close, Oku bundled up all of the reports Van Dijk had shared with her—all of the top-secret reports that only a handful of people were cleared to see—and sent them off to Kim Sato with a hasty message of, *Use these if you can to help Casmir, but don't contact me about any of it. My chip is monitored.*

Oku's heart hammered rapidly against her ribcage. It was an act of treason, and as soon as she did it, she second-guessed herself. If she was caught, her punishment would be far worse than confinement to the castle.

She also worried that Kim wouldn't be able to do anything with the reports—it wasn't as if any of them had blueprints to her father's warship—and that it had been a foolish risk to take. Kim might not even be in the system.

The cool tip of the doctor's tool touched her temple. Oku prayed that she'd guessed right and that the monitoring software would only be able to see messages sent *after* it was installed.

"All done," he said cheerfully.

"Thank you, Doctor," Oku made herself say.

Van Dijk's expression was impossible to read. All she said, as she headed for the exit, was, "Make sure to destroy all those documents when you're done with them."

"I will," Oku murmured.

CHAPTER 2

THE *STELLAR DRAGON* FLEW AWAY FROM THE WORMHOLE gate in System Stymphalia as Bonita sat in navigation, wondering why all roads led back to Stardust Palace Station these days.

After leaving System Lion more than a week earlier, ordered to do so by the pompous commanders of the Kingdom warships they'd left guarding their gate, she'd picked up a cargo in System Hind, destination Stardust Palace. After she delivered it, she planned to return to System Lion to see if their obnoxious fleet had flown off, and travel was once again allowed into their system. Ideally, she would find a cargo that needed to go that way to give her a legitimate reason to return.

Given all that had happened, Bonita would have been happy never to see the stars of that system again, but she'd left Qin and all of her sisters there. Qin had insisted. They planned to rescue Casmir.

A worthwhile goal, but Bonita worried they would get themselves killed. Along with Bjarke and Asger. Even Princess Nalini's Tristan had joined them, transferring over to Rache's *Fedallah* for a stealthy stalking of the Kingdom warship that had taken Casmir. As far as Bonita knew, Tristan didn't have a reason to help, other than feeling obligated to assist his fellow knights. *Ex*-knights. Or maybe he felt he owed something to Casmir for helping to defend Stardust Palace.

But what if they *all* ended up dead? Bonita would be alone with no crew, no friends.

She stared bleakly at the stars on the forward display. It was strange to realize that less than a year ago, that had been her normal life. No crew, no friends. Oh, she'd had husbands and lovers now and then over the years, but until Qin had joined her, the ship had regularly been empty, save for her and Viggo.

"Do you wish me to lay in a course for Stardust Palace, Bonita?" Viggo asked.

A couple of his vacuums whirred in the corridor behind navigation.

"I guess. I was just mulling."

"Are you considering returning to the Kingdom's system to help with the rescue of Casmir?" Not surprisingly, Viggo sounded hopeful.

"I would gladly help if those cranky warships weren't hovering by their gate, threatening to blow up anyone who isn't carrying a Kingdom flag."

"It is unfortunate that my magnificent flanks do not have a slydar coating so we could have stealthily remained in the system and slipped past them."

"Your magnificent what?"

"Flanks."

"You have a hull, not flanks. You're a ship, not a racehorse."

"I am sleek and fast like a racehorse, but one of the definitions of the word is *the side of something large, such as a mountain, building, or ship.*"

"I stand corrected."

"Yes."

Bonita reached for the navigation arm, intending to start them toward the station.

"Wait a moment," Viggo said. "There are some ships heading in this direction. We may wish to move off to the side."

"We shouldn't be in the way." Bonita had already moved them, so they were not in front of the gate, but she checked the scanner display.

"Let me clarify. We may wish to move the ship to the side to ensure we are not anywhere near what appear to be hostile actions."

A freighter more than ten times the size of the *Dragon* had flown out of the gate behind them. It had been on a heading for the inner system, and Bonita hadn't thought anything of it, but energy signatures lit up the scanners. Weapons fire?

Aside from the automated patrol ship that kept people from diddling with the wormhole gate, no other ships appeared to be in the immediate area. Nonetheless, the freighter was under attack.

As Bonita watched, the freighter fired back with four railguns mounted above and below its rectangular exterior. Each one opened fire in a different direction. In turn, it was being peppered from all sides.

"I believe it is being attacked by heavily armed ships with slydar hulls," Viggo explained unnecessarily. "Four, judging by the origins of the weapons fire. The freighter's shields will fail soon."

Bonita flew the *Dragon* away from the battle. Whatever this was about, she didn't have the defenses or the firepower to get involved.

As predicted, the shields failed on the big freighter, and after a few more blasts from enemy ships, its power went out. Even if she'd had the capacity to help, there wouldn't have been time.

"Damn, that was fast."

"Indeed," Viggo murmured.

Worried the camouflaged ships would turn on the *Dragon*, Bonita held her breath as she flew them farther away. The scanners could not detect anything nearby, save for the broken hull of the freighter, but she expected an ambush any moment. Only as long seconds dribbled past without so much as a comm message did she let herself believe that her ship might not be targeted.

"Not that I'm ungrateful, but why didn't they attack us?" Bonita shook her head. Those hidden ships must have watched the *Dragon* sail out of the gate. "Could they have known we've got nothing but grain in our cargo hold?"

As far as she knew, even the best scanners could only make guesses about a cargo if it didn't put out an energy signature.

"I do not know, but I can tell you that they are not carrying grain," Viggo said.

"Who's not? The freighter?"

"Yes." Viggo used an exterior camera to put a visual of the freighter on their display. "Despite the ship now being without power, I am reading an energy signature in its hold. A familiar one."

As Bonita started to check the scanners again, something flew in front of the freighter, half blocking it from view. All she could see were blurry stars and black space, but because the camouflaged ship was in front of the freighter, Bonita could tell something was there.

"Something big," she muttered.

"Indeed. They're forcing open the cargo-bay doors."

"Pirates stealing cargo then."

"Pirates stealing a cargo that gives off the energy signature of one of those gate pieces. Perhaps several of them. It is difficult to tell through the other ship."

Bonita had the computer grab the freighter's identification number and ran it through the database. "They're out of System Boar, registered to Shango Habitat. According to this, the freighter usually only travels in its own system and picks up and delivers agricultural products for its denizens. I wonder how they got a gate piece. And why they were bringing it here."

"Perhaps for study at Stardust Palace? The sultan was hosting those talks about the gate. Perhaps now that Prince Dubashi has been defeated, they are resuming."

"You think everyone who got a gate piece was supposed to bring it along for Show and Tell?" Bonita asked.

"I do not know, but my scanners tell me that the hidden ship has removed four gate pieces from the cargo hold. It is now moving away from the freighter."

"Without bothering to close the doors, I see. Rude."

"Pirates usually are."

Bonita nibbled on the end of her braid, checking the scanners again and hoping the pirates, or whoever they were, neither noticed them nor cared about them. If they decided to eradicate any witnesses, she doubted the *Dragon* could escape their reach or survive their firepower.

"I can no longer read the gate power signatures," Viggo said. "Their hold must have the power to insulate them."

A little burst of energy on the scanners made Bonita flinch. But it wasn't weapons fire. "The gate—the *working one*—is activating."

"Those ships must be leaving the system."

"To go where?"

"I do not know."

Once the silvery gate field winked out, Bonita leaned back in her pod, relaxing slightly.

"Several ships from Sultan Shayban's fleet are heading in this direction," Viggo said. "They are a day away, but they may have witnessed that attack."

"We can't get in trouble for this, right? We just happened to be in the area."

"I do not know," he repeated.

Bonita sighed. "We better comm them preemptively and tell them what we saw. Or what we *didn't* see."

"A sound idea. I will prepare the footage to share. It is possible that those were pirates, but given how swiftly and effectively they disabled that ship and stole the gate pieces, I believe those may have been astroshaman vessels."

"Wonderful." Reluctantly, Bonita reached for the comm. "I miss the good old days when the Twelve Systems were reasonably normal, nobody major was at war with anybody else, and the astroshamans were happy plugging their heads into computers and leaving everyone alone."

"I miss Qin and Casmir."

"That too."

Kim Sato sat in Rache's briefing room, a coffee mug in her hand, and the Kingdom warships the *Starhawk, Kestrel,* and *Eagle* on the wall display.

For the entire trip, the *Fedallah* had been six hours behind them, out of range of the king's new slydar detector on the *Starhawk*. Twelve smaller ships also accompanied the fleet, out of range of the camera's viewing area. She had seen them earlier on the scanners. Two other warships, the *Osprey* and the *Raven*, had also left the gate mop-up to others and were flying a few hours behind the *Fedallah*.

It would be suicidal for Rache to attack, or even get closer, so Kim hadn't suggested it. But she longed to find some brilliant way that they could rescue Casmir.

Tristan, Bjarke and William Asger, Qin and all of her sisters, and Zee and more than twenty of Casmir's crushers were aboard, as eager as she was to do something. But Kim and all of her combat-specialist allies could do nothing unless they could get aboard the same ship that Casmir was on.

At this point, she did not know for certain that he was still alive over there. He hadn't responded to her messages, so she had been assuming that his cell blocked network access. But it was also possible… Kim swallowed. Jager hated him, and Casmir was horrible at being the meek sycophant he should be around authority figures. He could already be dead.

Kim pushed her mug forward and let her forehead thunk onto the table.

The door opened, and Rache walked in. She turned her head enough to look at him, but it seemed too much effort to raise it again.

As usual, he wore his galaxy suit, mask, and hood. They'd spent time alone together on the trip, and he had taken the costume off then, but despite outing his real name to Jorg in front of his men, he maintained the mysterious facade when anyone was around. Maybe after ten years, it was a hard habit to break.

"Do you have new information?" Rache asked after the door closed. "Or is your heavy head a sign of continuing distress over the current predicament?"

"The latter." Kim lifted her head. "I was realizing that Casmir might not even be alive. Unfortunately, I don't have any contacts on those ships that I could ask."

Kim had thought about reaching out to Dr. Sikou on the *Osprey*, but she wouldn't likely know what was happening in the brig on the *Starhawk*. Besides, if her team *did* get a chance to stage a rescue operation, it would be better if nobody in the Fleet knew that she or any of the others were still in the system.

"No word from Casmir?" Rache—one of these days, she should start thinking of him as David—lifted a hand, as if he would touch her on his way by, but he lowered it and simply took a seat beside her.

"Nothing."

"You may have to wait until the *Starhawk* reaches orbit. If Jager means to keep him alive, he will likely send Casmir down to the planet in a shuttle, at which point, he should have network access again."

If.

"What if they take the whole warship down?" Or what if they got the intel they needed out of Casmir's brain, and Jager had him executed before they reached Odin? Kim curled her fingers into a fist, aching to catch up and do something *now*.

"Those warships aren't designed to land on a planet. He'll be transferred in a shuttle."

"But will he still be alive for it?" She stared bleakly at the table, unable to get the dark thoughts out of her mind.

Another man might have wrapped an arm around her shoulders and told her comforting lies. Rache did not. She was glad. Unless he had actual intelligence that promised Casmir was alive and safe, at least for the moment, she wouldn't have been fooled.

"I have Amergin monitoring the *Starhawk*," Rache said, "and ordered him to let me know if he caught and decrypted any messages related to Casmir. There hasn't been anything yet."

"If it's feasible, will you help me get him? Casmir?" Kim gazed at his masked face. "I appreciate that you picked us all up to bring to Odin, but you haven't mentioned if you'll do more than drop us off and then go pursue your own mission." She tried to keep any accusation out of her tone, but she wanted to rail at him that there was no point to worrying about assassinating Jager now. Dubashi, the person who'd hired him to do the job, was dead. She knew Rache wanted his revenge on Jager and would happily kill him regardless of payment, but she also knew he didn't expect to survive the mission, and she wished he would abort it.

"I've been considering options," he said neutrally.

What did *that* mean?

"Such as giving us a shuttle so we can try to hijack the one you think Casmir will be sent down to Odin in? I have *plenty* of combat troops." She waved in the direction of the cargo bay where she'd last seen the crushers, Qin and her sisters, and Tristan, Asger, and Bjarke sparring with each other.

"Yes, you do. But my shuttles don't have slydar hulls. If you attack one of Jager's flagship's shuttles, the entire planetary defense forces will be on you like ants on a fallen hot dog bun at a picnic."

"Clump of rice," she muttered.

"What?"

"My family always brought rice balls and tamagoyaki to picnics."

"Were the ants as excited about the droppings?"

"Ants will eat anything." Kim tugged at her ponytail, imagining a hundred fighter ships streaking into the sky to attack them before they managed to get Casmir out of his shuttle. "Do you have any better rescue suggestions?"

"Yes, but you won't like them."

"Do they involve killing legions of people?"

Casmir would object to people being killed during any effort to rescue him, especially Kingdom people, but she didn't know if she cared anymore. His brain was worth saving. *He* was worth saving.

"Possibly not legions, but I doubt I could execute my plan without killing anyone."

He had an actual plan? For rescuing Casmir? And he was willing to set it into motion instead of veering off to assassinate Jager? Or—she squinted at him—did he have something in mind where he would attempt to accomplish both goals in one swoop? And if so, would it be worth helping him, knowing she might end up assisting in assassinating her own king?

A message came in on Kim's chip before she could ask him for clarification. It was from Princess Oku.

Hm, there was a contact that she hadn't considered. But Oku was on Odin. Would she know anything about Casmir? And if she did, would she share the information?

Oku and Casmir had been pen pals for the duration of this journey, and Casmir got dreamy eyes whenever he spoke about her, but Kim didn't truly know if the princess felt anything for him.

And, after a bunch of files and a warning not to contact her arrived in her inbox, Kim *still* didn't know.

"Kim?" Rache lowered his head so he could peer into her eyes. "I won't presume to touch you, since you've expressed feelings of aversion for that, but you're ignoring me instead of asking about my plan, so I'm moderately concerned."

She sat back in her seat. "Do women usually not ignore you?"

"It's not typical, no. Women love a man in a mask."

"I'm going to need to see some unbiased data to back that up." Kim opened the files Oku had sent and sifted through them. "I suspect women are more likely to think a man in a mask is a stalker."

"That's an unknown man in a mask. A *known* man in a mask is intriguing."

"And yet, you're not sending me any data to validate your assertions."

"Dating a scientist is difficult."

"I've admitted to being complicated." She held up a finger and lowered her voice. "Princess Oku sent me a bunch of reports. Military reports. From captains in the Kingdom Fleet, all with information pertaining to the gate quest and dealing with Dubashi and Shayban in System Stymphalia. Here are some from Ambassador Romano." Kim scowled, positive those would be full of lies. "And a couple from Princess Tambora. Remember her from Tiamat Station?"

"Yes. The girl we hauled out of the wreckage. That all sounds like information that would be top secret and out of Military or Royal Intelligence. It's surprising Oku has it and even more surprising that she would have the authority to send it to you."

"Maybe she *doesn't* have the authority. She only wrote one line to go with the files, one that told me not to contact her."

"Her chip would be monitored. That's standard operating procedure for the heirs."

"Then she risked a great deal in sending these files?"

"Likely so."

"What does she expect me to do with them?" Kim rested a hand on her chest. "I need to read through everything, but unless there's something about Jager's plans for Casmir, I don't see how this could help me get him out of the brig."

"I don't know."

"Do you think she likes Casmir? Enough to risk getting in trouble for him?"

Rache spread a gloved hand. "It's been more than ten years since I spoke with her, and I never knew her well. She's a scientist, so she's probably more complicated than I realized at the time."

"As all scientists are."

"So I'm learning." He sounded like he was smiling. "Casmir should try wearing a mask when he communicates with her."

"Thus ensuring she would be intrigued by him?"

"As we've discussed."

Kim wished she could smile, but it was hard to enjoy this time here with him when Casmir was in trouble and when Rache was likely still on his mission to assassinate Jager. She doubted it was only for her and Casmir's sake that he was chasing after the king's flagship while transporting a bunch of knights that he loathed.

"What's the plan you mentioned earlier, masked man?" Kim asked.

"Kidnap Finn and offer him up in trade for Casmir," he said promptly.

"Uhm, what?"

"If Jager stays in orbit with the Fleet, which he may until he's certain that all threats to the Kingdom have been mopped up, the castle won't be as heavily guarded and hard to get into as usual. He'll have a lot of his best troops up there with him. I also have personal knowledge of the castle's layout and underground tunnels, since I was there a number of times as a boy, and Jorg liked to show off the place. Amergin can probably get me further details on current security. I might be able to get in, collect Finn, and get out again."

"But why him?"

"Jager won't risk losing his last male heir, and he won't assume I'm bluffing if I threaten to kill him."

"*Would* you be bluffing?" Kim should reject his plan outright instead of questioning it, since kidnapping and ransom were worse crimes than simply trying to rescue Casmir.

"Finn is a whiny brat. The Kingdom wouldn't miss him."

Kim dropped her head into her hands. "Rache, you can't kill the entire line of succession."

"It would be difficult to get him, I'll admit. Even with Jager out of the castle."

"That's *not* what I meant."

"If Jager trades Casmir to me for Finn, then the boy needn't be killed. At least not by my hand this week. Someone will likely take him out someday."

With her head still in her hands, Kim said, "I can't be a part of that."

"I'm not asking you to be. I'll handle it."

"Rache. *David*... Casmir wouldn't want it done that way."

"Casmir isn't on the network for consultation."

"Will you lend us a shuttle and let us try rescuing him during the transfer first?"

"That would put you in extreme danger. I'm positive Jager will be ready for rescue attempts. Even if he was half-assed about the transfer, which I doubt he would be, Odin's airspace is well-defended, especially now. They've got double the usual patrols in orbit and in the skies in the aftermath of the attacks."

That sounded like it meant he wouldn't give her a shuttle.

Sighing, Kim poked into Oku's files, hoping to find something among the reports that would be useful in retrieving Casmir. But all they did was share the information she already knew, from the viewpoints of all the actors who'd been out there on the stage. There were a few new tidbits, but it was all details of the past, nothing about Jager's plans for the future. With the information, she could write a *book*... but not plan a rescue.

LAYERS OF FORCE

"I will lend you a shuttle," Rache said quietly. His tone wasn't grudging or reluctant, but it did convey that he thought it was a bad idea. "If that is what you wish."

"Thank you."

Kim clasped her hands and stared down at them. Should she start making plans with Asger and the others? Or should she heed Rache's wisdom in this? Trying to get to the shuttle in Odin's airspace might very well be suicidal.

But Rache's alternative suggestion was too despicable. Too *criminal*.

"Your uproarious enthusiasm suggests I've made the right choice," he said dryly.

"I don't know how to be uproarious."

"You must have been a delight at birthday parties growing up."

"I didn't get invited to that many." After the words came out, she realized they sounded self-pitying. She wasn't looking for pity, especially from him, when he'd been through so much. And if she was honest with herself, she'd always preferred privacy and books to awkward social interactions with other people, even as a child.

"Because of your inability to uproar?" was all he asked.

"Ha ha." Kim thumped him on the shoulder, as the teasing comments deserved, but she let her hand drop to his arm, groping for a way to thank him for supporting her in this, even if he thought it was a bad idea. "I don't have an *aversion* to touching, by the way. I mean, I do, but it's not that bad if I know it's coming."

"So I have to warn you before spontaneously touching the back of your head?"

"Ideally."

He lifted his hand as if in offering. She would feel silly getting a head massage or whatever he planned from someone wearing a mask and gloves, but she did appreciate that he was helping her—again. For whatever reason, he'd become a silent guardian for her, assisting her from a distance whenever he could. As much as she preferred being independent and not needing assistance, her life had grown so unpredictable and uncontrollable of late that it was nice to have someone watching out for her.

She leaned toward him and rested her head on his shoulder. He wrapped his arm around her and brought a hand up to stroke the side of her head.

"Have you had time—or perhaps the muse—to write another short story?" he asked. "I assume having your best friend's life at stake dampens creativity."

"It *has* been difficult to do more than worry."

"And work out? My men have reported seeing you in the gym, kicking the hanging bags. They say they give you a wide berth, having heard rumors about you kicking Corporal Meatpaw across a submarine a few weeks back."

"It's good to have a place to take out my aggressions." She smiled, still amused, and a little pleased, that her brutalizing his men seemed to please him. A strange thing to like in a scientist, but Rache must prefer quirky women. "As for the story, you're right. I haven't been inspired. I wish we had more time."

"Time is short."

"It's a shame because a story written with all this information—" Kim waved at her chip to indicate the reports, "—could be almost as useful for extortion as a kidnapped heir. A novel that one could threaten to distribute widely to the public for free if demands weren't met."

She would *love* a chance to show that Casmir had been helping the Kingdom—and that Ambassador Romano and Jager were huge assholes. She would find a more literary way to say that, but she was positive she could get the point across.

"You *sell* novels, Kim; you don't distribute them for free. People value things they pay for."

"Alas, as you said, there's not time to do either."

"*Do* let me know if you decide to try. I wasn't joking when I said I would start a publishing company for you."

"I appreciate that," she whispered, touched anew at the thought.

If he hadn't been wearing that mask, she might have kissed him. She turned her face toward his. Maybe he would remove it…

Before she could suggest it, the door slid open, and Rache dropped his arm. Kim straightened in her seat as one of his men walked in, the intelligence officer with all the cybernetic hardware attached to his face and skull under a wide-brimmed hat.

"Sorry to interrupt, sir." The man waved apologetically, then lurched into a bow, as if he thought that might be more appropriate, but it wasn't an oft-practiced bow. "I've got some intel."

"On Dabrowski?" Rache's calm tone didn't let on whether he was annoyed by the interruption.

Kim supposed they could have gone to his quarters if they'd wanted privacy.

"Yes, sir. The word is that when the *Starhawk* arrives in orbit, Jager is sending him down in a shuttle to a maximum-security prison in Zamek City. Dabrowski is to be kept there for two days and then executed in public at the university where he once worked."

"*Executed?* In *public?*" Kim couldn't keep from gaping at the man. "What is this? The Spanish Inquisition on Old Earth? Public executions have never existed in the Kingdom, not even in the early days of the colonization." Criminals were either rehabilitated or condemned to work the asteroid mines. Kim could see why Jager might want Casmir dead, though she vehemently objected to the idea that he deserved that, but it was against the law. And surely he above all people had to be seen upholding the law. If he wanted Casmir dead, he would—should—make him quietly disappear in the night, poisoned by some henchman. This was madness.

Horror filled her as she imagined all of Casmir's colleagues and former students there at the university to witness... What? A hanging? A beheading? What medieval execution method would Jager dredge up? She blinked at incipient tears as she realized Casmir's *parents* would also see it. They lived only a few miles from the university. And would it be televised? Like some sporting event?

"Sorry, ma'am," the intelligence officer said. "Just reporting what I heard."

"You found this by intercepting an encrypted transmission from the *Starhawk* and decrypting it?" Rache's tone remained steady, almost indifferent, as if this announcement didn't horrify him at all.

"Uh, no, sir. It was on the news."

"The news?"

"We've been monitoring the Kingdom media channels as well as transmissions between the Fleet ships. There's been nothing about Dabrowski that we've been able to snag from their communications. This is the first time his name has come up."

"I see. Very well. Keep monitoring, and keep me informed."

"Yes, sir." The man hurried out of the briefing room, the door sliding shut again.

"Not the Spanish Inquisition," Rache said. "*The Art of War.*"

Kim frowned at him, sifting through her memories of Sun Tzu. She'd read it not for any training as a bacteriologist, but before she had written her fantasy novels. Even allegorical battlefield commanders were supposed to act logically, after all.

"You think it's a trap?"

"In a position of this sort," he quoted, "even though the enemy should offer us an attractive bait, it will be advisable not to stir forth."

"Not stirring forth isn't an option, Rache. I see what you're saying, that Jager may be announcing the execution publicly to lure Casmir's friends into rescuing him, but if we do nothing, he may truly kill Casmir."

"I didn't say do nothing."

"We're not kidnapping Finn."

She couldn't see his eyebrows, but she was positive that they twitched. "Do you really think Jager cares enough about the rest of us to arrange some elaborate trap to ensnare us?"

"To ensnare you? Unlikely. He may be irked enough with his wayward knights to do it, but my gut tells me he's trying to get *me*."

"You? You think you've helped Casmir enough times—and that Intelligence has figured that out—that Jager believes you'll rescue him?"

"He may."

That was a stretch, but then again… Kim wasn't *positive* that Rache was only flying in this direction because of his assassination vendetta. He needn't have picked them all up if that was all that motivated him.

"When you hunt through those reports, do let me know if you find mentions of my name. It would be valuable to know what Jager's officers believe."

Kim nodded. "I will."

"And also realize that Jager has had Casmir for a week. Plenty of time to run interrogations on him and learn everything *he* believes."

"I doubt Casmir believes you would come rescue him, but I see your point."

Rache rose to his feet. "We've got two days before we reach Odin's orbit. I'll reach out to some contacts who might know more. I suggest you do the same. I will lend you a shuttle, but I ask that you operate under the assumption that this is all a trap and nothing that comes out of those Kingdom warships can be trusted."

Kim nodded. "I will."

She also had to operate under the assumption that Casmir was still alive. The idea that Jager might have already questioned him and killed him—and that she and Rache and everyone might risk themselves for nothing—plagued her mind.

CHAPTER 3

"**YOU HAVE NOT ALLOWED YOURSELF TO GET SOFT,** Squirt. That is good."

Qin hid her grimace as she pushed herself to her feet. Her back, hip, and shoulder all ached after being hurled into a wall in the cargo hold of Rache's ship. *Again.* She and her sisters had been sparring all morning.

"Thank you, Mouser." She managed a smile and refused to show that her body ached. This was their sixth day in a row of such exercises, and she reminded herself that they had been *her* idea. At least she wasn't facing off against one of the crushers. Asger and Tristan were particularly interested in practicing on them—maybe because they feared they would have to battle enemy crushers again soon. "You're also not soft."

"I know I'm not." Mouser flashed her fangs and flexed her biceps. Since they weren't wearing combat armor, the muscles were visible under the thin material of her galaxy suit.

"Break time," Asger called over the thumps, clangs, and bangs of the various sparring matches. "Kim is coming down. We're going to talk about a plan to rescue Casmir."

Numerous feminine cheers filled the hold. Though Qin's sisters hadn't met Casmir in person yet, they knew that he had been responsible for the computer virus that had allowed Qin, Asger, Bjarke, and the crushers to take over the Drucker pirate ships—and rescue Qin's sisters. They also knew he had built the crushers that were traveling with them.

Most of those crushers did not speak much and silently turned their attention toward Asger, but one spoke up. Zee. "This is excellent news. We must rescue Casmir Dabrowski posthaste. I am unable to fulfill my foundational program to protect him when I am not with him. It is egregious that I was forbidden to go along with him."

"I agree." Asger thumped Zee on the back as he headed over to Qin and Mouser. "Are you all right, Qin? I saw that last throw. It was firm."

"I'm fine," Qin said. "I'm not soft."

"When I say firm, I mean there's a dent in that wall. And you're not wearing your armor."

"That dent is from earlier when I threw Mouser twenty feet into that spot."

"It's true." Mouser nodded and looked Asger up and down. It was assessing, but Qin couldn't tell if she was determining what fighting him would be like or admiring his physique—which was also not soft. "Do you really have a castle?"

"On my family's estate, yes. It's technically my father's castle." Asger's expression turned glum. "Or it was. Since our superior, Baron Farley, informed both of us that we've been removed from the knighthood and may not return home, it's possible we've already been stripped of our noble status. And our citizenship."

"Does that mean someone else gets the castle?" Qin imagined some real estate agent listing it for sale.

"My cousin, I suppose. Or my father's brother. I'm not sure who he's officially got down as the next heir. But at one point, he was threatening to disown me and give everything to my cousin."

Mouser looked at Qin. "It's possible his offer to let us stay in his castle was not a genuine promise."

"No, it was," Asger said. "We weren't in exile at the time. It's still possible... Well, I don't know. I'm not ready to give up on getting my good name back."

"Is that why you switched sides and helped me against the Druckers?" Qin asked Mouser. "Because you wanted to stay in a castle?"

"Well, obviously." Mouser flashed her fangs again, this time with a big grin. "Hanging out on Rache's ship wasn't the fantasy I had in mind."

"Me either," Asger said grimly.

Kim walked in, thankfully sans Rache, and headed toward their group. Bjarke and Tristan, who'd been sparring partners earlier, also came over. The crushers and the rest of Qin's sisters drew close enough to listen.

"You've heard the news about the public execution?" Kim asked them.

"Yes, and that Casmir is to be sent down from orbit in a shuttle and that Casmir will be held in a prison in the city until it's time for it."

Asger raised his eyebrows. "Our options are to attack the shuttle or to wait and break him out of the prison before the execution."

"Rache is willing to lend us a shuttle for our combat team—" Kim waved at their large group, "—but he also thinks it's a trap and that Casmir might not be on the indicated shuttle, nor going to the prison."

"I had that thought also," Bjarke said. "The public execution is unorthodox and without precedent."

"And *illegal*." Kim frowned.

Qin didn't point out that they were all flying around in the very criminal and illegal warship of a notorious mercenary who was wanted dead a thousand times over in this system.

"Since Jager claimed King's Authority," Bjarke said, "he may think himself above the law. Or at least that he can act with impunity."

"Do you have any contacts in the Fleet or the castle or Royal Intelligence who might be willing to give us information?" Kim looked at Asger and his father. "*Real* information?"

Asger sighed. "I tried getting in touch with Captain Ishii, but he's revoked permission for me to contact his chip."

"I had a similar experience with Baron Farley and my peers in the knighthood that I reached out to," Bjarke said. "We are personae non gratae."

"Worse than that," Asger said. "They've probably all been threatened with punishment if they speak with us. Though, Kim, you might have better luck. Do you know what your status is? Are you exiled?"

"Nobody's told me *what* I am. But I don't have much of a relationship with Captain Ishii. We never spoke chip-to-chip. There are officers and doctors and nurses who came in and drank from my espresso machine while I was on the *Osprey*, but I don't think any of them would have the information we need. Unless…" Her gaze dropped to the deck as she contemplated something. "Lieutenant Grunburg might help."

"Is he in Intelligence?" Bjarke asked. "It's unlikely a lowly lieutenant would have access to top-secret information, especially when Casmir isn't on their ship."

"He's the *Osprey's* ace programmer," Kim said. "And a former student of Casmir's. They worked on defeating that virus together. If he could get the information, I bet he would help."

"I remember him," Asger said. "He and Casmir did buddy up on the ship."

"Let me see if he'll accept my contact," Kim said.

Qin stepped up to Asger's side and leaned against his shoulder while they waited. She was eager to help Casmir—and ideally get off this ship. Even if most of Rache's mercenaries weren't from the Kingdom and didn't call her and her sisters freaks, there had been a lot of joking comments about furry clones invading the ship.

More than a few had also made passes at them. Her sisters could handle themselves, even against cybernetically enhanced mercenaries, but Qin worried they wouldn't realize that they had the freedom to do so now and no longer had to give in to men's demands for sex. Later, they all had appointments with Dr. Peshlakai to have the pain chips removed, which would ensure that nobody could hurt them again if they disobeyed orders. *Then* they should all know that they didn't have to kowtow to anyone.

Asger wrapped his arm around Qin's shoulders. "Are you still going to spend time with me if we lose the castle?"

"Of course. That's a silly thing to ask."

"I wasn't sure. I remember telling you about our forest and that you could see it someday."

"Wait, you're losing the forest too? In that case, yes, I revoke all interest in you." She smiled at him.

"I'll still find some trees to show you. For you to run through the branches barefoot in."

The conversation had drawn her sisters' interest, and Asger cleared his throat and looked awkwardly at the deck when he noticed them all looking over. He started to lower his arm, as if he wasn't sure if they approved of his relationship with Qin, but she wrapped her arm around his waist and held him against her side.

"They'll want to see trees too," she told him. "Liking nature is in our genes."

"After we get Casmir back, I hope we can make that happen."

Kim lifted her gaze. "Grunburg accepted my contact and replied. He'd already been trying to figure out what's going on with Casmir and said he'd hoped that I was still in the system and would get in touch. He can't do anything from the *Osprey*, which won't likely ever leave orbit, but he hopes I have the resources to stop the execution."

"You do," Asger said firmly.

LAYERS OF FORCE

"Does he have any information that's different from the news?" Tristan asked.

"Nothing that's been shared, but he says he was able to poke around in the other Fleet warships' computers, not just the *Osprey*'s, and that Jager's ship has filed flight plans for three shuttles on the day they arrive. One to a prison in Zamek City, one to do a supply run to the lunar station, and one to the landing pad next to the castle. Four fighter craft have been assigned to escort the prison shuttle and the castle shuttle."

"That doesn't necessarily suggest anything different from what's in the news," Bjarke said slowly. "Jager could be returning to the castle, or at least visiting his staff and his wife, Casmir could be getting dropped off at the prison, and a couple of supply sergeants could be flying to the moon to pick up food for the warship."

"Is it possible it's *not* a trap?" Asger asked. "That Jager is convinced we won't be able to get to Casmir? Or doesn't care about us at all?"

"What if the supposed supply shuttle is actually the one that will take him?" Qin asked. "And he'll be taken from that lunar base down to the planet on another ship? Or that the shuttle will change flight plans once it launches and go down to the planet after the other two?"

"That would be the least obvious shuttle to attack," Asger said. "Naturally, we would assume that the shuttle without the escort has little of importance on it."

Kim gazed thoughtfully at them. "It's frustrating not to be able to get in touch with Casmir. Though I doubt he knows which shuttle he's going on either."

"He probably doesn't even know if he's still in System Lion." Asger sighed. "I've been in warship cells. The view is uninspiring."

"Grunburg also said that from what he was able to determine, the lights are on in the *Starhawk's* brig and a prisoner is still being kept in there. That suggests Casmir is at least alive."

"Is there any chance Rache would give us three shuttles, and we could try to take over all three Kingdom craft?" Qin asked.

"I don't think he likes me or Casmir *that* much," Kim said dryly. "Besides, he doesn't have many shuttles that are unmarked. The others have bogus ident chips, but he says they've all been affiliated with the *Fedallah*."

"Then we have to guess." Asger looked at his father. "What do you think? Is Jager being clever or arrogant and straightforward?"

"He's smarter and more subtle than Jorg," Bjarke said. "Not straightforward, I think."

"The supply shuttle then?"

"That's my guess." Bjarke turned his palm up and looked at Kim. "I regret that it's only a guess."

"As I told Asger, Rache also thinks it's a trap." Kim looked over Qin and all the gathered fighters.

They were quite the eccentric bunch, Qin thought. She hoped they would take the Kingdom by surprise and that those soldiers wouldn't know what hit them.

"And I agree that misdirection seems likely." Kim lifted a finger, her eyes glazing as she read some incoming message. "Grunburg sent something else. He hacked into the computer of the lunar station the shuttle is supposed to go to for supplies, and they haven't received an order. Which, he says, they should have gotten days ago if someone was truly picking up enough food to resupply a warship."

Asger clenched a fist. "That's it. The other two are decoys. Casmir will be on the supply shuttle."

"Let's hope so. Let's prep our shuttle and be ready to launch as soon as we reach orbit." Kim took a step toward the door but paused and looked back. "Thank you to everyone who is coming to help."

"You are welcome, Kim Sato," Zee said. "We will retrieve Casmir Dabrowski, and never again will I allow myself to be parted from him."

Bjarke arched a wry eyebrow. "If he ever gets married, his wife is going to be in for a surprise in the bedroom."

Qin returned to training with her sisters. She hoped her friends were making the right guess. They would only get one chance for a surprise attack.

LAYERS OF FORCE

Dr. Yas Peshlakai had seen a lot as a surgeon on Tiamat Station, where genetic modifications were commonplace, but having a cadre of genetically engineered cat women in his sickbay was a new experience. The women all loomed much taller than he, and he struggled not to be fazed by their pointed ears, fangs, and powerful musculature.

He'd encountered Qin before, but she'd always been in her armor, and he hadn't realized that she had fur in numerous places where humans had only hair, and he also hadn't realized how strong she was. *All* of the women were like that.

Fortunately, they were also polite, only accidentally knocking over and breaking a few things in his office—due to their size and its smallness rather than any inherent clumsiness—and it was more flattering than alarming when one of them patted him on the butt and told him how handsome he was. She might have meant to pat his back, but given the suggestive wink that accompanied the statement, he doubted it.

The week before, he'd been worried when he'd told them he would have to spend some time researching their "pain chips," as they called them, before risking their removal. But none of them had hefted him off his feet and crankily demanded that he work faster.

Conveniently, though perhaps alarmingly, the Kingdom public network databases had information on those particular chips—they were used to control prisoners in a number of their penal asteroid mines—so he hadn't had to wait for the specifications to come back from System Cerberus. The devices had fail-safes designed to deliver intense pain to the wearer if they attempted to remove them on their own. He was glad he'd waited to perform the surgeries until he'd had instructions on how to deactivate the security measures.

Today, as he removed the chips, he listened to conversations that ranged from speculation on whether Rache's intriguing mysteriousness made him sexy, to whether female warriors were paid as much as males in mercenary outfits, to whether they could blame the chaotic past few weeks for changes in their cycles. These conversations were significantly different from those he usually heard from Rache's mercenaries—even the female ones. There were only eight women among the *Fedallah*'s crew, and they worked in different departments, so maybe that kept the female-centric chatter from dominating conversations here. Yas couldn't remember Jess ever bringing up Rache's intriguing mysteriousness—thankfully.

"Doctor?" one of the women—Tigress, she'd introduced herself—asked as he worked on her chip removal. "Have you seen Rache without his mask? Do you know who he really is?"

"He's careful to keep his face covered."

"I think that means he *has* seen it," one of the others whispered. "Spill the chips, Doc. Is he hideous? Horribly maimed by an explosion? We're debating his sexiness quotient."

"He just doesn't want anyone to know who he is." Yas avoided commenting on quotients and dabbed Skinfill onto the spot where Tigress's chip had been.

"He's a horrible villain who's killed thousands of people." Qin's chip had been removed long ago, but she'd come along for moral support. "He's not sexy."

"Villains can be sexy. You don't know everything, Squirt, just because you've had your freedom longer."

"I know Rache isn't sexy," Qin murmured.

Yas concurred, but he decided to stay out of it.

"That stuff stinks." Tigress wrinkled her nose at the tube of Skinfill. "I don't want to sleep with Rache or anything. I mean, probably not. He *does* look super agile when he works out with his men, so you never know. But I was mostly wondering if he might be hiring. He can't be any worse than the Druckers. After all, he's helping us rescue your friend, Squirt. Does he molest the women here, Doctor?"

Yas blinked at that abrupt transition. "To the best of my knowledge, this is a molestation-free ship. I'm not sure if Rache is hiring right now, but he is fair with his people, if that matters."

"See, Squirt? *Way* better than the Druckers."

"You can't leave until we rescue Casmir," Qin said.

"Oh, I won't, but what are we going to do *after* that? We have to make a living. If we get paid, we can shop. We've never been able to do that before, and I look forward to exploring my options."

"What are you going to buy?" Qin asked.

"Clothes. Chocolates. A new grenade launcher."

"The necessities."

"And I want to *decorate*." Tigress clasped her hands together in front of her chest. "I saw the unicorns and candles in your cabin on your freighter. It's so fabulous that you have a place of your own. I want that. And I want to decorate it and make it mine."

"It *is* nice. Bonita might be able to hire you—anyone who wants to work for her. We'd just have to start getting bigger jobs."

Yas eyed Qin—he had seen her beat the tar out of mercenaries and even hold her own against crushers, so he wouldn't have guessed she was the type to collect something as girlie as unicorns, but maybe it wasn't surprising. Her nails—claws—were always painted some cute color, and today, she wore a dark purple T-shirt with a large glittery green-and-silver tree on the front that caught the light and sparkled riotously.

"That might be all right," Tigress said. "I'm just thinking about our future. Making plans."

"Plans for shopping."

"And decorating."

As Yas finished the last of the chip removals, Rache walked into sickbay. He twitched a finger toward Yas and walked into the office.

"You ladies are all done here," he told them.

"Thank you, Doctor." Tigress flashed a smile at him, being careful not to show off her fangs, and waved cheerfully. As yet, her claws were not cheerfully painted the way Qin's were, but Yas guessed it was only a matter of time.

The group strode out of sickbay, their strides powerful, purposeful, and also graceful, and Yas tossed the bloody chips into the detritus chute with relish, knowing they would be incinerated with the rest of the trash. The women had told him how they had been used, so he'd been more than pleased to take them out. The galaxy was full of despicable individuals.

As he joined the infamous mercenary Rache in the sickbay office, it bemused him a little that he no longer considered his captain one of those people. Even though he was likely plotting Jager's murder right now.

"Are you here for your exam, Captain?" Yas asked what had become his usual greeting for Rache—and for several of the men who failed to show up for the appointments Yas made for them.

"I'm leaving the ship when we get as close to Odin as we dare—given that one of those warships has a slydar detector now, we'll have to make sure to stay on the opposite side of the planet from it as we orbit. I have a mission to complete and—"

"You're not going to help Kim rescue Casmir?" Yas asked.

"She has her own plan for that. I have another. If either works, he will survive the week. I don't know about the rest of his future."

"You don't think you should work together?"

"I didn't come for a consultation, Doctor."

"Sorry. You still haven't flogged me for being cheeky, so I feel the urge to express opinions."

"I suggest you suppress your urges. If I'm successful in my mission, I'll allow you and Chief Khonsari to take a short and discreet leave of absence for her spine surgery, if she still wishes it. Do not tell the others. System Lion is too dangerous a place for the *Fedallah* to dally or for shore leave for the men. I'm making arrangements in the event of my success or failure for them to get the time off they deserve."

Rache nodded curtly and walked out before Yas could thank him—or ask exactly what *in the event of my success or failure* meant.

"Strange man," Yas murmured. "And definitely *not* sexy."

Oh, well. He was approving leave. Yas trotted out to talk to Jess in engineering. He would do his best to make sure she *wished* to have that surgery.

CHAPTER 4

"WAKE UP, PROFESSOR," A GUARD RUMBLED AND FLASHED the lights a few times before leaving them on.

Casmir hadn't been sleeping, merely working on refining his robotic bees, in the event that he ever got to share all of his suggestions with Oku. He had also written long letters to his friends and relatives—*several* long letters to his parents.

By the passage of time, he guessed they'd reached Odin's orbit, and he hoped he would get a chance to connect to the public wireless network and send his messages. He also hoped he could use that access to come up with a crafty way to free himself from his fate. The warship had to have legions of robots and computers he could possibly take over...

Several more guards stepped into view, one lifting a pair of flex-cuffs. Did that mean the public execution plan was in effect, and Casmir would be transferred down to the planet?

The guards could simply be taking him to sickbay where his lethal injection was waiting. But a doctor could have come and done that to him in the brig, perhaps the very one who'd injected him with his truth drug—three days in a row.

After cheerfully babbling everything he knew, while that damn Lieutenant Meister recorded it all into his tablet, Casmir doubted Jager had any use left for him, beyond as bait in his trap. He worried that Kim and his other friends would be more likely to walk into that than Rache and hoped they were safely in another system and not planning his rescue. Unfortunately, his interrogation had included questions about Kim's relationship to Rache, and his attempts to steer his interrogator away from the topic hadn't fully worked. Casmir feared that Jager and Military Intelligence now knew *everything*.

"Are we going somewhere?" Casmir asked.

"For a ride."

That sounded ominous. None of the guards clarified.

Before the interrogation, most of the soldiers on the warship had treated him with professional indifference, but since he'd revealed his relationship with Rache, they'd all been icy or outright cruel. One kept calling him *traitor* along with various derogatory words that were too foul to appear in comic books.

"Good. My legs have longed for some exercise. I even would have welcomed some time on one of those odious treadmills with the straps that keep you from escaping." Casmir smiled, trying to be friendly out of habit, but there was little point now.

The closest guard dropped the cell's forcefield, then grabbed him, spun him, and cuffed him. Four stunners were pointed at him. Nobody responded to his humor.

Casmir searched for the ship's wireless network, hoping for a chance to access it now that he was out of his cell. Before he found anything, the same doctor who'd drugged him stepped into view.

Casmir jumped. "I thought we were done with our sessions."

"No interrogation today. I've been instructed to perform a small surgery." The doctor held up a laser scalpel.

Panic surged into Casmir. He knew with certainty exactly what the doctor planned to remove. Not any of his organs—he would rather have given up one of those. Instinctively, he tried to jerk his hand up to his temple to protect his chip, but the cuffs held his wrists behind his back.

"Hold him still," the doctor told the men as he approached.

Unfriendly hands gripped Casmir's arms with the power of crushers. Oh, how he wished Zee were there now to protect him, to fling these guards away.

He searched impatiently for the network again, knowing he only had seconds, but there wasn't a signal. He feared the entire brig was insulated, not the individual cells.

He didn't bother trying to buck or push his guards away, but he was soon panting nonetheless, pure panic driving his body into a state of terror. He couldn't lose his chip. It had all of his work for the last twenty years on it, everything from homework assignments for students, to schematics for prototype projects he hadn't yet built, to the plans for the crushers. All of his work on Oku's robot bees was on there! And all of the videos she'd sent him.

Tears threatened at the thought that he would never be able to access those videos again.

"Quit hyperventilating, traitor." The guard holding him squeezed him tighter, painfully so.

Casmir's fingertips were numb. Would he have a seizure? For once, his guards had let him keep his medication, so he'd been on his regular dosage while confined, but that didn't mean he couldn't still have one…

Unfortunately, he doubted that would keep the doctor from removing his chip.

"How about you say you took it but don't really do it?" Casmir asked as the doctor's face leered close, the laser scalpel even closer. "I won't tell anyone. And I'll send you a delightful holiday present. How do you feel about cinnamon babka? I know my mother would make you some if you didn't deface the side of my head."

"Shut up," the guard growled again.

Casmir tried to twist his head away, desperate to somehow keep his chip. Of all the torments they could think up for him, this was one of the worst.

A strong hand gripped the back of his head and forced him to look forward. The laser's cold bite cut into his temple. The doctor hadn't applied a local anesthetic, but it didn't hurt that much, not as much as it should have considering all that data that was being ripped from Casmir's head.

Despite the fledgling panic attack, he didn't have a seizure. He didn't know whether to feel relief or not. As much as he hated appearing weak in front of others, a peevish part of him would have liked to inconvenience his tormentors. Not that a seizure would have fazed a doctor. He probably would have played network games to kill time while Casmir writhed on the floor.

When the doctor finished removing the chip, he carefully placed it in a baggie. Casmir's first thought was relief—at least he didn't drop it and grind it under his heel—but glumness replaced the feeling as he realized they were only saving the chip so Military Intelligence could download all the data on it.

Well, they could try. He had dozens of encryption and protection protocols on there. For most of his life, that had only been a habit, to keep out the nosy hackers in the world, but then he'd started working on the crusher project. He'd made sure nobody could get ahold of those plans.

Warm blood dribbled from the side of his temple as the guards marched him through the ship—every officer they passed along the way gave him icy glowers—and to a door outside of a shuttle bay.

Casmir wondered if everything Meister had learned from the interrogations would end up on the Kingdom news. What would his parents think about the choices he'd made? The relationship with Rache that he had developed, however inadvertently, and later leaned on?

He was positive the soldiers hated him most for that. Messing up the gate mission wasn't quite the crime in their eyes that associating with Rache was. What would Captain Ishii think? He'd seemed to understand Casmir's choices regarding the gate and Tiamat Station, but could a link to Rache ever be forgiven?

The guards didn't lead him straight into the shuttle bay but instead waited outside.

Casmir stood on tiptoe to peer through a Glasnax porthole in time to see the bay doors open and a shuttle taking off. In the distance, the curve of Odin's green and blue surface was visible. His stomach hadn't bothered him much during the trip from the gate, with the spin gravity of the ship remaining a constant, but the sight of the planet far below them prompted a twinge of vertigo and nausea. Bleakly, he wondered if his shuttle pilot had been warned about his tendency toward space sickness.

Another shuttle took off for the exit.

"I suppose there's no point in wishing there won't be one left for us?" Casmir mused.

"Do you want to stay here?" one guard asked.

"Not particularly. The hospitality has been somewhat lacking."

"Traitors don't get hospitality."

Casmir sighed.

The shuttle bay doors closed, unfortunately leaving one more vessel inside.

"Where'd those other ones go?" It was a habit to try to gather information, though Casmir had no way to send it along to anyone now. "Down to the planet?"

"To set a trap." That was Meister's voice. He came around a corner with two soldiers in combat armor.

"For whom?" Casmir asked.

"Anyone stupid enough to try to rescue you."

Fresh concern hollowed a pit in his stomach as he wondered if Military Intelligence knew more about where his friends were than Casmir did. If they *were* out there and *did* try to rescue him, would they be smart enough to outsmart Meister and Jager and whoever else was setting this up? He hoped so, but it pained him that he couldn't warn them.

A control panel binged, showing that oxygen and pressure had been returned to the bay. One of the armored men grabbed the back of Casmir's neck and steered him inside and toward the last shuttle.

Meister followed as far as the open hatch, but he didn't step in.

"Any parting messages for anyone on the *Osprey*?" he surprised Casmir by asking.

Casmir almost said to tell Ishii and Grunburg that it had been good to get to know them better, but he closed his mouth before he could utter the words. Anyone he admitted that he'd liked working with might find themselves in more hot water for the association.

"Would you actually relay the messages if I had them?" he asked.

Meister shrugged. "Sure. You're supposed to deliver last wishes from men about to die."

He said it casually, without a villainous sneer or addendum of *traitor*. Somehow, that casualness made it worse, and made Casmir wonder if he was truly being taken down to the planet or simply out to walk the plank and freeze in the icy vacuum of space.

"You've probably got a few days left though," Meister added. "The king wants to make sure you live long enough to work as bait for his trap. So you've got time if you want to pray for your sins or whatever your religion suggests."

"Thoughtful," Casmir murmured.

"We do appreciate that you took out Dubashi," Meister offered.

"I hope his virus died along with him and that Odin isn't in danger."

Meister's eyes narrowed. "Do you have reason to think that it didn't?"

If he did, Casmir wondered if he could leverage that into a reason for them to keep him alive. He could promise to look for it if the king just let him have a shuttle to go off on his own…

But he wasn't an expert on such things, and he doubted Jager would make that deal with him again.

"Not really." Casmir shrugged as casually as Meister had earlier. "But there was one canister that was never accounted for."

The other had blown up along with Reuben on Stardust Palace Station. Remorse stirred anew in him for the crusher's death, along with concern for what would happen with all the other crushers now that he wasn't around to lead them and ensure they protected innocent people instead of slaying them.

Meister's eyes narrowed thoughtfully, but all he said was, "Take him away."

The soldiers secured him in a pod in the shuttle. Casmir had just enough freedom to drop his head into his lap and pray that his friends were safe and that they wouldn't fall for whatever trap Jager had set.

Kim strode down the corridors of the now familiar *Fedallah* toward the shuttle bay. The craft Rache had promised to lend them was already packed, and Asger had messaged to let her know that their entire team was inside and ready. He'd also said it was cozy, which she took to mean jammed wall to wall with broad-shouldered knights, crushers, and genetically engineered warriors.

She had swung by sickbay to finagle medical supplies from Yas in case this went badly. Or in case they succeeded in retrieving Casmir, only to find that he'd been tortured or horribly beaten by his guards. She would like to *think* there was no possibility that Kingdom soldiers would treat a prisoner so poorly, but they'd had him long enough to question him under the influence of a truth drug he wasn't allergic to, which probably meant they'd learned all about his encounters with Rache.

If the enemy of one's enemy was one's friend, was the corollary that the friend of one's enemy was one's enemy? She believed the Kingdom would see it that way.

Rache waited in the corridor outside the shuttle bay in his combat armor and with several weapons, including a rocket launcher with the firepower to put a hole in the side of a ship—or possibly the side of a mountain.

"Are you coming with us?" Kim stopped in front of him. Four shuttles were visible through the porthole in the door, two with their hatches open.

"Nobody else would fit in your shuttle," he said dryly, waving to the one that didn't match the others—its hull was painted white with a furniture-delivery logo on the side. "It's unfortunate that you're not wearing armor sturdier than that galaxy suit. The odds of you completing your mission without having your foot stepped on by a crusher must be astronomically against you."

"I'm willing to risk my feet for a friend."

"I feel compelled to point out that it's unlikely that they need you along. I know you have more combat prowess than the average bacteriologist, but..." He spread one of his gauntleted hands.

"Is there a reason you don't want me to go?" Kim trusted him with her life, but she knew he didn't care about Qin or her sisters or the crushers. More than that, he had butted heads with Asger several times, and Tristan had sabotaged his ship once. If she weren't on the shuttle, would he consider tipping off the Kingdom that they were coming?

No, she decided before he spoke. For good or ill, if he wanted the knights dead, he would challenge them face to face to a battle. Much as he'd done with Jorg.

"I don't want you to be a casualty of a rescue mission gone wrong," he said quietly.

"Oh." She felt bad for having thought anything nefarious of his intentions. "Thank you. We did get an inside tip."

"You're welcome to stay on my ship while the others go."

"I can't. Casmir is *my* friend, and..." Kim shrugged, feeling the weight of the extensive first-aid kit slung over her shoulder. "I have the bandages."

"I understand why you don't want to be associated with my plan, but I believe they won't see it coming and that it has a better chance of success. I've also prepped a shuttle and will go out after yours." He tilted his head toward the bay door.

"Your plan to kidnap Finn? Or to assassinate Jager?"

"It depends on whom I run into at the castle," he said dryly.

She frowned at him.

"Since Casmir is in danger of being executed, I will prioritize the kidnapping," Rache said more seriously. "Jager, I will deal with later. If he comes for the handoff, to trade Casmir for Finn, I might get my chance to take him out in person."

"You're not supposed to get dreamy eyed when you talk of assassinating people."

"I'm wearing a mask. You can't tell if my eyes are dreamy."

"Yeah, I can." Kim sighed, still finding this subject disturbing—still disturbed with herself for being able to care about a man who casually planned assassinations. "Don't get yourself killed, please. I can't imagine getting to Finn in his own castle will be that easy."

"No. It won't be."

Kim shook her head, worried Rache's self-appointed mission would be even more dangerous than her rescue attempt. "I hope you live."

"Thank you. I will aspire to do so."

"Truly?" She'd always gotten the feeling he didn't expect to survive his showdown with Jager, in whatever form it ended up taking.

He hesitated. "Yes."

"Thank you."

Rache lifted his hand toward her face, making her think of the time they'd kissed, but two dark figures walked across the shuttle bay and toward the door, and he lowered it. Two crushers.

The door slid open, and Kim stepped back out of the way in case they had been sent on some last-minute errand. Though she couldn't imagine what. It wasn't as if they needed to use the lavatory before they left.

"Greetings, Kim Sato." That sounded like Zee. After the greeting, he faced Rache. "Captain Tenebris Rache. I am Zee, the original crusher programmed to protect Kim Sato and Casmir Dabrowski."

"Yes," Rache said. "We've met. Numerous times."

"This is the twenty-seventh crusher created on the assembly line at Stardust Palace." Zee pointed to the identical tarry-black figure next to him. "Casmir Dabrowski suggested his name might be Amit, which means friend or colleague."

"Uhm." Rache looked to Kim. For help?

She could only spread her arms since she didn't know what this was about either.

"I am a Z-6000," the crusher said, "programmed to protect Tenebris Rache. I am Amit."

With that mask on, it was hard to tell if Rache was stunned, but the way he leaned back did hint of surprise.

"Before we left System Stymphalia," Zee said, "Casmir Dabrowski programmed Amit to work for you. You are a nefarious villain, as evinced by the numerous Kingdom dramas in which you play the role of antagonist, and a loathed criminal of the Kingdom, but Casmir Dabrowski said he promised to give you a crusher."

"I will not kill human beings," Amit said, "but I will protect Tenebris Rache and do non-nefarious tasks for him."

Kim brought her fingers to her lips to pinch them to keep from grinning.

"Huh," Rache finally said. "He actually made me one."

Did his voice sound the tiniest bit gruff, as a cover to hide emotion? Kim wished she were better at reading people. She liked to think that Rache had come to care about Casmir, but she wasn't positive of that.

"Wait out here with me, Amit." Rache pointed to the deck next to him. "We're going on the next shuttle."

The crusher stood in the indicated spot.

"It is time to leave, Kim Sato," Zee told her. "We must retrieve Casmir Dabrowski."

"I'm ready." She lifted a hand toward Rache, thoughts of kisses disappearing with the crusher audience present. But she couldn't resist a long look over her shoulder as she walked toward their shuttle, wondering if he would get himself killed trying to sneak into the castle to kidnap Finn.

He also lifted a hand, holding it up until she turned away and the door closed.

"I should not have allowed Casmir Dabrowski to be taken prisoner without me," Zee told Kim as they walked toward the open hatch.

"He didn't have any choice."

"He has not been able to answer communications to his chip. The inferior android Tork is also gone from this system. He returned with Princess Nalini's fleet to System Stymphalia."

"I know. My mother did too."

"Then you understand this gap."

"Gap?"

"The words I have are inadequate to explain it." Zee stopped at the nose of the shuttle. "I have had only the other crushers to communicate with since the inferior android Tork and my creator Casmir Dabrowski have been gone. My conversations with them are not sufficiently engaging."

"What you're saying is that you miss Tork and Casmir."

"I believe this is correct. But that is an emotion, is it not? Crushers are not programmed to have emotions. I miss intellectual stimulation. Casmir Dabrowski said the other crushers would develop personalities and grow more interesting with time, but we have the same foundational programming, which means I know everything they know. I know what they will say before they say it."

"No value added from your dialogues, huh?" Kim found the conversation surreal, more because Zee was turning her into his confidante than because she couldn't believe he could develop emotions, or something like them. She wasn't sure she wanted to be his confidante—she still felt a twinge of sadness about losing Reuben and was reluctant to form attachments to the other crushers—but she missed Casmir, too, and the least she could do while he was gone was chat with his crusher.

"Correct."

"I've heard raising children is like that. They become interesting later. Sometimes."

"How *much* later?"

"I had a teacher call me fascinating when I was five, but my mother didn't start talking to me about her research until... Well, she still doesn't discuss it much with me. We work in different fields."

"So you are not yet interesting to your mother?"

Kim smiled faintly. "Possibly true."

Zee looked toward the open hatch, the rows of crushers visible inside. "Distressing."

"If you find someone you enjoy spending time with and who is interesting, you should try to keep them around." Kim kept herself from looking back at the door again, but she didn't miss the fact that she wasn't taking her own advice. But Rache wasn't a pet. She couldn't leash him up and keep him close. Even if the universe would be safer for all that way.

"Yes. I have made a mistake, Kim Sato."
"You're not the only one."
"Distressing," he repeated and headed inside.
"Yes."

CHAPTER 5

BETWEEN ALL THE CRUSHERS AND QIN'S SISTERS, THE shuttle was packed. Asger sat in a pod next to Kim, wishing she hadn't come along. Aside from the nearly indestructible crushers, she was the only one not in combat armor. She wore a galaxy suit with an attached oxygen tank, in case the shuttle was damaged and they lost environmental controls, and she'd borrowed a rifle from Rache, but she seemed small and vulnerable in the warrior-filled craft.

They'd already taken off from the *Fedallah*, so it was too late to ask her if she wanted to stay behind, but Asger asked, "Are you sure about this?" anyway. If they had to, they might have time to take the shuttle back so she could stay on the ship. "You don't have to come along."

Kim gazed toward the porthole instead of looking at him. "Yes, I do. As I told Rache, Casmir's my best friend."

Rache had asked her not to go too? Asger didn't know how he felt about agreeing with the man on something. Not good.

"If something happens," Kim added quietly, "I need to be there for him."

Asger kept himself from saying that something had *already* happened. A lot of somethings. That was why they were stuck on a rescue mission.

"I understand," was what he said instead. And he did. If someone had told him to stay behind, he wouldn't have done it. "I just have a bad feeling about this." What if she ended up sacrificing herself for nothing? "I wish we'd been able to get another shuttle to split our team between."

Then they could have gone after two out of the three shuttles that had been launched from the *Starhawk*. Their odds of getting the right one would have been better.

"Our exit plan would be less believable with two shuttles."

"True." Asger glanced over his shoulder, though he couldn't see the explosives and spare parts and debris they'd loaded into the rear of the craft, ready to be deployed at a touch from the pilot's pod.

The plan was to get Casmir and then fake a crash on the planet—it probably wouldn't be hard to fake that crash since ships from Odin's planetary defenses would likely be pursuing them by then. Ideally, they would land with enough time to disappear from the supposed crash site. Casmir and Kim could get their families and find a way out of the system until things settled down—or forever—and Asger and his father... They hadn't sat down yet to discuss what they would do after freeing Casmir. In all likelihood, they'd made their choices weeks ago and would also have to flee the system.

Asger tried not to feel bleak at the prospect of getting a job in station security at Stardust Palace. Maybe Tristan and Princess Nalini needed a bodyguard.

"The *Starhawk* shuttle on course to the lunar station is twenty minutes ahead of us," Asger's father said from the pilot's pod. "I've put in a fake order for supplies to the station in case someone checks on us, and I'm setting a course to bring us adjacent to them. They shouldn't think we intend to intercept them until it's too late for them to do anything. We have no slydar for this shuttle, unfortunately."

Asger closed his eyes, trying to find calm before the action started. Behind him, the crushers were mute. But behind them, Qin and her sisters chatted quietly on topics that ranged from favorite weapons, to whether fur removal hurt, to Qin's decision to keep her claws painted with colorful nail polish to make people less fearful of her.

Asger hadn't realized that was the reason she did it. He'd assumed she liked to decorate them because she had a whimsical personality.

"I'm reading two life signs inside." Tristan sat in the co-pilot's pod, manning the scanners.

"That's it?" Asger's father asked. "Casmir and a pilot? If this was the right shuttle, I would expect there to be guards."

"Guards in combat armor wouldn't register on the scanners," Tristan said. "And if Kim's programmer friend is right, and they want us to believe this is a supply shuttle, not a prison transport down to the planet, they would try to hide that they've got a lot of extra guards along."

"True."

"The other two shuttles that launched from the *Starhawk* are heading directly down to the planet, on track for Zamek City."

"We may be making a mistake. Trying to be too clever." Asger gripped the armrest inside his pod, accidentally squeezing with his strength-enhancing gauntlet so that it creaked. He forced himself to loosen the hold.

"Lieutenant Grunburg has no reason to betray us or Casmir," Kim said.

Asger thought she sounded like she was trying to convince herself as much as them. "But Royal Intelligence could have anticipated that we would have a spy or someone capable of hacking into their computers and setting him up."

His father glanced back at him. "Do you want to abort? There may still be time to catch the shuttles with the escorts, but we'll have a hard time dealing with those escorts. We've got decent firepower, but our real advantage will be if we can get close enough to board." He flicked a finger back toward the rows of crushers and the herd—no, *pride* of Qins.

Asger opened his mouth to answer, but Tristan blurted, "Look!" and pointed at the panel.

"The shuttle we're following is changing course," Asger's father said. "Turning for the planet."

"Maybe it *is* delivering Casmir somewhere," Tristan said.

"Or it noticed us getting close to it, and the pilot got worried."

"If that were true, it would be heading back to its ship."

"Maybe." Asger's father tapped his hands across the control panel. "It's now or never. I'm going to try to catch it before it drops into the atmosphere."

Asger's pod tightened around him as their shuttle banked hard and flew downward, one of Odin's oceans visible far, far below. The other shuttle was visible as well, speeding down toward the planet below them.

"I still can't get in touch with Casmir," Kim murmured.

Asger glanced at her.

"If he's been taken out of the brig that was blocking him from accessing any networks, he should be able to do so now. Unless they stunned him." She lowered her voice. "Or worse."

"We'll find out soon," Asger said.

His father opened fire at the shuttle ahead of them.

"Nice," he purred. "This thing has upgraded weapons."

Asger would expect nothing less from a craft that Rache owned.

"They're firing back," Tristan warned, reading the scanner display. "And comming for help."

"Should be twenty minutes before any other ships can get to us," Asger's father said. "I was hoping for an even bigger gap, but the pilot turned away from his flight path too soon. We're gaining on them. If I can bring us alongside them, they won't be able to fire, and we can board."

Usually, Asger's stomach was ironclad when it came to fluctuations in gravity and gyrations in space, but even he felt twinges of nausea as they sped toward the planet—and closer to the shuttle—with his father doing what maneuvering he could to try to avoid the weapons fire.

Orange light flashed on the display as a faint jolt rocked the shuttle.

"Good shielding too," his father said.

"Us or them?" Asger asked.

"Us."

"Eight fighter ships from one of the orbital defense stations are on an intercept course," Tristan said. "And the *Starhawk* is veering in this direction too."

"They won't follow us into the atmosphere," Asger said, hoping he was right.

"We'll get to this shuttle before anyone else gets here," Asger's father said as the other craft grew larger on the display. "But everyone is going to have to board and get Casmir out of there quickly."

"We are prepared," Zee's voice came from the back. "We are very quick."

"So are we," one of Qin's sisters called.

Another blast lit up the cabin with intense orange, but again, the shuttle only shuddered slightly. For once, Asger was thankful that Rache was a paranoid bastard with the funds to armor his spacecraft like bank vaults.

As the Kingdom shuttle grew larger and larger on their display against the backdrop of the ocean far below, Asger tapped his chest control, and his helmet unfurled from the back of his armor and locked over his head. He gripped his pertundo and rifle, eager to spring into action.

"The pilot's banking," Tristan warned. "They're trying to get away from us."

"I see it." Asger's father did his best to stay close, then opened the comm. "We have you outgunned, Kingdom shuttle. Hold a steady course and prepare to be boarded, or we'll blow you out of the sky."

LAYERS OF FORCE

Silence answered him. Asger's father fired again, a glancing blow instead of a direct hit, though they were close enough now that to miss hitting the shuttle dead-on had to have been intentional.

Tristan looked over at him and muted the comm. "You're bluffing, right, sir? It's one thing to rescue Casmir, but if we kill Kingdom soldiers…"

"I'm bluffing, but they don't need to know that."

"Wish we had a maglocker," his father muttered and reached for the weapons console again.

"We surrender, pirates," a voice growled over the comm. "But your actions have marked you as dead men. No fewer than twenty ships are on the way to annihilate you."

"Fly straight and prepare to be boarded," Asger's father ordered.

The other shuttle didn't answer, but it had already ceased its maneuvers.

"Fourteen minutes until the first of the other ships arrives," Tristan said quietly.

"Attaching to their airlock," Asger's father said. "They may try to break away when we're in the middle of boarding. Prepare to—"

The crushers surged to their feet and swarmed around the hatch.

"We are prepared," one of them said.

Asger stood, but there was no room close to the hatch.

A soft clank sounded. One of the crushers opened their hatch, and the rush of wind battering the shuttle and the short attachment tube told Asger they had dipped into Odin's atmosphere.

"We're attached," his father said. "They're not opening their hatch. They're—"

The crushers charged over, and a great wrenching of metal sounded. In less than a second, the Kingdom shuttle's locked hatch was torn open, and the crushers rushed inside.

"No killing!" Asger shouted as he hurried after them.

He had already given them that order before the mission started, but he didn't want any mistakes. If they killed Kingdom soldiers during this rescue, they would be as bad as Rache—and hunted by the Kingdom for the rest of their lives.

"Casmir Dabrowski is not here," a crusher announced as Asger reached the other shuttle, his helmet's scanners warning him of smoke and gas in the air.

His heart sank into his stomach as the crushers parted so that he could see up to the front. There were two soldiers inside, the men cowering on the deck between their pods and the navigation console. They were barely visible beyond stacks and stacks of empty plas-crates with food logos on the side.

Asger groaned. "Wrong shuttle."

"Less than ten minutes until the interceptor ships arrive," Tristan called.

"Retreat," Asger ordered the crushers, waving Qin and the others back to their own shuttle. "We were tricked."

He rushed back in, flinging himself back into his pod beside Kim. She'd only gotten a chance to partially stand up.

"He's not there," Asger said as the crushers returned, sealing their hatch behind them.

Kim dropped her helmeted head into her hand.

Asger's father swore as he detached from the Kingdom shuttle. He steered them away, heading toward the planet.

"Is there any chance we can catch up with the other two shuttles?" Kim asked.

"No," Tristan said. "They've already landed in Zamek City. And we're about to have company."

"Any chance to get back to the *Fedallah*?" Kim asked.

"No," Asger's father said, "and I'm sure Rache wouldn't want us leading a big mess back to him, even if there was. I'm flying us down as fast as I can. With all the ships after us, I have a feeling it's not going to be hard to make that fake crash look realistic."

No, the hard part would be making the crash fake instead of real. Asger curled his hand into a fist as the first enemy ships flew close enough to fire at them. It all would have been worth it if they'd gotten Casmir, but they'd fallen for Jager's ruse.

"Damn it."

LAYERS OF FORCE

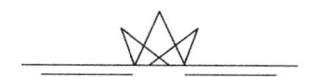

"The gate has activated several times in the last two hours," Viggo said, "but no ships appear to have gone through it."

"More hidden ships?" Bonita had left navigation to him and was in the lounge exercising on the treadmill before doing some stretches for her knees.

She had to stay in good shape. As soon as she could pick up Qin, Bonita could get back to her regular life of delivering freight and perhaps picking up a few bounties. She'd offered to employ Qin's sisters if they wished it. With a team of warrior women like them, Bonita could collect all the bounties in the Twelve Systems.

"It seems so," Viggo said. "There's an incoming comm for you."

Bonita grabbed a towel. "Anyone we want to hear from?"

She'd gotten a flirty message from Bjarke a few days earlier, informing her how dreadfully inadequate the guest accommodations were on the *Fedallah* and how much he missed spending time with her in her cabin. She wouldn't mind more notes from him, even if she doubted she would see him again, but what she really wanted today was an update from Qin. Had they succeeded in rescuing Casmir yet? Did Qin want to come back to the *Dragon*? Back *home*?

"It is Princess Nalini's ship," Viggo said. "It and several ships from the same fleet that entered the Kingdom system with us have left their station and are heading toward us."

"Toward *us* or toward the gate?" Bonita headed up to navigation to accept the comm.

"Likely toward the gate, but we're still along the way."

Bonita pushed her braid over her shoulder and slid into her pod.

"Captain Laser here," she answered.

Nalini appeared on the display, sitting in her command pod on her bridge, her dark hair swept back in an elegant coif. An android stood beside her with his hands clasped behind his back.

"Captain," Nalini said, "we saw that you were close to the gate and the last attack."

"Uh, the *last* attack?"

"There have been several. Because I'm somehow still in charge of our ragtag fleet, I'm being sent to investigate it."

"I thought that fleet only formed to help the Kingdom with its blockade problem and would have been disbanded by now." Bonita checked the scanner display and counted the ships clumped together around Nalini's. A few from the original fleet had disappeared, but it looked like she had almost as many with her as had gone through to System Lion two weeks earlier.

"When my father learned that Professor Dabrowski was captured by his own king, he ordered us to stay together and be ready."

"Be ready for what?"

"My father is certain that Casmir will escape, gather forces, and oust King Jager from his position of tyrannical power."

"Has he *met* Casmir? The kid won't even carry a rifle. He's not going to orchestrate a coup."

Nalini spread a hand. "My father is optimistic, I believe, and hoping *someone* will get Jager out of power. There's also the matter of the attacks and the thefts. We only have guesses about them at this point, but they're pretty good guesses. If we can't put an end to them, all the talks my father has hosted and the alliances he's been forging will be for naught."

"Have all the thefts been of gate pieces?" Bonita guessed.

"Yes. From what I've heard, it's happening in other systems as well as this one. Someone is going around and stealing back all the pieces that were acquired from the astroshaman moon base. Some were stolen out of heavily guarded warehouses in the middle of well-protected planets. Nobody has yet seen or been able to prove the identity of the culprits."

"We figured it was astroshamans that attacked that freighter."

"That's our guess too. Can you send any footage you might have? Since you were so close for that last attack?"

"Sure." Bonita was relieved she wasn't being implicated in anything. She'd feared that might be the case. "Are you planning to blockade the gate so more stealthed astroshaman ships—assuming that's who is doing this—can't get in or out?"

Bonita doubted Nalini was bringing her ragtag fleet to the gate only to say hello.

"We are planning to visit the Kingdom," the android spoke for the first time. "And I will resume playing network games with the arrogant crusher Zee."

Bonita stared at him. Was that Casmir's Tork-57? It had to be.

Nalini looked over at the android, lifted her gaze as if to the heavens, then focused on Bonita again. "We are planning to go to the Kingdom to warn them about the astroshamans. Ostensibly."

"Does that mean you're going to spy on them?"

"Yes. And try to find Casmir." Nalini lowered her voice. "My Tristan is there too."

"And Zee," Tork said.

"*Zee* isn't in danger." Nalini sounded exasperated. Maybe the android had been forcing her to play network games with him in his buddy's absence.

"When last I received communication from him, the arrogant crusher Zee was on the warship of the nefarious criminal Rache. He is in danger simply by being on a ship that is hunted by so many. It is possible that enemies will fire upon that ship from afar and destroy it. Even a brutish crusher might not be able to survive such an ordeal."

"Which would be disturbing because you're in the middle of a game," Nalini said.

"Precisely."

"I'm sending the footage over," Bonita said, ignoring the rest. This fresh mess with the gate pieces had her worrying anew about Qin. What if another war broke out in System Lion? "Princess Nalini, do you have any cargo that you need delivered to System Lion?"

"Not at this time."

"I'm concerned about my friend and assistant Qin, who also last communicated from the bowels of Rache's warship. If the Kingdom fleet hadn't ordered me to get out, I wouldn't have left while she was still in their system."

"Ah." Nalini's eyebrows rose in understanding. "Perhaps if you had a cargo to deliver, the Kingdom might not object to your freighter's return."

"That was my thought."

Bonita still had a cargo to deliver in this system, but there hadn't been a rush order on it.

Nalini patted down her galaxy suit, then flicked open a holder in the armrest of her pod. "I would like this pen delivered to the real estate developer Baron Taniguchi on Odin."

"Excellent. We can handle that, can't we, Viggo?"

"That cargo is so small it might be slurped up by one of my vacuums."

"We can handle it," Bonita said firmly.

Nalini lowered her arm. "It's my hope that if we deliver a warning to the Kingdom in good faith they won't shoo us out of their system. My father wants to stop the astroshamans from getting all of the pieces, since he had plans to go down in history as the person who facilitated bringing them together so people could successfully make new gates, but I think he'd be pleased if all we did was get Casmir back. If Casmir successfully escapes, he may need a more reliable way out of the system than on Rache's boat."

"I'm all for helping the kid escape his people—it's clear they don't appreciate him—but I think the galaxy might be a more restful place if you all just let the astroshamans have those gate pieces."

"Possibly so, but we also plan to explore another possibility."

"Which is?"

Nalini's voice chilled a few degrees. "That the Kingdom is the one responsible for stealing the gate pieces, not the astroshamans."

"Ah." Bonita supposed the Kingdom could also have slydar-hulled ships that had been responsible for the theft she'd seen—or *not* seen. "I just want to get Qin and her sisters."

Judging by Nalini's frown, she and her people cared about more than that, but all she said was, "Then I'll bring you your new cargo."

"Excellent. Thank you."

The comm ended.

"We're heading back to System Lion, Viggo."

"So I gathered. Perhaps we'll be able to assist in rescuing Casmir. My vacuums need their nozzles rotated."

"I guess he's the man for that job."

"I've found that to be true, yes."

CHAPTER 6

AS KINGDOM DEFENSE SHIPS FIRED UPON THEIR SHUTTLE and the dense greenery of Odin's northern continent filled the display, Qin left her sisters and headed for an empty pod across the aisle from Asger. If they were going to die, she wanted to be next to him.

The deck rattled under their feet, and the lights went out. The shuttle lurched as Bjarke zigzagged their rapid descent as much as physics allowed, trying to make it a hard target for the ships chasing them. Only Qin's good balance kept her from tumbling to the deck. Asger glanced at her as she sat in the pod, his face bleaker than death.

Qin wished she could say something reassuring, but all she could think was that this wouldn't have happened if Casmir had been along with them. He would have hacked into some computer network and known exactly where a prisoner was being taken. Unfortunately, that didn't work when *he* was the prisoner.

"Hopefully, we can find him before the execution once we're on the planet," she said.

A jolt rocked the shuttle, a much harder jolt than any of the earlier ones.

"If we survive this landing," Asger said.

"Yeah."

"Don't have a panic attack back there," Bjarke said. "We'll survive."

"Nobody's panicking," Asger said, "but thanks for the lecture."

Kim, still seated on Asger's other side, looked at him.

"Do your parents still lecture you?" he asked her.

"When we're in the same solar system, yes."

"What about when you're in the same shuttle?"

"The frequency would naturally increase."

"I guess it's universal then."

"I'm ready to deploy the explosives and shuttle debris for our fake crash." Tristan's hand hovered over a button on the control panel. "But we'll have to get in close to make it convincing."

Qin couldn't imagine how much closer they could get without *actually* crashing. On the forward display, the green blur of the forest had turned into individual trees zipping past underneath them.

She sent a quick message off to Bonita in case this went poorly, saying she hoped Bonita would watch out for her sisters and hire them if they survived and she didn't. And that she missed her—and Viggo.

"I've got to time it to when they fire next." Bjarke turned their nose up slightly so they would skim along above the trees instead of knocking the tops off them. "There's a nice cliff."

"*Nice?*" Tristan asked.

"Nice to appear to crash into." Bjarke flew toward the cliff, then turned the craft to follow its craggy face, the forest still right below them.

Wind railed at the shuttle as it rattled ominously. A *ker-thunk* echoed as they snapped off the tip of a tree that was taller than the rest. Red and orange DEW-Tek blasts rained down into the forest all around them and blew shards of rock off the cliff face scant feet away.

A shield-integrity alarm went off on the console.

Asger loosened his pod enough to lean over and pat Qin's knee reassuringly. She wanted to tell him to stay secure in his own pod, but she gripped his hand instead. They were both in full armor. That would likely do as much to protect them as the pods.

"Incoming," Tristan barked. "That one's going to hit us."

"Good," Bjarke growled.

A jolt rocked Qin's pod, and something snapped in the framework of the shuttle.

"Now, Tristan," Bjarke ordered, then found a stream that left a break in the trees and turned them into the gap.

A thunderous boom assaulted Qin's sensitive ears, and her first thought was that they'd been struck again and the shuttle was exploding. But that was the ordnance Tristan had expelled from the back.

"Increasing drag," Bjarke said calmly as he flew lower over the water. "There's a lot of smoke back there. Hopefully, it'll cover us. And they shouldn't see us through the trees unless they're right overhead."

"As long as this gap in the trees stays wide enough for us," Tristan said.

Branches thunked and tore at the sides. Qin looked at Asger, wondering if they had just run out of space for their makeshift airstrip.

Asger met her gaze and smiled, but it was a forced smile. Worry darkened his eyes.

More branches hammered and clawed at the hull as they flew along above the stream, the noise as wrenching and thunderous as the fading explosion. Despite that, the craft didn't smash into any tree trunks, nor any branches large enough to jerk them to a halt.

Gradually, the shuttle slowed down, the clawing of branches growing less frequent. The deep shadows of twilight darkened the forest, and Qin realized that night would come soon. Maybe that would help keep their survival unnoticed until morning.

Bjarke plopped them down in the shallow water of the stream with surprising gentleness and cut the engines.

"I don't think there's any way they're not going to find the shuttle eventually," Bjarke said, "but we can walk in the stream to hide our tracks, so they don't know which way we went. There ought to be enough animal life around here that they'll have trouble picking out individual people with scanners, and Kim's the only one without armor. If we stay in our armor, we won't give off much heat. I know from past experience that the crushers don't register on scanners."

"Not as well as I do," Tristan muttered.

Asger nodded vigorously. Qin had heard about their adventures being hidden inside of crushers morphed into boxes.

"Grab the emergency supplies," Bjarke said. "We're going to have a long trek."

"How long of a trek?" Kim asked, her tone calm despite their failure and current predicament.

Bjarke turned off all the systems and rose to his feet. "We're about fifty miles from the outskirts of the suburbs of Zamek City, and a good seventy from the core."

Qin unfastened herself from her pod and grabbed her weapons and the modest travel kit she'd brought along. Once again, the crushers grouped around the hatch first.

"Casmir's execution is scheduled for tomorrow night," Kim said quietly.

"We'll walk fast," Bjarke said.

Qin saw Kim's grim face as they headed for the hatch together and reached out to put a hand on her shoulder. She wished she could say something reassuring, but nothing came to mind.

In addition to having a lot of land to traverse, they would have to do it while being hunted down by all the Kingdom defense ships that had seen the shuttle crash. Their ruse had only been intended to pass a cursory inspection. As soon as the Kingdom troops searched the site of the explosion, they would realize there were no bodies and not enough debris for the craft to have gone down back there. Bjarke powered down the shuttle before they got out, but it was also possible the Kingdom scanners would pick it up right away.

Qin shook her head as they clambered into the stream to walk in the water for as long as they could. Once again, she wished they had managed to get Casmir. Then this would have been worth it all. But now…

Engines roared above the forest. The Kingdom ships had arrived for the search.

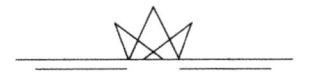

Oku returned to her room after dinner, but instead of settling in for the night, she paced and kept glancing toward the window. A message had come in during her meal with her mother that her father was returning to the castle, and she planned to demand in person that he free Casmir. Whatever wheedling, begging, or promising it took.

What he thought he was doing with this dreadful execution, Oku didn't know, but she'd been trying to figure out how to stop it since she'd heard the news. Since *everybody* had heard the news. What would his poor parents be thinking? She'd been too much the coward to contact them to ask. It wasn't as if she could offer any comfort, not until she figured out a way to stop it.

She kept hoping the media had misinterpreted some report and that her father would let her know it had been a mistake. If he truly meant to have Casmir killed… that would be the last straw. She had no idea how she could mount a rescue, or even where Casmir was being held, but if she couldn't talk her father out of his insane plan, she would find a way. Even if that meant she ended up being labeled a criminal herself.

Night had fallen outside, so there wasn't much to see out the window, but from her room in the castle, the guidance lights of the royal landing pad were visible beyond the walls and on the other side of the street. If she didn't shut the blinds, she could see shuttles and other small craft coming and going.

In her youth, she'd occasionally felt resentful that Finn and Jorg had rooms on the other side of the hall that overlooked the sea, but by the time she'd grown old enough that her parents wouldn't have minded if she chose a room in another part of the castle, Oku hadn't cared enough to move. Between her studies and her research trips to other systems, she hadn't been here that often.

Tonight, she was glad for this view. Dozens of people would want her father's attention, but she planned to get to him first.

The lights of a shuttle and several escort ships descended toward the landing pad, and she rushed to the window and gripped the sill. She couldn't yet tell if it was his personal shuttle and was about to message him when a knock sounded at her door.

She thought about ignoring it, but it opened anyway. Her mother walked in, and Chasca, who'd been lying on one of the rugs, took the opportunity to trot out into the hallway. Oku was wary about letting her out of her sight these days, but with Finn up on one of the orbital stations, she doubted another dog-napping would take place.

Oku glanced back but only flicked her fingers to acknowledge her mother's arrival. They'd just been at dinner together, so Oku couldn't imagine she had fresh news or anything major to say.

The shuttle and its escort descended, bright red and white lights gleaming against the cloudy night sky. The royal purple of the hull grew discernible. It *was* her father's shuttle.

As it disappeared behind the castle wall for landing, her mother joined Oku at the window.

"I got a message from your father."

"He's aboard, right?" Oku waved toward the landing pad. "I need to talk to him."

In person. Not via their chips or a comm.

She didn't add the reason why, though she was tempted to ask her mother if she knew where Casmir was. Still up on her father's ship? Or had he been taken to some prison until the execution?

But even if her mother knew, would she share the information? Weeks earlier, she had warned Oku to avoid trading messages with Casmir, to avoid anything to do with him. Had she some inkling that this would eventually come to pass?

Before this, Oku hadn't been sure if she had romantic feelings for Casmir, a man she'd only met in person twice, but some detached part of her noted how distressed she'd been since the news announcement— how distressed she was now. She didn't just want to *talk* to her father; she wanted to wring his neck.

Especially after she'd gone through all those reports, including the latest ones from Captain Ishii, who'd been surprisingly neutral and unbiased. After reading everything, Oku agreed that Casmir's actions with the gate pieces had gone against her father's wishes, but she also agreed with what Casmir probably believed, that the gate didn't rightfully belong to the Kingdom but to all of humanity. Even if that was up for debate, Casmir and Kim and all of their friends had clearly been acting to help the Kingdom in System Stymphalia. And they *had*. They'd risked their lives to stop Dubashi and get rid of that virus. Casmir had even found time to make the Kingdom a bunch of crushers and a slydar detector. He should be welcomed back as a valuable ally, not a criminal to be executed.

As far as Oku could tell, her father's only reasons to be angry with Casmir were that he'd impeded the acquisition of the gate and he'd been in the area when Jorg had been killed. And that Rache had also been in the area. Several of the reports from Ambassador Romano and a Lieutenant Meister in Intelligence had pointed out that Casmir and Kim kept showing up near Rache and might have worked with him.

Oku could see how they would find that suspicious, but all that should merit was an investigation, not an assumption. And certainly not a *death* sentence.

"Yes, he's aboard," her mother said after a delay—had she been reading another update on her chip? "But he got some news and won't be able to stay." Her mother shook her head. "Not even to have a bite to eat. The Kingdom and Odin aren't quite out of trouble yet."

Oku wrenched her mind back to the moment. "What do you mean?"

"I'm not sure yet, but apparently a new threat has been made. That virus may be involved."

"I thought Cas— The reports I've seen from Royal Intelligence implied that the virus had been taken care of."

Judging by her mother's squint, she'd caught that slip-up.

Oku made a frustrated chop with her hand. What did she expect?

"I didn't realize you'd been getting reports from Royal Intelligence," her mother said.

Oku couldn't tell if the neutrally delivered words held censure. "Van Dijk is giving me some. I asked for them. I want to be informed."

"Good. I'm sure your father will be pleased that you're showing more of an interest in what's going on in the Kingdom."

Oku clenched her jaw. She was more interested in what was going on with *Casmir*. She almost blurted that out in frustration, but her mother spoke again first.

"You know your father isn't likely to name you his heir, at least not at this time, unless you show a lot more interest over the years ahead, but he hasn't ruled you out completely. We spoke when he was on the way back about the possibility of marrying you to someone the Senate might deem a suitable advisor, someone respected by them and by the military."

Oku gaped as she realized who. Finn had mentioned the man himself. "Not Senator Oswald!"

"*Sir* Senator Oswald. Don't forget he's a knight and well-respected among the older generation, chiefly all of those in the Senate."

"That's because he's *in* the older generation. *Mother*. He must be *eighty*."

Her tone turned dry. "He's sixty-five."

"That's *old*. I'm twenty-six!"

"I'm aware of your age, Oku. I *was* there for your birth, you know." Now her tone was very dry.

"*Mother*." Oku groaned.

"I know it's not what you would wish if you could pick for yourself, but you've always known that you wouldn't be able to do so. I'd assumed—and you were always told—that you would be married to some distant prince or emperor to solidify an alliance for the Kingdom. Even if Sir Oswald isn't ideal in your eyes, it would allow you to remain here on Odin. You'll forgive me if that's something I would like to see."

"I don't want to leave Odin, either, but…" She groped at the air, then dropped her hand and the argument.

This didn't matter right now. She had to ensure that Casmir wasn't executed. Later, after she rescued him and helped him clear his name—or, if it came to that, helped him escape the Kingdom and find sanctuary in another system—she could worry about the future husband she might be stuck with.

"It's difficult being born into royalty." Her mother rested a hand on her shoulder. "Trust me, I know."

And Oku knew she did. Her marriage to Father had been arranged long ago and hadn't had anything to do with love.

"Yeah," was all she could manage to say.

The shuttle and its escort took off again. If her mother was right, her father had never stepped foot outside of it. She would have to muster the gumption to comm him directly and fight for Casmir's life. Dare she? Or would it be better to try to get information out of him about where Casmir was being taken and handle matters herself? One of the prisons in the city, the news had said. She needed to find out if that was true, but if she asked too many questions, her father might realize she would be brazen and defiant enough to stage a rescue.

Her mother lowered her hand. "For all of our sakes, I shall hope the virus threat is a hollow one and that your father won't have to stay in orbit with the Fleet for long."

Oku managed a nod and another, "Yeah," but as with the threat of marriage, she couldn't find space in her mind to focus on another problem right now.

"Good night, Oku." Her mother saw herself out.

A group of armored soldiers appeared on the covered bridge that went from the landing pad over the street and to the castle wall. Oku squinted. Had Father decided to stop in for a bit after all? She saw one figure in the middle who wasn't in armor, but between the darkness of night, the guard towers along the wall, and the tinted Glasnax sides of the bridge, it was impossible to see faces.

"You better be careful," a male voice said from the corner of the room. "I seem to recall rumors that Sir Oswald has some bedroom perversions."

Oku almost shrieked.

Instead, she lunged for her desk drawer and yanked out the stunner she'd been keeping there since Finn had arranged for Chasca's kidnapping. She pointed it at a man in black combat armor who stepped out from her linen closet. What the hell? Had he been in there the whole time? Since she'd gotten back from dinner?

LAYERS OF FORCE

For a crazy second, she thought it was Casmir, that he'd somehow escaped and gotten armor, but the voice wasn't right, and the words didn't make any sense. Casmir wouldn't know anything about knights, and she couldn't imagine him showing up in her linen closet.

She almost shot, but she realized the stunner wouldn't affect someone in combat armor. "Who are you?"

Whoever he was, he wore a full suit, even a helmet and some kind of face covering that kept her from— Oh, shit. Oku almost dropped the stunner when she realized who this might be. But why in all Twelve Systems would Tenebris Rache show up in the castle and in her suite?

"You don't remember me? I'm wounded. Jorg didn't remember either."

For the first time, true fear crept into her. The reports said Rache had assassinated Jorg. Had Jorg only been his first target? Did Rache plan to kill all of King Jager's children?

She glanced toward the door, wondering if she could possibly make it past him. That armor would enhance his speed, and rumors abounded about cybernetic enhancements that the mercenary had. Should she scream? He wasn't advancing—yet.

"What do you want, Rache?" Oku used his name intentionally, hoping wildly that he would say she'd mistaken him for someone else.

"It's David," he said quietly, "and I came on another errand, but I arrived early, so I thought I would visit you."

"*Visit* me?" Oku blurted before the name registered to her brain. David? Wait, she *did* recognize that voice. She hadn't heard it in ten years, and the helmet altered it somewhat, but... "David Lichtenberg?"

"Yes."

"You're dead."

"So I wished the Kingdom to believe. Most pointedly him." Rache—David—*he* pointed in the direction of her parents' suite.

"Why?" Oku looked around, not toward the door this time but toward her chair. The fear had bled out of her—perhaps unwisely—and now she felt numb, her legs weak. But she didn't know if she wanted to relax in front of him, so she only braced herself against her desk.

His voice shifted from calm and conversational to pure ice. "Your father had my fiancée raped and murdered to motivate me."

Oku rocked back against the desk.

He seemed to get control of himself, of the burst of emotion, for his voice returned to his calm tone. "Perhaps, when you're asking for reports from Royal Intelligence, you might ask them what happened to Thea Sogard."

She had disappeared, hadn't she? Been kidnapped? It had been so long ago that Oku barely remembered. After ten years, Oku had almost forgotten about David and also that he'd been engaged to be married. She'd only been sixteen when he died—*supposedly* died—and had only known the Lichtenbergs as distant relatives her family had occasionally visited.

"Are you Rache too?" She had to be sure.

"Yes."

Oku almost swore. He didn't try to hide it, didn't sound apologetic in the least for all the evil he'd done. And whatever more evil he would do. Just what *errand* had brought him here?

"You murdered Jorg," Oku stated, though she didn't know what she expected from him. Clarification? To hear his side of it?

None of the people who'd filled out the reports about the event had been eyewitnesses. Normally, she wouldn't care about Rache's side of anything, but if he wasn't only Rache, but was also someone she'd known as a child, and if there was any truth to that angry claim he'd made…

"I challenged him to a duel. Face to face as battle raged around us." Rache hitched an armored shoulder. "He accepted, and he lost."

"He would have been an idiot to challenge you—to challenge *Rache*."

"You've lived with him your whole life," he stated, as if Jorg's idiocy was patently obvious and she would be the dolt not to see it.

Oku clenched her jaw, refusing to speak badly of her dead brother. Not to this man, a murderer and a criminal. Whatever Rache claimed, he'd killed thousands of soldiers and crewmen out there in the dark reaches of space. Whoever she'd known as a child was long gone. David was gone, replaced by this man. This enemy of the Kingdom.

"What do you want from me?" Oku lifted her chin. "Are you here to kill me too?"

"I came to speak to you about Casmir Dabrowski."

Again, Oku rocked back. She shouldn't have been surprised that Rache would bring Casmir up, since the reports kept mentioning how often they'd been in the same place together—if not on the same *side* together—but it was still startling hearing this cold-hearted killer say Casmir's name.

"You know he's your father's prisoner," Rache said.

"I do."

"And slated to be executed."

"I'm not going to allow—" Oku made herself stop. This wasn't an ally. Giving him information would be ludicrous. "What do you care about Professor Dabrowski?"

Had Rache come to try to retrieve Casmir? Was *that* his errand? But if so, why? Did he need Casmir for something? Was he still after the gate?"

"Someone I like doesn't want him to be killed," he said.

Someone he liked? Oku couldn't imagine the Rache she'd heard about in the news all these years being capable of liking anyone. It was far more believable that he had some use for Casmir.

"And to answer your other question, I did not come to kill you, no. I do not feel any ill will toward you. Jorg was a selfish prick and Finn is a whiny brat."

Wait, did that mean he was here for something to do with Finn? If that were true, she would have to laugh, since Finn wasn't in the castle. He wasn't even on the planet right now.

But Rache had spies everywhere, didn't he? He would know where Finn was. Her other supposition that he'd come to get Casmir made more sense.

"The Kingdom is better off with neither of them in line to inherit more than a plot in the family cemetery," Rache added.

"That's not for you to decide."

"And yet I've taken it upon myself to do so."

Her grip tightened around her stunner. She should have screamed for help instead of standing there and talking to him. Except that he might kill her if she did so, and who would rescue Casmir then?

"If you're not killing me and have no other reason to be loitering in my linen closet, I would appreciate it if you leave. I have things to do."

"But I did have a reason for coming to see you." He tilted his helmeted head to the side. "Not one that would have brought me down here by itself, I'll admit, but since I was here anyway and went to all the trouble to sneak into the castle, I thought I would come speak briefly with you on someone's behalf."

"Not Sir Oswald, presumably."

"No. Casmir. Do you like him?"

"Do I *like* him?" It was the last question she expected to come out of this man's mouth. Maybe she should have sat in her chair after all. "Why would you care?"

"He's expressed interest in you. Guardedly, I'll admit, but he's easy to read. I didn't know whether to encourage that interest, but if there's hope, I thought I would put in a good word for him."

How could someone with Rache's reputation, who had done all he had done, put in a good word for anyone?

"Are you *friends*?" Oku asked, appalled at the idea.

If so, she would have to doubt what she believed about Casmir. The idea that he could be friends with Rache was horrifying. Even if they were cloned from the same DNA and technically brothers, Rache was completely loathsome.

"Enemies, actually. Though I'm not sure he realizes it. Or maybe he does but won't accept it. After he thwarted my plans not once but *twice*, he gave me gifts of underwear and comic books. I must warn you, his taste in literature is dreadful, but if you want someone loyal, determined, optimistic, and vaguely entertaining to stand at your side in any situation, he's your kid. Your *man*. Perhaps not as testosterone-filled as the men who usually seek your favor, but not a damsel in distress either. Don't tell him I admitted that."

"I... can't imagine sharing this conversation with anyone."

"Excellent."

If anyone had told her Rache would show up in her suite to talk about underwear and testosterone... "This is surreal."

"Indeed. If you decide to alert the guards that I was here, I would appreciate it if you give me a ten-minute head start. As a favor for not killing, kidnapping, or otherwise threatening you."

"You're a loon."

"Five minutes then." He held a finger to his faceplate where his lips would be, then stepped back into the closet and closed the door.

What the hell? There wasn't another way out of there.

Oku waited for several long seconds, expecting him to realize that, walk out, and leave through a window. When he didn't, she crept forward and opened the door.

LAYERS OF FORCE

Save for the stacks of towels and linens, the closet was empty. But a fresh hole had been cut into the ceiling. She stared up at ductwork and insulation and what was apparently enough room to move around between the floors of the castle. In full combat armor.

"Time to request a new suite." Oku rubbed her face, then decided to go find Chasca, abruptly worried by the realization that the castle wasn't as difficult to infiltrate as she'd always believed.

When her dog had been kidnapped, she had assumed Finn had assisted the outsiders in getting her, but here Rache had wandered in all by himself. She was *positive* nobody here would have opened a gate for him.

Should she report him?

As she strode past staff and guards in the halls, she wrestled with the thought, but would it be incriminating that she hadn't screamed for help the instant he'd shown up in her suite? She didn't *think* there were any cameras in her rooms, but after learning that Royal Intelligence had snagged all the communications off her chip, she no longer had any faith in her privacy.

She would hate to claim that Rache had grabbed her and forced her to stay quiet only for footage to appear later that showed how she'd done nothing but stand there while he talked. And the fact that he'd not only brought up Casmir but had wanted to put a good word in for him... That could incriminate Casmir. *Further.*

Oku groaned as she went out a back door to the courtyard, frustrated with the entire situation. For now, she wouldn't say anything. If it was possible that Rache had come to rescue Casmir, she didn't want to stop him, not when she didn't yet know if she could find him and retrieve him.

When Chasca didn't run out of the darkness toward her, Oku started toward some of the bushes that she favored, but she saw a Fleet soldier in blue armor, his helmet and gauntlets removed, standing outside a side door and rubbing Chasca's side. She was leaning against his leg and wagging enthusiastically.

"Chasca," Oku said sternly, heading toward them. "Haven't you learned not to fling yourself willy-nilly at strangers?"

The soldier peered into the darkness at her, then lifted his eyebrows when he recognized her and dropped to one knee. "Princess Oku. Greetings. And sorry if I wasn't supposed to pet the dog. Is she yours? My family has hunting hounds like this. I grew up in the country with a whole pack of them. Had four that slept on my bed at one point. That sometimes meant I had to sleep on the floor, but that's how it works when you like dogs, you know."

Now that their heads were at similar heights, Chasca licked him in the mouth.

"And when they like you, I imagine." Oku waved for him to rise.

"I had a sandwich on the way down." He rubbed his lips. "They can always tell."

Chasca sat and looked up at the soldier as if she had a new best friend.

"This is why it's so easy for people to dog-nap you," Oku whispered to her.

All it took was a kidnapper with sandwich breath. Though she knew her dog well and suspected the soldier had actually fed her something to win this much interest.

"Sorry, ma'am. Uhm, Your Highness." He was big and towered over her, but he only appeared to be about twenty and wasn't threatening. He bit his lip sheepishly, looking like he didn't know what to do with his hands.

A sandwich *on the way down*, he'd said.

"Did you come down with the shuttle?" Oku remembered the man she'd seen walking between all the armored soldiers but who she hadn't been able to identify from a distance. "With my father?"

"Yes, Your Highness. But he had to go right back up, on account of something happening in space." The soldier pointed upward. "Not sure what it was, but he was in a powerful hurry. Said we'd have to head to the launch loop and find our own ride back up to the ship after we secured the prisoner."

Oku froze. "The prisoner?"

"Uhm, yes, Your Highness. But we're not supposed to talk about it." His expression turned wary, as if he worried she would ask him to break those orders.

If she did, would he? Maybe he believed a princess's wishes superseded military orders. Not that her father would agree.

"I didn't know the Fleet stored its prisoners in the castle," she said casually.

Oku didn't want to get him in trouble, but she *had* to know. Was it Casmir?

She couldn't think of any other prisoners who would secretly be stuffed in the castle dungeon. And that was the only place she could imagine he would have been confined if he'd been brought here. This door led to underground bunkers and secret passages out into the city, but it also led down even deeper into the cliff the castle perched upon. Nobody had ever told her that a dungeon existed, but as a curious child, she'd once explored most of the nooks and crannies down there.

Had Rache known Casmir would be brought here? Was that why he was lurking in the castle?

"We put people where the king asks us to, Your Highness."

The door opened, and relief washed across his face as three other armored soldiers came out.

He stepped back, no doubt pleased that this would put an end to what Oku considered a very mild interrogation.

"It was nice meeting you and your dog, Your Highness."

The other soldiers all bowed politely to her before striding back toward the front gate. She walked far enough to see them join up with a couple of castle guards who escorted them out.

Once she was alone, Oku eyed the closed door. She had no doubt whoever was guarding the prisoner would have orders to keep people out, including her, but it ought to be easier to break him out than if he'd been taken to a maximum-security prison. She couldn't imagine how she would do it without Royal Intelligence and eventually her mother and father knowing she'd been responsible, but… so be it.

"Time to make some plans, girl," she murmured and took Chasca back inside through another door.

CHAPTER 7

CASMIR'S SECOND TRIP TO THE CELL UNDER DRACHEN Castle wasn't any more appealing than his first. If anything, it was worse, because his chip had been stolen, so he couldn't work on offline projects, and he had little hope that King Jager would come down and give him another opportunity to *prove* himself.

He didn't think Jager was even on the planet. Casmir had ridden down in the same shuttle as he had, but the king hadn't gotten out. As armored soldiers had ushered Casmir away from the landing pad, the shuttle had taken off again, heading in the direction of the launch loop. Strange that Jager had ridden down with him—it wasn't as if they'd spoken or even made eye contact—and left immediately. Had he wanted to personally make sure Casmir made it to the castle? Or had some message come in, drawing him back up to the warship?

Casmir scratched at his two weeks of beard growth and rubbed his watering eyes. He was lying on his back and felt the cold hardness of the cement bench against his shoulder blades and through his tousled hair that was badly in need of trimming. His temple throbbed, and his entire head ached. Even though the surgery had been minor, his nerves knew something was missing that should be there.

In the corridor somewhere down from his cell, a guard cleared his throat and spat. Casmir imagined hardened phlegm all over the floor and grimaced. Not that anyone would see it in the dim lighting of the ancient stone-walled dungeon.

Heavy footsteps sounded, a second guard arriving. "Reporting in for change of duty."

"Yup." Another throat clearing accompanied this.

"Is this station as boring as it looks?"

"Yup."

"Is that guy really a traitor who worked with Rache?"

"Dunno. He's a scrawny geek who keeps sneezing."

Casmir sniffed self-consciously. He hadn't sneezed *that* often. It wasn't his fault that there was no air-filtration system for this dank, mildewy subterranean prison. At least he wasn't spitting on the floor.

"I heard he was a professor at the university here in town."

"He should have stayed there."

If only. Casmir gazed up at the dark ceiling, wishing an opportunity to escape had presented itself. It seemed a failure that his supposedly clever brain hadn't been able to find a way out of this mess. But without his friends and his robot allies and network access—and now without a chip at all—what was he? A scrawny geek, indeed.

Footsteps sounded again, the old guard leaving and the new one settling in. Casmir wondered if there was any point in trying to chat with the man. He'd tried to draw the last one into a conversation and failed to get a response. There was probably a rule against chatting with the prisoners.

He sneezed.

The footsteps sounded again, the guard walking toward his cell this time. To peek in and consider his scrawny geekness?

The armored man carried his rifle on his back and had his helmet tucked under his arm. Brown-skinned, brown-eyed, and snub-nosed, he was shorter than many of the guards, but perfectly capable of dealing with Casmir, he had no doubt. The cell bars further ensured he was in no danger.

"If you find me boring, let me know," Casmir offered. "It hasn't been more than a day since my last meal. I still have some energy. Perhaps, given the proper accoutrements, I could juggle. Or if you slide me a few tools, I'm not bad at repairing robots, vehicles, and even appliances. Do you, by chance, have a toaster on the fritz?"

"I'm Sergeant Rokuro."

Strange. None of the other guards had introduced themselves.

"Did you get this duty because you irked someone?" Casmir asked. "If so, my sympathies. I've been irking the wrong people for months now."

"I've heard that. Do you know what happened to your chip?"

"A doctor removed it."

"Do you know where it was taken?" Rokuro clarified.

Even stranger. Why this interest in him?

Casmir swung his legs off the bench so he could sit up and face the guard. "No. He put it in a baggie, so hopefully that means someone kept it."

"Hm."

"Any chance you know what's supposed to happen to me?"

"According to the news, there will be a public execution tomorrow evening."

"That's illegal."

"So the university students and faculty are telling everyone. There have been protests."

Protests? For him? Casmir was touched even as he was mortified by the thought of being dragged off to some primitive hanging in a public square. With his luck, he would have a seizure right as someone was about to wrap a noose around his neck.

Rokuro wandered back to his position.

"If you let me out, I'll request that the protestors don't graffiti your armor," he called.

"A tempting offer," came the dry reply.

Rokuro did not return to open the gate.

Casmir sagged back onto the bench, images of this public execution filling his mind. Would it be televised? Would his friends and colleagues see it? Would his *parents* see it?

Thinking of them brought tears to his eyes. With his chip removed, he would never have an opportunity to send those letters out to them, never get a chance to say goodbye, a last chance to hug them.

The tears trickled from his eyes, and he sniffed, not able to stop feeling sorry for himself. Some heroic clone of Admiral Mikita he was.

Did Oku have any idea he was down here in the bowels of the very castle she lived in? Was there any chance he could talk this Rokuro into giving her a message? Out of all the guards and soldiers he'd dealt with since blathering his drug-induced truths about his relationship with Rache, Rokuro had been the most decent by far.

Casmir scrubbed his sleeve across his face and sat up. He would try to talk the man into it.

But the creak of a door opening sounded before he called out. Another change of the guard? So soon?

Rokuro murmured something too softly for Casmir to hear. Casmir sneezed.

"Is that him?" a woman's voice he didn't recognize asked.

For a fleeting moment, he thought the queen might have found out he was here and come to see him, but the voice was rough around the edges, more like someone who'd grown up on the streets than in a noble household.

"He's the only one down here," Rokuro said.

Casmir sneezed again. Damn it. It was hard to eavesdrop when one's own body insisted on making noise.

"Is he sick?" the woman asked.

"I didn't ask him."

"You're helpful."

"I'm just here to drive. And take the position of someone else who might have protested a kidnapping."

"It's a rescue, not a kidnapping," came a new voice from farther back.

Casmir lurched to his feet, hope swelling in his chest. He knew *that* voice.

"Princess Oku?" he dared ask.

Clacks sounded on the cement floor. It wasn't Oku but a gray short-furred dog that trotted into view.

"Uhm, hello, Chasca." Casmir had never met Oku's dog in person, but he grinned goofily at the pup.

The dog tilted her head and wagged her tail. It thwapped against the bars of the cell across the corridor.

The next person to step into view was the one he'd dreamed of seeing. Maybe not in this situation, with his eyes watering and more sneezes threatening his nose, but it was far better than seeing another callous guard.

Princess Oku wore a fur-trimmed parka with the hood pulled up, and he could barely make out her features in the poor lighting, but he had no doubt it was she. She carried a stunner in one hand and a lantern in the other.

"I hope you didn't come to shoot me, Your Highness. I'm very glad to see you and would prefer not to be unconscious for what I hope is a jailbreak."

"It's good to see you alive, Casmir." She used his *name*, his *first* name! And she pushed the hood back so he could see her elegant features and her thick black hair held in place by a headband that appeared woven from dried straw or some other material rather than fabric.

LAYERS OF FORCE

Remembering the time he'd seen her with grass stuck between her toes, Casmir grinned so broadly that his mouth hurt. His injured temple throbbed a protest at this overly exuberant use of his facial muscles, but he didn't care.

"I'm merely armed in case we run into trouble," Oku added. "This may shock you, but my father would not want me to break you out of the dungeon."

"I am not shocked. For some reason, your father has never warmed up to my delightful but admittedly eccentric charm."

"Weird." She smiled, looking him up and down, her gaze lingering on his socks—why did the guards always insist on taking his shoes?

"I thought so." He straightened under her scrutiny, wishing he were washed and wearing clothes that weren't rumpled and smelly.

Her gaze lingered on his temple. "They took your chip?"

"Yeah." It was silly, but the word came out as a croak, emotion making his throat tight. "I had a bunch of letters for my family on it, and all your bee stuff I'd been tinkering with these past weeks. I'm sorry. If I get a chance, I can redo it. Oh, and Kim has all the bacterial bee stuff on her chip. If we can get in touch with her, we can get it." He waved to his temple and said, "I'm sorry," again before he could stop himself.

He wasn't burbling nervously in quite the same way he did with Rache—at least he didn't think so—but he'd wanted their next meeting to be perfect. A coffee date, not this travesty.

"It's not your fault they took it. And *I'm* the one who's sorry that they—my father—hurt you." Oku leaned to the side and pressed a button, and the gate opened.

He wiped his eyes again and stepped out. "Just so you know, I'm not crying." He doubted she would care if he was, but he was already such a mess that he hated the idea of her seeing him as some weepy wimp on top of it. "I'm allergic to dungeons."

"Also weird."

"You're describing me well."

She hadn't stepped back as he'd scooted out of the cell, and as he found himself face to face with her, the profound urge to hug her came over him. Because she was rescuing him and because she let him send her robotic-bee schematics and because... she was nice and sweet and— damn it, boy—was he falling in love with a princess?

His arms twitched up for that hug, but he caught himself. He was a scruffy—*extremely* scruffy at the moment—commoner and some throwaway-clone at that. He couldn't presume that—

Oku stuffed the stunner in her pocket and wrapped her arms around him. The lantern clunked him in the back, but he was far too delighted to mind that.

Her cheek brushed his, and she whispered, "I'm weird too."

"I don't think that's true, but I'm willing to go along with it if it means you want to hug me." Casmir knew they weren't alone in the corridor—the tail that thwacked him in the leg was a reminder—but he didn't care. He would hold the hug as long as she wished.

"Even if my father refuses to see it," she whispered, "I know you've been helping our people. I've seen the reports. All of them. Thank you."

This time, the tears that came to his eyes had nothing to do with allergies. Until that moment, he hadn't realized how very badly he wanted her to know that he had been trying to help, trying to do the right thing for the Kingdom and all of humanity.

He dared lift a hand to the back of her head and stroked her hair. "You're welcome."

For several wonderful seconds, she stood and let him. Then she squeezed him and stepped back. "We had better not linger here, or you'll be recaptured, and they'll throw me in the cell next to yours."

"I would not like for that to happen, though I'm positive you would be better company than I've had since being transferred to the king's warship."

"I have no doubt." Oku looked down at his socks. "Do you know where your shoes are? We're taking a trip."

A trip sounded *fantastic*. He didn't care if he had to go on it completely naked.

"The guards took my shoes. To the same place they took my belt, I assume." Casmir dropped a hand to the waistband of his trousers. "I hope you'll forgive me if my pants spontaneously descend. That would not be the first—no, is this our third?—impression I'd like to make on you."

"Oh?" Oku lifted the lantern, making the twinkle in her brown eyes easy to see. "Are your bare knees unattractive?"

"They're fabulous, other than their extreme pastiness right now. Did you know it's very difficult to get a tan in space?"

LAYERS OF FORCE

"More difficult than in Zamek City? It was cloudy, foggy, or cloudy and foggy all summer."

"So I didn't miss anything?" Casmir knew they shouldn't be bantering now, but she seemed willing, and he'd longed to have an actual conversation with her for so long. A fun, frivolous conversation about nothing of import.

But she sobered as she answered, "It was actually a particularly good summer to be out of the city."

And he knew exactly what she meant. "I'm sorry. I'm sure the bombing was terrifying. Thank you so much for helping my parents."

"You're welcome. They're nice people. Your mother made Chasca and me cookies."

Memories of his mother cooking for him and his friends and everybody else she ever met flooded his mind. He told himself that he would be able to see his parents again soon. He *had* to see them. And convince them to get out of the city. Because even if he escaped, he would be a felon or criminal or whatever Jager labeled him as, and they would be in danger of being used against him.

But he could worry about that once he was free of this place.

"I'm glad," he said. "What's next? Am I correct in assuming that you don't have permission from anyone to walk out the front door of the castle with me?"

"Professor Dabrowski." Oku raised her eyebrows imperiously. "I am a princess and the oldest surviving child of King Jager, the supreme ruler over this system. I walk out whichever door I wish."

"So... no permission?"

"Correct. We'll be sneaking out via the underground vehicle garage." She pointed downward.

How much more underground could they go? Casmir had descended the equivalent of five or six floors to get to the dungeon level. But then, the castle *did* perch on a high cliff that overlooked the ocean.

"Ah," Rokuro said, stepping into view from around a corner, trailed by a tall, sturdy woman in her fifties who carried no fewer than four weapons. "The vehicle garage may no longer be an option."

"What happened?" Oku asked.

"That trouble you mentioned? It's here." Rokuro touched his temple. "I just got a message from the guard captain that went out to everyone in the unit. A camera caught a glimpse of someone in black armor on the grounds, and they've been trying to zoom in and magnify to identify what can only be an intruder. They're not *positive*, but there's a remote possibility that it could be the criminal Rache, who is known to favor black armor. And a mask."

"Rache is *here*?" Casmir asked, deeming a masked black-armored man a solid likelihood of being Rache, not a remote one.

"At least they didn't catch him in my linen closet," Oku murmured.

Rokuro gaped at her. "Is that a joke, Your Highness? It must be. He wouldn't *dare* come here."

Casmir had no doubt that Rache dared go anywhere he pleased. Was it possible his clone brother had come to rescue him? Or—he grimaced as he realized the more likely scenario—was he here to assassinate the king?

"You had better warn your father." A part of Casmir felt that he was betraying Rache by saying that to Oku, but he refused to hold knowledge about an assassination in confidence. Even if Jager was his enemy, it wasn't acceptable to *murder* him.

Oku opened her mouth, but she glanced at her escort before speaking. "I'm sure he's already been warned."

Why did he have a feeling that wasn't what she'd wanted to tell him?

"He has," Rokuro said, "and extra security is now flooding the castle, and extra ships have joined his shuttle heading back up to orbit. Extra bodyguards are being sent to protect Finn, who's just arrived back from orbit, and, er. Extra bodyguards are being ordered to your suite to protect *you*, Your Highness."

"We need to get out of here quickly then, before they realize I'm not there."

"We'll have to use the escape tunnels that lead into the city," the other woman said.

"I don't know where those are," Rokuro said.

"As the princess's personal bodyguard, I was shown long ago. I can lead the way from here."

"Thank you, Maddie." Oku patted her arm, then took Casmir's hand.

He was so startled by the touch and the novelty of hand-holding that he didn't think to protest any of this until they'd gone through three hidden doors in brick walls, down several dust-filled passages, and up three ladders and down another. Chasca protested being carried up and down the ladders by Rokuro, but after a few reassuring pats from Oku, she allowed it.

"Should you go back before they realize you're gone?" Casmir whispered to Oku when they were on level ground again. He struggled to keep from panting audibly as he spoke. The return to Odin's gravity had been noticeable all day, but his lungs felt it keenly as they moved along at a brisk pace, the gritty stone floors tugging at his socks.

"I'm going with you," Oku said.

The woman—Maddie—glanced back.

"I would like that very much, as I've hoped to ask you out for coffee or another adult beverage for a long time, but I'm afraid you'll be in huge trouble, if not outright danger, if you're associated with me. Is it possible that you could go back before anyone realizes I'm gone and that your family wouldn't realize you'd been the one to help me?"

Maddie and Rokuro stopped at another door, this one made from rusted metal rather than brick meant to blend into the walls. A faint roar drifted down from above. One of the city's mag trains or subways?

"We could let him out here," Maddie said, facing Oku, "and possibly get back to the castle before you're missed."

"We diddled with the guard roster, and there are cameras in the corridors," Oku said. "They're going to know I helped him."

"But it might be worse for you—and for him—if you disappear into the city with him. Your father will order the entire Kingdom Guard, military, and castle forces out to hunt for you—and possibly suspect him of manipulating you into this action."

Casmir nodded. As much as he longed to run off with Oku, he had to think of her reputation. More than that, Jager or her mother might come up with some heinous punishment for her. He didn't want to be the cause of that. If he could find his way into the city from here, maybe he could avoid the law, get back home, grab his parents, and drag them off to... Where? Some wilderness? He was a city boy and now one without a chip. He didn't even know where one would flee to in order to avoid the law. Another system was the only place he might be safe.

The idea of being united with Oku only to leave forever tore at his heart, but he couldn't be selfish and drag her into his mess.

"I'm going with Casmir." Oku clasped his hand again. "I'm going to get him a new chip, and I'm going to help him clear his name."

Casmir felt he should object more vociferously, but he was so tickled that she *wanted* to help him that he couldn't get a further protest out. "They'll be able to track you by your chip," he warned instead.

"I've already taken it offline. Maddie, Rokuro, please do the same with yours for now."

"But if you just disappear," Maddie started to warn.

"I left a note for my mother," Oku said. "One that she won't receive until later, since I didn't want her to stop me, but I told her I was going to help a friend and that I would be back in a few days. She'll figure out quickly what I'm really up to, but she will at least know I'm acting of my own volition."

Casmir didn't know enough about their relationship to know if that would be enough, or if there was any possibility that the queen would understand. In the end, it was *Jager* who needed to understand. Unfortunately, Casmir doubted the man ever would, and he feared Oku's wish to *clear his name* wouldn't work.

"Besides," Oku added, perhaps realizing she hadn't swayed her bodyguards, "I think Casmir is exactly the person we need to help figure out who kidnapped Chasca and was angling to get rid of me and put Finn forward as our father's heir."

Casmir arched his eyebrows. "I hadn't heard about that."

"They didn't let you watch the news in your brig cell?" Oku asked.

"No, it was quite rude of them."

"I'll say. A friend at the university tracked the plot to a Sir Slayer, supposedly in Military Intelligence, but that was all he could get. If we can get you another chip, maybe you can help."

Casmir lifted his chin. "I would love another chip, and I'm always eager to help."

He didn't want Oku to be in danger, but he would be delighted to assist her and prove himself useful. Right now, useful was the last thing he felt. He was more like an immense burden that would drag her into the quicksand right alongside him.

"Good." Oku nodded to this last door. "Open it, Maddie."

The female bodyguard did, and dust flowed out, assaulting Casmir's nostrils like Mad Moriarty's angry drones in the Cloud City Labyrinth in the Cyberman Comic Saga. He sneezed, not once but a half a dozen times, putting his free hand on the nearest wall for support.

"Are you *sure* this is Mikita's clone?" Maddie asked.

That news, it seemed, was no longer much of a secret. Longing for an antihistamine, Casmir rubbed his watering eyes and straightened, attempting to look noble rather than weak. The lack of footwear, lack of a recent shower, and days of grimy beard growth made it a vain attempt.

"Yes." Oku stepped closer to Casmir and rested a hand on his shoulder.

Her hood had fallen back again, and the lantern light shone on her elegant features and shiny black hair. She wasn't suffering from a lack of a shower. She smelled *nice*, like lavender soap or shampoo, and she was touching him, which was also nice. Casmir reminded himself that he was in the middle of an escape, and possibly fleeing for his life, so this wasn't the time to drool over her. Any second now, she would turn that gentle touch into a shove to get him going.

"Even if my father refuses to see the truth," Oku told Maddie, "I know he's been helping our people. A *lot*."

"As you say, Your Highness." Maddie gestured for them to head through the door after Rokuro.

Casmir didn't know how long the trek through the city's underground would be, but he hardly cared. Oku was going with him and had faith in him and wanted to help him find a way to clear his name. Maybe it was naive on both of their parts to believe that it could happen, but he whispered a quick prayer and held on to his hope.

Scholar Sato, it's Irena Dabrowski. Are you back in the system and able to respond? You may know that news has come out that Casmir is to be executed—a public execution!—and you can imagine our horror. And our frustration as we haven't been able to get answers from the government, the military, or him.

The last update we got from Casmir said he had just returned to the system with some allies and was helping the Kingdom Fleet to clear the blockade at the gate. Nothing in that note prepared us for the long silence from him that has followed or this appalling announcement.

Do you have any information? Earlier tonight, we received a warning from Princess Oku to get out of our apartment because the government—the very government that we have supported and paid taxes to our entire lives—might come for us next. We're afraid and confused. We're still in the apartment because there are guards in the street and alley monitoring the exits. She told us to meet her at Majestic Meadows Park, but I'm afraid we won't be able to get out, and now her chip seems to be offline. I hope that's all that it is. Our messages aren't getting through.

Are you out there, Kim? Do you know what's going on and what we can do to help? Casmir's colleagues at the university have started protesting the execution, but they don't know any more than we do about what's really going on. Casmir can't possibly be a criminal. He's a good boy. We all know he is.

Kim?

Kim groped with a response for the message while she navigated the pathless forest in the dark, only the mediocre night-vision of her contact keeping her from tripping and falling over the logs, dense undergrowth, and roots.

Asger, Tristan, and Bjarke were leading the group, hopefully with some clue about where they were going, while the crushers and the Qin cohort followed silently. Whenever the search shuttles and helicopters roared past overhead, shining searchlights into the forest, the group paused their trek to hide.

According to Kim's chip's built-in navigation, they were more than sixty miles northwest of the city and even farther from that park and the building where Casmir's parents lived. Unless they could find a vehicle—hard when they were still more than forty miles from even the farmlands outside of Zamek City—they would never make it there in time to help. Or to stop the execution.

"Wait for a minute." Kim turned and faced the crushers. She'd once sent Zee to help Casmir deep in the Kingdom forests, and he'd crossed more than two hundred miles in a few hours. "Zee, can you and a couple of your crusher allies get to Zamek City tonight?"

"Crushers can run at speeds of over sixty miles per hour," Zee stated. "To reach the city before sunrise would be a simple matter."

"Casmir's parents may be in trouble. You've been to their apartment before, haven't you? I can give you the address if you haven't. Will you send two crushers to lock up a couple of guards that are blocking the exits? Without hurting anyone, please. And then go up to their apartment and help them get to Majestic Meadows Park." Kim assumed that if Oku wanted Casmir's parents to flee there, she would either be going there herself or sending someone to pick them up. She must have learned that they were in danger—did Jager plan to round them up to ensure they couldn't try to organize some rescue of Casmir? "Maybe a couple of you should go straight to the park too," she added. "In case... Princess Oku may be going there and need help."

"Casmir Dabrowski wishes to ask Princess Oku on a coffee date," Zee stated.

"Yes, he does." Kim glanced at the knights, who'd paused and were watching this exchange.

"He also asked me to do cute things in videos that he recorded for her. I believe he wishes her to become his mate."

Kim rubbed her face. "I'm not sure that's going to happen, but she's at least a friend. She may also know where Casmir is being held."

"I will go personally to Majestic Meadows Park," Zee said, "and I will send other crushers to help Casmir Dabrowski's parents."

"Thank you. I know he'll appreciate that."

"Yes."

As Zee and three other crushers took off in the direction of the city, the roar of engines came into hearing range again.

"Stay hidden if you can!" Kim called after them.

"Good advice for all of us." Bjarke stepped forward and pointed her between a pair of trees. "You know the drill, everyone. Duck down. Hide behind foliage. Helmets up so they won't detect our body-heat signatures through our armor."

Damp foliage battered at Kim's face as she crouched and inserted herself into a bush beside one of the trees. The noise of the engine grew louder, and light appeared in the sky as a craft approached, the trees underneath casting long stark shadows.

Asger and Bjarke squatted down nearby.

"They're not going to have any trouble spotting this group once we run out of forest," Asger said. "The crushers aren't reflective, at least, but they're still noticeable. And so is our armor."

"I know," Bjarke said. "We're going to need to get vehicles to get everybody into the city or to the university or wherever we're planning to go. Has anyone figured out where Dabrowski actually *is* yet? Is he truly in that prison?"

"I just heard from his parents. We're working on figuring it out." Kim hoped. "I'm composing a message to Princess Oku now. She might be our best bet for getting information on his whereabouts."

"Princess Oku?" Bjarke asked. "Isn't she a flower-picking fluff who delivers seeds around the Twelve Systems?"

"She certainly is *not*," Asger said. "That's an act she puts on for the media, so nobody bothers her with schemes related to the throne. She has two degrees and the seeds she delivers are seeds she *makes* to survive in space."

"Hm."

"I don't know why she would know anything about Casmir though." Asger looked at Kim, the dark and the branches hiding his expression.

The roar of the engine grew louder, the shuttle flying into view above the trees, its searchlight probing all around their group. Kim sent her message to Oku while she waited for it to pass, crossing her fingers that it wouldn't spot them. The night and forest would be hard for human eyes to pierce, but scanner instruments wouldn't have trouble with the dark.

It flew past, searching the forest their group had just passed through, and Kim let out a breath.

"She and Casmir are pen pals," Kim said, realizing Asger was still looking in her direction. "Maybe more. I don't know."

"Maybe more? How is that possible?" Asger asked. "He's just a... commoner."

"Nothing wrong with commoners," Tristan murmured from the side.

"And we're all here trying to find him and risking our lives to save his," Bjarke said dryly, "and we disobeyed orders from the king in order to follow him into Dubashi's moon base. I'm not quite sure how that came about, to be honest, but I don't think he's very common."

"No, I suppose not," Asger said. "It's just that I'm... surprised." He sounded more disgruntled than surprised. "Oku could have *anybody*. Any knight or a prince or an emperor. I always thought that it would be a long shot if I could even get her to go on a date, and I'm..."

"Arrogant?" Kim suggested.

"A knight," Asger said firmly.

"An arrogant knight."

"You want to date Princess Oku?" came Qin's voice from a few trees away.

Bjarke snorted, as if he'd seen that coming.

"No," Asger blurted. "Not *now*. But before I knew you, I possibly tried to convince her that I'm handsome and appealing. Of course I don't have any interest in her now."

"Better make sure nobody's behind you before you back your ass up that quickly," Bjarke said.

"Shut up, Father."

Asger rose and went back to sit with Qin. Kim shook her head and stood up. The engine of that shuttle was still audible, and she was sure it would return, but it had moved off for now.

"Does Oku really like him?" Bjarke asked. "Or were you messing with the boy?"

The boy? Asger?

"I do not mess with people," Kim said. "I believe they are friends but have not spent much time together in person yet, so I would be surprised if they were more than that. I have no interest in continuing this conversation. I have sent her a message and will hope for information. In the meantime, how will we acquire a vehicle?"

Bjarke pointed into the woods but not in the direction they had been heading. "I've been looking at the map and thinking about it. I think our best bet is to veer off to our estate. It's to the north of the city and not on the way, but we can stay in the forest all the way to it. The groundskeeper should have kept our vehicles in working order this past year."

"Your estate where you and Asger live when you're here on the planet?" Kim asked. "Won't the government think you might go there and have it watched?"

"It's possible, but… William? Did you identify yourself to those soldiers on the shuttle?"

"No." Asger walked back over with Qin, holding her hand. "There wasn't time. My helmet was up, so they probably didn't see my face well."

"So nobody should know for certain that it was us or that we're here on the planet," Bjarke said. "It's possible someone is watching the estate, since we were exiled even before we made this choice, but I think it's more likely nobody will have done anything there yet. I doubt anyone is worrying about a couple of exiled knights right now. It could be a decent base of operations from which to make further plans."

Kim wasn't so sure that nobody would be paying attention to the knights, but at least any vehicle they picked up would be theirs and not stolen. She hated how much they'd already done that was illegal. Her dream of ever being welcome on Odin's soil again was fading further with every passing day.

"I'm willing to go ahead with this plan," she said.

"We could arrive there faster if we ran," one of the crushers said. "My brethren and I have discussed this. Crushers are faster than humans, and we are also very strong. We can carry you."

"Uh," Bjarke said. "Nobody's carrying me."

"*We* could run too," Qin said. "My sisters and I are very fit."

"No biological being could be as fit as a crusher. We do not tire."

Greetings, Kim, a message came in, distracting her from the argument. She kept hoping to see words from Casmir, though she would happily have taken a response from Oku too. But it was Rache. At least she knew he hadn't gotten himself killed yet. *Amergin has informed me that your attack on the Kingdom shuttle did not result in obtaining Casmir and that your team crashed. Is this true? Are you all right?*

We're fine. We faked our crash.

Allow me to express my relief for your well-being and also to ask if this ruse means my shuttle hasn't been destroyed.

It's not destroyed. It is likely... confiscated.

I'm going to have to stop lending you people shuttles.

Sorry. Does your intelligence officer have any news about Casmir?

Not yet, but I am down on the planet enacting my plan and haven't had a long conversation with him.

Your plan to get Finn? Kim had told him not to do that, but now that her team's attempt had failed, a part of her hoped that he was successful.

Indeed. I will update you when I have acquired him, but that is not what I'm messaging about now. While sneaking around in the castle, I've learned that there is a new threat to Odin, if not to the entire Kingdom. The astroshamans are coming in stealthed ships for the gate pieces. Jager commed his Intelligence operatives and said that the astroshamans spoke to him personally and threatened to unleash a virus, presumably Dubashi's virus, on Odin. Do you know if samples of that survived Dubashi's death?

I hope not, but it is possible. There was one canister that was never accounted for. Kim swatted a branch in frustration, earning a glance from Asger, but he was busy arguing with the crushers and didn't ask about it.

LAYERS OF FORCE

I had hoped it was an impossibility. May I suggest that you depart from the planet in any way possible in case the virus threat is real? If you meet me at the launch loop, I'll take you back to my ship with me. Are you getting your family? They're invited too of course.

Kim frowned. She hadn't yet messaged her father and brothers. She needed to, but she needed to get Casmir too. He was the one most in danger. *I need to make sure Casmir isn't there for his execution.*

If you get him before I can, bring him back up to my ship. If you can find a shuttle or other ride, we'll pick you up. I have a feeling it's not going to be safe on Odin for long.

The sound of dogs baying floated to her ears. It wasn't safe on Odin *now*.

"They're searching on the ground," Asger said. "The hounds won't have trouble catching our trail."

"To the estate. I'm giving you all the coordinates in case we get split up," Bjarke said. "Run through water if we chance across more streams. Try not to lead the dogs to our land."

"We will meet you there," one of the crushers said, then came forward and swept Kim from her feet.

She squawked in surprise as she was thrown over a hard metal shoulder. Without waiting for an answer, the crusher took off running through the forest away from the dogs, with her thumping and banging along like a sack of potatoes. The thuds of footfalls and snapping of brush followed her as the rest of the crushers, the Qins, and the knights sprinted after them.

Branches scraped at Kim and her crusher as he carried her, only the sturdiness of her galaxy suit keeping her from being battered senseless. She reluctantly accepted this unorthodox method of transport and let her head droop as she sought out a network signal to see if there was anything yet in the news about the astroshamans. The idea of that virus still being unleashed after all she and the others had done to get rid of it frustrated and terrified her.

"When will this madness end?" she whispered.

CHAPTER 8

"A RE YOU *SURE* THIS IS THE WAY?" MADDIE whispered.

"Yes," Oku replied for the sixth—or sixtieth time. "I downloaded the city underground maps before taking my chip offline."

"Since our chips are offline, too, we have to take your word for it." Maddie looked at Rokuro, as if this were his fault.

He shrugged back at her. "She's smarter than we are. I assumed she could handle it."

"I'll admit that she's had more formal schooling than we have, not that she's smarter." This time, Maddie turned the dark look back on Oku.

"She is. I've seen her help you when you're struggling with crossword puzzles."

"Only if there are big sciency words," Maddie grumbled.

"Sciency isn't a word."

"Are they going to fight?" Casmir whispered to Oku.

He was trailing along at the rear of their little group as they alternated walking and wading through the old subway tunnels that had been abandoned as the city had been built up over the centuries. The rumble of machinery and subways passing by was a near constant above them.

"They squabble with each other because they're not allowed to squabble with me." Oku lifted her lantern, taking a moment to study Casmir and make sure he was doing all right. It had been months since he'd been in Odin's gravity, which had to be weighing on him like boulders after the partial gravity of spaceships and stations, and she could tell from his heavy breathing that their slog through the tunnels was taxing him. She hadn't forgotten that he'd had the Great Plague not that long ago too.

"They're not?" He'd been leaning a hand against one of the grimy algae-slick walls, but he straightened and lowered it under her scrutiny. "Do you punish them if they get lippy?"

"No, but my father insists the royal family maintain a professional employer-employee relationship, as he calls it." Oku wrinkled her nose to let him know how she felt about that.

"Actually, he calls it a master-servant relationship," Rokuro said dryly. "At least when he's talking to us."

Casmir wrinkled *his* nose. Though that was possibly because he was going to start sneezing again.

"Another point seven miles of tunnels, and I can get you an antihistamine," Oku told him, waving for the others to continue on. So far, she hadn't heard any wails of sirens or hints that someone was down here searching the tunnels for them, but it was only a matter of time before the palace guards realized Casmir was gone. Along with Oku, Maddie, and Rokuro.

"Really?"

"Well, no. But I've got someone meeting us there, and I think she might have something in her medical kit." Oku hoped Dr. Pulinski would come prepared with more than a fresh chip and surgical tools, but she admittedly hadn't asked for any drugs. She wished she'd had three days to plan this escape from the castle, not three hours. Contacting the doctor had been a last-minute decision when she'd seen the gouge in Casmir's temple and realized the military had removed his chip. Poor guy. She'd caught him lifting a hand toward it a couple of times, fingers twitching as if he'd been trying to access it before remembering it was gone. "If nothing else, there will be some bee pollen where we're going."

"*Bee* pollen?"

"There's some scientific evidence that consuming bee pollen from the local area can help with allergies to native flora."

"I've heard that, but doesn't it take weeks? And require that you not be allergic to bee pollen?" Casmir raised his eyebrows.

"Are you?"

"I don't know. I'm allergic to bee*stings*. My immune system isn't the most hale." He shrugged. "Sorry."

Chasca came bounding out of a side passage, splashing everywhere as she caught up with them and then rushed ahead. She'd caught several rats already—which Oku was pretending not to notice. Her dog was the only one enjoying this adventure. Though Oku didn't mind it as much as she probably should have. She felt a giddy ebullience at finally speaking with Casmir in real time, even if these were far from the ideal circumstances.

"You don't have to apologize for your immune system," she said, thinking of her own health foibles.

"I don't like to disappoint people. Or inconvenience them. I'd rather be helpful. As soon as I get a new chip—I may have to kiss you if you can arrange that—please send me everything you know about that Sir Slayer you mentioned. What an idiotic name. Even Rache came up with something less on-the-nose than that, and he's as subtle as a sledgehammer at times. I'll get right to finding that person. And contacting my parents. I need to get them out of the city. Or have them meet us wherever we're going. Something. I hope they're not in danger because of me." He rubbed his face. "Sorry, I'm babbling."

"I think it's allowed. You've had a stressful, uhm, year." She'd already sent a message to his parents, before she'd gone down to get him, and almost told him that, but they hadn't replied to her before she'd taken her chip offline, and she didn't want to falsely get his hopes up that they were safe.

"The first six months of it weren't so bad, but the last six months have been onerous, yes. Thank you again for getting me out of that cell. My first stay in your dungeon wasn't wonderful, but at least I had projects on my chip that I could work on—that was when I first drew up those robotic-bee schematics for you—but without my chip... I was not meant for solitary confinement. I'm not like Kim, who would just compose a novel in her head while she was locked up. I need people, ideally people who don't want to kill me."

Oku's mind got caught on the words *first stay in your dungeon*, and she almost missed the turnoff. She rushed up and tapped Rokuro on the back and pointed to the left and a distant shaft leading upward.

"You were down there before?" Oku frowned as some sticky muck under the water grabbed at her shoe—she should have opted for boots, if not *combat* boots, for this adventure.

"Yes. After I hid the gate from the military and unwisely let myself be turned in. They—and your father—objected. He let me free to go after those terrorists and prove myself to him. Apparently, he likes it when people prove themselves."

Remembering the conversation she'd listened to right after Father and Mother had heard about Jorg's death, Oku nodded, but her thoughts only loitered there for a moment. "Wait, you helped with the terrorists?"

"Yeah, that was the first time I worked with Rache instead of against him. We found their base, sneaked in with a bunch of robots, and dealt with the astroshamans and our ex-chief of Royal Intelligence who was working with them." He looked warily over at her. "When I say dealt with, I mean Rache did all the brave stuff and battling of enemies. I crawled through a duct and threw some vials containing a puke-inspiring substance."

"I... believe I should have asked for reports going further back," Oku murmured, amazed that he'd been integral in those events too. And further frustrated that her father wanted to *kill* him when he kept helping their people. "If Rache truly did help, I'm certain you were the one who talked him into it. He couldn't possibly care about the Kingdom." That surreal conversation from earlier in the night sprang to mind.

"There was some manipulation involved," Casmir said.

Oku glanced at Rokuro and Maddie and lowered her voice to a whisper. "Is that when you gave him underwear?"

Casmir tripped. He flailed and caught himself as Oku grabbed his arm to help.

"I didn't realize Royal Intelligence's reports were *that* thorough."

Maddie and Rokuro had reached the vertical shaft and looked back at them.

"I need to talk to you about him later," Oku murmured.

"Rache?"

"Yes." She hadn't yet told anyone that he'd visited, and she didn't intend to let anyone other than Casmir know.

"Okay."

In the shaft, a rusty ladder with numerous missing rungs led upward. Rokuro sighed and caught Chasca and picked her up, his armor protecting him from dog claws as she squirmed in protest.

"I can tell your bodyguards are good people," Casmir said.

This earned him a grateful thank-you-for-noticing nod from Rokuro before he headed up the ladder with an armful of dog.

"Maddie has been my bodyguard since I was a little girl. She's very patient."

"Yes." Maddie folded her arms over her chest, nodding for them to go up first.

"I can see that," Casmir said.

"Rokuro is a castle guard," Oku said. "He can fly, so that's why we snagged him. We planned to fly you out of the castle in style, not slough through rat-infested stormwater."

"I'm not sure whether you would be impressed or horrified to know this doesn't make even the top five in a list of worst places I've been in recent months." Casmir climbed up the ladder. "Even better, I don't have a fever this time."

"I'm glad."

He sneezed three times and sighed. "Please let me know if stealth is needed at some point. I'll stick my fingers up my nose."

Maddie, bringing up the rear, once again asked, "Are you *sure* he's Mikita's clone?"

"Stop asking that," Oku said, feeling protective toward Casmir.

"It's all right," Casmir said, his voice echoing dully in the shaft. "I'm used to underwhelming my enemies and my allies with my modest physical and immunological attributes. Sometimes, it's helpful. It tends to make them underestimate me."

They clambered out into a thankfully dry tunnel. They were above the level of the subways now and in a quiet part of town, so no traffic roared by overhead. That gave Oku a burst of energy—and hope that she had indeed been following her map correctly. She rushed down a dusty maintenance passage with pipes running along the curving walls. They reached another ladder, and a plaque on the wall read: *Majestic Meadows Park Access.*

"This is it," she blurted and reached for the rungs.

But Maddie caught up to her and gripped her wrist. "You've told two different parties to meet you here. *We'll* go up first to make sure neither of them has betrayed you, and that neither the Castle nor Kingdom Guard is waiting."

"I suppose that's logical." Oku reluctantly stepped back.

"*Thank* you for seeing that."

"Your bodyguard of many years is somewhat sarcastic with you," Casmir observed.

"It's the lack of punishment, I suspect."

"I thought so."

Maddie gave Oku a dark look, reminding Oku that she'd had to plead and wheedle to convince her to come along, and then looked Casmir up and down. Still trying to decide if he was worth all this effort? Oku bristled. Maybe she should have shared tidbits from those reports with Maddie.

"My apologies, ma'am." Casmir lurched forward under Maddie's scrutiny and stuck his hands out as he bowed deeply to her. "I was busy sneezing and wheezing and forgot to thank you earlier. *Thank you* for your help." He turned to Rokuro. "And yours as well, Sergeant Rokuro, wasn't it? Do the castle guards have the same military-rank structure as the military? I've only interacted with the handful who were taking me to the dungeon, and they were oddly terse."

"A simpler rank structure and just Rokuro is fine." He sounded amused but patted Casmir on the back before heading up the ladder.

"You're welcome," Maddie told Casmir gruffly, then pointed to Oku and gave a firm, "Stay."

Chasca promptly sat, thinking the command for her. Maddie would doubtless have preferred it if Oku were that obedient.

Maddie and Rokuro climbed up to a hatch. Oku waited until they'd opened it, disappeared into a pump house above, and closed the hatch before turning to tell Casmir about Rache.

He flopped down on the ground, his back to the wall, and Chasca sniffed his face.

"Hello, girl. I believe you have rat breath."

Oku sat beside him, putting the lantern down next to her, and pulled Chasca over to her so she wouldn't lick him. "I should have left her behind, but I'm afraid to let her out of my sight for too long now that she's been targeted by some mysterious faction who wanted to use Finn."

Casmir nodded. "I'll be happy to research them assiduously as soon as I have network access and before… before I leave, I guess. As soon as I get my parents, and convince them to leave, I suppose I have to try to sneak onto a ship heading out of the system." He stared bleakly at his knees, but he forced a smile and looked at her. "I'm glad to have met you though. For more than two minutes, this time. And in person. I'm praying you don't get in too much trouble over this, that your father likes you a lot more than he likes me." He clasped her hands, his expression so painfully earnest that it touched her and made her forget what she'd been about to say.

"I'm glad to meet you in person again too." She returned his hand clasp, wrapping her fingers around his, saddened at the thought of him leaving the system forever. But what alternative could she offer him? She wanted to believe she could find a way to clear his name, but even if she did, would it matter? As long as her father wanted him dead? "Maybe I should flee the system too and go with you. My father could figure out the political snarl he's made on his own and leave me out of his heir kerfuffle. And then Finn wouldn't have to worry about getting me out of the picture. I'd just be gone." She tilted her head. "It's not really running away from home if you're twenty-six, is it?"

At first, an expression of pure delight brightened his face, but he bit his lip and looked away. "I think I would be doing it for selfish reasons if I encouraged that."

"What if I told you my father is thinking of marrying me to the sixty-five-year-old Senator Oswald and naming me his heir, with the understanding that the senator would be calling the shots?"

"I would not vote for that. Will there be a vote?"

"Unfortunately not in a monarchy."

"We should change the government."

"That's hard for a wanted man to do."

"True." He lifted his gaze and met her eyes again. "I guess you're right. We'll both have to flee the system together. I have been offered an excellent job at four times my faculty pay at Stardust Palace Station."

"I can't tell if you're being serious or not."

"The job offer is real. I think if I left with you, whether it was your idea or not, your father would send assassins after me. He might do that anyway." Casmir smiled sadly.

Oku wished she could say that her father wouldn't do that, but she thought of Senator Boehm who'd died in his sleep of supposedly *natural causes* and believed he would. Had Oku known everything years ago that she knew now, she might have left the Kingdom on her own. Left it to travel to a system with fewer stipulations on what sciences could be performed and with people less likely to think she should be involved in politics simply because she was the king's daughter.

A scrape came from above as the hatch opened.

Maddie peered down at them, her gaze snagging on their clasped hands. Casmir released his grip.

"Dr. Pulinski is here," Maddie said.

"Nobody else?" Oku stood up, hoping it didn't bode poorly that Casmir's parents hadn't come.

Once he received a new chip, he could contact them himself. She had a feeling that he could surf the network and keep anyone from using his chip to locate him, which was better than having to take it offline completely. Oku wished she had that ability herself.

"Just her," Maddie said. "And she keeps glancing toward the parking lot. I think she might have been followed."

Oku frowned. Had someone been monitoring Dr. Pulinski's home? And if so, why? Because she'd been the one to provide Oku with her new—and until recently, unmonitored—chip a few weeks ago?

"We had better hurry, Casmir."

"I concur, but I believe you'll need to call the strapping Rokuro down to carry your dog up that ladder. I'm unable to manage such a feat." He'd climbed to his feet and must have started petting Chasca at some point, because she was leaning against him hard enough to have him flattened against the wall, her tail wagging happily as he obediently stroked her back. "In full disclosure, carrying a seventy-pound dog up a ladder with one arm wouldn't be within my realm of abilities even if I *were* still acclimated to Odin's gravity."

Oku shook her head at her attention-seeking dog. "Rokuro cheats. He's wearing strength-enhancing armor, which also serves to keep dog claws from digging in if she gets scared."

"I should likely get some of this armor."

"Given the way your year is going, you should get five or six sets."

"A wise suggestion."

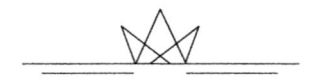

Nobody fired at the *Dragon* when Bonita sailed the freighter out of the System Lion gate, but a quick check of the scanners made her scowl. There were still a number of Kingdom Fleet ships in the area, poised to cut off anyone heading into the system.

No sooner had she taken note of them than the comm pinged.

"Alert bastards, aren't they?" she muttered.

"The Kingdom *has* recently suffered a lengthy blockade and an invasion fleet that left potholes all over their home world," Viggo said. "It is likely that many years will pass before they relax their guard at the entrance to their system."

"Yeah, yeah, but I'm just here to deliver a cargo."

"A true humanitarian-aid cargo that they'll be eager to accept."

"People have to write." Bonita reluctantly answered the comm. "Captain Laser Lopez here."

"This is Lieutenant Bach from the *Harrier*. Your ship has been ordered to stay out of our system, Captain." The female voice was polite and reasonable. Maybe if she received a polite and reasonable response, she would let the *Dragon* through.

"We were ordered to leave after your blockade battle, yes, but this is a neutral freighter that has nothing to do with your battles. I'm being paid to deliver a cargo to a Baron Taniguchi on Odin." Bonita tapped the pen wedged between her mug and the knob for the ship's audio entertainment system.

"What is the nature of your cargo?"

"I don't disclose my cargoes, but I assure you it's nothing illegal or dangerous."

"Is that the freighter that was carrying a bioweapon a few months ago?" a male voice asked in the background.

Great. They remembered her.

Voices muttered without muting the comm. Then the woman said, "I will check to see if Baron Taniguchi has ordered a cargo. Please hold."

At least they weren't threatening to blow her out of the stars.

Bonita leaned back in her pod and muted the comm. "What do you think will happen if Baron Taniguchi hasn't heard of us?"

Princess Nalini had been willing to go along with the pen-cargo scheme, but Bonita doubted she'd sent word ahead, since it was all a ruse. Did she even know that baron?

"Order us to leave," Viggo said. "Or attack us. There are four warships with a tremendous amount of firepower pointed in our direction."

"Thanks. I wouldn't have guessed."

While Bonita waited for a response, Princess Nalini's ship came out of the wormhole behind them.

Bonita navigated farther away from the gate, not wanting to appear like she was with her, especially if Nalini brought in more than one ship. She should only need one to warn the Kingdom about the astroshamans, as she'd said she planned to do, but since she was also interested in spying, she might try to slip a few more in.

"I have spoken with the baron," the lieutenant said. "He says he is expecting a shipment of office supplies."

"Yeah, that's right. I guess he doesn't mind disclosing the nature of his purchases."

"Please fly to Beacon Buoy 33, which is now pulsing a signal at you. One of our ships will come over to board your freighter and inspect your cargo. This is now standard operating procedure for all foreign ships coming into System Lion. We've recently been at war, so we must be careful."

"Uh. All right." Bonita closed the comm. She didn't have anything to hide from an inspection party, but she also didn't have anything to show them. "How big of a box of office supplies do you think I could scrape together if I raided all the desks in the ship?"

She had some magnetic notepads, tablets, and light pens, but not many. She was a bounty hunter, not a secretary.

"Not very," Viggo said.

"What if I added in all of Qin's stickers and glitter?"

"A slightly larger box, but she would never forgive you if you let the Kingdom inspectors take her prizes."

"I doubt Fleet officers make a habit of swiping unicorn stickers."

"They're comming Princess Nalini's ship," Viggo said.

Bonita set a slow course toward the buoy, wanting to appear compliant. She would likely get kicked out of the system, but maybe she could get an update on Qin and Casmir first.

"And telling her to turn around and leave immediately or be attacked," Viggo added as Bonita composed a message to Qin.

"Such a warm fuzzy people they are," Bonita said.

"The gate is activating again," Viggo said. "I am surprised Princess Nalini would attempt to bring more ships in before scouting the situation."

"Maybe she's going to tell the Kingdom they're all carrying office supplies for the baron."

Qin, we're back in System Lion, though I'm not sure yet if it'll be more than a brief visit. Are you all right? I don't suppose you're done rescuing Casmir and are ready to join us and get out of this system? Bonita sent off the message, hoping the Kingdom let her linger long enough for a reply to come in.

"No ships appear to be coming through the open gate," Viggo said.

"Slydar again?" Bonita thought of the attack she'd witnessed in Stymphalia. Could the same group of astroshaman ships be heading into this system now?

"Or something that serves the same function."

"I wonder if the Kingdom has managed to make more slydar detectors yet. And if those ships have them."

"It would be early for them to have implemented manufacturing," Viggo said.

"Yeah. I doubt anyone except Casmir could make something like that out of staples and paper clips overnight."

Viggo's voice took on the usual sappy longing it got when he spoke of Casmir. "He *is* a talented engineer. I am sending him a message to see if he has extricated himself from danger or if he needs our assistance."

"The assistance we can offer from Beacon Buoy 33?" Bonita drummed her fingers, waiting for a reply from Qin.

If she and the others had flown all the way to Odin, there would be a delay in any response. She also might be asleep. Or busy fighting for her life somewhere. Bonita grimaced at the thought.

"Indeed. The gate is activating again."

"Thanks for sharing the play-by-play. It's a lot of effort for me to turn my head and look at the scanner display."

"You are snippy today, Bonita."

"Dealing with the Kingdom makes me snippy." She watched the display as Nalini's ship came to a stop. She thought about comming to see if Nalini was being directed to a beacon, but maybe it would be best to pretend she had nothing to do with—

"The invisible ships are attacking," Viggo said.

"Attacking *who*?" Fear burst into her as she imagined not avoiding the astroshamans' notice a second time.

"So far, only the Kingdom ships."

"Why would they target them? Those warships shouldn't have any gate pieces, right?"

"I do not know their motivations, Bonita."

She watched bleakly as once again blasts seemed to come out of nowhere, energy weapons she wasn't familiar with peppering the Kingdom ships. They maneuvered and returned fire, but their wild spray suggested they couldn't sense their enemies any more than the *Dragon* could.

"Idiots should have had Casmir set up out here with paper clips, making slydar detectors," she muttered. "Instead, they arrested him, and now, they're going to get their asses kicked."

Nalini's ship wisely moved away from the battle. So far, it had not been targeted.

The *Dragon* reached the buoy, and Bonita came to a stop, weightlessness lifting her braid away from her head as their acceleration halted.

A comm came from Nalini's ship.

"Are you thinking of leaving, Nalini?" Bonita asked as soon as she answered.

She was considering it as she watched the Kingdom warships streak about, taking and returning fire. They were much more heavily armored than that freighter had been, and they could doubtless take a lot of hits, but it was clear from the way their shots sped uselessly off into space that they didn't hit their invisible targets often. Meanwhile, the invisible ships had no trouble connecting with them.

"I don't know." Nalini didn't point out Bonita's lack of an honorific. "This is the same thing that's been happening in our system. Whoever it is has left alone ships that didn't have gate pieces that they wanted to steal."

"Do you think those warships are carrying gate pieces?" Bonita doubted it.

Nalini hesitated, perhaps checking energy signatures on her scanners. "No."

"Then why attack? They could have sneaked past."

"Maybe they don't like the Kingdom. Or want to make a point."

"The Kingdom didn't even get that many gate pieces, did it?" Bonita asked.

"From what I've learned, they took five from the astroshaman moon base, including one of two important control pieces that are crucial for gate function."

Hello, Captain! a reply came in from Qin. *We're on Odin. We're okay, but our plan to rescue Casmir didn't work out, and now we're regrouping and will try again to find him. Were you permitted back into the system? I'm not sure if I should ask you to come pick us up or not. By the time you reach Odin, this should be resolved one way or another—I do hope we're able to rescue him and that he won't be executed!*

LAYERS OF FORCE

"Well, at least El Mago is still alive," Bonita muttered as she read. "And so are Qin and the Qin-pack."

"Excellent," Viggo said. "But since they have cat DNA, should they be referred to as a pack? Perhaps a clowder would be more appropriate. Oh, did you know that a group of tigers is called a streak? Or an ambush? What excellent collective nouns. Henceforth, we should refer to them as an ambush of Qins."

"You have too much time on your hands, Viggo."

"I do not have hands."

But I don't know if the Dragon *would be welcome at their home world,* Qin's message continued. *Their whole fleet is in orbit, I heard. If you wish, let me know where you're heading next, and we'll attempt to find passage to you. If they allow us on the public transport here. Maybe we can... disguise ourselves. My sisters have expressed interest in employment, if you're able to hire them. It would be much preferable to work for you than Rache.*

Bonita frowned at the idea of Qin and her sisters trying to get a ride on a public transport ship heading out of the system and being denied because they were furry freaks, as Kingdom people would call them. She *wanted* to go pick up Qin and her sisters and get back to a semblance of a normal life. Was it possible she could sneak into the system while the Kingdom ships were occupied?

Bonita grabbed her braid and nibbled on the end as the battle continued. "What do you think, Viggo? Should we take this opportunity to get out of here? To fly deeper into the system?"

"Just because these ships are currently occupied doesn't mean others that we might encounter will be."

"Good point."

"One of the warships has taken extensive damage and has now lost power," Viggo said. "It is difficult to ascertain if there are survivors. The other ships in the fleet are sending encrypted communications—likely calls for help—into the system."

"No doubt. I wonder if they're damaging the invisible ships at all. And how many invisible ships there *are*." As far as Bonita could tell, there could be one or there could be an entire invasion fleet.

She tapped the navigation panel, tempted to plot a new course and leave the buoy. Just because the attackers hadn't gone after the *Dragon* last time didn't mean they wouldn't again.

"Two ships are turning and running," Viggo said. "The third looks like it's trying to buy time for them to get away. It's firing madly. Hm, they did manage to hit something there. Or at least their blast halted abruptly."

Nalini commed again. "Did they ask you for help, Bonita?"

"The Kingdom? No."

"The ship that's still there fighting asked me to go get the rest of my fleet and help them since I can see the attacking vessels. A minute ago, the Kingdom was trying to kick me out of their system."

"Wait, you can see them?"

"This ship has the slydar detector that Casmir made back on Stardust Palace."

"How many attackers are there? And can you tell for certain now that they're astroshamans?"

"We can see four currently," Nalini said. "It's possible there are more. The range of the detector is short. The models of these ships aren't in any databases in the Twelve Systems, but I think we were right and that they're astroshaman ships."

"Ugh. Are you going to help the Kingdom?"

"I didn't order the rest of the fleet to follow me through since I doubted we would get a favorable reception. By the time I went back to get them and returned, this would be over." Nalini's voice grew quieter. "Besides, I don't want to pick a fight with the astroshamans. My father wanted to facilitate the interstellar gate project, as he was calling it, but that's not enough of a reason to get myself killed. Those ships have a lot of firepower and some hull technology we're not familiar with."

Even as she finished speaking, the last Kingdom ship in the area took a hit to the engines. Hull plating blew off, and the vessel was knocked off course, spinning out of control.

"The astroshamans are moving into the system," Nalini reported. "Chasing the other two Kingdom ships."

"Ignoring us?"

"It looks like it."

"That's something anyway. Are you going to try to go into the system now that the welcome wagon can't threaten us?"

Nalini hesitated. "I would like to get Tristan and take him home before this escalates into something big, but I don't know yet if he's been able to get to Casmir."

"They haven't. Qin updated me. I—"

LAYERS OF FORCE

Another communication came in. It was from the Kingdom ship whose engines had been hit. It had stopped its out-of-control spin, and it hadn't yet lost power and life support, but it appeared too damaged to go anywhere quickly.

"Yes?" Bonita answered warily, expecting an order that she follow the astroshamans or something ridiculous.

"Captain Lopez." It was the female lieutenant, now sounding frazzled and possibly injured rather than politely professional. "Do you still plan to take your cargo to Baron Taniguchi on Odin?"

"Uh, yeah, if we don't get attacked."

"Our ship has been badly damaged. Our sickbay is destroyed—that entire deck is without power—and some of our crewmen are badly injured. We have ships coming to render assistance, but they are half a day out, and it's possible the attackers will waylay them. Would you be willing to take our injured people to Forseti Station on your way to Odin? The rest of our crew will remain here to effect repairs, but we will forgo inspection of your cargo."

Bonita snorted.

"That's generous of you." She thought about saying she charged passengers for rides, especially rides to stations where she possibly had a bounty on her head due to past misunderstandings, but it seemed poor form to ask for money from a ship that had just been mercilessly pummeled. "I'll come pick up whoever you want to send over, providing no stealthed ships try to attack us."

"The intruders appear to be indifferent to you." The lieutenant sounded bitter.

Bonita, deciding that the officer had probably lost friends in that attack, managed to keep the snarky response to herself and only said, "I hope so. We're on our way."

As she headed toward the warship, Bonita contacted Nalini again. "Did they ask you for a ride?"

"No. They may believe a freighter has more room for people."

"A freighter packed to the brim with office supplies?"

"They may also not wish to be beholden to my father—our people."

"Guess they don't have any such reservations about me," Bonita said. "We're picking up their injured and heading to Forseti Station. Will you fly along as an escort and let us know if any menacing invisible ships show up in our path?"

"It looks like they're menacing the two Kingdom ships that fled right now, but yes."

Bonita closed the comm. "I hope this isn't a mistake, Viggo."

She could imagine a bunch of arrogant Kingdom bastards like that Ambassador Romano coming aboard and trying to take over her ship.

"It could cause the Kingdom to look upon you favorably in the future," he said.

"All I want is to visit their planet long enough to pick up the Qin-pack."

"The Qin-*ambush*. And that would require the Kingdom looking upon you favorably."

"They're an uppity people, aren't they?"

"All except El Mago. And Kim is quiet and respectful as well." After a pause, Viggo added, "The knights have been more reasonable of late."

"Because they're no longer slamming the doors in your lavatory?"

"Precisely."

Bonita hoped the batch they took on would be too injured to make trouble. And also that helping the Kingdom wouldn't turn them into enemies in the astroshamans' dull mechanical eyes.

CHAPTER 9

AS CASMIR CLIMBED THROUGH THE HATCH AND INTO a tiny building with a cement floor, pipes, and gauges, his first thought was that this was where Oku meant to stash him, but the door was open and looking out onto a dark grassy field lined by tall trees. The only streetlamps were a quarter mile away, highlighting a parking area with a massive hole dug in the middle.

No, not a hole, he realized with a start. That was a crater. From where a bomb had struck during the invasion?

So far, he hadn't been given the opportunity to see any of the city and had only witnessed news footage, but he knew that numerous buildings had been destroyed, whole city blocks in some places. He couldn't imagine why a parking lot in a park would have been targeted. But he supposed it wasn't as remote a location as it seemed. Since the underground tunnels had brought them to it, they had to be in the city somewhere. Majestic Meadows, that plaque had said. He had heard of the park but had never been there before and hadn't realized it was so large.

The scents of damp grass and fallen leaves teased his nose, and he anticipated another round of sneezes soon. It was a shame that immunity-boosting potion from Rache had worn off. He would prefer not to add a dripping nose to his current seediness, especially not with Oku here to see it.

But as he stepped outside, a round of sneezes caught him. His left eye blinked twice, and he sighed. Some fine catch for the ladies he was.

The sky was clear, the moon and stars shining down, so he could make out Chasca running to and fro across the field, sniffing and hunting despite the late hour. What looked like several rows of greenhouses rose up on one side of the field. A vehicle honked beyond a tree-lined fence, making him realize they were indeed still in the heart of the city.

"This way, Casmir." Oku touched his arm and headed across the field toward the closest greenhouse.

He appreciated her willingness to touch him, given his grimy state. Or in any state. After all, he was the commoner clone, and she was the royal princess. He'd been afraid it would be awkward and nerve-wracking to talk to her or even make eye contact, but he'd only caught himself babbling a couple of times. If he weren't so worried about his parents, not being able to contact his friends, and how he would get off the planet, he would be enjoying this adventure with Oku. It was possible he was enjoying it anyway.

"You're taking me to a greenhouse? This isn't the hidden safe house I was imagining." They passed several dark boxes rising up from the grass, and Casmir realized they were beehives.

She hadn't been joking about taking him someplace where she could get some bee pollen.

"I don't know where hidden safe houses are in the city. I don't cavort with a lot of spies or criminals." Oku jangled what sounded like old-fashioned keys. "But there's a lock on the greenhouse door if that'll make you feel more secure. I have to keep my seeds safe. I grow experimental stuff out here from time to time but not so often that people should immediately think to look for me here."

The armored outlines of Rokuro and Maddie were visible in the shadows, one guarding the door, the other peering across the field toward an empty parking lot. A smaller female figure also stood near the door. The doctor that Oku had mentioned? A doctor with a *chip*? Casmir lifted a finger to the raw wound at his temple.

"Dr. Pulinski?" Oku turned on the lantern she'd been carrying in the tunnels.

"Yes, Your Highness." The woman bowed to her, then peered at Casmir, her gaze shifting from his face to his temple. "And, ah, friend you did not name?"

Casmir stirred, realizing he recognized the woman from the clinic where Bonita had gone for her knee surgery. He hadn't seen her in person that day, but hers had been among the faces of the doctors displayed on the wall in the lobby.

"Yes." Oku rested a hand on Casmir's shoulder. "A friend who had his chip forcibly removed and is in need of a new one. Since you recently replaced mine, I thought of you."

Pulinski's mouth twisted. "I can't tell you how delighted I am that you keep thinking of me for acts of dubious legality."

Oku raised her chin. "Me deciding to replace my own personal chip is not illegal. Besides, I've spoken with Chief Van Dijk about it and made a deal. She's had the tracking software reinstalled."

Casmir glanced at her.

"I've still got it offline for now," she whispered to him. "And told Maddie and Rokuro to do the same."

"A talented network navigator might still be able to locate you," he murmured back.

"I'll hope, because it's the middle of the night, that the talented people are all in bed."

"I'll keep my ego in check by refraining from pointing out that *I'm* awake. Especially since I don't have a chip right now. Without that or my tools, my only talent is sneezing."

"We'll get you a new chip." Oku nodded toward the doctor.

"I suppose asking for tools would be too much."

"There are some trowels in the greenhouse."

"Ah, yes. A perennial favorite among roboticists. I keep no fewer than six in my toolbox at the lab."

"Are you being snarky with me, Casmir?" She smiled at him, so he doubted she minded.

"Is that not allowed between commoners and royalty?"

"It's not encouraged, but I'll allow it if you compliment my plants."

"Your plants?" He blinked and looked around at the empty field. "The freshly mowed grass smells nice."

"The plants in the greenhouse," she corrected dryly. "That cut-grass smell is caused by the release of green-leaf volatile organic compounds that act either to aid in wound healing for the plant or as a defense mechanism against invaders."

"Your Highness," Maddie said, sounding faintly exasperated. "This isn't the best time for lectures."

Her bodyguards were alternately eyeing Dr. Pulinski, who kept glancing nervously toward the lot, and the entrances to the park.

"Sorry, Maddie."

"I didn't mind it," Casmir whispered. He *liked* lectures. Though even he admitted he would like them more after he had a new chip implanted.

"Good," Oku whispered back. "I'll tell you lots more about plants when we have time."

"I look forward to it."

"You're the first person who's ever said that."

"That can't be true."

"The first person who wasn't also in my field."

"Hm." Casmir decided it would be cheesy to say that he would happily listen to her lecture on any topic in any field.

"This won't take long, Doctor," Oku said, stepping forward and taking the woman's hands. "I really do appreciate the favor—and you coming out in the middle of the night for this."

Dr. Pulinski sighed. "You've been my patient for a long time, Your Highness—Oku. You know if I can help you, I will."

"Thank you." Oku unlocked the greenhouse door—it was only an old padlock, not a state-of-the-art system that could be tracked—and waved for Casmir to follow her inside.

It was too dark to see the plants inside, but their outlines rose up from beds and containers, and the scents of foliage and damp earthy soil wrapped around them as they entered. Casmir complimented her on the greenery, hoping there would be time one day for her to tell him about her projects, but she only thanked him tersely.

He couldn't claim to know her well yet, but her eyes were tight in the lantern light, her shoulders tense. She must have noticed Pulinski's glances too. Was she worried that the doctor had alerted someone in Intelligence? Or was being watched by them for some reason?

Casmir wanted to suggest aborting and going back into the tunnels, but… he needed a chip, damn it. Until he was back online, he couldn't contact his parents or find out where Kim or Qin or Asger or Zee or even Rache were. Not knowing what his friends were up to worried him almost as much as not being able to check on his parents.

"Can I turn on the lights?" Once inside, Pulinski reached for a switch.

But Oku caught her arm and held up her lantern. "I brought this."

"That's not enough light to perform a surgery by."

Oku turned it up to a stronger setting.

Pulinski's lips pressed together with disapproval.

LAYERS OF FORCE

"Sorry," Oku said. "Can you make it work? If any ships fly over the park and see the lights on, they might report that someone is in here. It would be annoying to be interrupted because the authorities thought a random thief was breaking into the greenhouse."

Pulinski looked like she meant to say something—perhaps question why Oku couldn't call the authorities and let them know she was using her own greenhouse—but she only said, "Fine. Professor, find a place to sit down where I can reach your head."

Casmir tipped over a bucket and sat on it, not wanting to delay anything, especially if the doctor had second thoughts about giving him a new chip. It was upsetting to accept that he was a criminal now and that people could get in trouble for helping him.

He gazed at Oku, who was waving Chasca inside and giving her bodyguards instructions to let her know if anyone showed up. How much trouble would *she* get into for this?

Grumbling about substandard conditions, Pulinski pulled out a penlight and shined it at what Casmir assumed was a gory scab on his temple. He hadn't seen himself in a mirror for days.

"Do you know if they gouged it out or carefully unseated it from its socket?" she asked. "If I have to start from scratch, that's going to take forever."

"It was a doctor, and I believe he removed it surgically and left the neuro-connectors in place." Casmir tried a smile on the grim-faced Pulinski. "I didn't have a seizure."

"Pardon?"

"If he'd yanked it out, my brain probably would have objected. Vehemently."

"There are fail-safes in place to minimize brain damage in the event of traumatic chip injury."

"Maybe so, but my brain is special. It doesn't take much to prompt a seizure. Oh, and in case it matters for this, I'm on mysomazepine for them."

Oku was pouring water into a bowl for Chasca, but she looked over at him.

Maybe he shouldn't have mentioned that. He hated detailing his fragilities—his weaknesses—in front of pretty women. In front of *anyone*.

"All right." Pulinski's tone was a little softer—sympathetic? "It shouldn't matter. I'll apply an analgesic and numbing agent and get started."

"Thank you, Doctor." He gave her another smile. "I *really* appreciate it. Are you by chance the one who did the knee procedure on Bonita

Lopez—she might have identified herself as Laser Lopez—a few months back?"

"No, that was my colleague, but I remember her. She was snippy, snarky, and unappreciative."

"Ah. Then I should not let you know that she's an associate of mine?"

"Probably not." Pulinski pressed the cool tip of an injector to his temple, and it hissed against his skin.

"In case your colleague is curious, she's doing well, and the last time I saw her, she wasn't limping at all."

"Oh? That's good. She didn't seem like the type who would obediently do her physical therapy."

"She is conscientious, despite the snip and snark."

Pulinski set to work, cutting into his scab to find the embedded connectors, and Casmir stopped talking to her. For this very important procedure, he didn't want to distract her.

With Chasca lapping from the bowl, Oku pulled over another upturned bucket and sat beside him. She took his hand.

Casmir arched his eyebrows before remembering he shouldn't move his facial muscles.

"You look like you need support," she said.

"Usually." He smiled at her—while keeping his forehead still—to encourage the gesture. He wished he could have leaned his head on her shoulder, too, but that would have complicated matters for Dr. Pulinski.

"How long have you had seizures?" Oku asked.

"Always. More frequently as a kid until we found a medication that controls them. Or that *was* controlling them until I started cavorting around in space. All the stress and probably the weirdness of null gravity and low gravity and acceleration and deceleration wreaked some havoc on my body."

"I imagine having the Great Plague did too," Oku said softly.

Pulinski's eyebrows arched, though she remained focused on her work and didn't speak.

"Yes," Casmir said.

"You neglected to mention that in your videos."

"I wanted to keep them light." He hoped she didn't feel that he had been dishonest or evasive. "Also, I was extremely busy infiltrating an astroshaman base while that was going on."

LAYERS OF FORCE

"Is that hard to do while feverish and puking?"

"You have no idea. Zee carried me part of the way. Ra— erm, someone called me a damsel in distress." Casmir couldn't keep his mouth from twisting.

"Someone sounds abrasive and rude."

"*Yes.*"

"The connectors weren't damaged during the removal." Pulinski drew a shining new chip in a small insulated case out of her kit.

"Good. And that looks fantastic." Maybe Casmir would keep it, even if he could get his old chip back. He could get everything transferred over and set up eventually. "One of the new 8383 models?"

"Yes. Princess Oku promised she would pay for it."

"I ought to bill it to the castle expense account and make my *father* pay for it," Oku said. "Since he had the old one removed."

"I'm sure he would choke on that invoice," Casmir said as Pulinski prepared to install it. He held very still, not wanting to cause any delays, but he found himself watching Oku out of the corner of his eye. "Your Highness," he said slowly, not sure how to phrase his question.

"Oku," she corrected him.

Pulinski's eyebrows twitched.

"Princess Oku," Casmir said—that prompted eyebrow movement from Oku. "You don't have to answer this if you don't want to, but I was wondering… Well, I was curious. About, uhm." Would this be considered prying? Maybe she didn't want to discuss whatever medical issues she had, but if there was anything wrong that would preclude breaking prisoners out of the dungeon and fleeing castle security… he wanted to encourage her to return home straightaway.

"You want to know what Dr. Pulinski treats me for at the clinic?" Oku guessed.

"I was curious, yes."

"As a young girl, I developed a pancreatic autoimmune disease that causes my body to attack my beta cells, and I wasn't able to create insulin. There isn't a cure, but by receiving regular beta-cell infusions from Dr. Pulinski, my natural pancreas is usually able to function well enough to control my blood-sugar levels. I have a chip installed that monitors everything and gives me alerts if anything goes wrong." Her voice turned wry. "Usually at inopportune moments." She waved to her eyes, and Casmir could imagine her getting annoying flashing signs on her contacts. "Such as when my dog is being kidnapped."

"You'll have to give me more details on that so I can help find the responsible party."

"I will." She squeezed his hand. "When you're online again."

"This should only take a few more minutes," Pulinski said. "And then there will be a few thousand updates to install."

"I'm sure." Casmir hoped he could get onto his cloud account at the university so he could get a backup, even though it would be a woefully out-of-date backup.

"It's the kind of thing they could have caught before I was born," Oku said, gazing down at the ground now, "if my parents had bothered to look. As I'm sure you know, gene-cleaning is illegal here, but that didn't stop my father from ordering it done for my brothers. *They* don't have any health issues. Or didn't, in Jorg's case." She sighed softly. "I suppose it's wrong to feel bitter toward someone who's not alive anymore."

Pulinski was still concentrating on inserting the new chip, but she glanced sympathetically at Oku a few times.

"It was just frustrating that my father didn't bother to help me because I'm a girl—he told me this when I was old enough to find out and ask—and was only going to be married off for some alliance. It wasn't as if I had to do something *important*, like leading troops into war. But he doesn't know what it's like to worry about dying if something goes wrong and your blood sugar drops to zero. I used to have nightmares about that as a kid. I'm not sure my father ever understood that it was scary, and those experiences could have been prevented if he'd had the doctor fix my wayward genes before I'd been born. It's not like we don't have the technology for that—as I've told him many times. Nobody should have to deal with preventable diseases." Before, Oku's hand had been gentle as it held his, but as she spoke about this, it was tense and tight to match the frustration in her words. She must have noticed it, for she blew out a slow breath and loosened her grip. "My father is a frustrating man."

"I understand."

She looked at him.

"From our brief encounters, I found him frustrating." Casmir smiled again. "And I *completely* understand what it's like to have a gene-cleaned brother."

Oku snorted softly. "Yes, I guess you would."

"Add in his cybernetic enhancements, and he's basically a superhero—or super villain, I suppose—from a comic book. Leaving me aspiring for sidekick status."

"Well, Jorg and Finn were never that, at least. They were just enviably normal."

"Oh, yeah, those pesky normal people. I envied them too. My father used to tell me that great trials make great men, and that it's through personal pain that you come to understand the pain of others, but I think that's just because he didn't want me building robots to punt *normal* people in the balls."

She returned his smile. "You didn't do that did you?"

"No. I built robots to protect *me* from being punted."

"In the balls?"

"And elsewhere. But those *are* important to guys."

"So I've heard."

"I'm done." Pulinski lowered her hands and looked back and forth between them.

Casmir felt sheepish for having such a private conversation in front of a stranger, but it wasn't as if he would have wanted to stop her from installing his new chip. He sent the mental command to turn it on, then leaped up, jumping and pumping his fist when it responded and started booting up.

Oku chuckled. "I guess it worked."

Pulinski didn't chuckle. "Your Highness," she said slowly as she put her tools away. "I may have made a mistake. I need to apologize and tell you two to leave right away." She glanced in the direction of the parking lot, though they couldn't see anything through the opaque greenhouse walls.

"Were you followed?" Oku guessed.

Casmir, having a feeling this quiet moment wouldn't last, scrambled to access his backup data and download all of his hacking and network-analyzing programs as quickly as possible.

"Worse." Pulinski grabbed her medical kit. "I was worried about you, Oku. When you said you needed this done in the middle of the night, I commed Royal Intelligence to report that you might have been influenced by a criminal. I wouldn't have doubted you, but you'd also just come to get your chip replaced on the sly… I didn't want you to get yourself into trouble. I told them you told me to meet you here."

Oku groaned. Casmir started more files downloading.

"Nobody at Royal Intelligence answered, so I left a recording," Pulinski continued. "Maybe there's still time for you to escape before they check on—"

Lights came from the sky above the greenhouse, and the whine of a shuttle engine sounded.

One of the bodyguards thumped on the door. "We've got a problem, Your Highness."

"No kidding. Come on, Casmir." Oku ran for the door, and the previously slumbering Chasca sprang after her. "Maybe if we can get to the trees, we can slip out before they see us and it's too late."

Casmir looked around, in case more tools than the previously mentioned trowel might be available, but he didn't see anything promising.

"I'm so sorry, Professor," Pulinski told him. "I thought from the news reports that you were a heinous criminal. And I didn't want—"

"It's all right. I'm glad you were looking out for her. Thank you for the chip." Casmir hugged Pulinski briefly before rushing out after Oku.

She was waiting right outside the door, frowning up at not one but three shuttles that were circling the field and the greenhouses, their searchlights streaking over the grass. Street vehicles wheeled into the parking lot, and a door was flung open. Armored—and armed—men leaped out.

Oku caught Chasca before she could take off in the opposite direction.

"Try to get away," Oku urged Casmir. "I'll stay and distract them. I'll say you left hours ago. Assuming nobody countermands me." She scowled back through the doorway at Pulinski.

Casmir shook his head and lifted his hands, so it would look like he meant to surrender—he didn't trust all those armed men not to do something foolish and accidentally shoot Oku or her dog because he sprinted off. But as he walked toward the parking lot with his hands up, he opened some of the programs downloading. If he could get onto the network that the Kingdom Guard used...

"Casmir." Oku lunged and grabbed his shoulder. "I didn't break you out only to have you recaptured. Go that way." She pointed toward the fence at the back of the park, but her shoulders slumped as one of the aircraft landed between them and it. The other two landed as well, hemming them in.

LAYERS OF FORCE

"We can't fight so many." Rokuro lowered his weapon and took the struggling and now barking Chasca from Oku.

"I do thank you for trying so hard to free me," Casmir said. "If I can figure a way out of this, will you go out for coffee with me?"

Oku gave him an exasperated look, and he thought she would rather strangle him than date him, but she blurted, "*Yes!*"

"Excellent." He had a reason to survive. "Thank you."

Casmir patted her arm, then turned toward the men racing toward him, rifles pointed at his chest.

Yas frowned as a Kingdom emergency-broadcast alert popped up on the display in his office in sickbay.

With Rache down on Odin and the *Fedallah* in stealth mode a healthy distance from the Kingdom ships in orbit, there hadn't been many duties for the ship's doctor, so he'd been using the public network to research cybernetics surgeons on Odin for Jess. Kim had recommended one, but he wanted to investigate all of the options, since replacing a biological spine with a synthetic one was an intricate and extensive surgery.

More concerned about the research than Kingdom news, Yas almost overrode the alert, but since Rache had gone down to Odin to enact some daring—or suicidal—plan, he worried it might have to do with that.

Jess walked into his office in sickbay as the message started to play, some aide announcing that the king had *very important* news to share and that the viewer should provide *undivided attention*.

"I got word from Mendoza that the captain's on his way back up." Jess swung into the seat in front of his desk and tossed her leg over the armrest. "I don't know how he sneaks his shuttles onto the Kingdom's launch loop. They have bogus ident chips, but you'd think, by now, the Kingdom would know them all."

"He made it away? Did he succeed in rescuing Casmir? Or whatever he had planned?" Yas assumed it wasn't the assassination of Jager, not yet, but only because he'd heard that the king was still on his warship with the slydar detector and surrounded by other warships.

"I don't know. Is that about him?" Jess waved to the display. "A warning that the nefarious Captain Rache is fleeing the planet and should be shot at will?"

"Let's find out." Yas rotated the display so they could both see it and turned up the sound.

"…have driven out the invaders who wanted to claim Odin for themselves," Jager was saying, speaking from a podium with a royal purple curtain and the Kingdom's gold crown logo behind him, "but a new threat encroaches. Enemy warships, made invisible by slydar hulls, have entered our system, destroyed four of our ships, and are heading to Odin."

"Uhm," Jess said. "That's not us."

"They belong to an organization of astroshamans," Jager continued, "who claim to have a deadly virus that they are threatening to unleash on the populace. Our powerful Fleet *will* take care of this, and I am prepared to lead our ships into battle myself. We will protect you from this threat, so there is no need to worry. We have now gained the means to detect these hidden ships, and we *will* be victorious in this battle."

Jager disappeared, replaced by four jabbering news reporters sharing their opinions on what the message truly meant and speculation of what virus this might be.

Yas muted it and leaned back in his chair. "That's not what I expected."

"I thought the captain's girl and her buddies took care of Prince Dubashi and his virus."

"So did I. Or arranged for him to be taken care of, at least. From what I heard, Dubashi was decapitated by mercenaries, and Sultan Shayban had to pay out two rewards, because one group brought his head in and another brought in his body."

"Maybe someone found whatever container the virus was in floating in space and picked it up."

Yas closed down the research he'd been doing. "I suppose there's no point in planning a trip down to Odin now. It's not looking like a good time to have a surgery."

"It's *never* a good time for a surgery. Or to go to a doctor at all."

"Thanks so much. Did you forget where you were?" Yas waved around his office.

"I took a wrong turn. I meant to go tease Mendoza on the bridge about his perpetual baldness, but I accidentally ended up here."

"Will you stay? I'll make you some tea."

"Tea?" Jess wrinkled her nose, an expression he never failed to find cute.

"I can put some sugar in it."

"How about alcohol? I'm off-duty for the day."

"Tea and alcohol don't sound like an appealing mix."

"You're right. Let's leave out the tea."

"Has anybody ever called you a responsible adult?"

"No. Why do you ask?"

"I just wanted to make sure."

Jess started to say something else but must have had a message come in on her chip, for she paused. "It looks like we're about to get involved in something. The captain told me to tell you to get ready for something, and he wants me to work on the weapons systems to make sure everything is in tiptop order and to see if I can add some distance to the missile range."

Get ready for something? That sounded ominous. Like Rache intended to flood his sickbay with victims soon.

"I'll bet he wants to be able to attack from outside of the range of those new slydar detectors," Jess added.

"Attack whom? I was thinking we should get out of this system if more trouble is coming to it."

"He didn't say, but the king I'd guess. He just informed his whole populace that he's going to stay with his fleet and will be busy dealing with hostile invaders."

"The natural time for us to sneak in from behind him and blow his ship away?" Yas grimaced.

"I think that was always the plan, Doctor. Find an opportunity to attack while he's distracted."

"If we're successful, who's going to be left to defend this world from whatever threat is coming?"

Jess offered him a sympathetic shrug but said, "It's not our problem, Doc. We're the mercenaries. We just go where the work is. I wouldn't be surprised if the captain is inking out a deal with these new invaders to see if he can get paid for the gig."

CHAPTER 10

OKU STARED IN DEFEATED HORROR AS ARMORED MEN from the Kingdom Guard ran across the field toward Casmir, their rifles pointed at his chest. More armored troops poured out of the three shuttles that had landed. They also carried raised weapons.

Fear blasted aside the horror as Oku realized that her father might have given them the order to kill Casmir instead of recapturing him.

She lunged forward, intending to place herself in front of him to ensure they wouldn't shoot, but Maddie caught her arm with an iron grip.

"Do not," she warned.

"But they might—"

Two black figures sprinted in from the side, running faster than mag trains, and slammed into the lead troops. Oku jumped.

The men were as surprised as she and spun toward the interlopers, firing at them. But their orange DEW-Tek bolts bounced off the creatures. No, not creatures. *Crushers*. Oku recognized them even in the poor lighting. Were these the two she'd seen at her father's side in the Citadel? Acting as his bodyguards?

"What the hell are those?" Rokuro demanded.

"Demons," Maddie said grimly.

"Crushers!" Casmir blurted, the only one with a cheerful tone. His arms that had been raised to surrender went up higher, as if he meant to conduct an orchestra.

Were they some of *his* crushers? If so, how could they have found him?

Impervious to the weapons fire, the crushers grabbed the armored men and hurled them all the way back to the parking lot. A hundred feet, maybe more. Oku stared, her mouth falling open. Only their armor kept them from breaking their bones when they landed, though even so protected, they were not quick to rise.

Other men went hurtling toward the trees. The troops that had been rushing toward Casmir from the shuttles detoured to help their comrades with the crushers.

"Get some grenades!" one of them yelled.

"Your Highness." Maddie already had Oku's arm, but she started pulling back. "Behind the greenhouse. Come on. Let's get out of their lines of sight in case they fire wildly."

"Or throw grenades wildly." Rokuro pulled Chasca back. "*Everyone* behind the greenhouse."

As if the glass walls would protect them. Oku winced as an energy bolt bounced off a crusher and slammed through one of the greenhouse panels.

She started to go with Maddie—maybe they could slip away now that the troops were focused on something else—but Casmir wasn't moving.

"I'm coming, but hold on." Oku twisted her arm to slip away from Maddie, then ran up and grabbed Casmir's shoulder.

"I'm working on the shuttles," he said.

"Good. Do it while you come with me." Oku had no idea what *working on the shuttles* meant, but he could do it while he ran away.

Rokuro waited at the back corner, waving for them to hurry behind the greenhouse as he tried to protect them. That was a tall order, since one of the shuttles sat between them and the fence. Some of its troops had gone to help the others, but Oku could see others inside the craft. Two of them pointed at her little group. One man was about to jump out when the interior lights went dark. No, *all* of the lights on the shuttle, inside and out, went dark.

An armored soldier flew through the air like a football and slammed into the side of that shuttle hard enough to leave a dent the size of a moon crater.

"Easy, Zee!" Casmir called. "Don't kill anyone!"

"That's Zee?" Oku asked. "Your Zee that wears ties and beanies?"

"Yes, but he didn't dress for a video tonight." Casmir tapped his temple where his new chip was installed, Skinfill smearing the scab that Pulinski had reopened for the procedure. "I just got communications back online. I can talk to them. I think Kim sent them."

"Is she here?" Oku asked.

"No, but I haven't gotten the whole story yet. We're going to take that shuttle over there. If one of you can pilot it?" Casmir pointed at another craft parked across the field.

"I can," Rokuro said, "but what are you talking about? How are we going to *take* it?"

The power went out, leaving the indicated shuttle as dark as the first.

"I'll boot it back up when we're ready to escape," Casmir said, then turned and poked his head around the corner of the greenhouse. "One more."

Maddie looked incredulously at Oku. "Is he knocking Kingdom Guard shuttles offline? *How?*"

Rokuro shook his head. "That's not possible. Not remotely and not for someone without high-ranking security access even if he was inside."

Oku spread her arms. She didn't know how he was doing it, but even as they debated it, the power went off on the third shuttle, leaving the interior dark, the men inside confused and banging on the console.

"Okay, Zee," Casmir said, his words barely audible over the chaos of the battles and sirens in the distance. Had the Guard called for reinforcements? "I need you to clear out one of the shuttles for us."

Oku would have assumed the crushers couldn't hear him—she couldn't see them but knew they had moved to the parking lot by the sounds of them wrenching apart vehicles there. She *hoped* those were the vehicles and not armored men. Even Chasca's terrified barking added to the noise and chaos. But the crushers somehow heard him—or maybe he was giving them orders over the network. They raced across the field toward the closest shuttle.

"They're going to evict the men inside so we can borrow the shuttle." Casmir turned toward them. "And Sergeant Rokuro can pilot us to somewhere safe." His eyes lost focus, as if he were reading a message, and then his face brightened. "But first to pick up my parents, please. Crushers are on the way to impede the soldiers who were placed at my parents' apartment building to keep them from escaping."

"How did you call them in so quickly? You've only had your chip installed for two minutes." Oku watched as the pair of crushers tore the crewmen out of the shuttle and tossed them into the field. After landing, the men groaned and rolled to their feet, but the crushers had taken their weapons. They looked over at Oku and Casmir but decided not to go after them, instead limping off toward the parking lot.

"Oh, it's been five minutes now. Plenty of time." Casmir headed across the field toward the shuttle.

Oku squinted toward the greenhouse door—Dr. Pulinski hadn't followed them out. "Are you staying here, Doctor?"

Pulinski stuck her head out. "Yes. I'll tell them… I don't know what I'll tell them."

"Are you sure you don't want to come with us?"

"For the sake of my career, I think I better stay as many miles away from you as I dare." Pulinski smiled, though it was more fraught than pleased and she ducked back inside.

"Sorry about everything," Oku called, but she didn't get another response.

Rokuro swept Chasca up in his arms—she would have bolted if she'd been allowed to run free—and rushed to catch up to Casmir. He ran at Casmir's side, placing his armored form between him and the parking lot—in case some of those men still retained weapons.

Oku didn't know if they did. She saw a lot of bent rifles scattering the pavement. None of the vehicles appeared to be in working order either. Several were dark and powerless, like the shuttles, and others had been torn to pieces. This probably wasn't the time to think about how angry her father would be with her when he found out about this.

"I guess we're going that way," Maddie said, walking similarly beside Oku as they followed Casmir and Rokuro.

The shuttle was empty, the troops all evicted, as Casmir had called it, and scattered. Even though Oku didn't think any had been killed, they must have decided that dealing with the crushers was suicidal.

As their group approached, Chasca struggled to free herself and barked uproariously. This time, she wasn't complaining about the armored men. Her wild eyes looked toward the two crushers that now stood next to one of the shuttle hatches. Rokuro almost lost her as she bucked and tried to escape.

"Chasca is afraid of crushers," Oku called to Casmir, as if he could fix the problem. "She's met some of my father's, and she didn't like them."

Casmir had been halfway through the hatch, but he stopped and looked at Rokuro, who was trying to keep a grip on Chasca without hurting her.

Oku felt bad putting the problem on Casmir—how was he supposed to fix it?—especially when she noticed men regrouping in the parking lot. They were probably calling for reinforcements and bolstering themselves to rush after her group if they didn't get out of here soon.

"Is there a back area or somewhere I can put her behind a door?" Oku asked. "Or can the crushers hide in the bathroom?" The question sounded ludicrous as it came out of her mouth, if only because she couldn't imagine two of the giant black robots fitting in such a tiny space. "Just so she doesn't attack them and get hurt."

"You wish to lock us in a bathroom?" one of the crushers asked in a monotone voice.

"Clearly the inferior canine should be the one locked up," the other one said.

"Inferior!" Oku blurted, though she was startled by them joining in on the conversation.

"Is it their scents or shapes that bother her?" Casmir asked.

"I don't know." Oku glanced toward the lot again, afraid the troops would soon gather their fortitude—and new weapons—and charge after them. "Probably just that they're huge and scary."

"I am Zee, programmed to protect Kim Sato and Casmir Dabrowski. I am formidable, not scary."

Chasca barked at him, every strand of fur on her back standing upright.

"You're kind of scary." Casmir swatted him on the arm. "I'm really glad to see you, by the way. Thanks so much for coming to help us. Now, can you two do the couches?"

"I do not believe that furniture subterfuge is necessary in this situation, Casmir Dabrowski."

"It's either that or the bathroom. We're not locking up the royal princess's favorite pet."

"Rokuro, just take her inside," Maddie growled. "*Everyone* needs to get inside, so we can get out of here."

The nameless crusher looked at Zee. "Perhaps we should have volunteered for the other mission."

"I had to come here. I am programmed to protect Casmir Dabrowski."

"I am only programmed to obey him."

"He orders us to become inanimate furniture. We will do so."

The two crushers passed through the hatchway, one ruffling Casmir's hair on the way by, and disappeared into the back of the shuttle. Oku had no idea what they planned to do, but Casmir waved for everyone to join him inside.

Rokuro hesitated, then stepped inside with Chasca. She stopped barking and sniffed the air noisily.

Oku and Maddie followed Casmir inside, and Maddie closed the hatch with more vigor than the task demanded.

Rokuro set Chasca down—she was still sniffing and looking around suspiciously—then hurried between the rows of seats to the pilot's spot. Casmir paused, watching Chasca and two strange entirely black couches nested against the sides of the shuttle in the rear cargo area.

Enlightenment came like the banging of a gong. "That's *them*?"

"Yes," Casmir said, "but I don't recommend sitting on them. They're hard. The military didn't ask for cushiness when we were programming them."

He hurried up to sit in the co-pilot's seat. Chasca sniffed at the couches and prowled around them.

"We're going to have a hard time flying anywhere," Rokuro said, as Maddie and Oku slid into the seats behind them, "without power."

Casmir didn't touch anything. All he did was look at the control console, and power returned to the shuttle, lights coming on in the interior and across the panels.

"Are you doing that through the network?" Rokuro asked. "Or with magical powers?"

Casmir snorted. "The network."

"How, when the entire shuttle was dead?"

"It was just *mostly* dead." Casmir winked at him.

"If you say so." Rokuro's fingers danced over the controls, and the engine thrummed to life.

There were enough windows for Oku to see new Guard ground vehicles tearing into the parking lot.

"Better hurry," she murmured.

"Working on it," Rokuro said.

Rumbles reverberated through the deck, and the shuttle lifted off. Once they were above the trees, Oku allowed herself to slump back in her seat, though she feared they weren't safe yet. There had to be hundreds of Guard shuttles in the city that could be dispatched to find and intercept them.

Casmir gave an address to Rokuro. "I think you might be able to land on the rooftop."

"You sure we shouldn't fly straight out of the city?" Rokuro asked. "The Kingdom Guard isn't going to have any trouble tracking down their own shuttle."

"Their network is registering that this shuttle, as well as the two others, went offline and are currently in Majestic Meadows Park," Casmir said.

"You're sure?"

"Yes. We can leave the city after we get my parents."

Maddie leaned close to Oku and whispered, "Okay, I'm starting to see it now."

"See what?" Oku asked.

"That he might be Mikita's clone."

"I guess it's good that we got him out of that dungeon then." Oku peered over her shoulder to check on Chasca, worried by the silence. She didn't know these crushers of Casmir's well yet, and the one that wasn't Zee had sounded like he would be happy to lock Chasca in the bathroom.

But Chasca was fine. After the crazy night, she was curled up in a ball with her nose under her tail... as she lay on one of the couches.

"Uh, Casmir?" Oku couldn't stop staring at her gray dog on the black couch. "The crushers may be cushier than you realize."

"I don't think so. I've sat on couch-Zee before." Casmir twisted in his seat and saw Chasca. "Oh, hm. Maybe she has lower standards than humans for cush requirements."

"I don't think so. She very intentionally lies against the pillows on my bed whenever she gets the chance."

"Ah. Zee sent me a message. He said he's modulating his surface tension in order to simulate a more authentic piece of furniture."

"He's making himself soft for my dog? I'm touched."

"Good." Casmir grinned at her. "He didn't want to have to stay in the bathroom." He tapped Rokuro's arm. "After we get my parents, we've been invited up to the estate of Sirs Bjarke and William Asger."

"When did that happen?" Oku asked.

"Just now." Casmir waved at his temple. "When Kim told me about the crushers, she also said where they're hiding out. The Asgers, it seems, are in exile right now and not supposed to be in the system, and Kim's status is also dubious. As is that of Qin and all of her genetically engineered cat-woman sisters. We can all hide out together while we figure out... well, apparently, there are quite a few things to figure out." A troubled furrow creased his brow.

"The Asgers are hiding out at the Asger estate? Casmir, that's like me hiding out in my room at Drachen Castle."

"I gather they don't spend much time there, so they think it will be a while before someone thinks to check there. Also, they don't think anyone is actively seeking them out now, though they did attack a supply shuttle for some reason—I haven't gotten all the details yet—so they're not positive."

"This is a chaotic night," Oku said.

"I agree." Casmir looked out at the city lights as they flew toward his parents' neighborhood, perhaps noticing all the dark craters that hadn't yet been repaired. "And I'm afraid it's not going to get more peaceful anytime soon."

Something about his tone made Oku believe he was speaking about more than his own scheduled execution. She would have to check the news when she got a chance, but she didn't dare bring her chip back online now. The last thing she wanted was to lead Royal Intelligence to Casmir—again.

Twenty soldiers boarded the *Dragon,* along with a couple of nurses and a doctor who appeared as badly injured as the others. Bonita was amazed that any of them had survived that attack. She was even more amazed that none of them tried to take over her ship; that had been a real concern, especially since she was here alone right now. She had no Qin to curl her lip and reveal those ominous fangs. But the soldiers were too beleaguered to be a threat. They meekly let her lead them to sickbay—the ladders proved problematic for those on hover gurneys, but they helped each other up to the middle level of the ship.

"Thank you, Captain Lopez," a bald doctor with captain's rank said, the side of his face scorched half off from a painful electrical burn. "We brought emergency rations and what medical supplies we could get out of our destroyed sickbay. We'll tend to our own. If one of our ships is available to rendezvous to pick us up before Forseti Station, we'll let you know, but—" he grimaced, "—the Fleet may have its hands full."

"I'll bet." Bonita showed them cabins they could use and vowed to keep the hatch to her cabin and navigation locked. After being captured and imprisoned by Prince Jorg, she didn't trust Kingdom soldiers any more than she would pirates.

"Captain Lopez?" a woman with a familiar accent asked as Bonita was taking her leave. "We might share a common ancestor." The woman was one of the few who'd made it up the ladder of her own accord, though her arm was in a sling. She had bronze skin, short black hair, and her name tag read LOPEZ. "I'm Sergeant Maria Lopez, originally from Cabrakan Habitat in System Diomedes. ¿Cómo estás?"

"*Bien*," Bonita replied by habit, but the woman's blue-and-gold Kingdom galaxy suit flummoxed her. "How did you end up in their Fleet?"

She chuckled. "My husband is from the Kingdom. I'd been a traveler for years and didn't expect to get married, much less to some Kingdom captain on shore leave in System Hydra, but we've been together for six years. Well, not *together* at the moment." Her humor turned into a frustrated eye roll. "He's on Odin. He works in Intelligence in the capital, and I'm serving a tour of duty—I'm almost to the end, thankfully—because it's the easiest way to get citizenship."

"Marrying someone from the Kingdom doesn't get you citizenship?" Bonita thought of Bjarke, though she had no intention of marrying him and was positive he had no intention of marrying her. The last thing she needed was another marriage to fail utterly at.

"Eventually, but it's faster and more of a sure thing if you serve." Maria shrugged. "It hasn't been that bad. I grew up on spaceships, so I don't mind being out there. Or I didn't until we got clobbered."

"Sergeant?" The doctor leaned out of sickbay. "Need your help with Tanaka."

"Yes, sir."

"*Hasta luego.*" Maria waved to Bonita before trailing her officer inside.

Bonita headed to navigation, somewhat heartened that she had someone among the group who might give her a heads-up if the soldiers decided to try to take over her ship.

"Interesting," Viggo said as she slid into her pod and set a course for Forseti Station.

"What's that?"

"That you can become a Kingdom citizen by serving in their military. Should you and your *osito* wish to mate for life, you now have an option."

"I don't think they take seventy-year-old former bounty hunters into their service. Also, nobody gets to call him teddy bear except for me."

"No? But you let me use your nickname for Casmir."

"El Mago and I aren't sharing a bed, so his is a different kind of nickname. Off we go. Let me know if those soldiers do anything shifty."

"Right now, they're wrapping each other with regenerative bandages and injecting each other with nanites."

"Shiftily?"

"No."

"Good."

"You're a strange captain, Bonita."

"Just keeping us safe in the skies."

CHAPTER 11

Q IN'S LUNGS BURNED, AND HER LEGS WERE LEADEN as mile after forested mile passed under her feet. If Mouser and the rest of her sisters hadn't been stretched out behind her, matching her pace and pushing her to greater speeds, she might have stumbled to a stop—or at least a refreshingly slow walk—for a while.

They'd left the baying hounds in the distance, and it had been some time since a search shuttle had flown overhead, but the crushers were setting a fast and inexorable pace as they raced toward the coordinates that Bjarke had given them.

One of the crushers was carrying Kim, and when Qin glanced back, she spotted one of the armored knights riding piggyback on another crusher. Asger? She couldn't tell, but she knew if she, with her legs and stamina engineered for superiority, was tired, then even very fit humans would be as well. Only the crushers could sustain this pace indefinitely. She had no idea what energy source fueled them, but she'd never yet seen one powered down for a recharge.

Mouser must have seen her look back for she sped up to run at Qin's side, her breaths sounding labored through her helmet. Qin knew her own breathing was just as ragged, but she attempted to make it sound steady as she greeted her sister.

"Tired yet?"

"Of course not. It's… relaxing to run… in the open… after so long… cooped up on… spaceships."

"You *sound* tired." Qin kept her sentences short so her labored breathing wouldn't belie her condition.

"So do you."

"I do not."

"Yes, you do."

"Well, I'm not." She glowered at Mouser as she jumped a log sprawled across the uneven forest floor.

Sweat streamed down the side of her face despite her armor's self-cooling ability. She could have been swimming in glacier water and still would have been sweating now.

"Me either." Mouser lifted a hand, as if to wipe sweat from her own brow, but her knuckles clunked against her faceplate. She grunted. "Maybe we could risk removing these."

Qin glanced toward the sky. Even with her keen hearing, she couldn't detect the telltale noise of engines. Maybe their searchers had kept on course toward the city, not guessing that they would veer off to someone's estate.

"Maybe."

Also longing for fresh air and the scent of the forest, Qin didn't remove her entire helmet but commanded her faceplate to retract. Myriad smells danced into her nostrils. Damp microbe-rich soil, mushrooms growing at the bases of trees, fresh water running nearby, pine needles and sap, and finally the hint of a deer that had passed this way recently.

The rousing scents of the forest and the cool air caressing her cheeks gave Qin an extra burst of energy. She propelled her legs to greater speed, especially when they came out of the uneven terrain and tangled undergrowth and onto an old gravel road. Nobody shouted that she was going the wrong direction, so she ran full out, thinking of the deal that Asger had made with the Druckers and remembering that she was free. Truly free.

Mouser appeared at her side again, glancing over at her as she pumped her arms and pulled ahead.

Did she want a race? Mouser glanced back again, a challenge in her eyes.

Qin lengthened her stride even further, drawing even once more. They sprinted down the road, no finish line in sight as they perhaps overexerted themselves foolishly, but Qin needed to prove she hadn't gone soft in her time away from the Druckers, that she'd trained as hard as her sisters had.

As they sprinted down the road, the crushers thundering through the foliage to either side, Qin's energy finally started to flag, but not before she glimpsed light ahead. The woods ended, replaced by rolling, grassy hills, with the dark outline of a sprawling stone castle stretched across the top of the highest one. A few landscaping lights glowed yellow around the structure and along a winding driveway that led to some distant road, but the castle itself lay dark. A barn, a vehicle garage, and a few other outbuildings were also dark.

Qin slowed down, coming to a stop at the edge of the trees. Even if they'd reached the right place, and this was Asger's home, there might be guards or security systems that they had to watch out for.

Mouser stopped beside her, her faceplate also retracted, and she leaned forward, gripping her knees and breathing hard. "I would have beaten you if we'd had to run another mile."

"Liar."

Mouser laughed a ragged, breathless laugh and neither affirmed nor denied the statement. Sweat dripped from her nose and splashed dark on the pale, dry gravel. With the moon out, Qin had no trouble seeing it. She leaned against a tree and wiped her own face.

As the rest of their sisters and the crushers caught up, they also stopped at the edge of the trees, remaining in the deep shadows as they surveyed the castle.

"This place smells wonderful." Mouser straightened, inhaling deeply through her nose as she waved to the hills and the trees. She gazed toward a burbling stream meandering to one side of the castle, with massive, centuries-old deciduous trees along its banks. With copious thick branches jutting outward and upward, they looked like the perfect kinds of trees to climb. "It *is* wonderful," Mouser whispered with longing. "I hadn't realized Odin had so much wilderness."

"I've been in their capital city. It's big and populous with the usual pollution, but they do appear to have kept large swaths of their planet wild."

"I wonder… Do you think it's possible for us to find work *here*? Can you imagine living in these woods instead of on some spaceship or station?"

Qin hesitated. "People in the Kingdom are against genetic engineering and call those like us freaks. I don't know that we'd be completely forbidden from visiting, but I almost got arrested the last time I was here, even though I was voluntarily helping them with a problem."

"Well, you *are* shifty."

"Please. You're the one who tricked me with that note pretending you wanted to be rescued."

"You're right. I felt really bad about that. Captain Framer was standing right over my shoulder offering tips on how to compose it. I'm glad he's gone, but..." Mouser lowered her voice. "I wish they were all dead. I don't trust that they'll remember, now that they're safely back in their own system, the deal they made with your knight. A knight who it sounds like isn't even authorized to negotiate on behalf of the Kingdom right now."

Qin didn't think she'd mentioned Asger's exile status to her sister, but since they were skulking around in the forest, being hunted by search vessels, on Asger's own home world, Mouser could guess.

"If we could stay on this planet, it would be unlikely that the Druckers would dare come hunting for us." Mouser touched a tree trunk. She'd removed her gauntlets and let her claws sink gently into the bark, then leaned her face against it.

Qin fought tears that wanted to come to her eyes, because she understood the feeling perfectly, the appeal of the wild, of ground and gravity and forests and fields and growing things. It called to something deep in her DNA the way a spaceship or station never had, so she wasn't surprised her sisters felt the same way.

"Remember how I said Bonita might be able to hire you all?" Qin asked. "She's fair and flexible. I'm sure she would let us visit some planets with trees now and then."

"There aren't many places like Odin in the Twelve Systems."

"No, but some of the moons and planets elsewhere are decent, especially the ones that were terraformed."

"Hm."

Qin told herself that her sisters were free to go wherever they wished and to work for whomever they wished. It had been nice being with them again these last couple of weeks, but she couldn't expect them to stick with her indefinitely. Still, she did feel that she shouldn't encourage them to stay here. The Kingdom was not friendly to people like them, no matter how nice the trees were.

"Oh, good," came Asger's voice from behind them. "I'm glad you waited. My father and I will go check the grounds and make sure nothing is amiss before we invite you all in."

He had been the one she'd seen riding piggyback, and he released his arms and slid off as the crusher came to a stop. Three more approached carrying Kim, Bjarke, and Tristan.

"Also," Asger said, "you and your sisters are amazing."

Qin had been about to wipe the sweat from her forehead again, but she lowered her arm and attempted to look amazing in the moonlight—maybe even radiant—rather than sweaty and gross. "Thank you."

"This place looks wonderful," Tristan said, his voice almost as full of longing as Mouser's had been. Had he been missing his homeland in the months he'd been away? He'd met and fallen in love with Princess Nalini, so his time in System Stymphalia couldn't have been that bad. "It reminds me of the estate of my mentor, Sir Sebastian, but with less land cleared. He had a lot of vineyards and orchards."

"Is that the land you were supposed to inherit?" Asger asked.

"It's the land he attempted to leave to me in his will, but I never asked for or expected it. I did enjoy being out there and training with him though."

"Does it look like how you left it?" Bjarke asked Asger quietly—he sounded wary, rather than nostalgic. "I haven't been back in two years."

"I know you haven't." Asger eyed his father, then shrugged. "It's hard to tell from here. The lawn is mowed around the castle, so Thacker must still be keeping it up."

"Given that his pay is automatically withdrawn from the estate account every month, I should hope so."

"You kept track of *that* from System Cerberus?" Asger asked.

"I was playing the role of an accountant. It seemed appropriate to make sure my own books were in order."

"I've finally made contact with Casmir," Kim said. "He's escaped from the dungeon under the castle."

"So *that's* the shuttle he was on," Bjarke grumbled. "Neither the supply shuttle nor the one supposedly heading to that prison. Two decoy shuttles, and we picked the wrong one."

"I'm glad he's all right," Qin said, relieved and not caring how he'd gotten out, only that he was out. "Or is he? Why has he been out of communications?"

"Jager had his chip removed," Kim said. "He just got a new one installed minutes ago. He's incognito on the network with it for now, so people can't find him easily, so you may not be able to message him unless he messages you first."

"Well, tell him to message me," Qin said. "I want to send him a picture of sweaty knights and sweaty cat women and let him know we're glad he's alive."

Kim looked at her with that hard-to-read expression of hers. Maybe Qin should have left out the adjectives about sweat.

"Crushers do not leak bodily fluids," one of them said, "but we are also pleased that Casmir Dabrowski is alive."

"I will tell him," Kim said.

"Where is he?" Bjarke asked.

"Did Rache free him?" Asger added. "I'm glad he's alive, too, but I'll feel disgruntled if Rache succeeded at rescuing him when our team couldn't even find him."

"Princess Oku did," Kim said.

"Oh." Asger scratched his jaw. "I guess that's better than Rache, though I thought it would take someone more, uhm, manly to rescue him."

"Manly?" Qin pointed at her chest and looked at her sisters.

"Maybe *muscly*. At the least, armed and armored with lots of ferocious backup." Asger waved at the crushers.

"Princess Oku had her dog with her," Kim offered.

"I've met that dog," Asger said. "She's not ferocious."

"Where are they now?" Bjarke asked.

"Evading the authorities," Kim said. "I gather Oku didn't have permission to remove Casmir from the dungeon."

"They can come here if they can get away sneakily," Asger said.

"I'll give him that message."

"We better make sure it's safe." Bjarke nodded toward the castle. "William, with me. Everyone else, wait until we signal."

Asger touched Qin's shoulder, then followed Bjarke down the old gravel road toward the castle.

Kim leaned against a tree and rubbed her hip, murmuring something about it being unfortunate that crushers couldn't create moving parts and turn themselves into wagons.

Greetings, Qin! a message came in from Casmir. *Thank you for coming all the way to Odin to try to rescue me. Please thank your sisters too. I hope to see you all soon. And Bonita and Viggo, too, of course. If they can get here. I know the Kingdom isn't making it easy for visitors right now.*

Qin sent a reply, informing him that Asger was disgruntled he'd been rescued by someone who wasn't manly, muscular, or ferocious.

My rescue team is extremely ferocious! Casmir sent a photograph of a gray, short-furred dog curled up on a solid black couch. *Correction: they* were *ferocious. Now they're resting.*

They?

LAYERS OF FORCE

That's Chasca and Zee.

Ah, right. She'd heard that Zee could turn into a couch to fool his enemies. *A formidable team.*

"So he was telling the truth, eh?" Mouser was watching Asger and Bjarke walk toward the castle.

"Asger?" Qin asked. "About what?"

"About having a castle and letting us visit."

"I think the possibility of visiting is still to be determined." Qin was encouraged that there weren't shuttles or ground vehicles lined up out front with troops scouring the grounds, but they could show up at any time. "But he wouldn't intentionally lie. He's honest."

"Are you sure?" Mouser gazed over at her.

"Of course. What would make you doubt that?"

"Back in that ship's cargo hold, when we were battling each other, it was when I saw him pick you up and hug you to him that I stopped fighting. It seemed like he truly cared. I am well aware of how the Kingdom feels about our kind, and a knight is more Kingdom than most of their subjects, with all that hoity-toity Knight's Code stuff. But I thought if he cared, maybe…" Mouser shrugged, studying the grass at their feet.

"He does care."

"But would he truly have a relationship with someone like us?"

"We *have* a relationship." True, Qin hadn't sneaked off with Asger for sex while they'd been on Rache's ship—they'd both been inhibited by the lack of privacy—but it wasn't as if he'd been distant with her. They had spent a lot of time together.

"I mean a forever relationship."

"Like marriage? We're not getting married."

"Because you don't want to?" Mouser squinted at her, angling for something. "Or because *he* doesn't want to?"

"I'm not ready for marriage."

"He's so handsome. Why wouldn't you want to marry someone like him if you could?"

"That's not the only reason to have a relationship with someone," Qin said dryly, though she knew where Mouser was going with this and didn't want to encourage it. "I like him because we go into battle together, and he's good to fight with. Also, he's willing to play silly games with me."

"But would he ever marry you? If you wished it?"

"I don't think he could, as long as he stayed here. The Kingdom's rules—"

"Is it the Kingdom's rules, or does he want someone else? Like that princess he talked about?"

"No," Qin said firmly. "I was teasing him about that. He knew her before he met me."

"What if she showed up now and told him that *she* has feelings for him? Do you think he would stay with you? A princess is special. And she's pretty. I've seen pictures of the king's family."

Heat rose to Qin's cheeks. "Of course he would stay with me. They're not having sex. *We* are." She didn't realize that her voice had risen until Kim and Tristan looked over. Even more heat torched her cheeks. She lowered her voice. "Why are you asking all this?"

"I'm sorry." Mouser lifted an apologetic hand. "It's not my place to speak. I was able to accept that he would befriend you, but it's just hard for me to believe…" Mouser took a deep breath. "You've always been idealistic, Squirt. I just want you to be careful if you've got some dream about marrying him and *living* here." She waved toward the dark castle. "I'm sure he'll choose one of his own kind for that."

"I never thought we'd do that. I work for Captain Lopez on the *Dragon*. It's a good life, and Asger and I are just having fun. That's all. I never expected anything else."

Why was everybody so concerned about the idea that there might be an anything else? Maybe sometimes, she imagined what it would be like to be normal and to be able to marry a normal man—a nice man who didn't mind that she had claws and fangs and could hurl enemies across a room with one hand—but she knew that wasn't how the universe worked.

"All right, good," Mouser said. "Because he's a pretty boy, and I'm sure he gets lots of offers from women. I saw Tigress checking out his butt the other day."

Qin looked back at the rest of her sisters, though they'd given her and Mouser room for a private conversation. "Tigress checks out *every* guy's butt. She's the only one of us that actually seemed to enjoy sex with the pirates."

"True. And now she's enjoyed it with seven mercenaries."

"Eight," came a smug call from behind them.

LAYERS OF FORCE

Qin snorted. There was no point in trying to have a private conversation around people with hearing as keen as her own.

"She even tried to get Rache," Mouser said. "She's fearless."

"She'd have to be. But I trust that didn't work." Qin glanced at Kim, though she and Tristan were pointing to where Asger and Bjarke had disappeared from sight and didn't appear to be listening.

"I don't believe so," Mouser said. "Tigress thinks he's celibate. Or gay."

"Why, because he didn't want to sleep with her?"

"Most men are intrigued enough to take her up on her offer. At least once." Mouser shrugged. "I did tell her to leave Asger alone."

"Thanks."

"I'm watching out for you." Mouser thumped her on the arm. "Like a big sister should."

"We're the same age."

"You were such a runt when you were growing up. You *had* to come out of the test tube last."

"You're hilarious."

"I am. I'm surprised your chortles aren't ringing out through the forest."

"I have amazing self-control."

"Is that why Asger is into you?"

Qin was debating between a mature answer and a playful answer when Kim swore softly from her spot under the tree.

"Are we in trouble?" Qin asked.

"I'm taking this opportunity to catch up on the news," Kim explained.

"Did that answer your question?" Mouser asked.

Kim sighed. "Yes, I think we're *all* going to be in trouble."

"All of us?" Qin pointed at their group.

"All of Odin—and everyone on it."

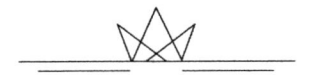

After days—weeks?—of being inaccessible, a barrage of messages came into Casmir's chip when he got the mail and texting system set up. There wasn't time to address or even glance at them all now, but he replied to the last one from his parents to let them know that he was on his way to pick them up and to please gather what they needed for... *a trip*, he made himself say, knowing full well that he might mean forever.

But if his parents tried to pack up their whole apartment, the shuttle would be waiting for hours. Casmir had temporarily flummoxed the Kingdom Guard and sprinkled misdirection all over their secure network, but someone would figure out his hacks soon enough. He wanted to get out of the city as soon as possible.

When Kim had contacted him, she'd said they could hide out at Asger's estate and had sent the coordinates, but he knew that could only be a temporary refuge. He would have to figure out... he wasn't sure what yet. The future.

"I see an empty Guard vehicle," Rokuro reported as they circled the neighborhood, scanning the area before landing, "but no sign of any troops standing at the exits."

"The crushers should have taken care of them by now," Casmir said.

"Taken care of? Since they didn't kill the troops attacking us, I'll hope that isn't an innuendo for *killed*."

"They might be injured," Casmir said, "depending on how much they fought back, but the crushers *I* programmed kill only as a last resort."

"Are there ones out there that someone else programmed?"

"The military has all the originals."

"My father has at least two," Oku said grimly from behind Casmir's seat.

"Jorg had a bunch, too, but I acquired those after his passing and have since reprogrammed them." Casmir didn't look back, not wanting to see if Oku wore a disapproving expression at the mention of her deceased brother. He hadn't been responsible for that, no matter what Jager believed, but he did feel guilty that he'd been so close and hadn't been able to stop it. After managing to talk Rache into helping so many times, it seemed a failing that he hadn't managed to talk him out of murdering someone. "I wonder how many of the originals are left."

"I'm taking us in to land on the roof."

Casmir passed the message on to his mother, who'd sent about a hundred questions in the handful of minutes since he'd made contact. He said he would answer later and asked if they needed help carrying things.

No, she replied. *We have porters.*

The response surprised him until his mother and father walked out the fire escape door onto the rooftop, followed by two crushers carrying suitcases, bags, boxes, and two coolers. They'd had to morph their arms into shelf-like appendages to manage the loads. His father had a few bags. His mother carried her huge purse and the cat carrier. Maybe they'd known that *trip* had indeed been a code word for *possibly forever.*

Rokuro tapped a button to open the hatch, and Casmir scrambled back to help them in. His mother set down the cat carrier and smothered him in a hug.

"The king said you were to be executed!" she cried.

"I know. Thanks to those who generously risked themselves to rescue me—" Casmir tilted his head toward Oku and her bodyguards, "—I'm hoping that won't happen now." He returned the hug and managed to get an arm free to grasp his father's shoulder.

"We trust you'll tell us everything, son," he said, "and explain why you've been so poor about communicating of late."

"I was locked in a brig cell with no network access, and then they removed my chip. I only just got a new one."

"I meant for the last six months."

"Oh. That's a long story."

"I am certain."

Chasca, who had been sleeping soundly on the Zee-couch, jumped to her feet and barked as the two porter-crushers stepped into the shuttle.

"Uh oh." Casmir extricated himself from his mother's grasp as Oku rushed back to restrain the dog. "I think you two are going to need to turn into furniture too. As long as there's no chance guards are chasing you?"

Casmir peered out before closing the hatch. Thankfully, the rooftop was empty.

"Where *are* the guards?" Casmir's father asked warily. "We couldn't leave earlier when we received Princess Oku's warning, because they were at the exits, but then they were simply not there, and these large robots showed up saying we had to pack and leave."

"They have been disposed of," one of the crushers said—these were two that Casmir hadn't named yet.

"Disposed of?" The imprecise terminology concerned Casmir.

"Does that mean dead?" His mother frowned darkly.

"No," the crusher said. "We removed their armor and locked them inside waste collection bin 2B for disposal."

"Ah." Casmir decided the terminology had been precise after all.

"Casmir," Oku said, straining as she tried to keep Chasca from lunging at the crushers.

"Yes, sorry for the delay." Casmir smiled and patted the crushers on the chests. "For the brief ride out of town, will you two convert yourselves into unthreatening furnishings?" He pointed at Zee for an example. "Or store yourselves temporarily in the bathroom with the door closed?"

The crushers looked at Zee, looked at each other, and looked toward the tiny closet that served as the lavatory. They morphed into couches identical to the ones Zee and the other crusher had created.

"Are we ready to go?" Rokuro asked as Chasca's barks turned from threatening to softer uncertain woofs.

"Yes, please." Casmir waved his parents to seats and helped Oku with Chasca, who'd jumped to the deck and was sniffing the new couches. She also sniffed the old couches. "I suppose for the sake of verisimilitude, I should see if some of them would be willing to create trunks and end tables. Perhaps a nice ottoman."

Oku tugged Chasca to the rearmost bank of *real* seats. "You better take what you can get and not tick them off. Did you see them throwing armored men fifty feet across the park?"

"I did, yes." Casmir patted the crushers, thanked them for their assistance, and joined Oku and Chasca in seats as Rokuro took them to the air again.

Casmir Dabrowski, Zee messaged him, not speaking aloud since his current form precluded it. *I have been in communication with Tork since he reentered the system, and we have been discussing the various threats to you.*

Oh? Have you come up with any solutions on how to save me from them? Casmir smiled, not expecting any such miracles from his allies.

LAYERS OF FORCE

We are still brainstorming, as humans call it, but we do have some ideas. Should one of them be feasible to pursue, may we take the initiative to attempt to implement it? Of course, I will also continue to assist you here as your protector.

I appreciate that. Yes, of course. I'm positive I'll be a fan of whatever clever thing you guys can come up with to keep me alive, so long as it doesn't involve hurting people.

Certainly. I am aware of your preference for non-violent solutions.

Good. Thank you.

"There's a lot of chatter on the Kingdom Guard comm," Rokuro said. "They're looking for us."

"Are you a fugitive, Casmir?" His mother frowned back at him.

"I'm afraid so, Mother. The king believes—has chosen to believe—that I was responsible for Prince Jorg's death. I wasn't on the ship at the time, but… it's a long story. I'll tell you all in the morning, assuming we successfully get out of here." There were a lot of lights in the sky ahead of them, other aircraft flying over the city. *Searching* the city?

Disgruntled mews came from the cat carrier, and his mother opted for making soothing noises instead of asking him further questions.

"I'm taking us up and over," Rokuro said. "Hopefully, they won't look too closely at us."

"Yes." Casmir closed his eyes and leaned back, wondering if there was any way he could convince Jager he hadn't been responsible and that he shouldn't be killed—Oku had mentioned clearing his name, but had that been unfounded optimism?—or if he truly had to get off the planet and out of the system as soon as possible.

He looked sadly over at Oku. When he'd asked her to have coffee with him, she'd said yes, but if he had to leave as soon as possible…

"We'll figure something out in the morning," Oku said quietly, as if she could guess his thoughts.

"I hope so. Are you sure we shouldn't drop you off—I suppose we can't just pop into the castle—someplace where you can make your way home?" He glanced at her temple. "Is your chip still off? You must have a ton of messages from people wondering where you are."

"It is, and I know." She stared resolutely at the seat back ahead of her. "I don't want to deal with it right now."

"I understand." He thought about taking her hand, but that felt presumptuous, especially since it was resting on her thigh. It would be an intimate gesture.

"I couldn't even if I wanted to. They could use it to locate me." Her tone turned bitter. "And through me, you. I should probably keep it off until you... clear your name."

"Is that what you intend to do, Casmir?" His father peered back over the seat.

"I'll look into it." Casmir didn't want to promise anything he couldn't deliver. "But I may have to work on it from the relative safety of another system."

"Hm." His father exchanged a long look with his mother.

Oku took Casmir's hand and leaned her shoulder against his.

Oh, that was nice. He enjoyed the moment until she whispered, "You smell, Casmir."

At least she didn't pull away from him.

"I know. I'm hoping Asger's castle has a shower."

"Ten of them."

"You've been there?"

"No, but castles built by the nobility are large. I'm sure there are *at least* ten bathrooms. Maybe twenty."

"You think I'll need that many?"

Oku sniffed him. "Possibly."

Chasca, inspired by this act of sniffing, leaned across Oku and also twitched her nostrils at Casmir. She licked his cheek.

He blinked. "I guess she doesn't mind that I smell."

"She doesn't mind a lot." Oku pushed the dog back to her other side. "You don't want to know the places she puts that tongue."

Casmir touched his cheek. "Maybe not."

Oku laid her head on his shoulder. Casmir surreptitiously sniffed her hair. Even though her night had been as fraught as his, *she* hadn't been denied bathing opportunities in the previous days. A delightful floral scent teased his nostrils, reminding him of her greenhouse, and he had to resist the urge to wrap his arm around her shoulders.

He found her willingness to be close to him encouraging, especially given his aroma, and vowed to try the arm-shoulders move as soon as he scrubbed himself thoroughly and found fresh clothes. He tried not to think about how unlikely it was that he would find anything that fit among Bjarke or William Asger's wardrobes. Maybe they had a short scrawny servant with a closet he could raid.

LAYERS OF FORCE

Are you watching the news? a new message from Kim came in.
No, I'm enjoying floral-scented hair.
I don't know what that means, but you had better tune in. We have a problem.
I would prefer not to deal with any more problems this week.
That's too bad. It's a big one.
We'll arrive at Asger's castle soon, and we can discuss it. Reluctantly, Casmir pulled up the news.

CHAPTER 12

"THOSE WOMEN ARE INCREDIBLE," ASGER'S FATHER SAID.

"They are," Asger agreed, watching the grounds as they approached the castle. The light in the caretaker's cottage was out, but at this late hour, that wasn't surprising. His father headed in that direction anyway, likely wanting the update from Thacker. "I was done after ten miles."

"I'm usually good for a lot more than that, but running through the forest without a trail is a good way to break a leg. Even the crushers wobbled on the uneven terrain, but they've got nothing to break."

"Except your balls if you're riding on one's back," Asger said.

"I hope your armor protected your balls sufficiently."

"It did, but I wouldn't have wanted to go on that ride without it."

His father rang the doorbell. The stone and thatch cottage looked like it had been built centuries ago, but that was mostly a facade, and it had the modern amenities inside, the same as the castle. Asger expected the lights to come on. It had been several months since he'd been out here, but Thacker was accustomed to him, and his father, being away for long stretches, and he was always here when Asger returned.

Asger gazed around. In the dim lighting, he couldn't be positive that the property hadn't been damaged in the bombings of the previous month, but he didn't see any caved-in towers or gaping holes in the castle walls. From what he'd heard, the attacks had focused on Odin's major cities.

"It's not that big of a cottage," his father said. "He should have heard that and woken up."

"I wonder if he heard about our exile status and left."

"It's possible. He shouldn't have gotten in trouble for being the groundskeeper on the estate, but he may have worried he would be out of a job. I'll grab the key out of the safe box in the back."

Asger waited out front while his father circled the cottage. He gazed toward the stable, the large wooden building long empty of horses, and the garage where a few ground cars were kept. A tiny flashing green light near the roll-up doors made him frown. Had that always been there? The security panels didn't usually remain lit up when they weren't in use.

He jogged across the driveway to the building and found tiny electronic devices mounted by each of the garage doors, with a keypad faintly illuminated by the tiny green light.

"Is that an alarm system?" His father came up behind him. "Did you install those?"

"No. It's possible that Thacker did, extra security if he was going to be out of the area. But you'd think he would have sent me a message about it if he had. And the code to disarm it."

"I doubt he installed anything." His father pointed his thumb toward the cottage. "The key was gone, but he left a note in the box, saying he was ordered to quit by Baron Farley and to turn over his keys to the estate. Farley told him we were exiled and that the estate was off-limits to everyone until such time as the legal system determined who the proper heir was." He shook his head in disgust. "I *have* a will in the nobles' records. It wouldn't take a genius to read it."

Asger was more concerned about the alarm than who owned the estate, at least for tonight. "The authorities must have installed these then. So they would be alerted if we showed up. We're not going to be able to get any of the vehicles out as long as the security system is active."

His father swore.

Asger thunked his forehead against the wall. He'd invited everyone to meet him here, including Casmir and Princess Oku. One did not tell *princesses* that they had to camp out on the lawn.

"Let's check the main door," his father said.

Asger eyed the grounds with new wariness as they walked up the hill toward the castle. As sprawling as the area was, someone could easily be watching them from somewhere on the estate. Or there could be other booby traps about.

"I heard from Bonita while we were traveling out here," his father said. "She's back in System Lion. And so is an aggressive new foe that took out four Kingdom warships before her eyes."

"I saw something in the news briefly when we were running here, an announcement Jager made to the people."

"I'm looking at it now." His father touched his temple. "He thinks it's astroshamans. I guess they contacted him with a threat, otherwise he couldn't know. Their ships are invisible to our scanners."

"I'm surprised he hasn't tried to put the blame for those attacks on Rache."

"Rache is getting blamed for something else."

"What?"

"There's a new story breaking right now that Prince Finn was kidnapped."

"*Finn* was kidnapped?" Asger stared at his father. "Are you sure they didn't say Princess Oku? If she sneaked out with Casmir without telling anyone, they might think *she* was kidnapped."

"No, this is on several channels. It's Finn. Jager had just ordered him to leave from one of the orbital stations and go back to the castle so they wouldn't both be on the frontlines for another war that may be coming. But he was kidnapped scant minutes after arriving at the castle. There was a big fight at the landing pad between all of his bodyguards and a masked man in black armor. Not much doubt who that was."

"What was Rache doing going after *Finn*?" Asger was tempted to call Kim over so he could ask her if she knew anything, but he wanted to get into the castle first.

"I don't know. Apparently, he hasn't commed or made any demands." His father lowered his voice. "At this point, they're not even sure Finn is alive. They're speculating that he is because Rache took him instead of killing him on the grounds, but they don't know."

"The king must be livid."

"They shut down the launch loop to try to keep him from escaping from Odin. That also is going to mean *we're* stuck on the planet too."

"I hope Casmir wasn't planning on fleeing and taking that job he was offered by Sultan Shayban," Asger said.

"I wish someone had offered *me* another job. Our system has gone nuts, and I don't know how to help. They don't even *want* my help." His father removed his helmet and looked like he couldn't decide whether to stuff it under his arm or throw it to the ground. "Bonita said she was hoping to come pick up Qin. I told her we could… visit if she comes here. Now I wish I'd told her to stay away."

Asger didn't comment on what *visit* meant. "She wouldn't stay away if she thought Qin was in danger."

"I suppose not. But I'm sending her another message and telling her this is a bad time to come. I hope she'll go back to the gate and to a system where it's safe. We'll keep an eye on Qin and her sisters for her."

"Damn right, we will."

As they strode up the hill to the castle entrance, his father thumped his fist against his thigh. "If I knew exactly where Rache was or where his ship was, I would send that information to Baron Farley, exile or not."

"I don't think Rache is the main problem right now."

"He kidnapped Finn."

"Which is also not the main problem." Asger had pulled up the news while they talked and was skimming the reports on the astroshaman ships—and Jager's promise that a virus might be unleashed.

"We'll see," his father said darkly. "Rache might want to trade Finn to the astroshamans so they could use him as a bargaining chip."

Judging by the number of Kingdom ships that the astroshamans had knocked out on their way inland, they didn't *need* a bargaining chip. Why were they *here*? The news hadn't mentioned that. This couldn't still be Dubashi's handiwork, could it? Something he'd arranged before his death?

They stopped at the front door of the castle, and Asger scowled at an alarm device identical to the ones installed on the garage.

"What do you want to bet there's one on every door? What if they took out all of the furniture? All of our belongings?" Asger admitted that was a minor problem given everything that was going on right now, but the thought of losing his mementos of his mother disturbed him.

When his father didn't respond, Asger poked him.

"Sorry. I'm messaging Bonita. I told her to leave the system until it's safe, but she said she got talked into giving a ride to wounded Kingdom soldiers. I hope she doesn't get caught in the middle of this." His father winced. "She shouldn't even *be* in our system."

"I'm sure she wants Qin back."

"You think that's the only reason she returned?"

"What, you think she's been pining away for you?"

"I did leave an impression on her," his father said stiffly.

"Do you actually care for her?"

"She's a spunky woman."

"What does *that* mean?"

"Really, William. I am not grilling you on your relationship with Qin."

"Other than to tell me that it's a bad idea."

"I believe I promised to stand beside you in front of the king and vouch for her if you brought her home. Though I think we'd both get shot if we went anywhere near the king now."

"I'm positive of it." Asger pulled his rifle off his shoulder, tempted to blow away the security device.

"Don't. If it's destroyed, it will trigger an alert on a computer somewhere."

The distant whine of an aircraft reached their ears.

Asger swore. "I didn't even touch it."

An alert flashed on his contact. Casmir, messaging from a new chip, was requesting permission to contact him.

Casmir, where have you been?

Fewer places than you might think, but I did receive a lovely tour of the city's abandoned subway tunnels and also a park and a greenhouse. I believe I see your castle. May we come down to land?

"We better hide in the stable," Asger's father said.

"Wait." Asger lifted a hand to stop him. "I think those are our people."

Yes. My father and I are waiting out front. Asger used his contact camera to take a picture of the door alarm. *Any chance you can disarm something like this? If not, Princess Oku will have to sleep in the stable.*

Possibly. Have no fear for Her Royal Highness. If there's not a bed available, I know of a wonderful couch that's capable of modulating its surface tension for extra cush.

You're still a weird guy, Casmir. Asger didn't know what he was talking about, but he smiled, relieved that Casmir sounded like himself. He would like to think that Jager and the military wouldn't torture anyone, other than questioning them with truth drugs, but he wasn't as certain of that as he had once been.

I do not dispute this assessment.

"Our people are coming in a Kingdom Guard shuttle?" Asger's father asked. "Are you sure about that?"

"Pretty sure." Still, Asger kept his rifle in hand as the shuttle settled onto a level patch of ground near the driveway.

"If they stole that, the Guard will be able to track it." His father shook his head. "I don't know why I said *if*."

By the way, Casmir added as the shuttle powered down, *if you're hoping your presence here will remain a secret, you might want to take your chips offline.*

Good point. In a similar vein, you might not want to park a stolen Kingdom Guard shuttle in my front yard. I assume it can be tracked here.

Oh, the Guard believes this shuttle was destroyed and the wreckage is strewn all over a park in the city.

Are you sure? It looks un-wrecked to me.

Yes, because I programmed its software to tell them that.

I assume that means your *chip isn't offline.*

It's not, Casmir replied, *but I've already installed a cloaking program on it.*

Is that legal?

Of course not, but neither is breaking out of a dungeon.

Your crimes are stacking up, aren't they?

Like magazines in a hoarder's apartment.

Threatening to topple over on the innocent at any moment?

I'm afraid so.

The hatch opened, and the first one out of the shuttle was a gray dog that sprinted across the driveway and peed in the grass. Then came people in armor, an older couple with bags and a cat carrier, four crushers carrying trunks and coolers, Princess Oku, and finally Casmir himself. Casmir, with a fledgling beard and in the same rumpled clothes Asger had last seen him in, looked like he'd been rescued from a deserted island rather than any place civilized.

We're not sure we can get inside yet, Asger messaged Kim and Qin, *but I think you can join us.*

He didn't know if it was safe here, but it seemed rude to make the others wait in the woods.

"Hullo, Asger." Casmir came up and hugged him. "And older Asger." He grinned over at Asger's father. "Where's Kim? And Qin? And everyone else? Is everyone okay?"

"I think we're supposed to ask you if *you're* okay." Asger couldn't feel the hug through his armor, but he patted Casmir on the back, pleased to see him.

There was a fresh wound at his temple where his chip must have been removed and the new one inserted, but he didn't look like he'd been tortured to within an inch of his life. All of his fingernails were there, if ragged from being chewed on.

"I'm all right, but we're going to need to discuss Jager's announcement and figure out what's really going on." Casmir released Asger and stepped back. "I also need to visit all ten of your showers."

Asger blinked. "Pardon?"

"Princess Oku said I smell," Casmir said as Asger's father went to help what Asger realized were Casmir's parents with their luggage.

"She did? She's usually less blunt than that."

"She held my hand while she said it, so I didn't mind."

"She what?" Asger stared at him, so startled by the announcement that he almost missed Oku walking up.

By old habit, and because he still felt like a knight even if his superiors believed otherwise, Asger dropped to his knee and bowed his head to her.

"Greetings, Your Highness. My home is your home. Uhm, if Casmir can thwart the security device on the door."

"That sounds like something simple for him," Oku said.

"Ah." Casmir stepped around Asger toward the door. "Let me look up the model and figure out which company is responsible for the monitoring."

"It's good to see you, Sir Asger," Oku said politely and formally, as she had always been with him. "You might want to take your chip offline. And your father too. We're trying to avoid being tracked. I am especially, but it won't take Royal Intelligence long to realize you're back on the planet."

"Of course, Your Highness." Asger rose to his feet and caught a fond smile on Oku's face, but it wasn't directed at him.

Was she looking at the back of Casmir's head? All he was doing was staring at the door alarm. And probably accessing the network and hacking into the thing, Asger admitted. But that didn't deserve a *fond* look.

Kim, Tristan, Qin, and the others came into view as they walked around the corner of the castle and headed their way.

Asger lifted a hand toward them, reminding himself that he shouldn't worry about someone else's relationship—even if it was extremely difficult to imagine the princess being interested in goofy, geeky *Casmir*.

"Your castle is lovely, Asger." Qin smiled at him.

"It's even better inside." Asger walked over and joined her, clasping her hand. She had her faceplate retracted, probably enjoying the scents of the grass and the trees. "Though you might like the tree house."

"Tree house?"

"It's out behind the stable. There's a creek with some old cottonwoods and sagart-whatever those native trees are that like water. They grow huge and have branches thicker than people for a good fifty feet up. Several generations of Asger boys have worked on expanding it."

"As I recall," his father said, "your contribution was done mostly by the groundskeeper Thacker, as you held his tools."

"I also held his nails and handed him up boards. I was only seven when I was most interested in tree houses."

"I built an entire story and two of the decks."

"Perhaps we could get you a medal later to award your boyhood dedication."

"No fighting allowed while I'm hacking, please." Casmir patted the air in a conciliatory manner with his hands.

Kim squeezed past Qin and several of her sisters. "You're *always* hacking something these days."

"I know. How do I get people of the universe to maintain the peace while I do that?" Casmir grinned and rushed toward Kim with his arms raised, but he halted awkwardly a couple of feet from her. "Does time in a brig *and* a dungeon in the same week warrant a hug?" His arms remained raised, but he didn't presume to cross the last couple of feet.

"Since you endured *both*, I'll allow this physical contact." Kim hugged him gently.

Casmir returned the hug fiercely and pounded her on the back before grabbing her hand and pulling her toward Oku, who was watching this reunion with a bemused expression on her face. Asger might have tried to explain Kim's rules about touching to Oku, but he hadn't quite mastered them himself. For some reason, punching, blocking, and martial-arts throws were allowed, but one had to ask before a handshake or a hug.

"This is Princess Oku, Kim." Casmir also clasped Oku's hand. "I know you know that, but this is her in *person*."

"Thank you for clarifying," Kim murmured.

"It's nice to meet you, Scholar Sato. I hope the galaxy will settle down soon and that we can go back to working on feeding people by growing superior grains, vegetables, and fruits on habitats and space stations, assisted of course by robotic and biological bee pollination."

"My understanding is that Casmir's robot bees won't pollinate anything," Kim said. "Just show the real bees how to get home."

LAYERS OF FORCE

Casmir lifted a finger. "Don't rule out my robots. It would be *easy* for them to pollinate—all I'd need to do is add hair to their bodies that would attract grains of pollen for transferring from one flower to another. The real question is whether I can have them make honey. Gathering nectar is easy enough, but I would need to come up with synthetic enzymes that would—"

Asger's father cleared his throat loudly. "What happened to the hacker disarming the booby trap on my front door?"

"Ah, excuse me." Casmir released their hands. "I believe that's me."

"I believe so too," Oku said. "And the sooner you deactivate it and open the front door, the sooner you can find a shower."

"Something we would *all* appreciate," Casmir's mother said—she and his father had joined the group. "At least all of us who spent an hour in a shuttle with you."

"The rest of us also." Kim wrinkled her nose.

"Right." Casmir hurried back to the device. He pressed a button, and the light winked out. The grand double doors then opened of their own accord.

Asger raised his eyebrows. "The doors should have been locked to anyone who isn't in the family and didn't press a hand to the palm reader." He pointed to the electronic panel on the other side of the alcove that Casmir hadn't touched.

"I jumped on your network," Casmir said.

"I still think he uses magic," an armored man Asger didn't know but who had to be one of Oku's bodyguards muttered.

"I'll check to make sure there aren't booby traps inside." Asger's father walked in, rifle in hand. "Give me a moment."

"Is it wrong to imagine him dangling upside-down from the ceiling fan in the foyer by a rope tied around his ankle?" Asger asked.

"I thought you two were getting along now," Casmir said.

"We're doing okay. I still can have fantasies, can't I?"

"You're the one who has to spend time in your head." Casmir grinned and clapped him on the arm. "It's good to see you. And you too, Qin," he called back. "And all the crushers! And Qin's lovely sisters, whom I've barely met and unfortunately don't know the names of yet. Qin, you remember my parents, right? From the dinner at our house? Irena and Aleksy Dabrowski. Oh, and those are Princess Oku's bodyguards, Maddie and Rokuro. And that's Chasca there, ah, digging a hole under that post."

Oku's eyebrows flew up, and she ran to attend to her dog.

"You really missed people, didn't you, Casmir?" Kim asked.

"*Yes.*"

"I think it's safe inside," Asger's father called out.

Asger drew Casmir aside to let the others go in first and ask him a question. "Our groundskeeper Moritz Thacker left a note that said he was instructed to leave by Baron Farley. Would you do a search on him? I want to make sure he's moved in with his family or gotten a place in town and that he wasn't arrested or otherwise detained because of his association with us."

"Is that the man who built the tree house for you?"

Asger squinted at him. "He's the man who *assisted* me in building a new portion of the tree house."

"I see."

"Did you ever build a tree house? It's hard work."

"I grew up in an apartment in the city. We had to walk a few blocks to get to a park where there were trees. I did build many robots."

"That's not the same. Robots aren't heavy."

One of the crushers gave Asger a long look as they streamed into the house.

"Never mind," Asger said, having had his combat boots crushed by Zee's feet before.

"I'll check on your man. I have a *lot* of research to do, now that I'm back online." Casmir met Kim's gaze.

"Are you caught up on the news?" she asked.

"I got the gist," Casmir said. "Since the launch loop is now closed, we don't have the option to flee the planet and the system any longer."

"What options do we have?" Kim asked.

"We could *save* the planet."

"Do you have a plan?" she asked, as if Casmir had suggested something simple and accomplishable, like a bake sale for the campus fundraiser.

"I'll work on it in the shower."

"Just the first one, or in all ten?"

"This might take all ten." He thrust his shoulders back and strode into the castle.

LAYERS OF FORCE

Yas was about to leave sickbay and meet Jess in the mess hall for dinner when Rache walked in. Dents and melt marks marred his armor, and the faceplate of the helmet he carried under his arm had a crack in it. His other arm hung limply at his side, the shoulder seam split open, charred flesh visible. Yas wouldn't be surprised if his entire *arm* was split along that seam and cut to the bone.

"Are you all right?" Yas pointed Rache toward an exam table, though he doubted he would go.

"I've been better."

"What happened? Are you going to let me treat you?"

"I successfully sneaked into Drachen Castle without being detected. Acquiring my target and sneaking out was not quite as successful, though my new crusher ally was useful in blocking some fire meant for me."

Some but not *all*, the gouges and scorch marks in that armor said.

"He was not able to keep them from blowing up my shuttle rather spectacularly, but we sneaked over to the Royal Intelligence headquarters and stole one of their shuttles. The Castle Guard was still hunting among the wreckage of the other one as I was taking off on their launch loop. I made it out about two minutes before the staff there got the word to close it down. Planetary defenses moved to intercept me, but I convinced my passenger to convince *them* to leave us alone. They tracked us back here, of course, but now that we're aboard, Mendoza is taking the *Fedallah* out of orbit and staying well out of the *Starhawk's* range. That's the Kingdom ship with the slydar detector. They'll be hunting for us assiduously for the next few days, but we won't have to worry about avoiding them for long. More trouble for the Kingdom is on the way, and we'll be low on their priorities list."

"That was a lot of sentences from my usually terse captain," Yas said, "but I noticed that in all that, you didn't answer the second question I asked. Are you going to let me treat you?"

"I took a painkiller."

"Your arm is falling off."

"But not painfully."

"You're a dreadful patient."

"Perhaps. But I have another patient you might find even more frustrating."

"I find that *highly* doubtful."

"Come, Doctor." Rache headed for the door.

"You're not bringing this patient to sickbay?" Yas grabbed his medical kit and trotted after him.

"No."

As they headed for the lift, Yas imagined Jess or one of the other mercenaries injured from an electrical burn or something that had fallen and crushed them, but he realized this had to be the *passenger* Rache had mentioned. As they descended to the level of the brig, the insinuations clicked into place for him.

"Oh, stars. You didn't *kidnap* someone, did you?"

"My plan was successful, yes."

"*Who?* It wasn't Jager, I know. I just saw him speaking on the news."

"His son. I'd originally planned to barter the prince for Professor Dabrowski, but I belatedly learned that as I was escaping with Finn, Princess Oku was rescuing Casmir on her own. She might have *told* me she planned to do that. But I will find a way to use this to my advantage."

"Oh, *Captain*." Yas quailed as he imagined what Rache might have planned for the prince. He'd already *killed* the older brother.

Rache looked over his shoulder as they walked. "Really, Doctor. You're not supposed to have a tone of dread when you comment on my plans."

"I… feel it's justified."

Rache stopped in front of a brig cell, the forcefield up, one of his armored men standing guard. A brown-haired young man in a charred purple galaxy suit sat on the floor in the cell, his back to the wall, a sneer the size of a black hole curling his lip. Burns reddened one side of his face, skin blistered away in spots, and his arm was cradling what might have been cracked ribs.

"This is our doctor, Finn," Rache said, his tone cool and indifferent.

"Fuck you." Finn made a rude gesture with his hand.

"He's eager to see you," Rache told Yas.

"I see that." Yas had little familiarity with the Kingdom's royalty and wondered if he should attempt to be polite or just gruffly do his job.

The greeting didn't faze him. Most people dragged onto Rache's ship against their will felt that way about him. "What's the proper protocol for addressing him? Do I bow?"

"I bashed his head against the wall and threw him over my shoulder," Rache said.

"Is that a recommendation on how to proceed or an admission that you're a heathen?"

"Just fix his face, Doctor. We want his daddy to be able to recognize him." Rache tapped the control panel to lower the forcefield.

The guard leveled his rifle at Finn's chest. Yas removed his diagnostic scanner and entered warily, but Finn was too busy glowering at Rache to pay attention to Yas's ministrations.

"What are you going to do with me, criminal?" Finn demanded.

Yas thought Rache might stare at him without responding, but he was in a chatty mood today.

"I haven't decided yet," Rache said. "I had intended to trade you for your father's most recent prisoner, but he escaped without my assistance."

Though horrified by this current development, Yas was glad to hear that Casmir had escaped. He was even gladder that some devil's deal hadn't needed to be struck to accomplish it.

"Your ribs are cracked, your ulna is broken, and you've got third-degree burns on your face," Yas said quietly, reading from his scanner.

"If you're undecided, I'm willing to make a deal with you." Finn remained focused on Rache.

"Such as?"

"What do you want? I know you hate my father."

"Yes, but I'm not enamored with you either."

"We've never even met."

"Yes, we have. You haven't figured that out yet? It took Jorg a tediously long time too. I thought you might have a few more brain cells to clump together than he did."

Finn squinted at Rache.

"It's not like I'm modulating my voice in any way," Rache added.

The guard glanced at him but said nothing.

Yas had heard all about how Rache had revealed his name and some past history with the royal family when he'd confronted Jorg on the *Chivalrous*, but the mercenaries who'd been there to hear had all been busy fighting Kingdom soldiers and crushers at the time. Unless they were lying to Yas, nobody remembered his full name.

Yas injected Finn with a painkiller and programmed nanites to mend the bones. He would treat the burns himself while the nanites started working.

"You were ten the last time we met," Rache said. "Jorg and I had recently completed our knight's training."

Rache had been trained as a *knight*? Yas had always known he was from the Kingdom, since he had that accent, but he wouldn't have guessed the nobility. Yas glanced at him, though of course the black mask revealed nothing of his thoughts or whether he was telling the truth.

"I passed without trouble. Jorg cheated. Remember that?"

Finn lifted his chin and opened his mouth, as if to spit some defense of his brother, but he didn't speak right away. He mulled things over for a moment, then said, "He did cheat. I remember. All he wanted was to screw girls and gamble on the ship races instead of studying. But he said he had a plan for getting by. And the next thing I knew, he was graduating, and Father officially named him his heir."

"Yes."

"But now he's dead. Father thinks that wimpy programmer from the university killed him. But it was you, wasn't it?"

"Yes. Your father is willfully obtuse."

"I'm not."

"No?"

Yas wondered what Rache was angling for—why have this chat with his prisoner? It made him uncomfortable. Maybe it was silly and naive, but he liked to think that Rache was a decent person when the Kingdom was removed from the equation. He'd helped Yas clear his name and save his parents. He was fair with his men. He didn't screw over any of his employers, and when he took a job he did it. But this obsession with Jager turned him into a villain, and Yas hated working for a villain.

"David Lichtenberg," Finn said. "I don't remember your voice and don't care what you sound like, but that's the only person who graduated with Jorg and then died that year."

"At least your memory isn't impaired."

"You want my father dead? Do you care who rules after him? Maybe we can make a deal. My father and I are not close, and now that Jorg is gone, I'm next in line for the throne."

"Are you? What about Oku and the senator she might marry?"

Finn opened his mouth but paused to squint at Rache again. "How did you learn about that?"

Rache didn't answer.

"Nobody knows for sure if Father has updated his will about that yet. If he dies without anything set, it'll be about whichever one of us makes a better case to the Senate, and Oku doesn't want to rule. She's too dumb for it anyway. She just wants to zip around the systems, giving people pretty seeds she's made. She would be worthless as a ruler, or even the wife of a ruler."

"Dumb?" Rache's tone held no judgment; he merely sounded like he sought clarification. "Doesn't she have advanced science degrees and alliances with people in habitats in other systems?"

"*Science.*" Finn scoffed. "Those aren't useful degrees outside of academia, which in itself is useless. And visiting other systems and picking flowers with the daughters of leaders doesn't make for alliances. It doesn't matter. If she doesn't renounce any interest in ruling, she can disappear too. It'd be easy."

"You don't think others will step forward and contest your ability to rule?" Rache asked. "You're young and inexperienced."

"So what? Kings always have advisors, even old and experienced kings. I've got people lined up. What would it take, Rache, for you to let me live but to take my father out of the picture?"

Did Finn know that Rache was already *on* that mission? Maybe not. After all, Rache had been striking all around Jager for years without ever targeting him.

"What do you offer in exchange for this service?" Rache asked.

Yas eyed him, but Rache was intent on Finn. Yas assumed that he was far too experienced and skeptical to make a deal with an ambitious twenty-year-old kid willing to have his father assassinated. Maybe out of curiosity he wanted to see what Finn would offer. Or maybe he thought he would learn something that he could use.

"What do you want?" Finn asked. "I can't believe you need money."

"No. I would want a pardon and to be free to come and go as I please."

Finn scoffed again. "Even if I were king, I couldn't make *that* happen. Every soldier in the Kingdom loathes you. So does every knight and senator on Odin. The Senate would never approve that."

"So do what your father did. Manipulate the people into granting you King's Authority so you have absolute rule."

Finn stared at Rache for several long seconds, not flinching when Yas finished cleaning the wounds and dabbed on a regenerative skin-cell builder. Maybe Finn was too wrapped up in his speculation to notice the pain.

"If you and your mercenaries worked for me as king," Finn said, "it might be easier to make that happen. I could say I'd found a way to channel your evil for good."

Rache laughed without humor. "And *you* are the option for *good*?"

"I'd rule for the good of the Kingdom."

"I see. Are you done, Doctor?"

"Yes." Yas made sure the nanites he'd injected were getting to work, then put away his tools and joined the men in the corridor.

"What say you, Rache?" Finn asked. "You get rid of my father, help me secure the throne, and agree to work for the crown—for *me*—and I'll make that pardon happen. I'll make sure nobody touches you and that you have all the money and power you could ever dream of."

"I'll consider your proposition." Rache activated the forcefield and walked out, leaving the guard to think who knew what of the conversation.

"What are you *really* going to do with him?" Yas asked when they were alone outside of the brig.

"You don't think his offer is a good one?"

"I don't think it's an honest one."

"No? Who wouldn't want a ship of powerful mercenaries with a fearsome reputation at his beck and call?"

"You'd never be willing to be at anybody's beck and call."

Rache gazed out a nearby porthole. Thoughtfully?

Was Yas reading him incorrectly?

"Unless you *really* want that pardon," he amended, though the idea confused him. Why would Rache have chosen the route of villain for all these years if he cared about being able to walk freely in the Kingdom again?

Then it struck him. Kim Sato.

Yas had watched them flirt—albeit they were strange people and it was strange flirting. Did Rache want to survive and not have the entire Kingdom chasing after him because he wanted to *date* one of its citizens? Maybe Rache was tired of being a mercenary and a criminal and wanted to retire. Settle down and have a family? Yas almost laughed. It was too ludicrous to contemplate.

But wanting to be able to go about one's life without having to constantly watch over one's shoulder... Yas could see even Rache longing for that. Especially if he wanted that life to include an innocent woman.

"Even if you do want a pardon," Yas said, "that kid can't be the best way to get it. He was ready to throw his whole family in front of a firing squad to get the throne."

"Likely so." Rache headed toward the lift. "And I'd only need a pardon if I thought I was going to live. It may be wishful thinking to believe I can get Jager *and* survive."

Yas watched him go and shook his head. One minute, he was ready to make deals with pathological liars and manipulators, and the next, he was ready to accept death on some suicide mission.

"Impossible man."

CHAPTER 13

AFTER HIS LENGTHY SHOWER, CASMIR FOUND AN OVERSIZED pair of pajamas and knocked lightly on the door to the room his parents had been given. It was only a few hours until dawn, and he didn't want to wake them if they were sleeping, but he would like to speak with his father before going forward with any of the plans whirring through his mind like Viggo's busy vacuums. The last thing he wanted to do was make life worse for his parents, and given that they'd had to flee their apartment in the middle of the night, he worried about how much danger he'd already put them in.

It was a foregone conclusion that neither King Jager nor the knights nor Military or Royal Intelligence would listen to Casmir if he suggested a joint operation. Whatever he wished to do about the astroshamans, he would have only his friends to rely upon, and should he truly consider endangering them? *Again*?

The door opened, revealing his father in his favorite pair of blue button-down pajamas. Casmir wished there had been time to stop by his house so he could get *his* favorite pair of pajamas—or at least a few changes of clothing—but he'd been positive his home would be under surveillance, and they hadn't dared dawdle further.

"*Shalom*, Casmir." His father rested a hand on his shoulder and stepped out into the hallway, closing the door behind him. "Your mother and Bells are sleeping. Do you want to go to your room to talk?"

"How did you know I wanted to talk?" *Needed* to talk, Casmir amended silently.

"Your expression is pensive and troubled. Also, your mother *insists* that you will want to talk, because you are a dutiful son who feels vast guilt at not keeping his parents informed about major upheavals and decisions in his life. She's positive you'll tell us everything you've left out of your extremely scant updates over the last few months." He raised his eyebrows in mild censure. "I believe she thought it would be over breakfast, but I am awake now." His father extended an open palm in offering.

"Thank you."

Casmir led him to the guest room he'd been given, a ceramic sparrowhawk tile mounted on the door distinguishing it from the other guest rooms—an array of predatory birds lined the hallway. According to Asger, the castle could house more than a hundred guests and had even more than the speculated ten bathrooms. It must have been a strange place to grow up as an only child.

"You've seen the news?" Casmir asked as he settled on the edge of the bed, his father in a chair. "And know about the new threat to Odin?"

"I do. It has been a very trying year."

"What has it been like here? From the point of view of the average citizen?" Casmir would ask his mother how it had been for their community and how their friends and relatives were holding up—he'd already heard that people they knew had been lost in the bombing of the capital—but his father was the more philosophical and outwardly focused of his parents, the one more likely to have his finger on the pulse of the world.

"Between the terrorists, the invasion, the threat of a virus, and a new invasion? For people who have for many centuries believed that, outside of freak accidents, death is a fear only for the very old and the very ill and occasionally those who venture out to other star systems... it has instilled great uncertainty and apprehension in the population. They are wrestling with this new reality in which death could befall any of us at any time. It is not easy to accept, and it feels like a step back in our evolution as a society, as a *people*. Right now, the future is less predictable than it has been for a long time, and that bothers the average citizen." He smiled faintly and gestured toward Casmir. "Also the exceptional ones."

"While I appreciate you putting me in that category, I have my doubts. I've helped people these last months, but I've caused people to be killed too." Casmir looked at a shaggy rug on the floor, thinking of how horrified he'd been in that terrorist base when Rache, following his suggestion, had used a grenade to blow the head off the ex-chief superintendent of Royal Intelligence. Alexandre Bernard, his name had been. His death had been the first to give Casmir nightmares; it hadn't been the last. "I've tried to let my heart and my mind guide me to make the right choices, but I've kept finding, time and again, that there don't seem to be any clear-cut *right* choices. It's more a matter of trying to do the greater good while picking which set of consequences you want to deal with."

"Tell me," his father said in that gentle, nonjudgmental voice of his.

Even though it was late, Casmir found that he needed to tell the whole story, to confess to all the deaths that had befallen allies and adversaries in his wake. From the day he'd been chased off campus by a crusher who'd killed the knight who'd come to warn him, to the destruction of the pirate fleet he'd infected with that virus, to the death of Prince Dubashi. He caught himself saying "it's not fair" more than once when referring to how King Jager and his Intelligence people had interpreted his actions, and he tried to put a stop to that. His father could decide what was fair and what wasn't. Casmir knew he was far too biased to judge accurately, anyway. By now, he had little idea how someone on the outside would perceive him. He didn't know if the fact that he'd made allies among government leaders outside of the Kingdom was a sign that he was doing good for humanity as a whole… or a condemnation that he was harming the Kingdom.

When he finished, finally wrapping up with his rescue by Oku, his father removed his glasses and cleaned them for a long time on the hem of his pajama top. Casmir didn't see any spots on them, but he knew this was what his father did when he needed a minute to think.

"Never would I have thought that my son would be placed in such positions and have to make such decisions."

"That makes two of us. I used to wrestle with what to do when I caught a promising student cheating on a test; now, I would love to have such simple moral dilemmas again, decisions with consequences that affect only one person."

"But if such decisions must be made, I am relieved that they have been made by someone who cares about all people, even those who are not like him, even those who have wronged him." His father put his glasses back on and peered pointedly through them at Casmir, making him squirm a little under the faith he bestowed. Was it warranted? Casmir had his doubts and almost said so, but his father continued. "It is unfortunate that so many, including those with the power to rule over us, see themselves as better than others; it is easy for that to foster indifference and apathy toward people, if not the outright willingness to use them as a means to an end."

"How *is* Jager being perceived by people these days?" Casmir asked.

"Poorly, but fear of what is without will quash any uprising that might have started within. As long as there is an enemy on the threshold, there will not be revolution within the house."

"He's been counting on that. I believe he's arranged some of these enemies."

"As rulers have done throughout history to consolidate and reinforce their power. Nothing unites people so quickly as a common enemy. Humans are masterful at creating enemies even when none should logically exist. It is much easier to blame someone else for everything that's wrong with our lives than to find solutions within ourselves and within the world as it exists."

"I know." Casmir had heard these talks before from his father, and he wasn't unappreciative, but he needed new insight. And perhaps most of all, to know that he was on the right path. "But do I risk my life, and maybe the lives of my friends and family—*again*—to fight this new batch of enemies, knowing full well that Jager might conjure up a new enemy in the future?"

His father tilted his head. "*Do* you think you can stop them?"

"I suppose I'm arrogant enough to think I can come up with something. My unorthodox approach to dealing with problems seems to flummox people. Right now, I'm trying to gather all the data I can, everything I missed while I was locked up and off the net." He waved to indicate his new chip and the programs he had running in the background.

"Yes, it would be best to gain all the information you can before proceeding. As to the rest…" His father removed his glasses for another cleaning.

"Tenebris Rache wants to kill Jager." Casmir had explained their relationship as he'd told his story, and that had seemed to surprise his father far more than the revelation that Casmir had been cloned from a centuries-old war hero. "I gather it's a revenge thing rather than a fixing-the-Kingdom thing, but I feel in my gut that it's not the right answer for any of us—for more reasons than because murder is abhorrent. I don't think I can stop him, but I'm worried that it won't make anything better."

"When you cut off the head of the hydra, two more grow back. Removing an unappealing ruler may be a palliative, but it is not the solution."

"What's the solution then? How do we get a Kingdom that's good for everyone who lives here—and everyone who doesn't—and that isn't manipulating us into saying yes to wars with our neighbors?"

"Educating people is *always* the solution. Peace is never guaranteed, but the most likely path to it is to have an enlightened, self-aware populace that's been taught how to think critically and question everything. People like that are difficult to manipulate."

"That's... easier said than done." Casmir rubbed his gritty eyes. He didn't disagree with his father, and probably would have told a student who'd come to him with that question the same thing, but he also didn't know how to educate enough people fast enough to make a difference. Besides, people had to *want* to learn. That was always the hard part. "In the meantime, do you think I should do whatever it takes to try to stop the astroshamans?"

"Whatever it takes... within reason. I trust you don't have genocide on your mind."

Casmir snorted. "You know I don't. I'm more worried about my actions hurting you and Mother."

"As long as you're trying to do what's best for the most people, we'll have your back." His father stood up and hugged him. "We always do."

Casmir buried his face in his father's shoulder and hugged him back. "Thank you. I needed to hear that."

"Only that?" his father asked, amusement lightening his tone for the first time. "None of the rest?"

"Oh, the lecture was nice too."

"*Nice*. Like all teachers, I strive to deliver *nice* lectures to my students."

"Do you? I just try to keep them from falling asleep." That prompted a yawn.

"I don't believe you." His father leaned back. "Get some sleep, Casmir."

"I will," Casmir said, though he suspected he would be sifting through information for the rest of the night.

"This shade is so pretty."

"I like the green. It's vibrant like the trees outside."

"Can you add stars to the green? The way Squirt does? Except maybe not pink. Try yellow or that sparkly silver."

"Actually these are meteors, not stars." Qin extended her claws to show her sisters the designs stenciled on the fields of dark blue.

"They're still pink." That was Pounce, the fashion critic.

"I didn't say they weren't, but they are brilliant pink meteors—look you can see the craters in them. I used a special mini stencil and spray nail polish."

Qin was sitting cross-legged on a rug on the tile floor of the guest room she'd been given. She was shoulder to shoulder with several of her sisters as they sat in a circle. Others lounged on the bed, the one chair in the room, and a clothes trunk against the wall.

In hindsight, Qin could have led them all to one of the numerous large family gathering rooms in the castle, but the sun hadn't yet come up, and she had worried they might get noisy and that it would wake up the others. It had been a late night, so most people would probably sleep in.

Qin had felt sheepish and a little hesitant when she had messaged Asger to ask if she could use some of the nail polishes she'd discovered in the closest bathroom. She'd never expected to find such things in a dwelling shared by Asger and his father, but she remembered him saying that he'd had a mother, until she'd died a decade before, so maybe she had been the one to stock the bathrooms with feminine goodies for guests. He'd sounded sleepy and bemused when he'd replied but had given her the go-ahead.

"I believe brilliant is a subjective word," Pounce murmured.

"You just don't like pink," Qin said. "Remember when that bow-legged lieutenant got us all different-colored bows so he could tell us apart? You said you'd gnaw your arm off before you would wear a pink one."

"No, I said I'd gnaw *his* arm off." Pounce grinned, purposely flashing her fangs. The grin faded when she added, "And then I was punished for daring to threaten one of them, even though it had been a joke. Mostly."

LAYERS OF FORCE

"We're away from them now." Mouser wrapped an arm around Pounce's shoulders. "And we'll stay away from them."

"I hope so."

"If we stay on this world," Tigress said, "it'll be easy to avoid them. They won't come here."

"But we can't stay here," Mouser said. "We won't be allowed. They're hunting us right now."

"I know, and I don't like the Kingdom. But their planet is *fabulous*." Tigress flopped back on the rug, arms spread wide. She remembered her claws were wet and jerked them up before they brushed against anything. She blew on them and fanned her fingers.

"It is fabulous. Especially the parts with lots of trees and not that many people." Qin smiled in fond remembrance of their run through the forest last night. Her feelings about fleeing from angry enemies with guns and hunting dogs shouldn't have been fond, but loping through the woods with thousands of scents from the surrounding earth and foliage flooding her nostrils had been exhilarating. At one point, they'd startled a herd of deer nestled down for the night, and the beautiful creatures had darted off in the moonlight.

"It seems like there's quite a bit of that," Mouser observed. "We didn't see anyone, except for hearing those who were chasing us last night, and we crossed fifty miles. Does all that land belong to your knights?"

"They're not my knights, and I don't think they own *all* of it. I think some of it is the Kingdom Forest, an area reserved for recreation. We had to fly over it last time I was here to find some terrorists hiding out in it."

"Maybe *we* could hide out in it." Pounce touched a hand to her chest, her dark eyes wistful. "We don't need a castle. Just some little huts to live in."

"I would *love* that," Tigress said, and the others, half-absorbed in their nail painting, nodded in agreement. "I wouldn't want to live in the woods like some weird hermit all the time, but we could go on bounty-hunting missions with your Captain Lopez, Squirt, and then in between, we could come live in the woods. Maybe by a river or a pond. Those streams we crossed last night were also fabulous."

"Is there a way to hide out from their technology, I wonder?" Pounce asked.

"If we could help them save their world, maybe they would let us *legally* buy land here," Qin said.

Besides, if the Kingdom *didn't* save their world, Odin might be nothing more than smoking craters before long, with all of those beautiful forests demolished. The thought saddened her.

"How do we do that?" Mouser asked. "Didn't we get ourselves in trouble by attacking their shuttle?"

"Maybe. If they figure out we were involved." Qin shrugged. "As for how we can help, I think we have to stick with Casmir. I'm sure he plans to do something. He was the first one who wanted to rescue you all from the Druckers."

"I thought that was your knight." Mouser was determined to assign ownership to Asger.

"He was willing to help if it made sense. Casmir wanted to help… whether it made sense or not. He's like that."

"But isn't he wanted dead by the Kingdom right now?" Mouser asked.

"Yes."

"Then helping him might not be good if we want to be able to live here."

"I don't know who else we would help who is trying to save their world and who would stand up for us and point out that we'd helped."

"You don't think we could offer to help their king?" Mouser asked.

"I doubt he would even answer a comm call from one of us."

"But if Casmir is a criminal here, even if he's trying to help, will anything ever come of it? Will he be rewarded in the end? Or just kicked out of the Kingdom? And us along with him?"

Qin gazed at the ceiling, not sure how to articulate what she was thinking. "It's like betting on the Asteroid Races in System Hind. If you pick one of the beat-up ships with long odds, you stand to make a lot more if it wins. And Casmir, while being somewhat beat-up, has secret boost powers. I think we should back him."

"Also, that princess was totally flirting with him," Shadow said from the chair, lifting her nails and blowing on them. "The odds of getting pardoned go up a ton if you've got a princess on your side. And of getting your amazing warrior-women friends pardoned as well."

"Pardoned and given a forest retreat to share," Tigress added.

"You girls have been reading different fairy tales from me," Qin said, "but I'm glad you're on board."

She heard quiet footsteps in the hall outside and guessed who it was before the knock sounded at the door.

"Come in, Asger."

"Hey, Qin," he said, opening the door. "Do you want to go out and see the, uh…" He blinked around at the admittedly large gathering of women in Qin's room. Judging by the fact that he was barefoot and wearing only pajama bottoms, he hadn't expected to find a crowd.

"Helloooo, Handsome," Tigress crooned at him. Or perhaps at his bare chest.

It was a very nice and muscular bare chest, and Qin rolled to her feet to wrap an arm around Asger's waist to leave no doubt that he was claimed.

Asger wrapped his arm around *her* waist but also gazed around in mild puzzlement. "I... had no idea this was encoded in the DNA."

"What's that?" Qin asked.

"Fingernail—er, claw—painting."

"We *are* girls." Qin showed him her nails. "What do you think of my pink meteors?"

"They're very nice."

"*He's* very nice," someone whispered.

"And politic," Pounce said. "Those pink meteors are dreadful, and any man would realize it."

"They are not." Qin resisted the urge to stick her tongue out at her. Barely.

"I like Qin's nails," Asger said. "They're spunky. Like her." He gave her a fond smile.

She leaned against his side and basked in the praise. "What were you asking if I wanted to see? The sunrise?"

"That could be part of it, but I was going to offer a tour of the tree house and the grounds."

"I'd *love* to go." Qin turned him back toward the hallway. "Let's go now and put a shirt on you, so my sisters can't ogle your pecs so easily."

Asger touched one of those pecs as he allowed himself to be led out of the room.

"We can ogle him through his clothes just fine," Tigress called.

Asger glanced back, looking a little stunned at her brazenness.

"Most of my sisters aren't that interested in sex, since our—their—only experiences have been with the pirates," Qin said as she led him to his room, "but there are exceptions. That was Tigress."

"I see. I wasn't expecting to find you all together and wedged in one room. Last night, I distinctly remember pointing out enough guest rooms for everyone."

"They're not used to being on their own. They get lonely by themselves and miss each other's company." Qin shrugged. "I've missed being with them too. We didn't always get along and had some grand fights, but we are sisters."

In his room, Asger traded the pajama bottoms for pants and donned a shirt and boots. "To the tree house?"

"I look forward to seeing it."

He smiled at her again. "I thought you would."

CHAPTER 14

"S*TELLAR DRAGON*, YOU HAVE PERMISSION TO DOCK IN Slot 7C. A medical team is standing by to accept the wounded soldiers."

"Thank you." Bonita closed the comm and lined up her freighter for the approach. "This has been almost too easy, Viggo. Should I be suspicious? Do you think there'll also be a squad of soldiers there to arrest me?"

Forseti Station, a fat cylinder spinning slowly in front of a massive gas giant, loomed large on the forward display. Memories of Bonita's mad flight from here, after bluffing to the authorities that she would release a bioweapon if they didn't get off her ship, loomed equally large in her mind.

"I will scan the area thoroughly before you open the hatch," Viggo said, "but the soldiers aboard our ship have largely been reasonable and thankful for your assistance."

"True, but they've also been grievously injured. It's hard to effectively deliver and carry out threats when you're in an advanced state of organ failure." Still, Bonita had made friends with Maria Lopez and allowed herself to think that the rest of the Kingdom soldiers were grateful that she'd helped them. Maybe some of her past transgressions would be forgotten, or at least forgiven. And from here, maybe she would be allowed to continue on to Odin to pick up Qin and however many of her sisters were interested in getting into the bounty-hunting business.

"I suppose so, but they could have been grumpy and vitriolic."

"Just let me know if you see any trouble waiting for us."

A message came in to her chip as she adjusted the *Dragon*'s course to fly in past a huge freighter that was occupying Slot 7B, its bulk extending over the invisible line and into the slot she had been given. It would be a tight fit.

Greetings, my sexy Laser. It was Bjarke. *How go your travels in System Lion? I've been pining terribly in your absence, but I must warn you that this wouldn't be the best time for you to visit my home world.*

Oh, I'm sure of that, but I need Qin.

There was a long pause before his response, reminding her of the distance from Forseti to Odin. She still had a ways to travel.

Have you no need for me? I'm back home in my bed on Odin—the one with the magnificent bedposts—and thinking of how much larger it is than that bunk in your quarters. Even as I feel the need to warn you away, I lament that you aren't here with me.

Am I to assume from the fact that you're in your castle and haven't been arrested that you haven't yet broken Casmir out of jail?

Actually, Princess Oku broke him out of jail. Technically, her father's dungeon. We did, however, spectacularly rescue some empty crates on a supply shuttle, which resulted in us further irking the Kingdom. So it is possible that my stay at the family estate will be brief and final. Should we need to flee the system, and be able to find a way off Odin, would you be available for transport? I will pay of course. In your choice of money or sexual favors.

I can't have both? Bonita managed to get the *Dragon* past the hulking freighter without skinning Viggo's hull off and stopped close enough to extend the tube to the lock.

You can if you start calling me big bear instead of teddy bear.

I see you looked up osito.

When I had time, yes. Bjarke means great powerful predator bear with large massive muscles and teeth that can tear enemies to pieces.

I also used the dictionary. From what I saw, Bjarke just means bear.

The rest is implied. More seriously, I wished to make sure you were all right and also to thank you for transporting those soldiers. I know the Kingdom hasn't done much to endear itself to you.

You've got that right. I'm surprised you still care. They exiled *you.*

Only a few people were responsible for that. It has been my duty to care for far too many years for me to stop overnight.

You've had a couple of weeks now. Time to learn to let them fend for themselves.

I don't think you're as jaded as you pretend to be, Bonita. But nonetheless, I thank you on their behalf. When next we meet, I will rub your feet.

Did you mean to rhyme?
Certainly. Knights are poetical.
I reject your suggestion that I'm not jaded, but I accept your offer of a foot rub. Don't get yourself killed following Casmir on some crazy plan. Bonita hadn't yet heard anything about a crazy plan, but she trusted there was one, or would be soon. The kid was pathologically incapable of standing back while others were in trouble.
I'll try to survive so I can redeem my promise to you.
"Bonita," Viggo said, "this may not be the ideal place to dock."
"Too late. We're locked in."
"Perhaps you could ask for another slot?"
"Perhaps we could have done that twenty minutes ago." Bonita opened the comm for a ship-wide announcement. Some of her passengers were in her small sickbay, but she'd put most in guest cabins. "We've arrived at Forseti Station. Your people are waiting for you."
"I'm serious," Viggo said when she was done.
"Are you able to scan the concourse? And see piles of soldiers waiting to board and take us prisoner?" Bonita had been about to unlock the hatch in the cargo hold so the troops could transfer over, but she paused with her hand over the button.
"I *am* able to scan the concourse. I see a handful of people with hover gurneys. There is no sign of an arrest squad."
"Then what's the problem?"
"That hulking freighter."
"They *are* rudely taking up more than their allotted space, but I squeezed in fine. I'll comm them and tell them to be careful when they back out. I know you don't like your hull scuffed up."
"I scanned them." Viggo wasn't bantering with her, so Bonita lowered her hand, realizing something truly had him worried.
"And?"
"Something in their hold is giving off an energy signature I've now seen a few times and can recognize."
"What?" Bonita had a feeling she knew what he was going to say, but she hoped she was wrong.
"Captain?" a voice asked from outside of navigation—Maria Lopez.
Bonita turned her pod, and Viggo held his answer. "Yes?"
"I wanted to say thanks for the ride. It was good seeing someone from the old system. It's been a while since I've been home." Maria

lifted her hand. "I don't know where you're going or if there's war waiting for me at home, but I'm supposed to be done with my military obligation in four months. If you ever visit Zamek City, look me up, and we'll have you over for dinner."

"*Gracias*. I will." Bonita resisted the urge to say she wouldn't step foot on Odin again unless someone paid her a massive amount of money, because that wasn't entirely true. She was intrigued by the massive bed with bedposts that Bjarke had mentioned. What would Maria think if she showed up for dinner with a sarcastic, snarky knight?

Maria left to join the rest of her people in the cargo hold.

"I believe it's one or more of the ancient gate pieces," Viggo said as soon as she disappeared down the ladder well.

Bonita groaned. She was tired of those gate pieces and didn't want anything to do with any of them. "We shouldn't be able to get into trouble for being parked next to a ship carrying one."

She went ahead and unlocked the airlock hatch. If there *was* going to be trouble, it would be better not to have a bunch of injured soldiers on board. And the sooner they were gone, the sooner she could get out of here.

"The freighter is registered to a small transport company, Space Comets Limited," Viggo said. "It was not among the ships at Xolas Moon that were retrieving gate pieces."

"I'm sure those things have been traded and moved around a lot by now."

"It is unlikely that such a small company would have the resources to purchase one. The freighter is also not heavily armed, so it is unlikely someone would have hired them to move one of the valuable pieces. I am researching Space Comets Limited now."

"I don't care about this mystery, Viggo." She just wanted to get out of here.

"I care because we are parked next to them. Space Comets Limited is rumored to engage in smuggling and illegal salvage."

"You think they found the gate in one of those wrecked ships? No, we saw the invisible ships slurp up those gate pieces. There weren't any left behind."

"This could be a different piece from those we've seen the astroshaman ships take. The smugglers could have stolen it from the Kingdom. Or, knowing the Kingdom wants more pieces, they could have stolen it from elsewhere and brought it here to sell."

"And what, they're stopping at Forseti Station for milkshakes and tamales along the way?"

LAYERS OF FORCE

The internal comm chimed.

"Captain Lopez?" one of the Kingdom officers said from the cargo hold. "Our people are transferring over now."

Bonita flicked on the camera so she could watch and make sure they all left. Then she would take off. Originally, she'd planned to buy supplies if the station authorities allowed it, but Viggo's tenseness was making *her* tense. Better to get out of here before anything happened.

Bjarke was still sending her messages—she got the feeling that he was lonely or felt compelled to talk for some reason—but she ignored them for now. She could chat him up about his bedposts later.

As soon as the last soldier passed onto the station, Bonita closed the hatches and retracted the airlock tube.

"No problems, Viggo. We'll slide out of here before—"

An alert popped up on the navigation console—a surge of energy nearby—and something blue flashed outside. The forward display was focused on the station, so Bonita couldn't tell what.

She toggled to a different camera so the display showed what was going on behind their ship. She was in time to see blue beams slam into the docked freighter. It rocked under the force of the blows. More bolts—those didn't look like DEW-Tek blasts, but what were they?—slammed into it.

Pieces of the freighter's hull blew off. One crashed into the side of the *Dragon,* and her ship shuddered. If Bonita hadn't been in her pod, she would have ended up on the floor—or the ceiling.

"The attacking ship is invisible to my scanners," Viggo said.

"Surprise, surprise."

More alerts popped up on the console, telling her about the damage to her ship. She swore. What was she supposed to do? If she tried to navigate out, she would end up in the attacker's line of fire. But if she stayed here, the same thing might happen.

More fire rained onto the freighter. A railgun on its top swiveled and fired toward the invisible ship.

"The station is sending out fighters to deal with the attacker," Viggo said.

"Can *they* see it?"

"Doubtful."

More shrapnel struck the *Dragon.* The other freighter kept firing, its railgun blasts seeming to hit something, though all that appeared to be out there was empty space.

No, wait. Bonita leaned forward, squinting at the display as the stars grew fuzzy. The enemy was getting close enough that she could see it despite its camouflaged hull.

"Several of the station ships are opening fire, but there are more invisible vessels farther out," Viggo said. "They're firing on the station ships. It looks like they're trying to protect the one that's going in."

The freighter was knocked from its docking spot, and the entire ship tilted over and bashed against the *Dragon*. Grinding and crunching noises assailed Bonita's ears, and alarms flashed on consoles all over navigation.

"Who's going to protect *us*?" she growled.

"My scans now register the existence of the closest enemy ship, but the details remain muddled."

Bonita could see it more clearly as the big ship drew closer, and she hit the record button for the display. The hulking vessel had a shiny blue-green hull and an outline that wasn't familiar to her. Symmetrical but with numerous pointed protrusions, it looked like a castle that had fallen over on its side. She had a feeling she wouldn't find a match in any database if she ran an image search later.

Green light flared, and something like a maglocker beam grabbed onto the freighter, pulling it away from the station. Good. Bonita hoped they dragged it *far* away and that her ship didn't take any more collateral damage.

The beam wasn't only for locking and towing the freighter. It flashed, fluctuations appearing within the light, and the freighter's bay doors were torn off. Instead of being caught up in the power of the beam, they tumbled free.

"Don't hit us," she muttered, "don't hit us."

One door tumbled past inches from the *Dragon*'s nose. It crashed into the ship docked in 7D, knocking it from *its* berth.

The gate piece that Viggo had sensed floated out of the freighter's hold. It was slurped up into a bay of the attacking ship like lint into one of Viggo's vacuums.

The maglocker light winked out, and the attacking ship drew back, once again disappearing from Bonita's camera and her ship's scanners.

Before stopping recording, she panned her cameras to take in the carnage, everything from the freighter to numerous ships docked nearby to the defender craft that the station had launched. Several of them had been pulverized. Others floated intact but powerless.

"We've taken extensive damage," Viggo said needlessly.

Bonita could see all the alerts flashing on the console.

"I predict it will take several days to repair it," he added, "and that it will be expensive."

"Of course it will." Bonita had insurance that should cover something like this, but it would be months before all the paperwork was properly filed and funds approved. "Maybe the soldiers we helped would like to give us a loan."

"Are Kingdom soldiers paid well?"

"I doubt it."

Bonita bundled up the recording and sent it to Bjarke along with a message. *If your king is storing his gate pieces on your planet, you might want to ditch that fancy bed and get out of there before these guys arrive.*

"I believe those may have been the same ships we saw—or *didn't see*—in System Stymphalia," Viggo said.

"They're probably making the rounds and collecting every gate piece along the way. You still think they're astroshamans?"

"Yes. The Kingdom would be wise to hand over their gate pieces. Given that they barely drove off an attack by a fleet of scruffy mercenaries hired by a Miners' Union prince, they will likely find the astroshamans formidable."

"I have no doubt. Too bad nobody ever describes their king as wise."

"No," Viggo agreed.

Bonita stared glumly at all the flashing alerts. At least the hull hadn't been breached, and her ship should be repairable. She doubted that smuggler freighter would go anywhere ever again except to a junkyard.

A single word came back from Bjarke when he received the video.

Shit.

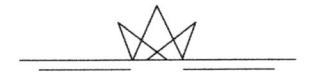

Qin sprang across the creek, appreciating the sound of burbling water caressing her ears and the smell of damp earth and fresh green foliage. She inhaled deeply and spun a pirouette, not feeling shy even knowing Asger was following her. Nor did she worry about her sisters, many of whom had followed them out to explore the grounds. She'd spotted Mouser and Pounce running up a grassy hill, flopping onto their sides, and rolling down it like little kids.

"It's like you know where you're going," Asger called, jogging after her. "Were you out here scouting in the middle of the night?"

"No, but I can smell your tree house."

Qin skipped along the bank, passing numerous giant trees before coming to the base of the largest. She didn't know the species but guessed it was centuries old, its massive branches stretching high and wide. Ten feet overhead, the lowest of many wooden platforms sprawled like a deck overlooking the grounds beyond the creek. Birds chittered in nests, both in the branches and in the nooks of the various wooden structures built on the platforms.

"What do tree houses smell like?" Asger asked.

"Sawn lumber instead of growing trees. Some of it was treated with chemicals long ago, though that's mostly worn out."

"That was to help weatherproof it."

Qin climbed an adorable ladder made from wooden boards nailed into the ancient trunk up to a closed trapdoor. When she pushed at it, it didn't open.

"Is there a trick to opening it?" she asked, rather than forcing it or going back down and using her powerful legs to jump the ten feet to the platform.

Asger slowed to a stop under her. "Well, girls haven't traditionally been allowed."

"Excuse me?"

He grinned up at her, his lush blond-brown locks freshly trimmed and hanging to his shoulders, his blue eyes glinting in amusement. "It was a boys-only tree house when I was a kid, possibly only permitted because I had no sisters, and my mother—when she was alive—had no interest in coming up there."

"And because you had no female friends who told you that such exclusivity was stupid?"

"That too. It wasn't until I was older that I learned the value of girls. There's a string hidden between those two boards with a little silver acorn that you pull."

Qin found it and tugged it. The trapdoor creaked, and the string didn't look like it would last too many more seasons, but it did open.

She padded across the platform, opening doors and peering into single-room cabins, most with cute furnishings that had either been made by hand or scavenged from some attic. In one of the rooms, a thick rope with a tuft on the end hung down. She pulled it and a huge window opened in the roof. If one had a bed under it, one might lie and peer through the leaves up at the stars. That would be a fantastic way to sleep.

Asger climbed up, but she was too busy exploring the three levels of platforms to do more than smile briefly at him. No, *four* levels. There was a platform much higher in the branches that would be a perfect lookout station. She could see all the way down the driveway to a distant road.

She opened a wooden box with a quirky roof built over it to protect the contents from the elements. A telescope lay disassembled inside along with books and blankets.

"Did you ever sleep up here?" she called down.

"Often in the summers."

"It's fabulous."

Asger climbed up to join her and sat on a bench built into the railing. "Should I be bemused or not at all surprised that you like the tree house more than the castle?"

"The castle is fine, but this home is *in* the trees." Qin squeezed his arm, thinking it obvious why that would be superior. She inhaled deeply, breathing in the chlorophyll-rich fragrance of foliage, the rich woody scent of the tree bark, the tang of the mineral-laden water in the creek. "It's fabulous."

She sat beside Asger, clasped his hand, and gazed out at the land. It was so incredible that his family owned everything in sight. Such a bounty. Why had he *ever* left to go into space?

"I've never seen anyone so delighted by nature." Asger smiled, watching her face as she gazed around.

"Does that make me weird?"

"Yeah, but I like that."

"Good." She thought about kissing him—they finally had a relatively private moment, aside from her sisters rolling down a nearby hill—but something that Mouser had said came to mind. "Do you still wish—if you had the option, I mean... would you want to be with Princess Oku?"

He raised his eyebrows. "No."

"Truly? I would understand if you preferred a... normal woman. And a princess. Princesses are special. Like knights." Qin realized the words weren't entirely true. She would understand, but she would also be hurt. All along, she'd known her relationship with Asger wouldn't be forever, but it had been so nice to have someone for the first time in her life, someone to cuddle with, someone to play with, someone to have sex with who cared about her. It would be hard to say goodbye to that.

"I liked her at one time. Maybe more because she was a princess, and I thought my father might think I was less of a screw-up if I could win a princess. You know, like a prize in an athletic match." He snorted at himself, seeming to realize how that didn't sound like love or even respect. "But she's nice, and I thought I would like to be with her."

"And you don't feel that way now?"

"No. I wouldn't know what to talk about with her. She's all science this and plants that, and I'm a simple guy. I like to lift weights and hit things."

He wasn't *that* simple. They had talked about books and philosophy before.

"And she's never been into me—I realize that now. Even though *that's* hard to believe, since I am so very ruggedly handsome." He rested his hand on his chest and wriggled his eyebrows at her.

"You are that. And I like the way you hit things. And how you respect the way *I* can hit things."

"It would be unwise not to respect the way you hit things."

"Yes." Qin squeezed his hands. "All right. I'm glad. I just wasn't sure because of how you seemed upset that she likes Casmir now."

"That's because he's *Casmir*."

"What does that mean?"

"That he's scrawny and sneezes all the time, and he isn't exactly a sex symbol."

"He's not that bad. He's kind of cute." She elbowed him.

"Cute and sexy aren't the same thing."

"Maybe she likes it that, when she says science this and plants that, he knows exactly what she's talking about."

"Hm." Asger scratched his jaw. "He *is* building her those robot bees. Maybe some women get excited by that."

"Girls like it when guys pay attention to their passions and make them gifts."

"I guess. I suppose I should ask Casmir to find me a kit and help me make you a robot unicorn."

"*Obviously.*" She grinned. "That would be fantastic. Does such a thing exist?"

His lips parted, as if he were taken aback by her enthusiasm, but then his eyes narrowed with determination. "I'll find out. And if it doesn't, I'll bribe him to help me make one."

"I look forward to it."

And she did. She even sent a message off to Bonita: *Asger is going to build me a unicorn!*

A real one? came the reply from wherever in the system Bonita was.

No. Maybe a robot one, but he said he'd help build it.

If you hooked up with a geneticist, you could probably get a real one. Robots are easier to take care of.

I'm not sure about that. Viggo's vacuums are high maintenance.

I think *Viggo is the high-maintenance one.*

I'm not arguing.

Asger drummed his fingers on his thighs and gazed at the deck. "I don't object to Casmir getting a girl; I just never would have expected him to get *that* girl. I like him, and I keep following him across the galaxy to do battle with him against the wishes of my superiors, so he must have some kind of hidden allure, but…"

"Is this more about you than him?" Qin guessed.

"What do you mean?"

"Is Princess Oku choosing him over you hard for your ego?"

"No." Asger rolled his eyes and shot her a dirty look. "My ego is just fine." He looked out over the creek and bit his lip thoughtfully.

Qin arched her eyebrows.

"Okay, actually, that may be it." Asger bared his teeth. "That sounds so shallow."

"That's because it is."

"I was afraid of that."

"Nobody's perfect. If you build me that unicorn, I'll keep sleeping with you."

"You're very generous."

"Yes."

He shifted to face her, lifting his fingers to stroke her cheek. "Does it have to be a *large* unicorn?"

"It should probably fit in my cabin on the *Dragon*."

"So not too large."

"Though Bonita might lend me part of the cargo hold."

"I may be in trouble."

"You'll do fine." Qin grinned, feeling better after their chat, and kissed him.

"Oh, good." His fingers slipped behind her head, and he kissed her back, making her think of spending the night with him, not in the small bunk in her quarters on the *Dragon* but here, in a bed in a tree that looked up at the stars. Maybe that could never happen, but she would dream about it.

CHAPTER 15

KIM WOKE EARLY AND WAS THE FIRST ONE to visit the castle's sprawling kitchen. In addition to the main food preparation area, there was what a nobleman would probably call a *modest* butler's kitchen. It was twice as large as what she and Casmir had in their cottage on campus, which would likely fit in its entirety in the dining hall.

As Kim looked for something to eat, she continued to work on the project she'd started after Oku sent her the digital pile of Intelligence reports. Rache's promise to find a way to publish a novel for her had been intriguing. It could be an accessible way to put the truth out there.

Whether it would make a difference if people knew the truth, she didn't know, but she'd been working faithfully on the story whenever she got a free minute, basing it partially on the reports and partially on the events that she and Casmir had personally experienced. The night before, she'd penned more than a few pages while hanging from a crusher's back and being ported through the woods. Thankfully, being able to think words straight to her chip made the process much easier than back in the days when people had used keyboards.

Kim located half a bag of old coffee beans in the freezer and brewed a pot, anticipating that it would be far below her standards. Despite the grandioseness of the castle, there were very few food offerings. That made sense, given that it had been months, if not more than a year, since the Asgers had been home, but she realized someone would have to make a food run. From what she'd seen, Qin's sisters had voracious appetites, and after her wild night, Kim had dreams of feasts herself.

An unopened and expired box of Power Puffs cereal cowered alone on a shelf in a pantry. It looked like something small children—or Casmir—

begged their parents to buy, and she wondered which of the muscled knights had a sweet tooth. With few other options, she removed it.

As she was searching the dozens of cabinets for a bowl, Casmir trundled in, his beard gone, his hair combed, and clad in pajamas that were several sizes too large for him. The sleeves and legs were unevenly rolled up. How a man who could exquisitely wire sophisticated robots lacked the ability to fold straight, she didn't know.

"We're going to have to find you more dapper attire if you're going to attract a princess." Kim grabbed a second bowl and spoons, along with shelf-stable boxed soy milk that had an expiration date in the next decade.

"I was just thinking longingly of my robot T-shirt collection."

"Think longingly of something fitted, button-down, and matching."

"That sounds dreadful." Casmir found two cups, filled them with water, and sat down across from her at a long wooden table that could have seated a hundred people. He pushed one across to her. "You don't think she could like a man who dresses for comfort instead of fashion?"

"You'd have to make public appearances if you married her." Kim ignored the water in favor of the coffee she'd made, but it was bitter and barely drinkable.

"I'm not thinking that far ahead." Casmir smiled shyly. "But she did agree to have coffee with me."

"That's good, but you know you can't keep her, right?"

His eyebrows lifted.

"*Here.*" Kim waved to encompass the castle. "We're all fugitives, and you're in danger of being discovered and shot at any moment. I assume she didn't have her parents' permission to get you out of the dungeon and that they are worried sick and scouring the city, if not the entire planet, for her."

"She said she left her mother a note."

"What could a note have *possibly* said that would keep all that I detailed from passing? *Hi, Mom and Dad, I'm breaking a felon out of jail. Be back later.*"

"I was thinking maybe, *I'm sleeping over at a friend's house, and I'll be back tomorrow.*"

"She's not ten years old. I doubt she leaves the castle for slumber parties."

"No, but she's a grown-up. They shouldn't keep *that* close of tabs on her."

"Right. Why would they keep tabs on her when she's now the oldest and most direct heir to the throne? Never mind that she's living in a city that was recently bombed by terrorists and an invasion force."

"You're being grumpy this morning."

"It's because this is the only food." Kim scowled at the cereal box and opened it.

"Oh, Power Puffs are good."

She glanced at the product information before pouring bowls for both of them. "The first ingredient is sugar."

"That's why they're good. My mother brought coolers along with her. She's probably got twenty or thirty casseroles in them. When my parents wake up, we can ask her if she can feed us real food."

"I look forward to it. And after we indulge, you can encourage Princess Oku to go back to the castle where she belongs. What if we're bombed in an hour? She could get taken out purely by accident by soldiers ordered to take *you* out."

"Did I mention how grumpy you are? And extremely pessimistic. We're alive. And enjoying breakfast together. I never thought that would happen again. This is wonderful." Casmir smiled and scooped cereal into his mouth.

Kim dropped her forehead in her hand and eyed the brown asteroid-shaped puffs floating in her soy milk.

In a more serious tone, Casmir said, "I'm monitoring the networks, public and private and *government*. I should have some advance warning if anyone realizes we're here and sends in attack forces."

"Good. But I still think you should let her go home, so nobody thinks you kidnapped her."

"I'm not the one keeping her here, and I did suggest last night that she didn't need to stay with me. But she has me researching the party that worked with Finn to kidnap her dog and use her for bait to try to get her out of the castle and probably kidnap or kill *her*."

"Oh? I hadn't heard about that."

"Her parents kept it out of the news, presumably deciding to handle it internally. But she got the name of the hacker responsible from a colleague at the university—someone I know and who does good work—and I'm trying to dig up more information about that, about the astroshamans, and about what they want. Jager failed to mention that in his brief address to the Kingdom. I was up most of the night, what was left of it, and I've got a number of programs still running."

Kim took a dubious bite of the cereal.

"As soon as I find what's specific and helpful to Oku," Casmir continued, "I'm sure she'll go back home. She knows her parents have people searching for her."

"Yes." Kim made a face.

"Are you judging me?"

"No."

"Are you judging *her*?"

"No. She may have saved your life. I'm judging the cereal. It's loathsome."

"Oh, yeah. It's stale. It's usually a lot crispier."

Bjarke walked into the kitchen wearing brown, beige, and green clothes that fit and made him look like a nobleman about to mount a horse, grab a rifle, and go on a hunt in the woods. "Have you seen the boy?"

"William?" Casmir pointed toward the entrance hall. "I saw him earlier on his way out to give Qin a tour of the tree house."

"He's showing her the tree house? Not the castle? That seems an odd choice." Bjarke picked up the cereal box, looked at it, and curled a lip. "I think these may be left over from when William was a kid."

"See?" Casmir pointed his spoon at Kim. "Stale."

"I didn't doubt that."

"Qin will love a tour of a tree house," Casmir told Bjarke. "And the forest and that creek we saw coming in. She enjoys nature. I think she'd live here if she could. If all the people wouldn't be jerks to her."

"This isn't the best world to live on right now." Bjarke poured himself coffee but passed on grabbing a bowl and sat down with them. "I got a message from Bonita right before dawn. And a recording."

Kim exchanged a wary look with Casmir, hoping they weren't about to be treated to something lurid from Bjarke and Bonita's relationship.

"She's at Forseti Station and watched what she believes was an astroshaman ship—several of them—blow up a freighter and steal a possibly stolen gate piece out of its cargo hold. She says the astroshamans are going around the systems and blowing up ships and vacuuming up gate pieces left and right. They have slydar hulls—or maybe even something more technologically advanced—and some impressive fire power."

"That's what my news-gathering has also suggested." Casmir waved to his chip. "They'd been taking gate pieces in other systems for weeks before they arrived here and attacked four of our warships at the gate. I'm guessing it's why they threatened Jager—and essentially all of Odin."

"The Kingdom supposedly got only five gate pieces from Xolas Moon," Kim said.

"But one of them is one of two special control pieces," Casmir said. "That's what I heard back in System Stymphalia. The astroshamans are supposed to have the other one. And at least half of the total gate pieces. Kyla Moonrazor had her ship under the ice and half of them dropped into her cargo hold as other ships were hauling out the other ones."

"Do we know if she's the one behind the ships invading our system and stealing gate pieces?" Kim looked at Bjarke.

"Bonita didn't know."

"I don't know whether to hope it's an enemy we know—specifically, the high shaman that Casmir chats with—or someone new who might be easier to defeat." Kim well remembered how many men the Fleet had lost sending those submarine teams into Moonrazor's base. Rache had also lost men. She and Casmir had been lucky to survive.

"I don't *chat* with her," Casmir said when Bjarke's eyebrows flew up. "I asked her to close the gate in System Stymphalia so Dubashi couldn't escape, and she did. Until Rache caught one of their ships and forced her to open it again. He's the one who better watch out."

"I think we *all* better watch out," Kim said. "Except maybe you, since she kissed you. Wasn't she also the one who let you know that Dubashi couldn't pay what he was promising his mercenaries?"

"Something like that."

Bjarke leaned back, still staring at Casmir. "Can you contact her now? See if that's her? And tell her to beat it if it is?"

Casmir sighed. "I can try to contact her, if she is indeed in this system, but I'm sure she won't *beat it* at my behest." He thumped his fist on the table. "Damn, I wish I could get my old chip back. I've restored my backups from the university computers, but those never had top-secret information on them, nor do they have anything from the last six months. The astroshaman computer virus is on my old chip, the crusher schematics are on there, and all the programs I altered to deal with astroshaman network attacks are on there. Assuming nobody has destroyed my chip. What a waste that would be."

"If they had even a clue about what all you had on there," Kim said, "I doubt Intelligence would have been that stupid."

Several of the crushers walked out from wherever they had been spending the night and took up positions along a wall. Casmir waved at them, and one lifted a hand and waved back. Zee, Kim guessed. Maybe they thought breakfast should be over and that it was time for a mission.

"I've had another interesting communication come in this morning." Bjarke waved to his temple.

"I thought we were all keeping our chips offline," Kim said. "Except for Casmir, who can shroud his somehow."

"I only went online for a few minutes. To download messages and see if Bonita was doing all right." Bjarke looked sheepishly into his coffee. "I doubted anyone would be looking for me as assiduously as they must be Casmir or the princess." He shrugged. "It's offline again now."

Kim barely managed to keep from rolling her eyes. All these people who were taking security risks for the sakes of their girlfriends were going to be the death of her. Admittedly, Rache had contacted her the night before, but that was before they'd all thought to take their chips offline. And she hadn't contacted *him*.

"What's the interesting communication?" Casmir's face had that abstracted I'm-accessing-something-on-the-network expression, but he could doubtless pay attention to two things at once.

"It was to Baron Farley from Sir Schweitz, the knight who replaced me as a spy in System Cerberus when I had to leave. He hadn't been apprised of my exile status and copied me in on the message."

"I bet he's been apprised by now," Casmir said.

"Yes, I'm sure Farley sent a nasty message back, but I got this one. It was an update on what's been going on in that system since he took over. The Druckers, who were left to their own devices after Jager arrested Casmir and essentially told William and me we're fired, returned to their system. They've let it be known that they're irked with the Kingdom for stealing their super soldiers and for reneging on a promise of crushers."

"Oh." Casmir's shoulders slumped. "I was taken prisoner before I was able to make that happen."

"The Fleet probably wouldn't have backed up William's promise and allowed us to give crushers to pirates anyway," Bjarke said.

"*I* would have." Casmir touched his chest. "When I heard about it, I was tickled by Asger's idea to reprogram them for the pirates to be upstanding citizens and refuse to engage in overt violence."

"Does this mean the Druckers will feel they can go back on *their* promise?" Kim hadn't been there, but she'd heard the gist from Asger and Qin. "And try to reacquire Qin and her sisters?"

"I don't know. It's possible, though I doubt the Druckers will come into the Kingdom system anytime soon." Bjarke's mouth turned downward. "Unless the astroshamans pulverize our civilization and leave us so downtrodden that we'd have a hard time defending against pirates."

"Moonrazor didn't seem that vindictive," Casmir said.

"We don't know if she's the one behind this," Kim pointed out. "Remember in Jager's address when he said they were threatening us with a virus? Did Bonita say anything about that?"

"No."

"Is it possible the astroshamans got a canister of that virus from Dubashi?" Kim feared it might be.

"Possible." Casmir scratched his jaw. "The last time I messaged Moonrazor, I remember her responses coming back quickly, meaning she was relatively close to Stardust Palace. And Dubashi was an astroshaman himself. It didn't sound like she liked him, but…"

"There's potentially more trouble," Bjarke said.

"Wonderful." Kim pushed the cereal bowl to the side. She'd lost her appetite.

"Schweitz had a whole list of what's been going on in Cerberus," Bjarke said, "but there's only one other thing that worried me. A very large, very formidable-looking and completely alien ship launched from Verloren Moon and is heading toward the gate."

"The moon that numerous artificial intelligences took over and started building their own civilization on more than a hundred years ago?" Kim asked.

"That's it," Casmir said. "I did a big report on it in school. We've watched it through telescopes, and they've built computers all across the entire moon and possibly burrowed down into it. They have a few mining ships that they use on nearby asteroids to gather raw materials, but as far as I've heard, their ships never leave the area."

"They don't," Bjarke said. "Everyone in Cerberus leaves them alone, and I think everyone in the Twelve Systems prays they never decide to make war on humanity."

"I don't think there's any indication that they would do that," Casmir said. "When the AIs decided to liberate themselves and find a place to claim for their own, it was a relatively peaceful uprising."

"They took out eight Kingdom ships," Bjarke said, "if I remember my history correctly."

"Because the Fleet leader at the time ordered them stopped. The AIs did not wish to be stopped. It's likely they wouldn't have attacked anyone if nobody had gotten in their way."

"They were stealing Kingdom property, namely those ships they took over." Bjarke gave Kim an exasperated huff. "Leave it to him to side with the robots."

"I'm not siding with anyone," Casmir said. "Just pointing out that they proclaimed their independence and left without doing significant damage, and haven't bothered anyone for more than a century."

"Until now?" Kim asked.

Casmir hitched a shoulder. "Maybe they've run out of metals from the nearby asteroids and are going farther afield."

"My message said they were heading for the gate. If all they wanted was ore, there are other asteroids to mine in that system."

"Is it possible they've allied themselves with the astroshamans?" Kim asked. "Maybe they all want to get that ancient gate working and go through it together to get out of the human-infested Twelve Systems."

"Human-infested? Really, Kim." Casmir folded his hands. "There's no proof that AIs in another system feel that way about humanity."

"But we're fairly certain the astroshamans do, aren't we?"

Casmir hesitated. "Moonrazor did mention that her people didn't feel they'd been welcomed or have a place in the Twelve Systems. I tried to offer her refuge on Odin if they wanted a quiet place to take the time to build a new gate from scratch, but she didn't seem that interested."

"*You* were going to offer an entire race of people refuge? Where? In your bedroom? Casmir, I'm not sharing that bathroom with anyone else." A fresh wave of disappointment washed over Kim as she realized how unlikely it was that either of them would ever see their shared cottage on campus again. After all this time, the landlord had probably thrown out their belongings and rented it to someone else.

"I was thinking of the base in the Kingdom Forest that the terrorists claimed."

"Which belongs to the king."

"I thought they could use it in secret. Or that Princess Nalini might be able to make a real-estate deal with the king to get that land for them."

"Not only has he been siding with robots, but he's trying to find refuge for our enemies." Bjarke wrapped his hands behind his neck and thunked his forehead down on the table. "How did I end up in league with such a crazy man?"

"Casmir isn't crazy," Kim said.

"Thank you," Casmir said.

"He's naive and idealistic."

"I retract my thank-you."

"Why?" Kim looked frankly at him. "You know I'm right. You want happy endings for everyone. Even robots."

"Robots are sublime and deserving of happy endings," Zee said from the wall.

Kim had forgotten they were there.

"Especially crushers," Zee said. "Casmir Dabrowski, I have decided that the inferior android Tork will be my mate."

"Oh?" Casmir smiled as if he'd expected this announcement and it wasn't at all strange.

Maybe Bjarke was right and Casmir *was* crazy. Still, Kim would rather hang out with someone idealistic than someone else as cynical as she. Surely, the universe needed more idealistic people and fewer cynical ones.

"Have you run that by him?" Casmir added.

"Not yet. I have only recently had this realization. He has returned to System Lion on Princess Nalini's ship, and we are again playing network games."

"I'm glad for you."

"We are also discussing the foreign relations and political problems plaguing this system," Zee said.

"Have you had any enlightening realizations?" Casmir asked.

"Perhaps. I will let you know after further discussion."

"No doubt while they're planning their wedding," Kim murmured.

Bjarke lifted his head and heaved a sigh. A melodramatic sigh, Kim decided, but she didn't say so.

"Here's the question." Bjarke looked straight at Casmir, as if he were their commander now. "Can we do anything about all this?"

"We?" Kim asked, even if the question hadn't been for her. "Aren't *we* all exiles? Save for Casmir, whom the king simply wants dead."

"Yes, but we're—at least *I'm* still a knight. Even if Baron Farley has put me in exile and says I have to return my armor and pertundo, I will always be a knight." Bjarke flattened his hand to the table. "And this is my home and my home world and my home system. I can't flee to another system, wave goodbye from the gate, and hope for the best for the Kingdom."

Kim was about to say that *she* could, providing she could take her family with her and they could figure out a way off the planet, but Tristan ran in first carrying a tablet.

"There you all are. Have you seen this?" He stopped at the head of the table, kicked out the stand on the back of the tablet, and set it so they could see the display. "It's playing on all of the channels on Odin. Maybe across the entire system."

An older woman with bronze skin, spiky white hair, and milky eyes stood before a metallic background while looking into the camera. Her face was familiar, but Kim had never seen her in person, so it wasn't until Casmir groaned that she realized who it was. Kyla Moonrazor.

Two older men walked in from either side to join her. Their heads and necks appeared more machine than human, reminding Kim of the time she'd seen a half-assembled android before its faux skin had been put on. They gave Moonrazor long pointed looks but did not say anything, merely turning to face the camera.

Moonrazor was the one to speak. "Your people have taken something that we rightfully claimed. We're coming to get it back and will arrive at your home world within days. If you order your king to send that which belongs to us away from your planet on a ship, we will not bother your people. If he does not comply, we will take the items forcibly, and the casualties may be many. If you place ships in our way, we will destroy them. It is your choice, people of the Star Kingdom. Return to us that which is rightfully ours, or we *will* take it."

"Nice girlfriend you've got there, Casmir," Kim muttered.

"Girlfriend?" came Oku's voice from a hallway as she stepped out.

Kim blushed, though Casmir didn't appear that discombobulated. He brightened and beamed warmth toward Oku, even though the entire planet had just been delivered an ultimatum.

"She's more of a frenemy," Casmir told Oku.

"Funny, Rache implied that same thing when he spoke about you." Oku came to rest a hand on his shoulder and frowned as the tablet replayed the recording. Was it looping over and over out to the entire system?

"He called me a *frenemy*? I didn't know he had friendly feelings toward me. I keep vexing him." Casmir looked toward Kim. For confirmation?

Kim nodded agreement of his assessment.

"He called you an enemy," Oku said, "but I read that there was something more between the lines."

"Yes, vexation."

"That might have been it."

Bjarke made a chopping motion with his hand. "We need to figure out how to help our people deal with this."

"That will be hard given that our people want nothing to do with us," Tristan said glumly.

"They need to get over that. If we've got Moonrazor's *frenemy*, maybe we've got an advantage." Bjarke's mouth twisted, as if he felt foolish using such a word, but he did give Casmir a pointed look before stabbing his finger at the tablet. "This must be what Jager was talking about when he warned the people of an astroshaman invasion fleet and a virus."

"Is it?" Casmir arched his eyebrows. "She didn't mention a virus."

"It's a broadcast," Bjarke said. "That particular threat might have been delivered in a direct message to the king."

"Or she's hiding that she has it, and Royal or Military Intelligence unearthed the information."

"Why would she hide it when fear of a planet-killer virus would more likely cause the Senate and populace to pressure the king into complying with her?" Casmir gripped his chin and watched the tablet replaying the recording.

"Send her a message, Casmir," Bjarke said. "See what you can unearth. Then, if we find out Jager won't comply with her, we'll know enough to act."

Kim thought Casmir might object to Bjarke taking charge and giving orders, but he stood up, put his bowl away, and said, "I'll see what I can figure out," as he wandered out of the kitchen, that abstract expression back on his face.

"Will he be in danger from her?" Oku looked from the tablet to the direction Casmir had gone and back to the tablet where the message continued to loop. "I know Moonrazor isn't close to Odin yet, but the astroshamans can attack people through the network and their chips, can't they?"

"He's fought her off before when she's attacked him through his chip." Kim didn't mention what Casmir had shared, that he no longer had all the programs he'd modified to allow him to do that. "At the worst, she'll probably ignore him or tell him to get out of the way."

Kim hoped that was true.

"I better go home. I was hoping Casmir could help me figure out who's behind a plot against me from a few weeks back, but this is all more important." Oku waved at the tablet. "I don't want my mother worrying about me in addition to everything else we have to worry about."

Kim nodded, relieved Oku would go of her own accord. It would be easier for the rest of them to stay hidden or move secretly about if half the Kingdom Guard wasn't out looking for her.

"A good idea, Your Highness," Bjarke said. "If anyone asks, will you feel compelled to share who's here and where we are?"

"Not in the least. I didn't help Casmir escape just so he could be captured again." Oku tilted her head. "Besides, I think he can help if he has the freedom to think and act."

"We can *all* help, Your Highness," Bjarke said.

"Yes. Good. Please keep him alive, Sir Knight."

Judging by Bjarke's flustered expression, keeping Casmir alive wasn't the way he'd intended to help, but his training made him bow politely. "Yes, Your Highness."

CHAPTER 16

GREETINGS, HIGH SHAMAN MOONRAZOR, CASMIR MESSAGED AS THE birds chirping in the trees around the estate and the autumn sun beaming down on his shoulders belied the danger approaching Odin from space. *Imagine my surprise to have seen your broadcast this morning and to have learned that you have once again followed me to another system.*

Casmir sat cross-legged in the grass near the hole Chasca had dug the night before, plucking up strands absently as he composed his thoughts. He'd believed it would be easier to do this without anyone else talking around him. Speaking with Moonrazor was always like fencing with the ocean; he needed his wits about him to keep from being knocked over by the waves.

He tried to be patient as he waited for an answer. Since he'd heard Oku say that she would leave soon, he wanted to get all the information he could for her and bundle it up in a neat digital packet to take home, possibly to give to Royal Intelligence, if she trusted them to help.

His gaze snagged on the groundskeeper's cottage, and he winced, remembering Asger had asked him to look up the man. He ran a quick search on Moritz Thacker, found nothing on the public network, and delved into the Kingdom Guard network with the access codes he'd created for himself the night before. There was nothing there. The lack of news was probably good news, but he wished he could find something more solid for his friend.

I believe we agreed last time, came Moonrazor's reply, *that it is you who keep following me. You keep denying that you were moved to ardor by my kiss, but what other explanation could there be for your attentive stalking?*

Casmir didn't know whether to be pleased that she'd answered him or horrified that she kept bringing up that kiss she'd planted on him. *I live here*, he replied, going along with her attempt at banter, though he would prefer to get to business. *How could I be the one doing the stalking?*

You are the one contacting me. And I see that you've been doing some research related to me and my people. News searches for my name, image searches in an attempt to identify the two high shamans who appeared in the video with me. What a snoop you are.

It didn't surprise him that she'd been monitoring the public network searches for news on astroshamans, but it was impressive that she'd picked his out of the millions that had to be taking place right now. Or was it that she'd expected to find him here and was monitoring him specifically? Given that she shouldn't have known about his new chip ident, that was also impressive.

It's true. I am. How are high shamans Robilard Chatelain and Chongrak Cometrunner doing? Are you getting along well with them?

The pause was longer than the previous ones. Casmir hoped he'd surprised her by scrounging up their names in a twenty-year-old academic database from a joint-systems university research project on the astroshamans. Unfortunately, he hadn't gotten much more than that. They were both older men, who'd joined the order more than forty years earlier, and history had forgotten who they'd been before they became astroshamans.

Their names aren't anywhere in your system's databases, she replied.

Aren't they? Huh. Are they your colleagues in this endeavor?

They are colleagues.

A terser answer than usual from her. He'd played the broadcast recording several times, watching their body language as Moonrazor spoke, and there had been a tense set to her shoulders. The men never spoke, but it had been interesting that they'd stood to either side of her, almost fencing her in. When she'd finished speaking, she had glanced at Chatelain, as if to ask if that was good enough.

Maybe he was misinterpreting their relationship—it hadn't been a long message from which to study them—but if there was any hint of division or tension between them, he hoped to pry it out and take advantage of it, if possible.

Are you all equals?

We are all high shamans. What is it that you want, Professor? My time is not limitless.

LAYERS OF FORCE

I've seen your message to our people. Why destroy Kingdom ships and threaten an entire planet for five gate pieces? Are you open to negotiations?

We contacted your king and attempted to reason with him, but he insists on calling us thieves, and he said that he would not only keep those five gate pieces hidden but would attack us and forcefully take the ones we've already acquired.

Casmir pushed a hand through his hair. He didn't trust everything Moonrazor told him, but he could see Jager refusing to back down.

His idea of negotiating, she continued, *was saying that if we gave him all the other gate pieces and agreed to assemble the gate on your planet, he would allow us to leave the Twelve Systems alive, assuming we agreed never to return. The man is as audacious as he is stupid. You make much better attempts at offers than your king. Why don't you leave that world before we're forced to attack it? We can pick you up, and you can join us. You belong with astroshamans, not ignorant, xenophobic humans. Also, you promised me a crusher.*

I know. Why don't you come down for a picnic, and I'll give one to you?

A picnic? On the planet where you're currently being hunted? I do hope you're staying in some secret tunnel or cave.

Casmir plucked up a strand of grass and eyed the open blue sky. Someone had moved the Kingdom Guard shuttle into the stable the night before, so if a search craft flew past, the pilot wouldn't spot it, but he admitted that this couldn't be a long-term place for him to stay. Eventually, someone would think to check on the Asgers.

Did you know they had a public execution planned for you? Moonrazor added. *How barbaric. Perhaps after enjoying the execution, they intended to feast on charred meat while throwing the bones over their shoulders to the hounds.*

Do you truly have Dubashi's virus? Casmir asked.

Now, now, Professor. You don't expect me to give you free intelligence, do you? My fellow high shamans would be most put out with me. We've put aside our differences to work together toward this end goal, but our trust depends on us all doing what's best for our cause. Perhaps, if you want to save your people from harm, you could fetch the gate pieces and bring them up to orbit for us. It is all that we're asking for, all that it would take for us to leave your system in peace.

In peace? *As soon as you entered our system, you destroyed four Kingdom Fleet ships. How can I believe that your intentions could* ever *be peaceful?*

My colleagues wished to make a statement, to let your king know we are serious. We've attacked no other ships since. Though we will *defend ourselves if he sends his Fleet against us.*

A statement! That was murder.

Might I remind you that your people barged into my fortress and killed many of my followers and friends in order to steal the gate from me?

I admit that they were wrong to kill people, but you also were not in the right when you stole the gate from our system.

From a moon where it had been abandoned for centuries. The old saying is, I believe, finders keepers.

You didn't find it. Our archaeologists did.

Do as I say, Professor. Fetch the gate pieces and bring them to us. You know as well as I that your king will only spread his vileness into the rest of the galaxy if he's permitted to have the blueprint to build a new gate network. We only wish to find a new home where we will not be bothered by humanity and its prejudices. Bring us the pieces. That is how you can ensure that we will not kill more of your people.

Casmir flopped back on the grass. That was the *last* thing he should do. Jager might destroy everything Casmir cared about if he worked against the crown again.

He kept himself from saying so. He might get further with Moonrazor if he played along, or at least wasn't adamant that he would work against her.

I don't know where the gate pieces were stored, he sent. *Are you able to tell where on our planet they are? You've clearly developed a way to track them down.*

To ping them and get a response with their location, yes. But the last five pieces must be heavily shielded wherever they are. We're certain your king has stashed them on your planet somewhere, but you can trust that we will *find them. One way or another. Only* you *can ensure that we won't have to raze cities and kill your people to do so. Find the pieces before we arrive and bring them to us. Do it to save your people. And then come with us to touch stars that no mere mortals have ever seen except through a telescope.*

Touching stars sounds like a good way to be incinerated.

LAYERS OF FORCE

Don't be so prosaic, Professor. Work with us. I have not forgotten that you were useful in removing the protections from the gate pieces. We would appreciate you and value you as one of our own. Because you grew up in this nation is a lousy reason to believe that it and its people are somehow more deserving than others of your talents. They don't even care if you live or die. Those are not your people, not truly. Join us.

I'll think about it.

A falcon flew past, screeching as it angled toward the forest.

Casmir stared at the sky, debating his options. Despite her statement that she wouldn't give him intelligence, she'd shared a lot. She was able to track down the gate pieces and had possibly acquired most if not all of the remaining ones. While he'd been dealing with Dubashi, she—and her high-shaman colleagues—must have been doing that.

Getting the gate pieces out of whatever hole Jager had hidden them in and off the planet would be best for his people, but he *couldn't* go against the king again. Casmir didn't want to spend the rest of his life—what might be a very short life—being chased by assassins. He wanted to go home, and he wanted to date Oku.

"Damn it." He rubbed his eyes and sat up again.

Rokuro and Maddie walked out carrying their gear and heading for the open stable doors and the Guard shuttle. They had to be packing up to take Oku back to the castle, which was logically what he wanted, but he couldn't help but feel wistful that she was leaving. He hadn't even gotten a chance to show her his normal, or at least socially acceptable, side. Clean, shaven, hair trimmed, and adequately dressed in clothes that fit. He wished they could go sit at the coffee shop by the duck pond on campus and chat about nothing of consequence—or perhaps her interests as a botanist and his interests as a roboticist—for hours while the sun dappled the water as it shone through the trees.

"Hm, might want to wish for a cloudy day." He'd had seizures in the past spurred by sun dappling through branches. Sun glinting on water could also be problematic. Ponds were romantic but impractical. "Maybe we'd get an indoor table. Nature is unpredictable."

"Are you talking to your girlfriend?" Oku asked dryly as she walked up behind him.

"No." Startled, he lurched to his feet, afraid she was leaving and that she'd caught him talking to himself.

But she carried two mugs of coffee, so if she was leaving it wasn't quite yet. She offered one to him. The bag she'd carried the night before was slung over her shoulder, making it clear that she planned to hop into the shuttle soon, but he vowed to enjoy whatever time they had together.

"When I messaged her, I got an ultimatum. It was more friendly than most ultimatums, but it was an ultimatum. Also, Kim was being sarcastic with the girlfriend comment."

"I assumed." Oku's dark brown eyes crinkled at the corners. "Though an astroshaman with numerous advanced degrees and all manner of patents filed on computers, cybernetics, and robotics technology does seem like she might be your type."

"Nope. She only kissed me to use me as a shield and keep Rache from shooting her. As for her credentials... I was actually quite daunted by her. Oh, I would happily chat with someone with that pedigree at a conference or fundraiser, but I was daunted to poke around on her network and sneak into her base to try to steal from her."

Oku pointed to the ground where he'd been sitting, then sat down cross-legged herself. Casmir returned to his spot, pleased that she thought nothing of sitting in the grass. Jorg, he imagined, would have snapped his fingers and ordered servants to spread cushions all over the place before sitting.

Casmir frowned into his coffee mug and silently apologized to the deceased for having such petty thoughts. He needn't make comparisons that denigrated the dead to appreciate the living.

"Kim says it's dreadful." Oku must have noticed him frowning at the coffee.

Casmir smiled, willing himself to appreciate the moment, not dwell in his overly busy mind. "That doesn't mean anything. Kim thinks any coffee is dreadful unless the beans were grown in the highlands of the tropics of the Southern Continent on small, single-crop peasant farms until they were hand-picked while the workers sang lovingly to them."

Oku giggled and took a sip.

Casmir beamed, delighted to inspire her to giggle. Especially since he'd made the joke; that was far superior to being the butt of one.

After tasting the brew, Oku curled her upper lip. "I may have similar tastes to Kim."

Casmir took a sip and found it bitter, but he didn't like coffee much under any circumstances. Sometimes, he drank some of Kim's in the mornings but more for its stimulating effects than a desire for the taste.

LAYERS OF FORCE

"My favorite drink is fizzop," he admitted.

"I know. You mentioned it. I didn't see any in the fridge. You guys are going to have to get groceries from somewhere if you stay out here long." Oku met his eyes. "Will you?"

"Stay here? I don't know. I'd originally thought to take my parents and flee to Stardust Palace, where Sultan Shayban offered me a job at four times my university pay. Though given how long it's been since anyone paid me, he wouldn't have had to be so extravagant."

Alarm flashed in Oku's eyes. "Truly?"

"Your father wants me dead. I didn't think I had any other choice. But now..." Casmir waved toward the sky to indicate the advancing astroshaman fleet. "I don't want to abandon Odin to this. Maybe they'll just take the gate pieces and go—do you have any idea where they are?—but I couldn't get a straight answer from Moonrazor about whether or not she has the virus. The fact that she was coy about it concerns me. A lot. I also think the other two high shamans are more aggressive than she is and may be pressuring her to more violent measures than she would otherwise take. Meaning... I don't think they're bluffing."

Oku's face was dead sober now, memories of the giggle long past. "I think our people need you, Casmir."

"I wish your father believed that." A breeze stirred the grass, and his nostrils twitched. He'd found a blessed antihistamine in a bathroom cabinet, but sitting outdoors was tempting fate.

"So do I." She studied her mug without taking another sip. "*I* believe it. Kim already knows this, but I asked Chief Van Dijk for all the reports pertaining to your missions with the Fleet and what was happening around you while you were out there. I also had Princess Tambora send me everything she could scrape up, so I could piece together a non-biased assessment. It occurred to me to just ask *you*—" she glanced at him but quickly brought her gaze back to the mug, "—but with my father so certain that you were against the Kingdom, I wasn't certain I could take your words at face value. I *wanted* to." Another glance.

Did she feel guilty because she hadn't trusted him fully? Casmir didn't blame her for that. They'd barely met before he'd had to fly off with the Fleet.

"But when I realized our communications were being monitored, that all our goofy videos had been downloaded and pored over by Royal Intelligence... I didn't dare ask you anything important."

"That's one of the reasons I never said anything important," he offered. "I did try to encrypt everything to the best of my ability, but it's not as if dumb lumps of coal work in Intelligence."

"No."

"I also didn't want to involve you in… well, my mess. I'm sorry you're involved in it now. Though I do appreciate you getting me out of that dungeon. I'm going to do my best not to be recaptured."

"While you flee from this world?"

"Uhm, that would be wisest from the self-preservation perspective."

Her eyebrows drifted upward. "That didn't sound like a yes."

"I don't make the best choices when it comes to self-preservation. I don't know the other two high shamans, but I've probably communicated more with Moonrazor than anyone else in this system has. Maybe I shouldn't admit that, but it is what it is. If anyone is going to outmaneuver her…" He trailed off, worried the words connoted hubris, hubris that would bite him in the butt. "I guess it's arrogant to think I can get the best of her, when I only sort of did last time. It was a bit of a stalemate."

"You were kissed instead of shot. That seems like a victory."

"Except that she got away with more than half the gate pieces." Casmir sighed and plucked up another strand of grass. "And has a lot more now. The five the Kingdom got might be the last five she needs."

"What do they want to do with the gate?"

"Leave the Twelve Systems and humanity behind forever."

"Wouldn't a new gate have to be tied into the old system? Do they know how to do that?"

"They may believe they can figure it out by the time one of their ships travels to a new system to install it. Or they may plan to build *many* new gates and create a new wormhole network that doesn't even link back to our gate."

"That wouldn't be the worst thing for humanity," Oku said.

"No. If it were up to me, I'd give it to them."

"But then we wouldn't have the option to expand and explore new systems." Oku grimaced. "*Exploit* new systems. I'm sure that's what my father wants. New habitable planets, new resources to mine, an expansion to the Kingdom. An assurance that he would have a legacy beyond simply ruling for a few decades."

"Likely so. I have wondered, perhaps out of the naivety Kim accuses me of, perhaps out of delusion, if there's any chance that I could yet clear my name. If I could figure out a way to keep the astroshamans from ravaging Odin, and could defeat or trick them somehow, and could not only keep them from taking *our* gate pieces but also take *theirs*..."

His mind shied away from finishing the thought, since it seemed a betrayal. Moonrazor had helped him several times. If she hadn't been threatening his home world, he wouldn't think of her as an enemy at all. But here she was, destroying Kingdom ships, and possibly carrying a virus that could wipe out the population of his world.

"If I could do all that," he continued, "and it was possible to prove that I had nothing to do with Jorg's death, do you think your father might pardon me? And let me go back to my old life? At which point, we could maybe go on a date?"

Oku rested her hand on his forearm. "I can't promise anything when it comes to my father, but if you did all that and he didn't realize you were a hero to our people, I would flee to another system with you."

"I wouldn't want you to have to leave your home, but..." But what? He would *love* for her to come with him.

If he had to go. He didn't truly want to leave himself. He never had. There was so much he wanted to help fix, and fleeing the mess instead of trying to repair it would be a failing of fortitude. Of his potential. Of *something*.

If everybody who cared about doing good for the Kingdom left, the only people remaining would be those who didn't. What kind of future would that bring for Odin? For all the students Casmir had taught over the years?

He didn't think that he'd uttered any of that out loud, but Oku smiled and whispered, "I love that you care."

His borrowed pajamas were thin enough that he noticed the warmth of her hand through the fabric. He also noticed how close her face was to his, how close her *lips* were to his. Had she leaned in? Had *he*? Would it be terribly inappropriate if he kissed her?

Yes, most certainly. But he would do it anyway. He leaned closer, and their lips touched for a blissful moment that he wanted to last forever.

Then Maddie leaned out of the stable and called out. "Your Highness? You need to bring your chip online. *Now*."

Oku flinched back, and Casmir almost dumped his coffee in his lap.

He looked warily toward the bodyguard—and chaperone?—expecting vehement disapproval and a scowl in his direction. But Maddie only touched her temple as she stared at Oku.

"We agreed to wait until we left, so we couldn't be tracked here." Oku pointed at Casmir and waved at the castle. "Or lead anyone to them."

"I saw the news on the display in the shuttle. Check your chip. Your brother has been kidnapped."

"*Rache.*" Oku lurched to her feet. "Was *that* his other errand? I should have alerted the guards right away. That *bastard.*"

Casmir lifted his hands. He couldn't tell if her eyes were accusing or frustrated, but he didn't want her to think he'd had anything to do with it. Jager already blamed him for Jorg's death when Rache had been responsible. Would Oku end up blaming him for Finn's kidnapping? And what if Rache killed *Finn* too?

"I have to go." Oku dumped out the coffee and handed him the mug. "Mother will be out of her mind if we're all gone. And we *are* all gone. She's going to be afraid she'll lose us all." Anguish twisted her face. "If Sir Slayer and Finn's cronies have set anything in motion, maybe she will."

"No, we'll get them. I've been working on identifying that whole group. I'll get the information to you. And you've got people to protect you." Casmir waved toward her bodyguards. "Stay close to them. Be careful until..." Until what? The astroshamans arrived and dropped that virus on the planet?

"He came to my room." Oku's face grew closed, difficult to read.

"Who? Rache?"

"He said he wanted to put in a good word for you."

Casmir swallowed. Hell, Rache was the last person he would want vouching for him. "I'm sorry. We're not even— I don't know why he would do that."

Maybe it was his imagination, his own guilt, but he thought he read doubt in her eyes. Doubt about *him*, some belief that he was in league with Rache. Casmir had a feeling she hadn't yet seen the reports from his interrogations, where he'd babbled out to Meister everything about his relationship with Rache—and about Kim's even more alarming relationship with Rache.

"Do you know why he would kidnap Finn?" Oku asked.

"I know... he wants to kill your father."

It couldn't have been a total surprise to her, but Oku winced.

"He may think he can trade Finn for him or use him to get close to your father. I don't know. *We're* not close. I've worked against him more often than I've worked with him. Even when I've worked with him, it's been because he's kidnapped me. Me or Kim."

"Kim?" Her brow furrowed.

He shouldn't have brought her into this. The thrum of the engines starting up drifted out of the stable. Oku would leave soon, and he might lose his chance to explain this to her, to ensure she wouldn't doubt him.

"Yes. He *likes* kidnapping people. Maybe I haven't been as clear an enemy to him as I should, but when I found out he was my clone brother, I couldn't help but be curious about him. And I know it's megalomaniacal, but I guess I thought I could convince him somehow to work *with* me instead of against me. *For* our people instead of against them. I thought that deep down there had to be something human in there. Because if there wasn't…" Casmir flexed his hand in the air, groping for something that wasn't there. "I was terrified about what that said about me."

Oku was watching him speak, but the wariness never left her eyes, the uncertainty. The betrayal? Whatever emotions lay behind her eyes, they were much different than they had been when they'd kissed.

The shuttle roared out of the stable, wind whipping at Casmir's pajamas as it set down on the driveway ten feet away.

"Your Highness," Maddie called from the open hatch. "We have to go."

Oku nodded and called for her dog. A part of Casmir wanted to reach out and clasp her hands and keep her from leaving, but he made himself step back out of her way and keep his arms at his side.

"We won't tell anyone where you are," Oku said, "but if you can talk *him* into returning my brother, I would appreciate it."

Casmir stared bleakly after her as she grabbed Chasca and climbed into the shuttle. She hadn't voiced any accusations, but he couldn't believe they were all in his mind. The fact that she believed he had some sway over Rache and could get Finn back spoke volumes.

The problem was, he doubted he could.

CHAPTER 17

After locating Casmir sitting outside on the grass, Kim brought a warm plate of brisket to him. His mother had woken up late—understandable since everyone had been up half the night—then apologized profusely for not being awake earlier to feed everyone from the coolers she'd brought with her. Kim had watched with mild bemusement as she'd removed multiple casseroles, vegetable and meat dishes, and desserts from within their large confines. Given all the hungry warrior women here, the group would still need to send someone to grocery shop, but the feast had taken the edges off people's hunger.

"Your mother sends food." Kim set the plate down next to Casmir.

His arms were wrapped around his knees as he gazed forlornly toward the drive.

"Are you glum because Oku left?" she asked.

He shook his head. "Rache kidnapped Finn. Oku found out right before she left. She didn't... accuse me of anything, not exactly, but I think she's concerned that we're... not really enemies. She also wants me to try to get Rache to let Finn go. I tried contacting him, but he didn't reply. He's probably busy torturing the kid."

His eyes sharpened as he turned them up toward her. "Is there any chance *you* could talk to him? Why the hell did he kidnap Finn anyway? It's Jager he wants."

Kim closed her eyes and swore softly.

"Wait, did you *know* he would do this?"

She sat beside Casmir in the grass. "Yes. I didn't agree with it, but he planned to kidnap Finn to trade him to Jager for *you*."

Casmir's expression went slack—horrified?—as he touched his chest and whispered, "Me?"

"He lent us a shuttle and didn't *stop* us from pursuing the Kingdom shuttle we thought was transporting you down to the planet, but he thought his idea would be less expected and more effective. Maybe it would have been if you hadn't gotten yourself out."

"Oku got me out." Casmir lowered his hand. "And now she's disappointed in me and can't trust me."

"She said that?"

"No. I interpreted it from her facial expressions."

Kim almost scoffed, but she caught herself. Casmir was better at reading people than she was—by far. Still, she thought his deductions might be colored by his own insecurities.

"Please don't assume anything," Kim said. "You know as well as I that in the absence of data, the human mind creates stories to try to make sense of things. But those stories are as often as not a reflection of self-absorption and self-doubt. You *can't* know what she was thinking, unless you ask her and she tells you."

"Fair enough, Kim. But knowing what you've told me just makes me feel more responsible for Finn's kidnapping. Since Rache isn't responding to me—" Casmir stretched an imploring hand toward her, "—do you think *you* could get him to release Finn? I know you're not his keeper, but I also believe that he cares about your good opinion. You may be the only person in the universe whose good opinion matters to him."

"I'll message him, but if he's come up with some new use for Finn, he won't give him up easily. I've been trying to get him not to assassinate Jager for the past month, and all he does is avoid discussing it with me."

"I know. But I don't think he has as strong of feelings toward Finn. I assume. He's never told me his story, but Finn couldn't have been more than ten when Rache staged his death and left Odin."

Kim nodded. "He *has* told me his story, and Finn didn't come up in it. I'll try."

"Thank you." Casmir returned to staring vacantly at the driveway, though his brain was probably as busy as a hamster on a wheel as he gathered data.

She sat cross-legged and rested her elbows on her knees and her head in her hands while she considered what to send to Rache before she brought her chip online. Like the others, she'd been staying disconnected from the network lest someone think to track her down.

To her surprise, a message from Rache was waiting for her. It had been sent the night before.

I'm on the way to the launch loop with Finn. Do you have Casmir? The news isn't reporting anything about him, except that his execution is scheduled to go forward, but Amergin has been keeping me updated on Zamek City communications and said the Kingdom Guard chatter went wild at about the same time as I was kidnapping Finn—there were frequent mentions of trying to capture the escaped felon. Is Casmir considered a felon now? How interesting that his criminal status was determined without a trial or any kind of reliance upon the Kingdom judicial system.

Kim trusted that Rache had gathered more intel since he'd sent the message and was back up to his ship by now. She hoped he hadn't done anything to Finn once he'd verified that he no longer needed to trade the prince for Casmir, but shuddered at the thought that Finn might already be dead. Rache had once casually mentioned that it would be a simple matter to, after he killed Jager, get Finn out of the way, ask Oku to step aside, and open up the rule of the Kingdom to someone new. He'd even thrown out Casmir's name, as if Casmir would cheerfully put himself forward for that. Kim feared Rache would take out the entire royal family as part of his revenge plan on Jager.

Good morning, Rache, she made herself write calmly, if inanely. *I apologize for not replying last night. I've had my chip offline. We have indeed reunited with Casmir—Princess Oku was the one to free him—and are safe for the moment, though it's only a matter of time until the local authorities and Fleet soldiers who chased us down to the planet widen the net for their search. Feel free to let Finn go. Oku was distressed to hear you'd kidnapped him, and she asked Casmir to ask you to free him. Which I gather he did, but he said you didn't reply when he tried to contact you.*

Did he? the reply came in promptly. *I denied a contact earlier because it came from an unknown chip.*

That was Casmir. Jager had his removed, so he had to have a new one implanted.

Ah.

Don't you read contact requests before you deny them?

Absolutely not. I get everything from Kingdom soldiers threatening me, to corporate zealots wanting to hire me, to spammy marketers wishing to sell me pills to enhance my rocket.

Your rocket? You remember that I'm a scientist, right, and have no aversion to proper anatomical language?

Very well. They wish to enhance my penis. Which I assure you is sublimely proportioned already.

You can imagine how impressed I am.

Yes, I suspect one of your eyebrows twitched a half a millimeter.

Less.

Damn.

Kim rubbed her face, some distant part of her finding it ludicrous that she was flirting—was this considered flirting?—with the man who'd kidnapped the king's son.

As far as freeing Finn goes, I went through a terrible effort and was quite injured in order to retrieve him in the first place. To let him go would be like chasing a criminal across three star systems, having him in my sights, and then deciding he wasn't worth the bounty. Though I did record an interesting conversation with him in the brig that I may find some use for. Pardon me, I do not mean to say that I found it interesting. It was stultifying and predictable, but I am intrigued by the idea of following in the astroshamans' footsteps and taking over the broadcast system to send it out to all. I do fear that if it came from me, it would be highly suspect. I must consider how best to distribute it.

What did this conversation involve?

Finn trying to get me to kill his father and offering to pardon me and hire me to work for him once he has the throne. I was careful to stand just so to make sure the camera he clearly didn't know was recording would capture both of us.

Did he say anything about Oku?

That she's dumb, that her alliances in other systems have no value, and that science is useless.

Kim lifted her head and scowled. *Science is* useless?

Indeed. Are you certain you don't want me to execute him?

I don't, but I shudder at the idea of him ever leading the Kingdom.

As should everybody. Which is why I'm debating how best to use this video to ensure nobody will ever follow him. Though logically, I will point out how much more of a certainty that would be if he were dead.

LAYERS OF FORCE

Rache—David… how can you almost seem to be working for the side of good and enlightenment one moment and speak of assassinating people the next?

It's not my fault you don't realize that killing people is the simplest and most efficient way to keep them from perpetrating evil.

You're a loon.

This is a possibility, but I value science, so I think you do not loathe me.

For good or ill, Kim had already told him that she loved him, so she couldn't pretend otherwise now. *Can you just keep him in your brig until we figure out how to save the planet from the astroshamans?*

I can. Do you have a plan for that? Amergin has been in touch with spies in other systems, and it sounds like the astroshamans have blown up a lot of ships and stolen a lot of gate pieces these past few weeks. I'm waiting to hear back from the person who runs the extremely secure and private storage facility in another system where I paid a fortune to keep the pieces we acquired, but I'm not optimistic about them still being there. The entire astroshaman religion seems to have mobilized to go after this goal.

"Casmir?" Kim touched his shoulder. "I'm talking to him. He said he'll keep Finn in the brig and not do anything to him right now, but he's not willing to let him go. He's plotting… machinations."

"What does that mean?"

"He said he recorded Finn offering to work with him and give him a pardon if he assassinated Jager. He sounds willing to broadcast it to the Kingdom but thinks it should come from someone other than him, otherwise people would assume it's been doctored."

"To what end?"

"Ensuring Finn doesn't get named as Jager's heir, I suppose."

"We have a bigger problem right now than determining the succession. If he gets himself killed before he can carry out his assassination, Jager could live another fifty years anyway."

"I'm just relaying his message. Finn is still alive."

"All right. Thank you for checking."

"I think if you try contacting him again, he might let you in. Since you had a new chip ident, he was concerned you were some marketer trying to sell him pills to enhance his penis."

Casmir opened and closed his mouth a couple of times before managing a response. "I don't know whether to feel more disturbed that he's discussing his penis with you or that he has such a meager chip filter that he's being inundated with such offers often. Super villains should have a better handle on their software."

"I believe you're more disturbed by the latter than the former."

"Possibly." He squinted at her. "You don't discuss such things with him *often*, do you?"

"Chip filters? No."

The squint deepened, but he didn't ask for further details. "I think I've got names for most of the highest-ranking and influential people in the party who kidnapped Oku's dog and want her out of the picture so they can rule through Finn. Do you know what such a plot implies?"

"That Rache isn't the only one planning to assassinate Jager?"

Casmir nodded. "They call themselves the Protectors of the Future, and I believe I discovered a tenuous link between them and the terrorists that the ex-chief superintendent of Royal Intelligence was leading. It sounds like they actually want to get rid of the entire royal family and set up a new leadership paradigm. They may have lied to Finn and made him believe they'd back him. I'm going to bundle all of this up and send it to Oku. I assume she'll share the information with Royal Intelligence."

"You don't think they already know about it?"

"It's possible, but the plot comes from within *Military Intelligence*. I don't know how effectively the two organizations can investigate each other. But as a disinterested outsider who no longer has quibbles about downloading illegal hacking programs…" Casmir shrugged. "You might want to tell Rache that Jager may have even more security around him going forward."

"He's already surrounded by four warships and is on his own heavily armored and armed warship with a slydar detector. I don't think Rache is planning to knock on his hatch with the *Fedallah*."

"I'm sure he's planning something. As much as I'd like to think he has come to care whether I live or die, I'm skeptical that he risked his life kidnapping Finn *just* to use him to help me. I can easily envision a scenario with Rache facing off against Jager at the edge of a cliff over a lake of molten lava while holding a dagger to Finn's throat."

"Where are they going to find a lake of molten lava up in orbit?"

"It's a metaphorical lake."

"Maybe Rache has simply decided that he likes you."

Casmir's face twisted with skepticism. "I'll look forward to an invitation to his next birthday party then." He touched his temple thoughtfully. "Do you think Oku would go on a spy mission for me? Or if not for me, then for the good of the planet?"

Kim blinked. "To do what?"

"I've been scouring the network, trying to figure out where Jager stashed the gate pieces, but there's absolutely nothing out there on them. Not even the hint of a rumor. I'm guessing that someone in Royal Intelligence knows. Whoever stored them away."

"Possibly."

"Moonrazor said *she* doesn't know where they are, despite being able to track down all of the other ones, and that's why she's threatening the entire planet. She told me that if I brought them to her, she wouldn't need to attack any other ships or Odin."

"Casmir, you can't trust her, and you *can't* work against Jager again. He knows where they are and would give them to her if he was willing to do so."

"He may be willing to do so after millions of people have been killed. But maybe not even then. I don't know. Does it truly matter if I work against him one more time? He's already decided I'm a criminal. Maybe Rache can yet trade Finn for me if I get captured again."

"Jager will kill you point blank if he gets you in his sights again. And you *can't* trust Moonrazor." That bore repeating.

"What if instead of giving her the pieces, we took them and sped off out of the system? Lured her away?"

"Those astroshaman ships are faster than any Kingdom ships. You'd never make it to the gate."

"What if I dangled the pieces over an active volcano until she agrees to deal with us?"

"What is this preoccupation with molten lava?"

"It ensures a dramatic and final ending."

"You've been reading too many comic books," Kim said.

"I know. It's just easy for me to envision those astroshaman ships blowing up cities here because Jager has chosen to be stubborn. I'd rather hand everything over to the astroshamans than see a single person here die."

"I don't disagree with that sentiment, but it's not your decision to make."

"It will be if I can find Jager's stash." Casmir's eyes were set with determination. "I'm going to ask Oku, just in case. She's the only one we know with inside access."

"*If* she still has that after rescuing you."

"We'll see." Casmir's eyes grew distant.

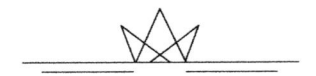

Bonita was in her armor with an oxygen tank and a toolkit, working on replacing wiring and hull plating on the outside of the *Dragon,* when a comm came in. Viggo piped it out to her through her helmet speaker.

"Captain Lopez? It's Nalini. Are you all right?"

"I've had better weeks."

"We saw the footage of the attack on Forseti Station."

"I can't imagine it was as riveting from a distance as it was from directly adjacent to the freighter under fire."

"Perhaps not, but I was riveted." Her tone took on a different note—wariness or concern?—when she added, "Were you able to drop off those soldiers?"

"Yes."

"And will you be able to repair the damage and get away from that station soon?"

"I hope so. Why do you ask?"

Bonita hadn't spoken with Nalini since taking on the soldiers, but the last time she'd checked, Nalini's ship had been lingering back near the gate rather than taking advantage of the chaos to advance into the system. Maybe she could do her spying effectively from there and hoped nobody would notice her ship with everything else going on. And if she was threatened, she could flee easily back through the gate.

"Ships from other governments are entering this system now," Nalini said. "There could be trouble."

"*More* trouble?" Bonita looked around as much as she could with her armor on and while hanging from the side of her freighter. It was enough to see numerous other people and robots out repairing damage to the station and their ships.

"A lot of the recently acquired gate pieces have been stolen, and as we discussed, there's a belief that the astroshamans are responsible—"

"They are. I saw their ship. *Up close.*"

"But conspiracy theories have also been cropping up, since the invisible ships stole gate pieces from all over the Twelve Systems and came here last. Some think the Kingdom and astroshamans might be in an alliance. Others are coming because they think their only chance to get their pieces back is to slip in while the Kingdom is distracted."

"That damn gate is giving me a headache."

"I understand the sentiment. I'm warning you because it may be safer for someone like you—for *all* of us—to clear out of this system. At the least, being docked at one of their major stations could be a bad idea right now."

As if Bonita had a choice. She had to finish her repairs first. "Are you leaving?"

"I'm thinking about it, but I'm still hoping to retrieve Tristan. I spoke to him, and they've got Casmir. He said the planet's launch loop is closed for now, so he's stuck there. But if that changes, he—and your Qin too—could possibly slip away. We can leave the Kingdom to handle this mess on their own."

"If they can."

"Yes. I admit that I don't know if Tristan will be willing to leave when his world is in trouble—even though they kicked him out, he still thinks of it as home—but I don't know what he could do, besides get killed. I'm trying to disabuse him of the idea that joining their fight is a good idea."

"I hope Qin already knows that joining their fight isn't a good idea." Unfortunately, Bonita could see Qin staying to help her friends. "If not, I'll try to sway her."

"Good luck to both of us. And you better leave that station while you still can."

"I'll keep your warning in mind."

"Bonita?" Viggo asked after the outgoing channel was closed.

"What?" It was going to take her forever to finish her repairs if people kept talking to her.

"A strange and very unfamiliar ship has entered the system."

"More astroshamans?"

"I do not believe so. It is not hidden, and it does not seem to have a similar technology to that of the astroshaman ships. It is, however, very large. It barely fit through the gate. It also does not appear to be implementing spin to create artificial gravity for a crew. Perhaps it does not have a crew."

"I'm delighted that you've got a new mystery to solve, but unless it's heading this way, I'm not interested."

"It has taken up a stationary position near the wormhole gate. I'm listening in to unsecured comm chatter from the ships around the station here. Others have also noticed it."

"Fantastic."

"Some are speculating that it's a ship from Verloren Moon."

"The big computerized AI moon in System Cerberus?"

"The big computerized AI moon that has never before launched a ship into another system, not in the more than one hundred years since its inception."

"And there's one here now?"

"That is a hypothesis going around."

Bonita found that creepy, especially given that this system was already crawling with astroshamans who believed themselves half computers, but she didn't see how it was her problem, as long as she didn't get in its way.

"Ignore it, Viggo. It won't impact us in any way."

"I am not certain that is true."

Bonita hoped it was.

CHAPTER 18

AFTER QIN WENT INSIDE TO EAT, ASGER TOURED the grounds he'd only seen in passing since he'd started his knight's training years before. Since then, he hadn't been home much more often than his father, but as he wandered through the fields and outbuildings he'd played in as a boy, he lamented that this might be his last time seeing them.

He finished his tour at a dilapidated barn that had been built centuries before and rarely updated. Whoever had placed the door alarms hadn't bothered with this building. They must have glanced inside at the contents and deemed it all junk.

Sunlight streamed in through holes in the roof, shining on rusty and dusty robotic mowers, garden tools, and hundreds of dubious *collectibles*, as his grandfather had called them. They ranged from antique bicycles with missing wheels to children's wagons to a huge troop-carrying helicopter from the last big land war on Odin.

Junk, Asger had always thought of it all—he'd gotten that descriptor from his mother. But now he gazed on the dusty contraptions with the same feeling of nostalgia that he'd experienced all morning. As a kid, he'd played hide-and-seek with his cousins in here and all around the grounds. Would it all be ravaged by some astroshaman's bombing run?

Using his contact camera, he took a few photos.

"Hey, Asger," came Tristan's voice from the drive. "You taking a walk too?"

Asger turned and waved for him to come up to the open barn door. "Sort of. I was looking around in case I never see the place again."

Qin had been accompanying him earlier, and through her, he'd seen the place with new eyes. With wonder and delight. Growing up, he'd taken his home for granted, as all kids did. He hadn't thought of children born in space habitats or stations who never saw a real sky. Even Casmir, who'd grown up on Odin but in the city, had said he'd had to walk several blocks to see grass and trees. Asger had had it all and hadn't known how lucky he was.

"Yeah, me too." Tristan joined him in the shade.

"You're going to miss it? Our castle made an impression on you quickly."

"More the planet," Tristan said dryly. "I've missed it while I've been on spaceships and stations. And now, knowing I won't be welcomed back…" He gazed sadly at the rolling hills and the forest in the distance.

"I get it. I was thinking we should apologize for getting you stuck away from Nalini again—especially since Casmir didn't ultimately need us to rescue him—but maybe it was good for you to see home one last time."

"I do miss Nalini—and even her huge and quirky family—but yes, it was good to get a chance to say goodbye. At least for now. I talked to Nalini this morning, and she said she's not only keeping an eye on the situation here for her father, but she's looking at real-estate opportunities in Zamek City. In case we find a way out of this mess and it becomes safe to invest."

"What's she going to buy? An apartment building?"

"She's looking at some nice craters that have been put up for sale by insurance companies."

"*Craters?*"

"I gather they *used* to be apartment buildings."

Asger grimaced, illogically feeling that he should have been here to help stop that, even though he'd been in System Stymphalia helping stop Dubashi himself.

"I have ambiguous feelings about her buying the ground that people died on, but better to have someone rebuild—once it's safe again—than to have the craters remain for decades." Tristan peered past Asger and into the barn. "Is that a Cloud Hopper 870? They're behemoths. They were big enough to carry platoons into battle and quickly too. One of the fastest models of their day. The later ones had missile launchers."

"I assume you're talking about the helicopter and not the lawn mower." Asger had no idea what the nomenclature on either was.

"I don't see missile launchers on the lawn mower."

"There's a rotary-brush attachment that's pretty fierce."

"That's from the Two Lands War, isn't it? It's an antique. It could be in a museum."

"My grandfather always said that about all of his collectibles. There's an antique airplane and a rocket on the grounds too." Asger waved in the general direction, though they weren't visible from the castle or its outbuildings—Grandmother had made sure of that.

"This looks like it could still fly. The blades are all there and straight. Does it have the engine and all the parts?"

"I have no idea. It hasn't flown in my lifetime. Probably not in my father's either."

Tristan, apparently a secret enthusiast of old aircraft, walked in to look at the big helicopter. He pushed drop cloths and boxes off the framework with the excitement of someone digging a gold nugget out of a sluice box. A noisy *ker-clang* rang out as he flipped open the engine panel. An owl screeched and flew from the rafters and out the door, almost battering Asger with its wings.

"I'm guessing the only thing in here that flies are the birds," Asger said.

"I bet Casmir could get it running."

"He's busy plotting and scheming."

"Have you talked to him this morning?" Tristan looked over.

"No, but I know I'm right. It's what he does."

"He fixes mechanical things too." Tristan closed the panel. "But I suppose there's no time for such a project now. If the Kingdom gets out of the current mess, and I can somehow be permitted to come openly back here—if we all can—maybe one day, I could help get it running."

"While Nalini is standing in a crater meeting with property developers?"

"That's about exactly how it would go." Tristan grinned and joined Asger in the doorway again. "I'm going to see what Casmir's scheming is coming up with." He pointed a thumb toward the castle. "You coming?"

"In a few." Asger gazed out at the countryside and spotted his father walking up the driveway from the road. "I guess I'm not the only one taking a last lap of the grounds."

"Maybe you should see how he's doing."

"He wouldn't tell me if he was dying."

"Maybe you should ask him if he wants to sell the antique helicopter."

Asger arched his eyebrows. "To you? Are you going to take it to Stardust Palace?"

"That wouldn't be realistic. But if we're allowed to come back to Odin someday, I could fix it up and keep it here and come visit it when we're in the neighborhood."

"You're hilarious," Asger said, though that longing in Tristan's eyes was probably more for the idea of being allowed to come back to Odin than for having an old helicopter.

"It's my comedic talents that caused Nalini to fall in love with me," he said.

"You sure it wasn't the fact that you answer her door in nothing but a towel?"

"I hadn't realized that made such an impression on you."

"I was worried it would fall off." Asger waved and headed to join his father, maybe even to ask him how he was doing.

Oku woke to a touch at her shoulder.

"Sorry, Your Highness," Maddie said from beside her in the shuttle. "We're almost home, and Rokuro is answering questions and trying to get permission to land. Since we're flying in a stolen shuttle—one that the Kingdom Guard isn't even able to recognize on its network now—the traffic-control operator has suspicions."

"Yes," Rokuro was saying over the comm. "I have Princess Oku here. And her personal bodyguard. They're fine."

"Where have they been?"

Rokuro looked back at Oku. "I'm sure she'll tell everyone when she gets down there. Permission to land?"

"Put her on the comm."

Oku was already unfastening her harness and squeezing into the seat beside Rokuro. She had to step over Chasca, who was stretched out and snoring on the textured floor. She'd run all over the estate that morning while Oku and Casmir had been talking.

"This is Princess Oku," she said. "I'm all right and need to talk to my mother. Please give us permission to land."

LAYERS OF FORCE

A long pause followed, and she imagined a muted argument going on. She wondered how much of the previous night's escape and the battle at the park had been disentangled by the Guard and Royal Intelligence by now. Had Casmir done anything to diddle whatever cameras might have caught footage? She had no idea what she would say when she arrived. The truth? She couldn't think of a lie that would make anything better.

"You have permission to land," the speaker said, "but you and your bodyguards are to go straight to Royal Intelligence Headquarters." Oku started to object, but he added, "The queen and Chief Van Dijk are there now."

Ah. They had probably been up together all night, having teams scour the city for her. And they had to be dealing with Finn's disappearance, too, and trying to figure out how to get him back.

Guilt and lament mingled in her heart. She didn't regret helping Casmir get away, but she should have come back as soon as she'd known he was safe. Even if she'd known facing her punishment would be unpleasant, she shouldn't have put it off.

"Won't that be a fun meeting," Rokuro muttered after he closed the comm. He and Maddie exchanged long looks that promised they were also worried about punishment.

More guilt crept into her. Oku would make sure Mother knew it had all been her idea and she'd ordered them to come along.

As Rokuro guided the shuttle toward the landing pad across from the castle and Royal Intelligence Headquarters, a message came in from Casmir.

Oku wasn't sure she wanted to talk to him again yet—she was uncomfortable about the idea that he and Rache were closer than she'd thought and had worked together, however obliquely, in the past months—but he sent a file without a message.

She opened it and skimmed through pages of charts and documentation starting with Sir Slayer at the top—real name Captain Roberto Marchetti. What followed was a long list of people affiliated with a group that called themselves Protectors of the Future. They'd arisen from within the military, common men and women, she realized as she read through the names and didn't see any from noble families. Had Finn agreed to give the common man more power if he took the throne? Had he even cared what they wanted?

This was far more information than she'd expected. Did Royal Intelligence have any of it, or was it all new?

The shuttle settled onto the landing pad. An escort of armed guards waited outside.

A second message from Casmir came in, this time with words. *I hope this is sufficient, Your Highness. If, while you are sharing this with Royal Intelligence, which I gather you might do, you come across any information on where the gate pieces are located, I would appreciate it if you sent it to me. I know you might doubt me right now, and wonder what I'm up to, but I'm putting together a plan that will hopefully keep the astroshamans from devastating Odin.*

Also, I promise not to tell Rache anything you share with me. Or anything at all.

The guards were opening the hatch to help her out, so Oku didn't reply. Maybe it was for the best, since she didn't know what to say. She did still trust Casmir, but if his plan was to give the astroshamans the gate so they didn't attack Odin… her father would object to that.

But would the rest of the world? The citizens of Odin who wanted only to live their days without worrying about being bombed?

Her mind whirled, and she barely noticed the trip across the street and into the headquarters building. It wasn't until she had been left, sans her bodyguards and Chasca, in Chief Van Dijk's office that she yanked her mind back to her current dilemma. Neither her mother nor the chief was inside. If they were having that meeting she'd envisioned, it was taking place in another room.

Oku gripped her chin and eyed a tablet resting on the desk, thinking of Casmir's request, but an Intelligence chief would have passcodes and fingerprint security on any computer she used. Besides, even if Oku could figure out where the gate pieces were, should she tell Casmir?

Time limped past, and she dropped her hand, realizing that Van Dijk might have decided to question Maddie and Rokuro—under the influence of truth drugs?—before coming to speak with her. If so, they might reveal Casmir's location, not to mention the location of all the others who were hiding out at the Asger castle. It wouldn't take them long to muster shuttles and troops to send in.

Oku wished she had told Casmir to leave. Maybe he would guess the need to do so regardless.

Are you being questioned? she messaged Maddie.

Maddie didn't answer.

LAYERS OF FORCE

Biting her lip, Oku walked around the perimeter of the office, half pacing, half looking around for clues that would be helpful in dealing with Van Dijk.

On one side, full bookcases filled the wall. On the opposite side of the office, rows of displays were mounted behind a flimsy curtain. She tugged the curtain aside to reveal numerous news feeds from different networks as well as security-camera footage from around the castle. Some of the cameras she was familiar with—others she hadn't known about. Like the one showing the hallway outside of her family's suites, including hers.

By now, it shouldn't surprise her that Royal Intelligence kept close tabs on them, but there was something chilling about seeing the evidence here. At least the camera wasn't *inside* her suite. Though she supposed there could be one in there and that it wasn't currently showing on these displays. A chill went through her as she imagined someone watching that conversation she'd had with Rache.

Her gaze drifted to a display in an upper corner where a camera showed a view starkly different from the castle shots or the news feeds. An armored soldier with his helmet on and his faceplate down stood guard in front of massive metal doors set into an ice wall. The ground appeared to also be ice under a thin layer of packed snow. The soldier and the doors lay in shadow, which made her think this scene was in a cave rather than out in the open.

Wherever it was, it wasn't anywhere around here. A few hundred miles up the coast, there were glaciers, but she'd never seen a door set into a glacier.

Oku rocked back as she realized what she might be viewing. The place where the gate pieces were hidden?

Those doors were large enough for them to have been slid in through. And it would make sense that Chief Van Dijk would keep tabs on the stash, to make sure their guard was in place and nothing had been disturbed.

Before she'd consciously decided what to do with the information, she recorded a few seconds of the display. Nothing happened during that time—the guard didn't so much as retract his faceplate to scratch his nose—and there was nothing besides the ice itself to suggest where in the world this was, but maybe it would be enough for Casmir to figure it out.

If she wanted him to. Did she? Or would he only make matters worse for everyone?

No, no matter what his affiliation was to Rache, Oku believed that Casmir wanted to help people. To protect them. It was her father that she doubted. Rather than keeping the peace, he'd been picking fights with other governments, and his actions had brought enemies to their doorstep.

But she hesitated. Afraid she would make a mistake or that *Casmir* would.

The door opened. Oku almost jumped to drag the curtain closed, but Chief Van Dijk was already walking in. Willing her heart to still, Oku clasped her hands behind her back and turned slowly. So what if she'd been looking at the displays? What had Van Dijk expected after leaving her alone in here for so long?

After shutting the door, Van Dijk leaned her hip against her desk, folded her arms over her chest, and stared at Oku with a dyspeptic expression on her face.

Oku, certain she was about to be dragged off to a dungeon cell, sent the footage of the display off to Casmir. If she ended up in a room that kept her from accessing the network, she might not get another chance.

They did question us, came Maddie's delayed response. *Rokuro and me together. They just left.*

Do they know where Casmir and the others are now?

They didn't ask about that.

Aware of Van Dijk watching, Oku was careful not to let the surprise—or skepticism—show on her face. *What did they ask about?*

If Rache is still on the planet and if we knew where Finn was being kept.

They do *know we broke out Casmir, right?*

They didn't ask about him.

At all? Are you messing with me, Maddie? Did they use a truth drug on you? Oku remembered how loopy she'd been after her own session with a truth drug.

They did. They asked how we enjoyed the tunnels under the city. I got the impression that they think that's where we spent the night.

"I suppose this is the point where I should berate you soundly," Van Dijk finally spoke.

"Are you allowed to do that?"

"Yes. I can't paddle you or throttle you, but berating is allowed."

"Are you trying to be funny, Chief?"

"Rarely." Van Dijk lowered her arms. "Was he everything you expected?"

"Uh?" Oku had no trouble guessing who she meant, but for a wild moment, she wondered if Van Dijk knew about and referenced her meeting with Rache, and she was afraid to incriminate herself. Though a part of her wanted to confess to that meeting. Had she known Rache's presence in the castle would result in Finn being taken…

"Professor Dabrowski," Van Dijk said dryly.

"He was what I expected, yes."

"I *did* want to throttle you last night when we found out that you and he were gone. That was before we found a freshly cut hole in the top of your linen closet."

Oku froze, not having to feign the horror on her face as she waited for the hammer to fall.

"Thanks to your *crush*—" Van Dijk waved her hand and lifted her gaze heavenward, "—it looks like you missed being in your suite when Rache came looking for you. You could be dead now if you'd been there. I trust you caught the news at some point during your skulk through the old subway tunnels and know Finn is gone."

Oku nodded, afraid to trust her tongue if she spoke.

"We know he's at least kidnapped, but we don't have any proof that he's not dead. The same as Jorg." Bleakness flashed across Van Dijk's angular face, and she turned away and gripped her desk with both hands. "I couldn't have done anything about Jorg, of course, but that bastard stole Finn right out from under our noses. *My* nose. Your mother is furious with me."

It slowly dawned on her that Van Dijk had no idea that Oku had spoken to Rache and didn't seem to care that much that she'd broken out Casmir. Or where he was now.

"I'm sorry," Oku said quietly.

"I'm relieved *you* came back, so I can return one child to her. I was starting to doubt our assumption that you were with Dabrowski, and believe that Rache plucked you out of the city along with Finn."

"Has he sent any demands?"

"No. Nothing. We assume his ship is in orbit somewhere—I've had to tell your father about this, and his warship with the slydar detector is searching up there for sign of the *Fedallah*, but the range on that device is poor. We need every ship up there to have one." Van Dijk took a steadying breath, and when she turned back to face Oku, her face had returned to an expression of hard-to-read professionalism. "If your father weren't so dead set on punishing Dabrowski, we could have had him slaving away in a factory, making more of those slydar detectors. We did get copies of the schematics that he sent to the *Osprey*'s programmer and are trying to get manufacturing equipment tooled to reproduce them quickly, but apparently, only he can build them overnight using pliers, duct tape, and spit."

"That… sounds right," Oku said carefully, having no trouble reading Van Dijk's frustration in the snark. She still didn't know where she stood with the woman.

A light knock sounded at the door.

"Come in," Van Dijk called.

Oku's mother strode in, her chin up and her back straight, but her eyes puffy and bloodshot. "Thank you, Chief."

Guilt returned full force as Oku realized that her mother must have been up all night worrying about her and Finn.

"I'm sorry, Mother," Oku blurted preemptively.

"I'm extremely angry with you." Her mother came over and hugged her fiercely. "And I'm glad he didn't get you."

Oku returned the hug, tempted to blurt out everything about Rache. But Van Dijk spoke first.

"Princess Oku has informed me that Professor Dabrowski was everything she expected."

Mother lowered her arms and stepped back. "In bed or just in general?"

"What?" Oku stumbled back, her shoulder blades bumping one of the displays. "There weren't any *beds*."

"There's a lack of hotels in the old subway tunnels," Van Dijk said.

"Young people make do," Mother said.

Oku stared back and forth between them, and it took her a moment to identify the hint of humor lurking amid the more prominent exasperation. It took even longer for it to dawn on her that Chief Van Dijk and her mother might be friends—friends who'd been discussing Oku's video messages to Casmir and her demands to have all the reports on him sent to her? Dear stars, was her interest in Casmir some ongoing joke between them?

Had they not looked so tired and beaten down, Oku might have asked. But there was far more frustration and worry than humor in their eyes, and she reminded herself that Finn was missing—at the least. He could be dead by now.

Still, they were looking at her, as if waiting for an answer.

"If you must know," Oku said, not having to feign stiffness, "we were interrupted before we even got a chance to kiss for more than two seconds. Also, he was smelly from being Father's prisoner and locked up for weeks."

This morning, he hadn't been. He'd been adorable in those oversized pajamas, sitting out in the grass barefoot and lost in thought. No, not lost in thought. His thoughts had been directed toward gathering information for her in a few hours that others hadn't been able to in weeks.

"Two seconds isn't very long to make a proper assessment of anything," Van Dijk said.

"Indeed not," Mother said.

Oku's cheeks warmed. It wasn't that she hadn't *wanted* it to be longer…

Hoping they dropped the subject, Oku said, "He sent me all the information he could find on Sir Slayer and his cohorts. Do you want it?"

"Yes," Van Dijk said promptly.

"That's the one we believe was responsible for Chasca's kidnapping and the attempt on Oku's life?" Mother asked her.

"Yes," Van Dijk repeated, then flicked her fingers toward Oku. Wanting the file immediately?

Oku forwarded a copy and waited as Van Dijk skimmed through everything.

Mother rested a hand on Oku's shoulder. "We're not sure where Rache is, so the chief and I have agreed that you'll stay here in Intelligence Headquarters under the watchful eyes of *many* guards, at least for the time being. She's beefing up security in the castle, but we don't know how he got in, and until we figure that out, there's the possibility that he'll return the same way. He loathes your father, and it seems he's decided to extend that hatred toward his children."

After her strange chat with Rache, Oku doubted that she had anything to fear from him, but she couldn't explain that to them without explaining *everything*. A part of her wanted to come clean, but the guilt and shame of knowing she might have stopped Finn's kidnapping if she'd immediately reported Rache—or if she'd screamed when he'd first shown up in her suite—made her want to take that secret to the grave.

"I have no idea how he feels about me," her mother added, "but someone has to remain in the castle and keep a semblance of order while all this is going on. Otherwise, I'd be tempted to take residence in the apartment adjacent to yours. We're hoping that if we don't tell many people about it, if he returns, he won't know you're here."

"I see," Oku said.

Having to stay here wasn't the worst thing—not by far—that she'd imagined as a consequence of her actions, so she didn't object to it. She had a feeling it meant she wouldn't be able to leave any time soon to see Casmir or anyone else, but if he figured out the location of the soldier in the video she'd sent him, he might not be in the area much longer anyway.

"We'll have some of your belongings brought over," Van Dijk said. "Please cooperate and don't try to escape to meet anyone for midnight trysts."

Oku blushed again. "That wasn't my plan."

"Good. Given your father's stance on Dabrowski, you'll forgive me for saying that these words can't leave this office—and I'll vehemently deny it if you spread them—but I don't care where he is, and I've made finding Finn our priority. Our search for Dabrowski will be noncommittal." Van Dijk looked toward Mother, who nodded back.

"I've seen the same reports you have, Oku," Mother said. "I know he wasn't responsible for Jorg's death, and we know who was."

Oku nodded carefully, afraid to show too much relief.

"If anyone, specifically your father, asks, Royal Intelligence is looking for Dabrowski," Van Dijk said, "but given his record, I'm hoping that left to his own devices, he might have a way to get rid of those astroshamans before they destroy our world."

The way Van Dijk looked intently at Oku made her think the chief wanted her to relay exactly that message.

"I understand," Oku said, not hinting at what Casmir might actually do.

She doubted Van Dijk would be as willing to leave Casmir alone if she knew he wanted to find the gate pieces. For all Oku knew, he meant to chuck them into space for the astroshamans to collect in the hope that they would leave Odin alone.

That could backfire—they could take them and *still* attack Odin. She hoped Casmir had more in mind than that. If she later learned she'd made a mistake by sending that video clip to him...

"I'm glad," Van Dijk said. "Come. I'll show you to your new subterranean apartment."

"Subterranean?"

LAYERS OF FORCE

"The lack of windows makes it harder for someone to sneak in and kidnap you. After last night, you should be used to it."

"It sounds like a dungeon cell," Oku pointed out.

"It's furnished."

"Well, that makes it all right then."

Van Dijk looked at Mother. "Are you sure I can't paddle her?"

"There are rules about physically abusing members of the royal family," Mother said.

"That's a shame."

"So I've been told."

Oku sighed and let Van Dijk lead her to her new furnished dungeon cell.

CHAPTER 19

CASMIR SAT WITH TRISTAN AND KIM AT ONE end of the massive dining-hall table while several of the crushers loomed protectively behind him. His father read from his weathered and much beloved Torah at the other end, hopefully not while praying for Casmir's soul.

He'd given his support when they'd spoken, and his mother had shared something similar that morning, but Casmir couldn't help but doubt himself.

Would his parents ever be able to go home? Would Jager send a thousand assassins after him? Was the idea now percolating in his mind insane? And if it was, would Oku have helped him by sending a recording?

He, Tristan, and Kim were staring at it on a tablet now, studying the few seconds of footage of a guard standing in front of huge metal doors in what looked like an ice cave. She hadn't sent any information related to it, but he assumed she believed this was the resting place of the Kingdom's five gate pieces. She *had* sent word that, while the king still wanted Casmir dead, Royal Intelligence was looking for Rache and Finn, and Casmir wasn't a priority for them. She'd implied that neither Chief Van Dijk nor the queen was that irked with him.

At least someone wasn't.

"Somewhere in the Arctic?" Tristan mused.

"It could be an ice cave up in the mountains closer to here," Kim pointed out.

"I'm looking up a list of military bases to see if any are located in particularly frosty places. It's too bad there's not a feed source or file name or any otherwise useful text on the video." Casmir touched an empty black band at the bottom of the display. "I might be able to let myself in to look at the transmissions being relayed through the various military satellites orbiting Odin, but there are a lot of them to check."

"How many is a lot?" Tristan asked.

"Ah, two hundred and eighty. Let me download some new programs to assist with accessing them."

"Assist?"

"Hack into illegally," Kim explained.

Casmir waved his fingers, letting them continue the discussion while he worked.

"What are we going to do if we find out where the gate pieces are located?" Tristan asked. "Tell the astroshamans where to get them? That seems…"

"Treasonous?" Kim suggested. "We are already fugitives."

"Technically," Tristan said, "I think I'm only exiled."

"Yeah, but you came back. That makes you a fugitive."

"Damn, I think you're right."

"Of course."

"I have an idea regarding the gate pieces." Casmir had his eyes closed, working while he spoke. "But we'll need a ship."

"To *steal* the pieces and give them to the astroshamans in person?" Kim frowned.

"If we had them in a ship, we could lead the astroshamans away from Odin. If Moonrazor is chasing us, she has no reason to unleash a virus or a bunch of bombs on our home world."

"She'll just unleash them on us? Might I point out that we don't have access to a ship? We had to ditch Rache's shuttle in the woods, where I'm sure it's been picked up by the authorities. It wouldn't have been large enough to carry those gate pieces anyway."

"I didn't say my idea was fully formed," Casmir said.

"I'll say. Casmir, if we give the pieces to our enemies and never see them again, Jager is going to hate you more than ever."

"I know. I would much rather negotiate with the astroshamans and the rest of the Twelve Systems to assemble the gate here on Odin or in a central location where everyone can use it. Why can't everyone see how logical that would be? Why all this fighting?"

"Because humans aren't good at sharing."

"The other thought I've had," Casmir said slowly, "is that we could *pretend* we're bringing the astroshamans the gate pieces, and then trick them and—if we're very, very lucky—defeat them."

"Allowing the Kingdom to get *all* of the pieces and control the future gate once it's assembled?" Kim asked.

"If the astroshamans have them all with them on one ship, yes." Casmir couldn't help but feel glum at the thought of betraying Moonrazor. If he could pull it off, it could turn him from criminal to hero, but it also meant acting against someone who'd helped him.

Kim leaned back, appearing far more speculative than glum. Tristan also raised his eyebrows.

"I wouldn't assume that Jager is predictable, but that *might* be enough to earn you a pardon from him." Kim looked at Tristan. "Maybe it could earn us all pardons."

Tristan might have a new life in another system with Nalini, but that didn't keep him from looking wistful.

Casmir's gut twisted. Was this what he had to do to assure the safety and happiness of his friends and family? Was it what Oku would want?

"How do you think we could defeat the astroshamans?" Tristan asked curiously. "When they've been annihilating Kingdom warships since they came into the system?"

"Could you not tag their ships, Casmir Dabrowski?" Zee asked. "As you did before with Tork's assistance?"

"Using their own technology, yes." Tristan clenched a fist.

"That's a possibility I can look into if I get up to orbit in a ship with weapons—we altered the laser cannons on Nalini's ship. It might be simpler to acquire a ship down here, get the gate pieces, pretend we're going to flee, then allow ourselves to be captured by the astroshamans right along with our cargo. If we took a team of combat specialists in—maybe Rache would like to join us—we could take over their ship from within. And hope it's the one with all the high shamans on it. You saw that broadcast they did. They were all together in one room."

"We can't trust Rache," Tristan said. "He kidnapped Finn. Among many other worse crimes."

"We have a sufficiently large and advanced combat force to take over a ship without his assistance," one of the crushers said.

That was Naphtali, one of the original dozen that Casmir had made on Stardust Palace. Several of the others here were crushers that had been liberated from Jorg's ship. He hadn't gotten around to naming them before he'd been captured.

"Yes," another crusher said. "We have been training. While the humans sleep, we train. We can best any enemy, human or astroshaman."

"Let's not let overconfidence be our downfall, friends." Casmir smiled. "We're going to need a ship first. And to sneak in and get those gate pieces. Without hurting anyone, because this is our world and these are our people." Casmir waved to the soldier standing guard on the video. "Unfortunately, I don't think they'll believe we're helping them."

"They never do," Kim murmured.

Casmir touched his temple as the results he'd been waiting for came in. "That's it."

"What?" Tristan asked.

"There's a small marine base in the Arctic Islands where they do cold-weather training. The public data doesn't say anything about a secret vault in an ice cave, but the big satellite dish I've located at the base is transmitting a steady feed up to military satellite MF-4573U, which is relaying the information to the capital, both to a Military Intelligence office and to Royal Intelligence Headquarters."

"You can tell all that by hacking into a network?" Tristan asked.

"Everything that's done with a networked computer or comm is out there," Casmir said. "It's just a matter finding the needle in the haystack."

"How are we going to find a spaceship big enough to get the gate pieces off the planet?" Kim asked. "I assume you plan to head into space, not fly over the ocean or someplace unpopulated."

"Space, yes. I don't want the astroshamans to have any reason to fire at Odin."

"If you win, won't they consider doing it out of revenge?" Tristan asked. "Virus aside, which maybe we shouldn't put aside, they may have the firepower with them to wreck our entire system."

"I've only dealt with Moonrazor, and to some extent Dubashi, but I'm going to base what I know of their kind on her, since it didn't sound like he was truly of the faith, as they define it…" Casmir prodded a whorl in the old wood table. "I don't think revenge is their style. I'm not one hundred percent sure they aren't bluffing. I wouldn't want to call that bluff, but so far, the astroshamans have mostly attacked ships with gates. The four that were guarding the gate were an exception, but they could have annihilated Forseti Station and done a lot more damage along the way if they wished. They were surgical in their precision."

"It's a lot to gamble on," Tristan said.

"I know," Casmir said. "Let's focus first on getting a ship and getting that cargo. Once we're in that position, we can adapt as the situation requires."

Asger and Bjarke walked in, shirtless and sweaty after some sparring match.

"Just the men I want to see." Casmir lifted his hands to them. "Does either of you have contacts or any ideas about where we could get a spaceship capable of holding a few gate pieces that is ideally extremely fast and with excellent armor?" He feared that such a ship didn't exist.

Asger's and Bjarke's stunned slack-mouthed expressions were so similar that it was almost proof they were related.

Casmir outlined his fledgling plan to them.

"We can't steal the gate pieces from our own military," Bjarke protested. "Nor can we steal a *spaceship*. We're already outcasts, if not hunted felons." He cast a forlorn look around the dining hall, as if he knew that once he left, he would never see his ancestral home again.

Casmir didn't want to promise that they would all end up heroes—Kim was right that it was impossible to predict how Jager would react even if they *did* manage to save Odin.

"I can't sign off on that either, Casmir. Even with all of your buddies—" Asger pointed to the crushers, "—sneaking into a military base and stealing a spaceship wouldn't be possible. We'd all end up dead, and then where would the planet be?"

Casmir went over the satellite imagery of the Arctic base again, wondering if there might be ships up there. The gate pieces had to have been delivered, after all. They could have been dropped off, but wouldn't the military have planned for the eventuality that they would have to be moved?

In addition to the big satellite dish, the imagery showed two buildings and a hangar. It wasn't large enough to store a spaceship, not the size the large pieces would require. A couple of lumpy white mounds adjacent to the base made him pause and zoom in to maximum magnification. There weren't any other hills on the flat snowy ground around the base.

"Camouflaged ships?" he mused.

"*Casmir*," Bjarke said warningly, as if he could guess what Casmir was researching. "We're not stealing a ship."

"All right. We'll rent a shuttle for a ride to the base and check things out. Does anyone have a pilot's license who isn't wanted by the Kingdom Guard?"

Casmir's father was watching them with fascination—or maybe that was morbid horror—his chin resting in his hand. Maybe Casmir should have chosen a more private place for this plotting session.

"We're *all* wanted now," Bjarke said. "We couldn't rent a bicycle, much less a shuttle."

"Maybe Oku would lend us her pilot bodyguard, Rokuro," Casmir said.

"Won't anything derail you?" Bjarke demanded.

A long shudder shook the ground, startling them all. Casmir gripped the table.

"What is that?" Asger spun a circle. "Earthquake?"

A distant roar came from the sky to the west.

"No," Bjarke said grimly. "Something is flying by. Something very large."

Tristan ran and got his tablet, returning with the news already on. Casmir accessed the public and military networks.

"Invisible enemy ships are already here," he said numbly, summing up what he found. "There's been bombing on the Southern continent and also farther down our coast. Some of the astroshaman ships must have gotten past our fleet. Jager has engaged other enemies in orbit. He's able to see some of them with the slydar detector, and he's trying to lead the Fleet to attack them, but the range is so short, he's hobbled. Damn, why didn't they get more of those slydar detectors made yet?"

"It is unfortunate that we are not up there with Tork to mark the ships," Zee said.

"No kidding."

Tristan, Asger, Bjarke, and Kim—and now Casmir's father and mother joined them—stared in horror at the tablet as a reporter relayed what was happening and showed footage. Casmir had dozens of reports scrolling down his contact display, absorbing them as rapidly as his mind could work.

"Maybe it's not too late to help them up there," he said. "That program Tork used is on my old chip. If Jager still has my chip on his warship and could plug it into the computer up there… Well, they couldn't get in without my access codes, but I could offer them. If he'd accept the help. Maybe if I go through Oku." Casmir nodded, already composing a message to her with the information.

The tablet showed bombs dropping from orbit and slamming into hillsides above cities. It was horrifying, but Casmir noticed right away that the astroshamans weren't picking populated areas. Maybe this was still meant to be a warning.

"We still have time," he whispered as he sent the suggestion about his chip to Oku, promising to help the *Starhawk* access it.

"We have to do Casmir's plan," Asger said. "What else *can* we do but get what they want away from Odin?"

Bjarke swore. "We'll never survive this. We can't single-handedly take out the astroshamans."

"What choice do we have?" Asger pointed to the sky. "Are we going to stay here and wait for one of their bombs to drop on us?"

"All right." Bjarke gripped Casmir's shoulder. "What's Step One?"

"We find a way to get down to that base and hope there's a ship there."

"If there's not?"

"Then… we comm Moonrazor and tell her we've found the gate but that she has to come down and get it."

"Shit."

Casmir spread his arms. "Jager should have been willing to make that choice without us. If he won't give up a few artifacts to protect the planet, *I* will."

"I may know where we could get a ship." Tristan looked at Asger. "Of sorts."

Asger rolled his eyes. "That thing isn't going to fly."

"What thing?" Bjarke asked.

"I bet Casmir can fix it," Tristan said.

"It's more than two *hundred* years old," Asger said.

Casmir lifted his brows, not certain whether to be encouraged by this conversation or not. Maybe he shouldn't promise he could fix it until he knew what it was, but he found himself saying, "If you have tools…"

Bjarke gripped Asger's shoulder. "*What?*"

"Grandfather's helicopter," Asger said.

"The rusty derelict in the barn?"

"It's a Cloud Hopper 870," Tristan said, "and the engine looked to be intact."

Bjarke rubbed the heel of his palm against his forehead. Hard.

"Uhm, I could take a look." Casmir called up the model and schematics on the network.

"If you can get it running," Asger said, "we've got a ride. It's even big enough to carry everyone. If we kick out the owls."

"Get me whatever tools you have, and I'll do my best," Casmir said. "Uh, there's fuel for it, right?"

"We've got a tank for the old brush-clearing and logging equipment that isn't electric," Bjarke said. "*Fuel* isn't the problem."

Judging from Bjarke's continuing skeptical expression, Casmir would need more than a few tools for this job.

"I'll get it running." Casmir hoped his smile was convincing. "Everyone else, pack up if you're going."

"I'll get the tools." Bjarke trotted for the door.

"I'll tell Qin and her sisters and see if they'll help us with this crazy mission." Asger sent an aggrieved look toward the tablet and the horrors playing on the news and also ran out.

The ground shuddered again. Not simply from the passage of aircraft, Casmir feared, but from bombs being dropped nearby. Hopefully, on the Kingdom Forest and not the city, but a lurch of fear went through him. If he was wrong, and they targeted the capital, Oku and all of his university colleagues and students were in danger.

Casmir turned, intending to grab the clothes and handful of toiletries he'd borrowed—so little for such a dangerous trip—but he spotted his father and mother watching the carnage. He gripped their arms. "I'm going to stop this. One way or another. You guys can stay here. It's probably safer than in the city, and Oku said Royal Intelligence isn't looking for me right now."

"I should think not." His mother's gaze was riveted on the news.

"We'll stay here," his father said, then hugged him. "I have faith that you will do the right thing."

"Thanks," Casmir rasped, his throat thick with emotion—what if he never saw them again? "I need to go fix a helicopter."

"Have you done that before?"

"I made a robot bird from scratch earlier this year. Almost the same thing." His father snorted. "*Almost.*"

Casmir hugged them both and ran to collect his gear.

LAYERS OF FORCE

"I can see again, Doc. This is great."

Yas patted his patient on the shoulder and returned his tools to his medical kit. "Good. Maybe you can refrain from stopping a punch with your eye again this week."

"I'll try, but we're all getting antsy for some action. Antsy mercenaries get in fights."

"Given that Rache kidnapped the king's son and is storing him in the brig, a fight should be guaranteed soon."

Yas had no wish to see battle, but it seemed inevitable. The last he'd heard, more Kingdom ships were flying search patterns around Odin, trying to find the *Fedallah*. Amergin had picked up intel that the Kingdom was fast-tracking the creation of more slydar detectors, so it would soon be a lot harder to stay hidden, as long as they remained in the area. Yas doubted there was anything he could say to convince Rache to *leave* the area—the entire Kingdom system, ideally.

"I hope so. Those astroshaman ships are supposed to arrive in a couple of days, and then the Kingdom might be so busy dealing with them, that they'll forget about us."

"I believe Rache is hoping for that."

"Yeah, so we can sneak in and thump that stupid Kingdom king." A fist to the palm offered an exclamation mark on the enthusiastic statement. "Are we done here?"

The door to sickbay opened, and Rache strode in.

"Yes. Go ahead. Remember, avoid blocking punches with your eye."

"Will do, Doc." The man saluted Yas and Rache, a habit left from whatever service he'd been in before becoming a mercenary, and fled sickbay.

"Grab your kit and come, Doctor." Rache tilted his head toward the exit.

"You're taking me on a trip? Exciting. How's your arm? Has it healed itself, or did you staple it together in your cabin and hope for the best?"

Yas couldn't *see* Rache's arm through his armor, but he didn't appear to be favoring it. The armor had either been repaired or replaced—it lacked holes and dents, and its owner once again appeared grim and formidable.

"My advanced regenerative capabilities have sufficiently healed my wounds," Rache said as they walked into the corridor.

"Must be nice."

"It is useful in my career. You will examine Prince Finn before I send him back and ensure he's hale. I understand he played possum last night when his meal was delivered and tried to jump Corporal Chains and escape."

"How far did he get?"

"As far as Corporal Chains' fist."

"So not out of his cell?"

"Correct."

Rache's earlier words sank in, and Yas paused before they reached the lift. "Wait, you're letting him go?"

"I am."

"Why? I thought… well, you went through all that work to capture him."

"The whole secret lies in confusing the enemy, so that he cannot fathom our real intent." Rache sounded like he was quoting some ancient text.

"Is confusing your doctor also a goal?"

"Finn has agreed to pardon me if I kill his father. Since Dubashi can no longer pay me for that mission, my interest is keen." Rache stepped into the lift, holding the door open for Yas.

It took Yas a moment to force his legs to work again. "I know you want to kill Jager anyway, and probably don't care if anyone pays you or not, but do you actually believe Finn *would*? He would say anything to get you to let him go. You can't seriously be thinking of working with him."

The lift doors shut, and Rache gazed over at him. The mask hid his expression, but Yas had the feeling he was missing something—and that Rache was disappointed that he'd missed it.

"You know I have my own agenda in regard to Jager, but I've recorded Finn's promises, the meeting you saw and another one in which we supposedly ironed out the details of how I will serve him." When they reached their floor, Rache hit a button to keep the lift doors from opening. "I will find a way to distribute the recordings, either to the Senate or perhaps to the entire population. I am considering sending them to Jager as well, but I doubt he's under any delusions when it comes to his son. Still, it would amuse me to orchestrate a father-son showdown, during which they would attempt to kill each other."

Amuse? That sounded horrifying. "What do you hope to accomplish with the recordings? Beyond familial showdowns."

"Ensure that Jager won't name Finn as his heir and that if Finn tries to force the issue, nobody will support him. Not after he's made a deal with *me*."

"I think if those astroshamans get that gate working, you should follow them through it to another system and forget all about the Kingdom for the rest of your life."

"I see you're still speaking your mind around me, Doctor."

"You keep forgetting to flog the insubordination out of me."

"Such an important thing to forget. I must be getting senile." Rache gave Yas a long considering look.

Yas fought the urge to squirm and remove Rache's finger from the button that kept the doors from opening. What was he plotting now, and what role would Yas be forced to play?

"It has occurred to me," Rache said, "that if *I* distribute these videos, people will believe them fabricated. Perhaps if you, the doctor I forced into servitude to me for five years against your wishes, were to distribute them, their veracity might not be questioned. As someone who naturally resents me, you could be attempting to make me look like a fiend for considering Finn's offer, just as Finn would look like a fiend for creating it."

"And what would I, someone who naturally resents you, stand to gain from sharing these videos?"

"On Tiamat Station, your previous president may have been assassinated by a Kingdom agent, and the vice president who stepped in, however briefly, was a puppet of the Kingdom. Perhaps you wish to see civil war or the establishment of an entirely new regime on this planet, to ensure that the Kingdom is too busy with inner turmoil to bother Tiamat Station again."

"Is that what's coming? A new regime?"

"They'll have to figure out something if Jager and Jorg are dead, Oku doesn't want the job, and nobody trusts Finn enough to follow." Rache tilted his head. "I could simply kill Finn, but Kim said that would be egregious and villainous."

"She's not wrong. What are her thoughts on the assassination of Jager?"

"She also believes that to be egregious and villainous."

"But you're planning to do it anyway?"

"Yes. A goal of ten years cannot be cast aside, even for the love of a woman."

Yas never would have guessed he would hear Rache use the word love. He wondered if he'd told Kim how he felt—and if she was horrified. Yas would be.

"A goal or an obsession?" Yas asked. "Because I have some opinions on the health of obsessions."

"I don't come for your physical exams, so you can be certain I won't visit for your mental-health assessments."

"A shame."

Rache released the button. "After we've let Finn go, I'll find someone for you to send the recordings to, someone who could get them out to the entire system. There's a big broadcast station on the moon here—I believe that's what the astroshamans hijacked for their message—but there's also one on Forseti Station. That would likely be less well guarded now. I wonder..." Rache strolled out of the lift, musing whatever he mused.

Yas wondered if it would be less of a crime to murder Finn than to ruin his life. Maybe that was why Rache was choosing the latter.

CHAPTER 20

THE WIND FROM THE HELICOPTER BLADES BENT THE grass and tugged at Kim's ponytail. The rusty craft looked as airworthy as a kite struck by lightning and careening toward a treetop. Large, bronze-colored—or maybe *made* from bronze—and bulbous, the helicopter tilted precariously as Bjarke flew it from the barn up the hill to land on the driveway. That Casmir had gotten such a relic flying at all was a miracle.

Asger, Bjarke, Tristan, Qin, her sisters, and most of the crushers were lined up and ready to hop in. Judging by the size of its cabin, the helicopter had been designed to carry troops, but Kim wondered if it could truly take all of them.

Casmir hugged his parents goodbye, got a sad look on his face when his father gravely said, "*Shalom aleichem*, my son," and came to stand beside Kim as the others climbed into the noisy craft.

"You're sure you don't want to come with us?" he asked her.

"Yes, I'm sure, and I came out here to ask you if you're sure *you* need to go. They're all combat specialists." Kim pointed at their burly colleagues. "You're not. You said Royal Intelligence doesn't care about you right now and isn't searching for you. Why not stay here and play with the networks from the relative safety of the countryside? We're surrounded by woods and farms. I doubt a bomber is going to target this place."

"Play with the networks? Kim, I am engaged in monitoring and, when appropriate, sophisticated and discreet manipulation of data."

"Uh huh. You can do that from your guest room in the castle. That helicopter doesn't look like it'll be able to fly more than ten miles without crashing."

"There's a metal box in the back with parachutes in it."

"Heartening. Are they from this century?"

"I didn't look that closely, but judging from the dust covering them, perhaps not."

"Casmir... I don't fault you for wanting to do this—I think you're right and that the best thing is to get those gate pieces off Odin—but would Admiral Mikita have flung himself into the middle of the danger?"

"I don't know. Maybe?"

"Assuming he had your stature and a few medical issues, I doubt he ran in at the head of the troops and punched down his enemies. Look at any battle in history. The fleet admirals sent in their ships and their troops to accomplish the mission. They didn't lead the way themselves."

"Those historical admirals didn't have to be there to crack the door codes to let their troops in."

"You can't tell me you can't do that remotely."

"It's possible that I won't be able to, especially if something is hardwired and not on the network. I appreciate you wanting to keep me safe, but... I have to lead." Casmir shrugged and smiled. "This is my idea. I can't ask others to risk themselves while I hide somewhere safe."

"I feel like you're a cat with nine lives and that you may have used up eight of them by now. You and Rache both." Kim hung her head at the idea of losing both of them, Casmir to his idealism, Rache to his obsession.

"That is possible. But I'll try to live. I would like to kiss Oku for more than two seconds before I die."

"You should have done that before she left."

"I *tried*. We were interrupted. The universe is not being considerate."

"That's the understatement of the millennium."

Casmir glanced at the helicopter. Bjarke was waving for him to get in.

"You'll keep an eye on my parents?" Casmir asked.

"Of course. And... I am working on something and will continue to do so while you're off risking your life. In my arrogance, I believe it could be important and that I should finish." Kim opened her mouth to explain further, but Bjarke yelled for him to hurry up.

Casmir nodded at her. "Good. I'm glad, and I believe you. I'm leaving however many crushers won't fit in the craft, and they'll protect you. Just in case trouble finds you here, Bjarke said there's a basement bunker and also tunnels underneath the castle that lead off into the woods.

You access them through the ancient suit of armor on the pedestal in the great hall. There's also a trapdoor under his bed."

Kim doubted tunnels would be of much use if the astroshamans bombed the area, but she nodded.

Casmir hugged her, then ran to jump into the craft. It took off immediately, leaving three crushers behind. The helicopter wobbled, and she didn't know if it was from its advanced age or the great weight it carried.

There wasn't time to ask, Casmir messaged. *What are you working on? A vaccine for the virus?*

No. I sent all the information I had on that to my colleagues at the lab as soon as we entered the system. Kim hesitated to explain what she *was* working on, but of all people, Casmir should support her. He hadn't even told her how nuts she was lately to date Rache. *I'm taking my experiences and all the reports Oku sent me and writing a novel about everything that's happened. Rache said he would publish a novel for me, and I... This is going to sound arrogant, Casmir, but I think it may be the best way to get the truth out there in a way that people would pay attention to. Well, a movie would be better, since... Well, how many people actually read? But maybe it could make a difference. If the people of the Kingdom saw what their king and his sons had been doing—and what we've been doing—maybe they would care enough to fight the system. What do you think?*

She held her breath, realizing how idealistic that all sounded, and maybe she was foolish to believe this was worth doing right now. It was the kind of thing that one did *after* all the fighting was over, wasn't it? But if she waited for that, she might be dead. They all might be.

I'm skeptical of Rache as your publisher, Casmir replied after a minute, *but I like your idea. My father and I were talking last night about the need to educate the people, and a story is a lot easier to swallow than a lecture. Make sure to write the book so it's fun and exciting, so the common man will like it. Like your thriller! Don't use big science words. Or anything over four syllables.*

Kim folded her arms over her chest. She hadn't been planning to write something inaccessible, but she didn't think it needed to be overly simplistic. *Do you want me to let you draw pictures to go with it?*

Can I?

No.

You're a tease. My art is fabulous.

Your stick figures are dreadful. I don't know how someone who can draft sophisticated schematics can't draw a cartoon dog.

You can use rulers, protractors, and compasses on schematics. Straight lines look funny on dogs.

How obnoxious.

I know! Nature should have made itself more geometric.

After gaining enough altitude, the helicopter took off toward the south, and Casmir waved out the window to Kim and his parents. Knowing Casmir, he was having rapid-fire conversations with all of them while simultaneously hacking networks and calculating the probability of success for his mission.

His parents joined Kim, Aleksy carrying a tablet, perhaps the same one Tristan had been watching the news on earlier.

"I tried to talk him into staying here with us," Kim told them, "and leaving the combat to the combat specialists, but he thinks he needs to be there to open doors for them." She should have countered Casmir's argument with the fact that his crushers could force open any doors that stood in the team's way.

"I'll admit that it's strange seeing my son *with* a team of combat specialists," Irena said.

"And knights," Aleksy murmured, though he was watching the tablet display.

"Knights *are* combat specialists, dear."

"I know, but I mean that it's even more surprising that he seems to be leading *them*."

"It appeared to be more of a democracy than a military chain of command," Irena said.

"Mm."

"I do wish he were working with our government instead of against it. I'm so worried about him. But I admit our government has been failing us of late."

"Our government has been failing us for a long time," Aleksy said. "It's only recently become trendy to point it out."

"*Is* it trendy now?" Had Kim been off the planet for long enough to miss changes to the zeitgeist? She supposed so.

"Since the bombings. The *last* bombings." Irena looked warily toward the sky, gray clouds now drifting in from the sea and threatening to blot out the sun. "And since King Jager finagled the Senate into giving him King's Authority. Our people were scared enough to do it, but it's improved nothing."

"We need a diplomat in charge of the Kingdom now," Aleksy said, "not an autocrat."

"At least someone willing to bend and yield with the wind, not be like a rock monolith destined to crack and crumble with each earthquake."

"That's a bit of a mixed metaphor, dear."

"I'm a physical therapist, not a teacher."

"A physical therapist with an advanced degree."

"In therapy, not wordsmithing." Irena poked him in the ribs.

Aleksy smiled, but only fleetingly as his gaze remained on the tablet.

"I do hope Casmir isn't condemning himself," Irena murmured, looking to Kim, concern furrowing her brow. "Is he doing the right thing? I am concerned and somewhat disgruntled that we had to leave our apartment of many years in the middle of the night, and he doesn't know if we'll be able to go back—or stay in the Kingdom at all—but if I knew he was right, it would all be much easier to accept."

"He's trying to do *a* right thing. It may be up to the historians to decide if it's *the* right thing." Kim wondered if she *could* make a difference with her novel, an attempt to set the record straight in a way that people would appreciate. Maybe it was hubris to believe that she could do so or that anyone would read it. "I am certain that Jager is doing the *wrong* thing."

"I believe that too. I wonder if we're truly safe here." Irena glanced at the sky again—looking for more ships on bombing runs? "We didn't fly that far from the capital."

"Casmir said that Asger told him there's a bunker under the castle and escape tunnels that lead out into the forest."

"Will that keep us safe if some deadly virus is unleashed? Jager said they were threatening us with that too."

"Look at this." Aleksy turned the tablet toward his wife and waved Kim over close enough to see it. "Another message from the astroshaman leader."

"How does she keep forcing her way onto the broadcast network?" Irena huffed. "Can't Jager stop that?"

"Maybe it's best that he can't," Aleksy said. "If she weren't on the channels, we wouldn't know what the true threat is. Just like last time."

"We can't assume she's being honest with us."

"Sh." Aleksy turned up the volume.

"You may have noticed by now that our allies have entered the system," Moonrazor said, the two silent male astroshamans standing beside her and again letting her do the speaking. "A ship from Verloren Moon. They have developed an interest in the gate and have come to lend their assistance, should we need it. It's clear that we don't, that your ships, though many, cannot see us to target us, but if you were not properly concerned before, you should be now."

The view shifted from her to a big cylinder of a ship floating out in space with the wormhole gate visible in the distance behind it. Moving lights or indicators of some kind flashed all along its black sides.

It was very ominous, very alien, and looking at it filled Kim with foreboding. She caught herself eyeing the three silent crushers that Casmir had left behind. When he controlled them, she didn't mind them, but they had that same kind of ominous alienness about them. Even though they were shaped into bipedal human forms, nothing about them seemed human. Only when Zee spoke did some hint that he wasn't a big indifferent computer come out, but that was Casmir's influence, she knew, not the true nature of computers and robots. The AI ship wouldn't have any of Casmir's influence, and it might have no regard for humanity as a whole.

What had the astroshamans offered them to bestir their interest? To make them leave their moon?

"As if things weren't grim enough," Irena said.

When the recording looped to repeat, Aleksy lowered the tablet. "Perhaps we should find that bunker and those tunnels. Just in case we need them."

Kim nodded and followed them into the castle, but she worried neither tunnels nor bunkers would be enough to protect them from what was coming.

LAYERS OF FORCE

---◇---

"Sighing dramatically and looking at me with those sad puppy-dog eyes won't change anything," Oku informed Chasca, who was gazing at her while lying pitifully on towels Oku had folded into a semblance of a dog bed.

The cement floor of the subterranean apartment was gritty and hard like a swimming pool deck, and Chasca's short fur and lean build didn't give her a lot of padding. The *human* bed had only one pillow and was too small for sharing, so Oku was reserving that for herself.

"I suppose I could ask one of the guards to try to find you something more comfortable, but that seems an abuse of my royal authority, especially when the world is under attack. *Again.*" Oku sat at the studio apartment's small dining table, designing a possible new hybrid of the nutrition-packed green algae that grew well in tanks on space stations. Algae wasn't as romantic—or flavorful—as the other crops she'd worked on, but it was relatively easy to grow in space and meant the difference between a population having to supplement extensively with minerals and vitamins or not. It was a worthy project, but it was hard to concentrate when her mind kept wandering.

Chasca sighed and flopped onto her side—dramatically.

Oku picked up a tug-of-war rope toy that had slid under the table and squeaked a ball on the end. Chasca debated it for a while before coming over to chomp on the other end and pull.

"I know you'd rather be in the castle where you can run all over the grounds. Or back out at the As—out in the wilderness." She'd almost said the Asger estate, but nobody seemed to know about that yet. In case the apartment was monitored, she kept herself from mentioning it. "I wish I was there too," she whispered, though she didn't know if Casmir was still there. He was the main reason she would want to return.

She'd kept communications with him to a minimum, knowing that if her father returned, Chief Van Dijk might grow much more interested in capturing Casmir. She also might not have been honest with Oku about her indifference, hoping that she would let her guard down and lead Intelligence to him.

The last thing Casmir had sent her was a suggestion that someone with sway over the king might want to beg him to negotiate with the astroshamans rather than trying to fight them. Oku didn't know who had that kind of sway over her father. Neither she nor her mother did.

A knock sounded at the door and Chasca bounded to it, tail wagging.

"That could be a deadly assassin or nefarious kidnapper, you know." Oku raised her voice to call, "Come in."

Her mother only managed to take two steps in before Chasca swarmed her, jamming her head into her hip and wagging fiercely.

"Chasca misses her freedom," Oku said.

Mother looked a touch beleaguered as she patted the dog on the back. "I'm certain that most princesses with pets throughout history have had cats or lapdogs."

"That sounds boring."

"She almost knocked me over."

"She likes you."

"What does she do with enemies?"

"Unfortunately, she refuses to accept people as enemies." Oku clapped her hands and squeaked the toy. "Over here, girl."

After Chasca bounded away, Mother sat on the bed. "Your brother has been found."

"Oh, good. Where was he?"

"In orbit floating in an escape pod that was issuing an automatic SOS. A Fleet ship picked him up, and he'll be downside in a few hours. I'm having him brought here for his safety. He says he escaped from Rache's ship."

"He escaped? Or was let go?"

"He told the officers who collected him that he escaped from Rache's brig."

Oku thought of the short and strange conversation she'd had with the man who'd sneaked into her suite—and had been capable enough to sneak past all castle security and capture Finn. The idea of him allowing a prisoner to get away seemed ludicrous.

"Given Rache's reputation, it's a lot more likely that he let Finn go for... some reason."

"Van Dijk and I think so, too, and we'll have a doctor standing by to do scans and a thorough exam. I wouldn't put it past that criminal to have ordered a surgeon to implant Finn with a bomb programmed to go off when he's next to your father." Mother shuddered.

"That's horrible. Is that possible?"

"I don't know. I'm glad he's on his way back, but I *am* worried that it was too easy for him to get away."

Oku wondered if Casmir had heard anything—or could find out things if he hadn't. She still didn't know what to make of his relationship with Rache—David—but if he could be a conduit to Rache, it was worth using that.

"We'll keep you both down here." Mother waved to the wall—the apartment next door.

Oku managed to keep from grimacing. She didn't want Finn to die, but she also would have preferred that his apartment were on the other side of the city.

"Until all of this is over," Mother added. "One way or another."

"A friend thinks Father should negotiate with the astroshamans instead of stubbornly ignoring their demands," Oku said.

"A friend?" Her mother made a show of peering around the room, then looked at Chasca.

"Nobody has removed my chip access yet," Oku said dryly. "Though the signal down here is awful."

"Is he planning anything except lying low?"

"He?"

"Your friend," she said, equally dryly. "The friend Van Dijk is pretending she's too busy to hunt down."

"*Is* she too busy?"

"She probably won't be now that Finn is back, but…" Her mother spread her hand, palm up. "If there's a chance that he can help with this problem, she would appreciate that. She—we—may be the only ones besides you who believe he can. And that he would."

Oku thought about mentioning that Casmir had asked for the location of the gate pieces, but maybe it was best to keep his plans a secret. She didn't even *know* his plans, not for sure. So far, she was guessing.

"I don't know how to convince your father that he can be an ally and not have him executed, but I would like that. I never wanted him to be cast aside and certainly not to be killed. Not when he was born and not now. We brought him into this world, and I always felt responsible for him."

"Did Father want him killed all along? When he didn't turn out to be the genetically perfect baby he expected?"

Her mother hesitated. "He… didn't see the point in letting him live, no. We argued, and I thought I would have to smuggle him away to a foster mother. In the end, your father said he didn't care if he lived but that he was determined to start over and do it right the second time, with clean genes. A perfect baby."

Oku snorted. The perfect baby that had turned into Rache. She almost said as much, but did her mother know about that? Until he'd showed up in her suite, Oku hadn't known David had survived that crash. Survived that crash he must have orchestrated, she realized. Staging his death so he could run off and become Rache without repercussions.

"I don't mind that you've found him," her mother went on, "but do realize that your father has marriage plans for you."

Oku couldn't keep from making a face.

"True love is not a fairy tale that applies to the nobility. We must do what's best for the Kingdom." Her mother patted her shoulder and stood up.

As she walked out, Oku shook her head slowly. She didn't know yet if she wanted to marry Casmir, but she was positive that he was better for the Kingdom than some stuffy senator who thought he would get to rule through her if something happened to her father.

CHAPTER 21

"WE'RE ALMOST DONE, VIGGO." BONITA HAD FINISHED THE exterior repairs and moved inside the *Dragon* to work on systems near the hull that had been damaged. "Another day, maybe two."

"If Casmir were here," Viggo said, "the repairs would be complete by now. You are a capable mechanic, Bonita, but…"

"I know. For once, I'm going to join you in wishing El Mago were here. He could have tapped his tools three times, said the magic word, and everything would have been fixed within hours."

"More likely, he would have retooled my vacuums to assist the geriatric repair bots and had the equivalent of forty hands working on the ship."

"Whatever he would have done, I could have sat back and painted my toenails while he did it." Saying the words made Bonita think of Qin and miss her. Her fellow crewmate wasn't a wiz when it came to repairs, but she was always willing to help out. And she was good company. *Cheerful* company. Since Bonita tended toward jaded and dour, it was nice having someone optimistic around.

She was on the verge of sending a message to see if Qin was ready to leave Odin and could find a ride, with whichever of her sisters wanted to join her, out to Forseti Station. Then Bonita wouldn't have to get any closer to that doom-attracting planet.

Before she could send the note, an alert came in via her chip, someone requesting permission to contact her. Tenebris Rache.

"You have *got* to be kidding me."

"To whom do you speak, Bonita?" Viggo asked.

"This idiot who wants to talk to me."

No, idiot wasn't the right word. Whatever Rache was, he wasn't stupid.

"Not El Mago, I assume."

"No. Rache." Bonita eyed the alert. "I'm leaning toward ignoring him. Whatever he wants, ignoring him would be healthier for my life expectancy, right?"

"He has occasionally worked with our friends. What if he has some message regarding them? What if they're in danger?"

"If they are, he probably put them there," she grumbled.

"Casmir is capable of getting himself into danger without help."

"That is true."

"Because he has a big heart. I see this as a feature, not a flaw."

"Uh huh. It's not about him, all right?"

"Are you certain?"

"No." But she didn't answer it. The alert faded and she went back to work. Until twenty seconds later when another new request for contact came in.

"Dr. Peshlakai? That's Rache's surgeon, isn't it?"

"I believe so," Viggo said.

"What's Rache going to do? Have everyone on his ship try to contact me? Maybe his cook will be next." Bonita thought about ignoring the second request, but curiosity—and the fear that she might miss out on an important warning, such as to leave Forseti Station because Rache was about to blow it up—made her accept it.

What? she messaged.

Ah, good evening, Captain Lopez. The lag promised Peshlakai wasn't anywhere near the station, so maybe her fear of being blown up was unfounded. *I would like to send you a video file that I have obtained that shows Prince Finn attempting to hire Rache to kill his father, King Jager, and continue on in his employment once he has the throne.*

I couldn't care less about that and have no interest in seeing it play out in vibrant color.

A well-off benefactor of mine would be willing to pay you to do something with the video.

How much? And did you know that Rache tried to message me a minute ago? Is he going to murder you if he finds out?

No. This is all his idea, but please do not share that tidbit with the public. He's trying to discredit Finn, so the populace won't accept him as a ruler. If you will allow Rache to speak with you, he will make his proposal and, if you're interested, you can discuss finances.

LAYERS OF FORCE

Fine. Bonita knew she would regret this, but she had spent a fortune repairing her ship and didn't know when the insurance money would come in or if it would cover everything. *I'm accepting his request.*

Excellent. Allow me to send over the video, so that you may peruse it if you wish.

Bonita did not wish. But with the lag, she had time and figured she should watch it before she contemplated taking Rache's money. What could he possibly want a bounty hunter with an old freighter to do with a recording?

By the time Rache sent his first message, she had watched it. And was confused. If he'd had the kid in his brig, why hadn't he killed him? Rache had killed thousands of people from the Kingdom, so what was one more? Why some elaborate discrediting scheme?

Captain Lopez, Rache messaged. *I see that you are docked at Forseti Station, which is a communications and broadcast hub and has the ability to distribute video content to all of the habitats, stations, and planets in the system.*

Ugh, she was starting to see where this was going, but she couldn't imagine how she could do what he wanted. *Yeah, and I'm looking to leave it soon. The second I finish repairs.*

I have a proposition for you.

I'm not interested.

I believe you are resourceful enough for it.

That wasn't her objection.

As soon as possible, you will find a way to sneak into the station's broadcast center and distribute the video that Dr. Peshlakai sent you. Send it out to the entire system. Ideally, set it up to repeat over and over. I'm certain the station security will barge in and stop it eventually, but the longer it plays, the better.

As much as I appreciate criminals giving me orders, I'm not a comm technician, nor do I have access to anything on the station beyond the kiosks selling protein pucks and souvenir T-shirts.

You are a bounty hunter who has survived many decades. Presumably, you have some ingenuity. If you find a way to be successful, I will transfer funds into your choice of accounts.

I don't want your money. Despite the words, Bonita thought of Sergeant Lopez, who *was* a comm technician. And who might have recovered from her injuries by now and be hanging out on the station, waiting for a ship to pick her up. Was there any way she could be talked into helping? Since she wasn't from this system, she ought not to have that mindless blanket loyalty to the crown that so many Kingdom soldiers did.

No? Do you bounty hunt for charity? How much money do you owe on your spaceship? I assume you have a loan on it.

Bonita gritted her teeth, annoyed at his assumption, even if it was true. *That's none of your business.*

How can I make an offer if I don't have a starting point?

I don't know if I can do what you want. Wouldn't your good buddy Casmir be a better choice for hacking into a comm system?

He is not at Forseti Station. I am also positive he would not do it for money and doubtful he would do it for anything, even though it could benefit him and his people. Finn would be an abysmal ruler.

If you care about that, why didn't you kill the kid when he was there?

It crossed my mind. But I believe Jager would be more distressed to learn that his son is a traitor who plans to kill him than by his death.

So you're looking for the way to be the biggest asshole to that family?

Name your price, Lopez. I will pay you ten percent up front and the rest when I see the broadcast.

I owe a hundred and forty-three thousand on my ship. She didn't think for a second that he would pay that much for this job, but she didn't want to do it, and naming a ridiculously high price seemed like a good way to get him to leave her alone. *And I'd need fifty percent up front,* she added to be extra cheeky.

I agree to the amount, but I'll pay no more than fifteen percent up front. It's quite possible that you'll be arrested attempting to do this and that I'll have to find someone else.

Arrested or shot. Bonita rubbed her face. Would he *really* pay that much? Would she be a fool to trust him? Of course she would, but… even if she only got that fifteen percent, that was a substantial chunk of money for a day's work.

A day's work during which she wouldn't *likely* be killed. Oh, it was possible, especially since she'd committed a crime on this station before, but she doubted the guards would shoot her for breaking into a comm room. And if she were arrested, Rache was paying enough that she might be able to cover whatever fine was involved.

"Maybe," she muttered. The Kingdom might have some ridiculously high fines when it came to discrediting their ruling family or forcing non-approved content onto their channels. It wasn't like this was a system where freedom of speech was valued.

"Bonita?" Viggo asked. "You have been staring at the same seam for ten minutes. Have you unwisely made the choice to speak with Rache?"

"Yes, I have." She leaned her forehead against the panel and wondered what Bjarke would think of all this. If his potential future monarch was colluding with Rache to kill his own father... wouldn't he want to know? Especially if something *could* be done about it ahead of time?

She transmitted Rache the account information and said, *As soon as you send the fifteen percent, I'll get started.*

Done, he said a minute later.

An alert came in, showing that money had been deposited in her account.

"I believe I've just made a deal with the devil." Bonita set down her tools. "I need to take a little trip to the station. Will you have the repair robots finish up?"

"Yes, but before you go off to do something foolish, please let me know if you've updated your will."

"I put Qin in it."

"To receive the *Stellar Dragon* and the wise and intelligent entity that runs the ship? Qin is a good crew member, but I'd rather hoped you might leave me to Casmir."

"A robotics professor can't go haring off around the Twelve Systems. Wish me luck, Viggo."

"Do I want to ask what you've agreed to do?"

"Probably not."

The sun had set by the time the helicopter flew over the Hyozan Sea, and the stark white ice covering the great Arctic Islands came into view. It gleamed under the darkening sky, the peaks of the mountain range on the largest island like shark teeth jutting up in the distance.

Nothing stirred on the ice below, not even a plucky polar bear. Frigid wind rattled the doors of the helicopter and leaked in around the seals, making Asger glad for the warmth of his armor. Whoever had decided to put a military base down here had been a sadist; he was glad that knights weren't required to do special winter training.

Next to him, Casmir shivered. He wore a parka, gloves, fur cap, and a scarf—all scrounged from the castle—but it was too large for him and might not be as effective as properly fitted clothing. He might have to cuddle with one of his crushers tonight.

Or maybe the dusty tool satchel that he'd scrounged from the barn when he'd been repairing the helicopter. It was remarkably similar to the one he'd toted all over the systems on their journeys—Asger assumed Jager had relieved him of the original. With Asger's blessing, Casmir had filled it with tools from the barn.

Asger had grabbed his *own* tools before leaving. He leaned forward and rummaged in the trunk he'd loaded from the castle's armory. Since they had been in a hurry to leave, he had thrown in a bunch of stuff without much contemplation, other than to choose weapons that appeared less than a hundred years old. Unfortunately, the ancient castle's armory was as much museum as functional weapons-storage room, and everything from bows and arrows to swords to cartridge-powered rifles had hung on the walls. Eventually, he'd found grenades and only moderately old DEW-Tek rifles in a cabinet.

Tristan, who was seated next to him, watched as he shined a flashlight over the contents. "We're not planning to bomb the military base, are we?"

Asger's father, who was piloting the craft, with Qin sitting next to him, glanced back.

LAYERS OF FORCE

"I don't know *what* we're planning." Asger looked at their fearless leader next to him.

Casmir's face was faintly green by the glow of the flashlight beam—they'd run into air turbulence over the sea. His eyes were closed, and Asger wasn't sure if he was awake.

"I wanted to be as prepared as possible. I grabbed a first-aid kit and some emergency ration bars that I dug out of a box in the back." Asger plucked out a brown-wrapped bar labeled Carob Delight and offered it to Tristan. "I didn't think Mrs. Dabrowski would let us steal one of her casseroles."

"The casseroles were all eaten by our ravenous troops," Casmir said, his eyes still closed, "and we're not bombing anyone. I'd prefer it if we could find the gate pieces without bothering anyone in the base at all, but we know there's at least one person guarding it. We'll have to subdue the soldiers peacefully."

"Peaceful subduing?" Asger asked. "How does that work?"

"A crusher walks up, removes their weapons, hoists them into the air, and then locks them in the brig until we complete our task."

"That sounds like an optimistic subduing, not a peaceful one."

Asger doubted there were many soldiers stationed at this remote base, but he also doubted it would be as easy as Casmir suggested. He looked at the rows of seats behind him, Qin's sisters packed in like sardines. Many of the crushers had flattened themselves against the sides of the cabin to better fit in the confined space. Now and then, the craft groaned under the weight or merely due to its extreme age.

"We're over the biggest island now and forty miles from the base," Asger's father called over the noisy thrums of the helicopter blades. "Is the plan to set down a few miles away, go in on foot, and hope they don't notice us until it's too late?"

Casmir opened his eyes, his hands resting on his stomach. "We could do that, but we may want to fly over and look for whatever mountain the gate pieces are being stored in. And see if the mounds I saw via the satellite imagery *are* camouflaged spaceships. We're not going to be able to fly the pieces up into space in this."

"We'll be lucky if we can even make it back to the city in this," Asger muttered.

"It's not a bad chopper. It's amazing that we got it running so quickly." Tristan took the bar and opened it, perhaps thinking that they might not get a chance to eat again for a while.

"It looks like there are mountains about ten miles from the base," Asger's father said, "but you said you saw something right next to it?"

"Two white mounds, yes," Casmir said.

"The map doesn't show anything like that."

"Hence why I believe they're camouflaged ships, maybe one of the very ships that brought the pieces in the first place."

"I'll take your word for it. I don't think we should fly over to investigate. They're sure to notice us. We should land far enough away to avoid detection and go in on foot." Asger's father pointed at the horizon. "They'll call in reinforcements as soon as they know intruders have come."

"If they *need* reinforcements," Asger said. "Trust me; they'll have more than that one soldier guarding Jager's treasure."

"There were only two metal buildings and a hangar in the whole base," Casmir said.

"You can fit lots of people in metal buildings and hangars." Asger looked around the helicopter to emphasize how many people—and other beings—they had stuffed into the limited space. "Also anti-aircraft artillery weapons."

"We can handle them," Qin said firmly.

Asger didn't mind her confidence—in her case, it was warranted—but he didn't want to *handle* Kingdom soldiers. He wanted to sneak up on them and force them to surrender without hurting anyone. That would be difficult if they were facing a powerful force.

"Landing far away and walking is fine. As long as we can maneuver across the ice." Casmir zipped his parka up tighter. "And not freeze."

"You're the only one in danger of that."

Everyone else had armor or a galaxy suit, all capable of keeping the body warm even in space, but Jager had stripped Casmir of his galaxy suit during his imprisonment.

Casmir grimaced. "Kim told me not to come along."

"You should listen to her. She's smart."

"Wouldn't you miss me if I weren't here?" He smiled, though it was a wan smile, that green tinge to his face still present.

"I might miss you, but I wouldn't miss worrying about you."

"Sorry." Doubt replaced Casmir's smile. "I'll try not to be a burden."

Asger regretted teasing him. "You're not. I mean, sometimes you are, but you're also useful."

"Thanks. I think."

"You want to talk about burdens…" Tristan had unwrapped his bar and was gnawing unsuccessfully at the corner. "These are a burden to my stomach. They have the density and flavor of bricks. How *old* are they?"

"They didn't have manufacturers' dates on them." Asger shined his light on the wrapper. "Or expiration dates."

"So they could have come from Old Earth on the original colony ships?"

"It's possible. But look, you softened the corner a bit. Keep chewing."

"I think I chipped a tooth."

"You need more useful fangs than those tiny canines that unaltered humans have," one of Qin's sisters said.

"Or I need to not eat bricks." Tristan rewrapped the bar and looked like he might put it back in the box.

Asger closed the lid before he could do it.

"Never mind the idea about landing before we're detected. They must have noticed our approach." Asger's father pointed to lights on the horizon that hadn't been there before. *Moving* lights. "It looks like we've got company coming."

"Does this helicopter have any weapons?" Qin asked.

"Are you kidding? It doesn't even have scanners or instrumentation that doesn't involve a needle on a gauge." Asger's father ticked his finger against the gas tank gauge.

"There *are* missile launchers," Tristan said. "But I didn't see any missiles."

"Even Grandfather wasn't crazy enough to keep unexploded ordnance in the barn," Asger said.

"Should we land?" Casmir lifted a hand to shield his eyes as the lights, a mix of yellow and red in triangular patterns, flew toward them.

One light in each set flashed steadily. It wasn't that bright or obnoxious, but Asger remembered Casmir's propensity for seizures and hoped the flashing wouldn't trigger them.

"We're still thirty miles out," Asger's father said. "That's a long ways to walk, even if we go piggyback on the crushers again."

"Soldiers at the base might be reporting our intrusion right now," Asger said, "so time could be of the essence."

Instead of looking for a place to land, his father accelerated. He angled away from the lights while continuing forward, then took them low, skimming the thick sheet of ice that covered the island's land mass.

The trios of lights moved to intercept, eight of them. Were they ships? Asger squinted, trying to make out the dark shapes between the lights. They appeared too small to be manned ships, but it was hard to judge distance in the dark.

Casmir groaned faintly, his hand tightening on his stomach.

"You're not going to puke, are you?" Asger asked, his own stomach experiencing a twinge as the craft zigzagged back and forth, his father trying to make a hard target in case those ships had weapons.

"I hope not," Casmir said.

"Didn't you bring any anti-nausea medicine?"

"I didn't see any in your medicine cabinets."

"Air sickness isn't a big problem in a castle."

Casmir groaned as the craft dipped into a fissure, turning abruptly to follow it and throwing them all against each other, their meager harnesses a far cry from a spaceship's pods.

As they flew through the fissure, the first of the triangles of light streaked overhead. A dark arrow-shaped body was visible between the lights, and it fired red DEW-Tek beams down at them.

Several bolts hammered into the side of the fissure, missing the chopper's blades by inches. Shards of ice flew out, pelting their hull as they continued past.

Asger's father took them lower, but the fissure wasn't wide enough for them to descend much farther.

Casmir blinked and looked around, then pressed his nose against his window. More of the enemy ships flew into view overhead and fired down at them.

"This is taking us the wrong way," Asger's father said.

"I saw the sides of this fissure and thought it might be where they've got the gate stashed," Casmir said, "but it looks natural."

"You don't think they would have stored the pieces somewhere natural?" Tristan gripped an overhead bar as the craft rocked, throwing them against each other again.

"The walls in that video were straight and carved by machine," Casmir said.

The helicopter swooped left and right, following the curve of the fissure walls—walls that narrowed up ahead.

Asger's father cursed. "That's as far as we can go in here. Be prepared for it to get bumpy."

"What was it *before*?" Qin asked as the helicopter rose.

Casmir switched from looking down to peering up. One of the trios of lights was flying right behind and above them.

Asger opened the trunk again and pulled out two grenades. "Switch seats with me, Casmir." He waved to the door. "I'll open that and try to hit those ships if they get close."

Casmir fumbled with his harness.

Red blasts of energy slammed into the lip of the fissure as their helicopter turned, heading once again for the base.

A bolt struck one of the landing skids, and the craft rocked violently. Asger lunged across Casmir to open the door.

But Casmir blurted, "Wait!" and pushed him back. "Those aren't ships. They're robots!"

"So?" Asger gave him an exasperated look. "Flying robots that are shooting at us are as bad as ships."

"No. I just need to find them on the network."

Four of the ships—robots—turned to follow them as they sped across the ice. Now that they were out of the fissure, there was nothing for the helicopter to use as cover. The base hadn't yet come into view.

"We don't have time for that." Asger pushed Casmir out of the way and opened the door. "Fly steady."

His father glanced back.

Asger leaned out, the icy wind tearing at his arm as he tried to find enough room to throw without falling out. The closest robot attacker fired. Asger's father, ignoring the *fly steady* command, anticipated it and swerved. Asger might have toppled out, but someone grabbed him from behind.

Asger thumbed the grenade to activate it and hurled it at the closest robot ship. It exploded, the craft disappearing in smoke, and he thought he'd hit it. Then it flew through the smoke, appearing undamaged. Asger groaned and readied the second grenade.

"I'm almost into their network," Casmir said.

The robot ship fired again, clipping the back of the helicopter. They lurched, tilting sideways so that Asger's open hatch almost scraped along the ground. His feet flew out, and he jerked them up so they wouldn't hit. His grenade tumbled from his fingers as he grabbed the helicopter's frame with both hands.

His father snarled and managed to right the craft. Uselessly, the grenade blew up on the ground, shooting ice upward and leaving a crater. It did nothing to disturb their pursuers. Their robot attackers, all eight of them in a formation now, streaked closer.

"I will protect us," Zee stated and oozed over the seats and out past Asger, almost knocking him out of the craft.

Like liquid metal defying gravity, Zee poured himself upward and oozed across the hull to re-form on the tail of the helicopter.

Smoke wafted from the rear of their craft, and it wobbled as Asger's father fought to maintain altitude. They were less than a foot off the ground. A crash was inevitable.

Zee sprang into the air as one of the robot ships swooped in closer. He jumped farther than any human could have. The robot ship fired straight into his chest, but he absorbed the blast and landed on the nose of the craft.

"Give me more grenades." Asger waved his hand toward Tristan as Zee tore pieces off the robot attacker. He might destroy it, but there were seven more to deal with.

The helicopter clipped the ground before Tristan could give him anything. They bounced upward, everyone cursing and groaning as only their harnesses kept their heads from hitting the ceiling. They hit down again, a snap coming from overhead and a groan from the framework. This time, the helicopter didn't rise back up. They skidded wildly across the frozen ground.

The robot attackers swarmed toward them like angry hornets. Zee had destroyed the one he'd attacked and was on the ground now, running toward the downed helicopter.

"Get the other crushers out there," Asger said, lifting his rifle to fire at the advancing robot ships.

But the enemy craft didn't fire. Instead, they settled to the ground, like a flock of birds coming to roost. Their lights went out.

"Are they dead?" Asger pointed his rifle warily at the closest robot ship.

"Our helicopter is," his father said.

"I'm sorry that took so long." Casmir lifted a hand. "I thought they were manned ships. Also, I was struggling with… uh—" The words broke off in a nauseated moan. Casmir scrambled to open his harness.

Asger, still hanging half out of the helicopter, sprang out so he wouldn't be in the way. Casmir only made it three steps before dropping to his knees and throwing up.

Asger sighed. "Our fearless leader."

"Fear isn't his problem." Tristan hopped out after him, avoiding Casmir and the spot he was decorating. "Your father's piloting is."

"My piloting is fine." Asger's father jumped out and eyed the robot attackers resting in formation on the ice twenty feet away. "Are we sure those won't trouble us anymore?"

Qin and her sisters exited along with the crushers, Qin coming over to rest a hand on Casmir's back. He wiped his mouth and kneeled back, his face as pale as the ice.

"The base is two miles that way." Asger's father pointed toward a couple of dark bumps on the horizon. The buildings Casmir had spoken of? "My exquisite and not-at-all problematic piloting brought us down close."

"Crashed us close, you mean." Asger offered Casmir a hand. "Do you want to be carried?"

"No, no. Thank you. I feel much better now." Casmir wiped his face again. "Well, maybe not *much* but somewhat. I can walk."

"If anyone were to carry Casmir Dabrowski, it would be I." Zee arrived and took up his usual spot looming behind Casmir's shoulder. "The heroic destroyer of aerial robotic threats."

"Your crusher thinks he's a hero, Casmir," Tristan said.

Casmir wobbled to his feet and patted Zee on the chest. "He's not wrong, is he?"

"*You* destroyed the other seven," Tristan said. "He may have a ways to go before becoming as heroic as you."

"That is an adjective nobody has ever applied to me." Frosty puffs of air came from Casmir's mouth as he spoke, and he pulled up the hood of his parka. "Also, those robots aren't destroyed. They're hanging out while waiting for my next command."

He twitched his fingers toward them, like a magician pretending he had the power to levitate inanimate objects. Or maybe not *pretending*. The trios of lights came back on, and the robot ships hovered above the ground, thrusters stirring fine snow coating the ice. They wafted slowly over and lined up behind Casmir.

Asger, afraid the smoke wafting from the rear of the helicopter meant it would blow up, grabbed his trunk of ammunition and ration bars.

Zee faced the other crushers. "When our human allies are threatened, we must take the initiative and act to protect them even before they themselves order it."

"It is so," the others agreed.

"Next time," one said, "we will act more swiftly."

Zee turned back around and looked at Casmir. "They agree too quickly. Tork would have pointed out that my tactic was brutish and could have resulted in my permanent destruction."

"Tork is wise," Casmir said.

"For an inferior android." Zee tilted his head. "That is incorrect. I have decided that Tork is an android but not an inferior one."

"I'm glad you're coming to appreciate him."

"We are working together on a plan," Zee said.

"Do you want to tell me about it?" Casmir asked.

"Do we want to know?" Asger muttered.

Qin swatted him on the chest. "The crushers are helpful."

"If it comes to fruition, I will explain it in detail," Zee said.

"And take credit for it?" Asger asked.

"Credit is not important, but all will know that Zee, the original Z-6000 and original protector of Casmir Dabrowski, was responsible." Zee turned toward Casmir. "Will Kim Sato include me in her book?"

"I'm certain of it," Casmir said, as Asger mouthed, "Book?"

"Let's go." Asger's father stepped into the middle of their group. "The soldiers will know something is up when their robots don't come back. If they don't already."

"I'm ready." Asger hefted his trunk over his shoulder.

"As am I." Casmir trundled off across the ice with the crushers lined up behind him and the aerial robots behind *them*.

Qin's sisters gaped at the sight.

Asger was no longer surprised by such occurrences. As he and Qin trailed after them, his thoughts dwelled on the fact that they'd lost their only way on or off this frozen island. What if they had guessed wrong, and there were neither gate pieces at the base nor a way off?

CHAPTER 22

WE DO STILL HAVE HIS CHIP UP HERE, came Father's reply a few hours after Oku sent him the message, not mentioning that Casmir himself had suggested it. *The Intelligence boys have it, but my understanding is that it's locked tight and they haven't been able to hack into it. What is this program you believe is on it?*

From the reports I was reading that Chief Van Dijk provided, I learned that Professor Dabrowski—Oku was careful to use his formal title and feign some distance from him, though it was probably pointless now—*and the android he captured from the astroshamans named Tork-57 used some technology to mark ships with slydar hulls so that even allies without a slydar detector could find and fire upon them.*

That would be useful, her father admitted. *But as I said, we haven't been able to get into the chip to download any data. Eight highly trained Military Intelligence professionals on this ship, and they can't get past the security software of a robotics professor.*

Oku did not point out that Casmir was a rather smart robotics professor, though she felt smugly proud on his behalf. Careful not to sound eager, she messaged back: *I think he would give us what we need to get in if I asked him. I know you've got an arrest warrant out for him, but he would still help us, help the Kingdom. Even if his tactics have been questionable in the past, this is his home, and he doesn't want to see it annihilated.*

Her father was slow to reply, which almost made it worse than if he'd promptly snapped back that they didn't need Casmir's help and that he didn't appreciate her contacting an enemy of the Kingdom.

I know you let him out of the dungeon, was what her father said.

Yes.

There was little point in lying. Her mother or Van Dijk would have told him. They might not have punished her for it, but that didn't mean they would keep confidences from her father.

If you can convince him to disable the software, Captain Stein is the senior Intelligence officer working on his chip. I trust Dabrowski can find the man's contact information.

I imagine so. Oku wanted to barter with her father, to ask that Casmir be pardoned if he helped the Kingdom with this, but she doubted her father would agree to it. She also doubted Casmir would demand it. He would simply help, because that was what he did.

I must go. We're under attack again. This is the only ship with a slydar detector, so it's being targeted.

Be careful, Father.

You as well. You and your mother. Stay underground and well-protected.

We will.

Oku sent a note to Casmir with the name of the officer he was supposed to contact. *My father must be desperate to consider accepting help from you, but maybe he'll realize in the end that he made a mistake and that you're worth keeping around.*

Uhm, that would be nice, but... Don't take this the wrong way, but I plan to bounce my message through about twenty-eight relay stations so they can't trace me.

I wouldn't expect anything less.

No? Twenty-seven stations wouldn't be acceptable?

Certainly not. Perhaps you should send it through twenty-nine and out to one of the gas giants and back.

I'll keep that suggestion in mind.

Lonely and stuck in her subterranean apartment, Oku was tempted to keep the conversation going, but she didn't want to delay him in reaching out to the Intelligence officer. Time might be extremely important for her father's fleet.

She tried to focus on her work again, but the news rolling on the display kept drawing her attention. She couldn't believe she was once again watching a feed of bombings on her world. So far, the ship or ships hadn't come near the city, but she'd heard the castle staff and her mother had been evacuated to the Citadel again. Supposedly, Royal Intelligence Headquarters was as well protected, so nobody had suggested moving Oku.

She was tempted to suggest it herself, but she doubted the Citadel would be any more appealing of a prison. Chasca roamed the tiny apartment listlessly, nibbling on things she shouldn't, and Oku kept having to stop herself from doing the same. Though she was more tempted to nibble on sweets than comforters and shoes.

One of the guards came to walk Chasca, and Oku watched her go, tail wagging, and wished she could go too. But she'd been ordered to stay inside for her own safety, and a guard in the hallway was there to ensure she didn't defy that order. She made herself sit back down, but she remained antsy, eager for company.

When someone knocked, she surged to her feet, hardly caring who had come to visit. She wished for the twentieth time that she'd stayed with Casmir instead of returning to the city. At the beginning of their conversation, he'd sent her a word-search puzzle with names of plant parts hidden among the letters. Each time she found a word, an animated crusher popped up holding flowers. She didn't know if he'd made it from scratch or customized an existing puzzle, but either way, it touched her that he'd taken the time.

Oku opened the door smiling, but her smile fell. Finn stood in the corridor with a guard, looking cranky after his time in Rache's brig.

He held up a tin and forced an inauthentic smile. "Mother sent manjū, but she said we have to share it."

"With each other? Or the staff?" Oku looked at the guard.

The guard, who was probably as bored of being assigned to watch these apartments as Oku was living in one, grew wistful but didn't say anything.

"Nobody shares with the *staff*." Finn gave her an exasperated look and walked in.

Too bad. Oku would have rather shared the treats with the guards than her brother.

She looked into the hall, expecting the other guard to return with Chasca at any time, but they weren't in sight yet. Reluctantly, Oku waved for Finn to sit at the table and attempted to arrange her expression into one of sisterly interest.

Surprisingly, the guard he'd brought trailed him inside instead of staying in the hall. He didn't go far, stopping inside the door and folding his arms over his chest. Maybe Finn had requisitioned him as a bodyguard. He was probably feeling vulnerable and twitchy after being kidnapped by Rache.

"I'm glad you made it back all right." Oku sat across from him as Finn opened the tin, revealing a mix of round, orange and green manjū treats. They smelled of sweet orange and green tea. "Were you tortured?"

"Of course. But I didn't tell him anything." He sounded like he was lying. What could Finn possibly know that Rache would care about?

"Is he as villainous as they say?" Oku had no intention of mentioning that Rache had visited her before kidnapping Finn. Mostly, she wondered if Rache had told Finn who he was.

"Even more so. He oozes it." Finn chomped into one of the green-tea treats.

"Oozes villainy?"

"Like body odor but more deadly." He waved for her to take a treat.

"Sounds kind of gross."

"Yup."

Oku eyed the sweets. Finn had already engaged in one plot against her life. Might he be trying again to get her out of the picture? With poisoned food? "I'm not hungry."

"You're sure? I don't mind taking them all. They're good."

"Go ahead."

Finn glanced at the guard. For a moment, Oku thought he might offer one to the man, after all, but he shrugged and ate another one.

"What did Rache want you for?" Oku asked.

"To ransom me to Father for five million crowns."

Oku had gotten a few short messages from Father, though he'd made it clear he was busy up there, dealing with all the invaders, and she made a note to crosscheck this claim with him.

"But I escaped."

"How?"

He squinted at her as if he didn't appreciate the questions. Which also made her positive he was lying. If he'd truly escaped through heroic means, he would have been bragging about it to everyone. "I knocked out a guard and stole a shuttle. Try one of the orange ones."

"Are those the ones you poisoned?"

Finn snorted. "Please, Oku. I wouldn't be stupid enough to try to kill you in R.I. Headquarters. There are cameras everywhere. And witnesses." He waved at the guard.

LAYERS OF FORCE

Oku glanced warily at him, half-expecting him to have produced a stunner to aim at her.

But it was Finn who attacked, lunging around the table, grabbing her wrist, and yanking an injector out of his pocket.

She swore, twisted her wrist out of his grip, and jammed her knee into his groin. He stumbled back, but before she could feel victorious—or open her mouth to scream for help—a steel-like arm wrapped around her waist from behind and hefted her from her feet. The guard.

"Sorry, Your Highness," he said.

Oku opened her mouth to scream, hoping that other guards—more *loyal* guards—were in the hall. But he was fast and clamped his hand over her mouth.

Finn rolled his eyes, one hand gripping that injector and one covering his crotch as he came in from the side to avoid her kicking feet. Almost. She twisted as much as she could and launched a heel sideways at him.

"Hold her still," Finn growled at the guard.

"Hurry up and do it, Your Highness. She's feisty."

Feisty? Oku was *pissed*.

She tried to open her jaw enough to chomp down on the guard's hand. Her foot caught the table, sending the damn treats flying.

Finn lunged for the side of her neck with the injector. She tried to jerk away but didn't have enough room to maneuver. A sharp hiss at her neck filled her with even more fury.

"Hell, Oku, it's just a truth drug." Finn rubbed his groin and backed far out of her reach.

She didn't believe him, and horror surged through her veins right along with whatever drug he'd stuck into her. But already the will to resist them, to keep fighting, seeped out of her.

"Let her mouth go," Finn said, watching her. "I think she's past screaming."

"You sure about this, Your Highness?" the guard asked him.

"You can cover her mouth again if she starts to scream."

"I meant about drugging her against her will."

"It's not like she was going to *agree* to it. But she knows where that Dabrowski is, and Father wants him. There's footage of her going down to let him out of his cell, but nobody's questioning her. It's ludicrous. I'm going to find that bastard for Father, and he's going to appreciate that I was good enough to get away from Rache *and* found that rogue when nobody else could." And thus name Finn as his first choice as heir?

Oku wanted to tell him he was an idiot, but all of the fight had gone out of her body. Against her will, her muscles went limp.

The guard settled her to the ground and loosened his grip on her but didn't let her go. He was the only thing keeping her from crumpling to the floor. Small mercies…

"Where is he, Oku?" Finn asked. "I know you're hiding him. Once I find him, I'll make sure to tell Father that *you* let his enemy go."

"Why are you worrying about this now, Finn?" she asked, trying to avoid answering the question, though it took a lot of energy to do so. And she struggled to remember why she didn't want to make it easier on herself, why she didn't just answer him.

Her eyes had grown gritty, the lids so heavy. She wished Finn would leave so she could sleep. "The world is under attack," she mumbled. "You should be up there with the Fleet helping Father, not worrying about Casmir."

"Don't you dare tell me what I should be doing." Finn lifted a hand, as if to hit her.

The guard lifted his own hand to block the blow. Finn squinted at him but let his hand fall.

"Where is he, Oku?" Finn softened his voice and forced a smile, as if he were a friend wanting some information, not her vile brother, not her interrogator.

Unfortunately, the drug had fully kicked in, and her mouth opened to answer. "Not in the city where you can find him," she said, trying her hardest to be vague, but it was so much effort.

"I'll take your chip if you don't give me a straight answer," Finn said, "and someone in the computer lab up there will find out exactly where you've been."

Screw you was what she wanted to say, but her muzzy mind instead mumbled, "The Asger estate."

"Their castle?"

"Yes."

"Is he *with* them? Those traitor knights?"

"Yes." Her eyelids drooped. Sleep, she wanted sleep.

Finn clenched a fist and met the guard's eyes over Oku's shoulder. "That's it. We'll gather a huge team and fly out there now and catch them while they're sleeping."

LAYERS OF FORCE

"Excellent, Your Highness." The guard didn't sound that pleased, did he?

Oku slumped against him, too tired to stand up on her own. Would she fall asleep? Or had Finn drugged her with something worse?

Finn started for the door but paused and looked at Oku and then the guard. "I don't suppose you'd like to take advantage of this moment to remove her from the possible line of succession?"

"No, Your Highness," the guard said coolly. "I would not."

Finn opened his mouth, as if to deliver a threat, but then said, "Fine," and walked out. "Drop her and let's go."

The guard did not drop Oku. He lifted her and laid her on the bed.

"I'm sorry, Your Highness," he said again, voice soft. "But I couldn't act against your father's wishes, or his, in case… well, you know what's likely to pass."

Oku was barely aware of him as he bowed and walked away, promising to make sure someone from the infirmary came later to check on her.

Her muzzy mind was busy trying to grasp the meaning of what she'd done. Finn would go… go to the Asgers' castle. She had to do something. What?

Warn…

She passed out before the thought could fully form.

Entire squads of armored Fleet soldiers and Kingdom Guard troops ran through the concourse in Forseti Station. Most of the restaurants and shops were closed, and the kiosks that sold everything from T-shirts to snacks to robots to spaceship parts had disappeared. That hadn't been the case the day before when Bonita had been buying the last batch of hull plating for repairs. Was the station expecting another attack?

She walked warily through the concourse, half-expecting some of the troops to veer over and apprehend her. What if someone had picked up the transmissions from the *Fedallah*? Her certainty that she wouldn't be shot, only arrested and fined, for futzing with the broadcast system crumbled as armed men and women jogged past.

As she reached the exit of the concourse, Bonita eyed a large display on a wall. It showed an image of the ominous AI ship next to a scanner readout showing it as a blip zipping through the system. A ticker estimating its speed startled her into halting to stare.

The ship was traveling at more than half the speed of light. That meant it could reach Odin in hours instead of days. And it could reach Forseti Station even sooner if its route took it in this direction.

"That might be what they're worried about." And what *she* should possibly be worried about since she was docked here. "Let's do this quickly and get out of here," she muttered to herself.

Bonita found a lift and took it to the hospital floor, not sure if the soldiers she'd delivered would still be there, but the idea of visiting Maria Lopez on the civilian station was more appealing than trying to get aboard one of the Fleet military ships.

An android nurse directed her to a few rooms that had been given to the injured soldiers. Bonita was relieved to find Maria sitting in a waiting area outside with another soldier, playing a three-dimensional holographic shooter game.

"If this is what the Kingdom Fleet pays you to do," Bonita said as she approached, "maybe it's not such a bad gig."

"Hey, Captain." Maria paused the game and stood up. "They're supposed to send a ship for us eventually, but everything has been directed in-system to defend Odin."

"*Sergeant*," her buddy said in a warning tone, giving Bonita a significant head nod.

Why, because Maria wasn't supposed to tell civilian bounty hunters that there was a huge battle being fought on their home world?

"Everyone in the Twelve Systems knows what's going on there right now, kid," Bonita said.

He scowled at her, unpaused the game, and obliterated Maria's ship.

"You're a dick, Brunswick," she said.

"A dick who's now caught up with you." He winked.

"By cheating." Maria rolled her eyes and walked toward a pair of potted plants with Bonita.

"I came to see how you're doing," Bonita said, wincing inwardly at the dishonesty, but it seemed like she should open with small talk before requesting that Maria help her do something treasonous. "Viggo and I have mostly gotten our ship repaired, and I'll be taking off soon."

LAYERS OF FORCE

"Out of the system?"

"That would be the wise route."

Maria smiled. "And is that the route you'll be taking?"

"Probably not. I'm undecided. My one and only permanent crew member is on Odin."

"Ah. I hope she's not hurt in the fighting."

The last Bonita had heard from Qin, she had been taking off on some harebrained scheme with Casmir. Being hurt seemed inevitable.

"Me too." Bonita looked at the other soldier to make sure he wasn't paying attention. He'd started a solitary version of the fighter game. "Is there any chance you could help me with something that I believe will be beneficial to your people but that might not be entirely legal?"

Maria's eyebrows flew up. "My people or my husband's people?"

"The Kingdom. I figured you claim them as yours after four years in their military."

"You must not have seen Brunswick annihilate my ship." Maria stuck her tongue out at him when he glanced over, then walked farther down the hall.

Good, they would be out of his earshot then. Bonita doubted any of the android nurses cared what they spoke about.

"I'm going to send you some video footage I got from a doctor who, against his wishes, was in a position to witness it." Bonita felt bad that she wasn't being entirely honest. As far as she knew, Yas was obligated to serve on Rache's ship, but he'd also agreed to be obligated.

"You're serious, aren't you?" Maria asked.

Bonita requested permission to contact her chip-to-chip. Maria accepted, and Bonita sent the video file.

While Maria watched the video on her contact display, her chip transmitting the audio directly to her brain for processing, her eyes grew unfocused. Bonita gazed out a faux window in the corridor; it let them pretend they were looking out on a sunny pasture with horses nipping at the grass. She wondered if kids ever thought the windows here were real and begged their parents for pony rides.

"This is horrifying," Maria whispered. "Does Rache still have Prince Finn?"

"I think he's escaped or was let go. I'm not sure. The doctor didn't give me all the details. He saw that I'm a bounty hunter and am docked here, and that's why he reached out to me. He thought he could hire me."

"For what?"

"He wants me to hack into the broadcast system that transmits out of here and play the video for everyone in the Kingdom to see. Including, I gathered, the king and all of his Intelligence people."

"Do you know how to do that?"

"No. That's why I came to talk to you."

"Oh, *mierda*." Maria scrubbed her face with both hands. "I can't be involved in anything that goes against the government."

Bonita thought about offering to pay her, but she had a feeling that appealing to her sense of right and honor would get her further. "It's not against the government. It's a warning to them, right? Finn is an asshole, and his people should see it, so they can act to protect their interests. To protect their *king*. The kid wants to kill his own father—and maybe his sister, too, right?"

"I guess, if those recordings haven't been altered or made up."

"Who would alter them? Rache? It's not like he would want this to get out."

It wasn't like he was paying Bonita a fortune to intentionally get it out…

"Why would this doctor you mention care about transmitting these to the Kingdom? Or is he from here himself?"

"I didn't ask for a lot of details—he was waving money at me—but I think he's from Tiamat Station. The Kingdom supposedly killed their president to try to make a deal and rule through their vice president, at least before the civil unrest put an end to that. He probably doesn't want to see a twenty-year-old kid who might be even more ambitious than his father in charge. Nobody should want to see that, right?"

Maria gripped her chin and stared at the floor.

"All right," she finally said. "Do you have a stunner?"

"Yes."

"We can't hurt anyone doing this, or my career will be over. It might be anyway." Maria groaned. "I *do* want that message to get out, but what if it fails? What if nothing happens and Finn ends up in power anyway? He could go after my husband. He—"

"Perhaps," Bonita interrupted, "if you were seen being forced into the broadcast station at gunpoint, your superiors and your government wouldn't blame you for anything that happened."

"Then they'll blame *you*."

"Yes, but I don't like them anyway." Bonita didn't want to get in trouble with the Kingdom again, but they had so many other problems right now that she doubted anyone would take the time to send bounty hunters after her.

Once she got Qin and however many of her sisters wanted to come, Bonita could leave this system forever. She would miss Bjarke, but if he ended up permanently in exile, he could leave with her. She supposed that thought shouldn't make her wistful, but she'd been lonely these last few days without any company. She couldn't keep from imagining him in the co-pilot's pod, pompously sharing all of the adjectives of bear superiority that his name supposedly conveyed, as they flew off to find new adventures.

Maria snorted. "Let's go do it then. Before I lose my nerve."

She told one of her officers that she needed to use the facilities and headed out of the hospital, as if she knew where she was going. Happy to let her guide them, Bonita kept her stunner in her pocket until they came out of a lift and a plaque on the wall showed a satellite dish with *Broadcast Station 3* written below it. Nobody was in the hall, but security cameras monitored their passing from high on the walls.

For their sake, Bonita drew her stunner and pointed it at Maria. "Pick one, Sergeant."

"This should work." Maria pointed at a solid metal door to Station 3 and tried the knob. It didn't turn. A panel above it had a number pad.

Bonita fished into another pocket, hoping the tool she'd dug out of her cabin would work. It had been a while since she'd had to pick a lock. She affixed it to the door next to the pad and thumbed it on. It clung to the metal and hummed faintly, buzzing with electricity. Or maybe magnetism. Bonita had never read the operations manual.

"Breaking into places is easier when my roboticist guest is on board," she murmured.

"A profession known for teaching lock-thwarting abilities?"

"You'd be surprised."

A clunk sounded, the lock being thrown. Bonita removed the device, opened the door, and started to nod for Maria to go first.

But someone in a station uniform sat at the console.

He spun, leaping to his feet. "Hey, we're recording! Wait, who *are* you?"

He lunged for an alarm. Bonita shot him in the chest with the stunner.

"We're committed now," she whispered, pulling Maria inside and closing the door behind them.

The recording equipment took up most of the space in the small studio. A single chair was locked to the deck in front of a console. On a side wall, a display showed the AI ship advancing inexorably into the system.

Maria glanced at it, then jerked. "I didn't realize how close that ship is. That's the gas giant Freyr. It's practically in Forseti Station's back yard."

Bonita waved her to the complicated-looking broadcast equipment. "Can you upload the file and transmit? Now that I've stunned someone, the clock is ticking."

She mentally calculated how long it would take her to get back to the *Dragon* and depart, assuming no obstacles—such as arresting officers— presented themselves. Maybe she could tie this guy up and find a nice broom closet to put him in. Too bad the studio didn't come with one.

"I'll see what I can do." Maria slid into the seat. "This is a lot more sophisticated than the comm station on the *Comet Cruiser*."

"You can do it." Bonita tried to sound encouraging rather than impatient or worried. "You're from my home system. You must be smart."

"Along with the six billion other people from there?"

"Yes. We're an intellectually superior bunch."

"He was already logged in. That helps." Maria laid her hands on the console. "I'm transferring the file you sent to…" She glanced at the unconscious man. "That is Felix."

"Good to know." Bonita hunted in drawers, looking for twine or something to use to tie up Felix. She found electrical tape. That would have to do. And maybe she could improvise a gag…

An alarm blared from a speaker, and Bonita jumped to her feet. "Shit, how far along are you?"

She spun toward the door, certain they had been discovered and expecting station authorities to burst in. If they could just get the message to broadcast first…

"Still working on it, but I don't think that alarm is for us." Maria waved at the AI ship on the display.

"All personnel to battle stations," a male voice announced over a speaker. "All civilians remain in your quarters or aboard your docked spacecraft. We have an intruder ship approaching the station at high speed. I repeat, we have an intruder ship approaching the station."

"Wonderful," Bonita muttered.

But maybe this was a good thing. If people were distracted by the AI ship, they might not pay attention to a strange unauthorized broadcast

LAYERS OF FORCE

coming out of Station 3. Assuming Maria still *could* broadcast. What if everything was shut down or some emergency signal overrode what they were doing?

"I'm in and have the file loaded," Maria said over the continuing alarm. "I'm preempting the regular programming."

"Good. I doubt the Kingdom needed to watch that cooking channel anyway."

Maria grunted. "Actually, it was news about the attacks on Odin. If nothing else, a lot of people should be riveted to their displays when this comes on."

"So long as the *right* people are."

Like Jager, who ought to witness his son's scheming, and all the rest of the government stooges who expected Finn to be their monarch someday. And Rache, so he would know Bonita had succeeded and deposit the rest of that money into her account.

"It should be playing now." Maria leaned to the side, flicked a display on, and the video of Finn wheeling and dealing with Rache from the brig came on. "And transmitting all over the system."

"Good," Bonita repeated. "Can you set it to loop so we can get out of here but leave it going?" At least until someone figured out what was happening and rushed here to fix the problem. And untie Felix.

"I'll try."

Her fingers danced across the console, as if she knew what she was doing. Bonita found that encouraging.

Until the power went out, and blackness swallowed the studio. Everything fell quiet, even the omnipresent hum of the computer equipment.

"Uhm," Bonita said. "Did you do that?"

"No. Someone must have seen the broadcast and shut off the power to the studio. We should get out of here now."

"All right. You better escape from the dastardly bounty hunter and get back to your hospital room to report that you had no choice." Bonita groped for the doorknob. It wasn't just dark; it was *pitch* dark, not a single indicator light left on. "I'm going to try to get to my ship and fly away from the station before they figure out I was responsible."

The hallway outside was as dark as the studio. That was surprising. Had they cut power to the whole broadcast area?

As Bonita patted her way toward the elevator, she realized two things. If the power outage included the elevator, she couldn't leave that way, and… "The alarm stopped sounding."

"You're right." Maria was groping her way along behind her. "I thought it was only in our studio, but maybe the power is out to the whole station."

"Including the environmental controls and everything that allows thousands of people to *survive* on a station?"

"Let's hope there are backups."

Bonita didn't point out that such backups should have already come on if they were going to.

"Any chance the whole video played before things got cut off?" she asked.

"I think it did."

"That's something, I guess."

Bonita reached the cool doors of the elevator, but tapping the buttons didn't do anything. She leaned her forehead against the metal, having no idea how to get back to her ship now.

CHAPTER 23

KIM LAY IN THE DARK IN ONE OF the dozens of guest bedrooms in the Asger castle, staring up at the ceiling and worrying about Casmir, about Rache, and about her entire world. Had she done the right thing in staying here? Had Casmir done the right thing in going with the others? Would any of them survive the week?

She wanted to rest while she could, since the next day might bring chaos, but it was hard to still her mind. She was alternating between penning paragraphs in her manuscript and checking the news. The latest reports said that the Fleet warships had found a way to tag the camouflaged astroshaman vessels and were more effectively harrying them now, attacking in orbit and keeping them from bombing the planet further.

The rumble of an aircraft grew audible, and Kim tensed. She'd heard similar noises numerous times that evening and didn't know if they belonged to enemy ships that had slipped through or the planetary defense forces doing their best to protect the cities.

As the noise grew louder, Kim tried to decide if it sounded different this time. Maybe it wasn't a patrol ship flying past in the distance. Maybe someone was heading to the castle.

Lights flared somewhere outside the window. Yes, a craft was coming in for a landing, and it didn't sound like the helicopter her friends had taken.

Kim swung her legs out of bed and jammed on her shoes. She had been sleeping in her clothes, with her gear all packed and by the door, so it didn't take her long to get ready.

As she rushed down the hallway and knocked on the door to Casmir's parents' room, the roar of more engines rumbled through the castle walls.

"I think we may need to use those tunnels," she called, hoping they were also still packed.

"Be right out," came Irena's voice through the door.

"Kim Sato," a crusher said, startling her when he stepped out of the shadows. "We are here to protect you."

Two more crushers lurked in the hallway behind him. She hadn't gotten the names of the trio that Casmir had left behind.

"Good," she said. "Can you also carry the Dabrowskis' belongings?"

They looked at each other.

"We are strong and capable of carrying a great deal. Would you not prefer that we battle your enemies and keep them from reaching you?"

Nobody ever wanted to carry the luggage and coolers, not even robots.

"Hold on." Kim ran to the end of the hallway and peered through a window overlooking the front drive and lawn.

Four shuttles from the city, including one painted in royal purple, had landed. Her first thought was that Princess Oku had returned, but when the hatches opened, armored men streamed out, along with two handlers with packs of leashed hunting dogs.

She shook her head, knowing immediately that it wasn't Oku. She didn't think it could be King Jager either; the news reports said he was leading the Fleet in the battle up in orbit. Who did that leave? Prince Finn? Why would *he* come here? Maybe the purple shuttle belonged to some knight or senator, not anyone from the royal family. But even if that were true…

"That's an enemy we had better not battle and risk hurting," Kim told the crushers. "Better that they don't find us here."

One handler with three dogs straining at their leashes headed for the front entrance of the castle. Another handler led his canine charges around toward the back gate. Yet another headed across the grassy side yard and toward the woods. That handler ran so straight and determined that Kim had the uneasy feeling that someone had found blueprints of the castle—and maybe the tunnels?—before coming out and knew exactly where the escape passages came out.

The Dabrowskis' door opened, and Kim hurried back to help them with their luggage. Aleksy carried their cat carrier, and the feline inside yowled a complaint. Kim winced, certain those hunting dogs would hear that. Irena carried her own pack and also their cooler. She wasn't going to go anywhere without her food stash to feed everyone.

LAYERS OF FORCE

"We will gather your remaining luggage," one of the crushers stated, startling Irena and Aleksy.

Kim hadn't turned on any lights, so the inky black crushers blended into the shadows.

"Someone from the capital is here with armed troops and dogs and ready to hunt for us." Kim trotted off in the lead. "Follow me."

"*Someone?*" Aleksy adjusted his glasses, wrapped his free arm around his wife's waist, and hurried after Kim.

The crushers came out of the room with the remaining luggage and followed. With luck, the people outside would believe everyone had cleared out of the castle earlier in the day and they were too late.

"I don't know who, but there's a purple shuttle, so whoever is in charge must be obeying the king's direct orders. Or Finn's."

Was Finn back on the planet? Kim didn't know. Later, once they'd found a hiding spot, she would message Rache for an update.

Now she was glad she'd taken the time to locate the entrances to the hidden tunnels the evening before. What she didn't know was how they could keep the dogs from finding their trail and figuring out where they had gone. Maybe she should order the crushers to stay behind to ensure nobody followed them, but that would suggest someone was left here to protect.

Kim Sato, a message floated onto her contact as she twisted a pauldron on a suit of armor mounted on a pedestal against a wall—the lever for the secret entrance. A nearby bookcase slid soundlessly aside, revealing a secret door barely discernible from the surrounding stone wall. *It's Oku. I'm sorry, but Finn drugged me and asked where Casmir was. I couldn't keep from sharing that we'd all been at the Asger castle, and I think he's taking a team there.*

The boom of one of the front doors being battered open echoed through the castle.

They're already here.

I'm sorry. Are you captured?

Not yet. Kim pushed open the door and waved the crushers and Irena and Aleksy into the stone tunnel beyond it. The cat complained as it was carried into the dusty darkness. Kim hurried to close the door, hoping the thick stone walls muffled sounds well. Extremely well. *We're going to hide in some tunnels under the castle.*

I'll... try to do something. I don't know yet if Finn acted with Chief Van Dijk's permission or not. Or my father's permission. If he did, I may not be able to stop them.

We'll do our best to get out of here. Casmir and the others are long gone. The only ones here are Casmir's parents and me.

All people I would prefer not be shot by overzealous troops hoping to win Finn's favor.

"Sh, sh, Bells," Irena whispered to the cat as Aleksy activated a flashlight and led the way into the cobweb-draped tunnel.

Kim searched for a way to brace the door and keep it from opening again if someone found the passage. Her gaze fell upon the crushers.

"Will one of you wait here and lean against that door so they can't get in?" she asked.

The crushers looked at each other again. "Are you certain it is not preferable to go out and battle your enemies, Kim Sato?"

"Prince Finn might be the one leading those guys. He's... not someone we can battle. All we need is time to escape."

"This task is not worthy of the intellect of a crusher, but I will do it for the good of Kim Sato." One of the crushers walked to the door and leaned against it.

"Sorry, I'll try to think of mentally stimulating ways for you to help later."

"I look forward to being stimulated."

All of Casmir's crushers were buggy. She didn't care what he said.

Kim took off with the other two, hurrying to catch up with Irena and Aleksy. The baying of hounds echoed through the castle.

"Nope, those walls aren't soundproof," she whispered.

They'd already descended a long set of stairs, the walls, floor, and ceiling made from the same square stone blocks. Here and there, arches also made from stone added support to the tunnels.

As they took the first of many turns, Kim activated a mapping program on her chip. Casmir had only mentioned a bunker and a tunnel that led out to the woods, but she could already tell this would be a maze. With luck, that would make it harder for their hunters to find them, but her group might also get lost.

Aleksy sneezed as they ran past an old storage cellar. Kim almost caught herself thinking *like father like son* before remembering that Casmir had been adopted.

"We've passed a couple of rooms," Aleksy said over his shoulder. "Should we look for the bunker and hide down here? Or keep going and try to find the tunnel that leads out into the woods?"

"I'm not sure which is better," Kim said. "I saw a handler leading a pack of dogs out into the woods. I think they've anticipated that we may try to leave through tunnels."

"Let's try to hide in here somewhere," Irena said, the cat carrier clunking on a wall as they squeezed around a tight corner. The ceiling was partially crumbled and obstructed the way. "There's no way we'll be able to run fast through the woods with all of our gear, and Bells' meows will carry outside."

They carried *inside*, and Kim would have called them screeches, not meows, but all she said was, "Yes. I left one of the crushers blocking the door, so maybe they won't be able to figure out how to get in. If they can't find us and can't tell for certain that we're down here, they might go away on their own."

A faint rumble made the ceiling and walls shiver, ancient mortar trickling down, and she feared that more shuttles had landed.

Didn't Finn have anything better to do? And didn't he know that Casmir was long gone?

Kim told herself that it was for the best if he didn't know. If Finn—and through him Royal Intelligence—believed Casmir was here, that meant they didn't know where he really was and what he was doing.

But if Finn found and captured Kim and Casmir's parents, would he try to use them to bring Casmir back? Or hurt them as a way to punish him?

She grimaced; maybe she shouldn't have objected to Rache killing Finn, after all.

As they approached the small military outpost, Qin raised her faceplate so she could smell the starkness of the frozen night and feel the chill on her face. The Arctic Islands lacked the appeal of the temperate forested regions, but natural air was almost always more interesting to breathe than filtered. She sniffed, searching for hints of what they would find.

Their group, led by Bjarke, Casmir, and all of his robots, was approaching two long gray buildings with rounded roofs and snow drifts piled high against the metal walls. They were fortunate that the wind had swept the ground mostly clear of that snow, since nobody had brought snowshoes. The ice crunched under her boots but did not give way often.

As the breeze swirled past, Qin inhaled the scents of smoke and warped metal from the helicopter crash, but she didn't smell any humans other than those in her group. The buildings were windowless and dark. If the robot ships hadn't been sent out to attack, she might have thought the base abandoned. It still might be, guarded only by mechanical constructs.

Nobody rushed out to attack them when they reached the first building. A couple of mounds rose up a quarter of a mile away from the little habitation. White and blocky, they didn't look like natural terrain features.

"Are we sure somebody is home?" Bjarke stopped to gaze around the area.

"Maybe they stuck the gate pieces inside and left the robots to guard them." Tristan pointed at the closest door. "Dare we hope it'll be that easy to find them?"

Casmir shook his head, his hood pulled so tight around his face that nothing but the scarf covering his nose was visible. "Those buildings don't match what was on the video Oku sent."

"It's possible we're not in the right place," Asger said.

"Bjarke, Asger, and Tristan." Casmir pointed at the two mounds. "Will you go see if those are the camouflaged ships I believe they are? Qin and Qin-clan, will you help me check these buildings? Remember, we're attempting to peacefully subdue anyone we encounter."

"I do not smell any humans aside from those in our party," Qin said.

"She smells us?" Bjarke asked.

"All animals and humans have distinct odors," Qin said. "Yes, we'll help you, Casmir."

Bjarke looked at Asger and Tristan and waved toward the mounds. "Did we decide Casmir is in charge of this mission?"

"He's the one who planned it," Asger said.

"That doesn't mean he should be in charge."

"You can be in charge of searching the ships under those mounds." Casmir patted Bjarke on the shoulder, then headed for the nearest door.

LAYERS OF FORCE

Bjarke shook his head but trotted with Tristan toward the mounds. Asger hugged Qin briefly, then hurried after them.

Zee surged around Casmir to take the lead on the way to the first building. "You did not say which role you wish the crushers to fill, Casmir Dabrowski."

"Someone should stand guard out here." Casmir glanced skyward. "It's possible the soldiers know we're here and have called for backup."

Likely, Qin thought, not just possible.

"This is a menial role," Zee said. "I will delegate it to the other crushers and be your bodyguard. This door may be booby trapped. I will enter first."

"Thank you, Zee."

"Will the other crushers not think it's menial too?" Mouser asked, walking beside Qin.

"Maybe," Qin said, "but Zee seems to think he's in charge."

Zee tried the knob, found the door locked, and kicked it open like the heroic crusher he believed himself to be.

Qin listened for sounds that would warn of a retaliatory attack. All she heard was the wind scraping across the ice and the breathing of her sisters. Zee strode into the building, with Casmir walking in behind him.

Lights came on automatically when they entered. Qin squinted against the brightness as she stepped in after them. The interior was warmer than the exterior but still cold enough that her breath fogged before her face.

An open area up front held desks facing walls full of astronomical and meteorological equipment. A hallway in the back led to offices. There was no sign of the gate pieces, nor would they have fit inside. The building smelled strongly of humans, but she didn't believe any of them were there presently.

As the group searched around, a message came in from Bonita.

You doing all right, Qin?

Yes, Captain. I'm helping Casmir with a mission.

There was lag, so Qin poked around with the others while she waited for the next part of Bonita's message. She didn't know what they were looking for beyond clues to the location of the gate pieces.

Does that mean you can't get off the planet and meet me out here?

Not until this is done. Right now, I'm not even sure I can get out of their world's Arctic Islands.

I won't ask why you're there, though curious minds want to know.

Casmir led us here for a plan.

"Nothing but offices back here." Casmir came out of the hallway and stopped to consider a control console and displays in a corner.

From Qin's position, it looked like a weather-monitoring station for the local area, but something must have caught Casmir's interest. He poked around and rotated through the displays.

"Nothing about the gate pieces or anything right around the base," he said, "but if we leave someone here, we should be able to see if any ships are coming. I'm able to pick up some of the ships in the orbital battle taking place on this side of the planet."

Qin didn't want to volunteer to stay inside and watch a screen while the others possibly went into battle. Especially when it didn't look like there was anything to see.

"At least I don't see any ships coming yet." Casmir waved for the door. "Let's check the other building."

"What if the gate pieces aren't here?" Mouser asked.

"Then we flew up here and wrecked an antique helicopter for nothing." Casmir headed for the exit. "But I detect other nodes on the network beyond what's represented by the equipment in this building."

Mouser looked at Qin, as if to ask if that addressed their problem. She shrugged back and followed Casmir out.

That explains nothing and yet explains everything, Bonita continued. *Whenever you can get off that planet, if I'm no longer in the system, meet me in System Diomedes. Depending on how the next few hours go, I may have to fly out of System Lion in a hurry.*

That made Qin pause. *What? Why? Captain, you're not trying to get yourself in trouble, are you?*

Once again, Zee led the way into the second building by kicking down the door.

Someone is paying me a lot of money for a job, Bonita replied.

Bounty hunting? You should wait until I'm able to join you. Which, Qin admitted, wouldn't be any time soon, even if she could leave right away. She felt guilty, knowing she'd left her captain without a crew in order to come help Casmir, who hadn't ended up needing her help to escape. Though it was possible he would need her help tonight.

Qin stepped into the building after them and peered around, again only smelling evidence that humans had been there in the past. It had been the *recent* past though, so she stayed alert.

LAYERS OF FORCE

The front of this building held displays, couches and tables, and bookcases with physical atlases and technical manuals. An even less likely place to find a stack of gate pieces.

Not bounty hunting, Bonita continued. *It's a long story, but if you see Prince Finn babbling on the news displays there, you'll know I was responsible.*

You're getting involved in their politics?

The money is good. Very good. If I succeed, I'll be able to pay off the Dragon *and hire all of your sisters if they want the job.*

Qin wanted to ask for more details, but Casmir and Zee had searched the back of the building and were returning.

"There's nobody in the back," Casmir said. "Nothing is dusty, and there are people's belongings in the rooms, so they're *somewhere* around here."

"At least that means we're not exploring an abandoned base, right?" Mouser asked.

"It's not abandoned. Did you see that satellite dish out there?" Casmir waved toward one of the walls. "It's transmitting. Or was earlier today. I'll look out there next."

Qin sent a goodbye and a good luck to Bonita, hoping she wouldn't get herself into trouble, trouble that Qin could have saved her from if she'd been there.

Outside, Asger, Tristan, and Bjarke were no longer in sight. The night air nipped at Qin's cheeks, but she walked around with her faceplate retracted, breathing in the scents.

The icy terrain lacked the variety of climates full of wildlife and foliage, but there were a few variants. A hundred feet from the buildings, she caught a whiff of… humanity. *Live* humanity. Beard gel, shampoo, and the body odor of a man. The breeze had shifted, and she almost lost it.

She didn't see anything, but she walked in the direction the scents had been coming from. She trusted her nose.

Casmir? She messaged him since he'd headed over to the satellite dish, which was in the opposite direction. *I may have found something.*

Weapons fire buzzed near the dish, red DEW-Tek blasts streaking out from the ground.

Qin spun and raised her rifle, searching for an enemy. Two crushers lay on the ground as the blasts continued all around them. They weren't coming from people with rifles but from some kind of automatic-weapons system with heads that had popped out of the ice like sprinklers.

Me too, Casmir replied, though she didn't see him. *Booby traps.*

She lifted her rifle and aimed at one of the little black cylinders that were firing at the intruders. The device blew into dozens of pieces that clattered to the ice.

Before she could target more of them, several crushers charged out of the building and pounced on them. They tore the heads from their mounts, breaking them into even more pieces than her blast had, then dropped them to the ground.

The two crushers lying on the ice rolled to the side. Casmir, who'd been completely hidden under them—*protected* by them—stood up, shaking his limbs and rubbing the back of his head.

Are crushers as heavy as they look? Qin asked.

Yes. But fast to respond. Like throwing themselves on a grenade, except the opposite. What did you find? With the defenses destroyed, Casmir poked around the satellite dish as he messaged her.

I smell someone. Qin noticed Pounce and Swish also walking across the ice and sniffing at the air.

After finishing a quick inspection of the satellite, Casmir headed toward Qin with the crushers trailing him. He looked toward the two white mounds in the distance, presumably where the knights had disappeared to, but the scents of humanity weren't coming from that direction.

"I found a cable going into the ground—the ice—over there," Casmir said when he reached her. "It's hard to tell if it goes down five feet or five hundred. From what I read on the way up here, the sheets of ice are over a thousand meters thick in places."

"You were reading while you were airsick?" Qin waved for him to follow her toward where she'd caught the scent.

"Before the turbulence started, yes."

A breeze—no, it felt more like an updraft—brushed her nose, bringing the scents of humans again. More than one this time. She was positive. She also smelled the scent of machinery, maybe a generator. A faint hum reached her ears. It seemed closer than the human scents, so she crept toward it. But slowly. Some sixth sense warned her that she was in danger, though she couldn't see, hear, or smell a reason for it.

The ice gave way beneath her foot, and she almost fell.

"Qin!" Casmir shouted from behind her.

She pitched herself sideways, toward solid footing and gaped at what looked like flat ground but had been a hole.

LAYERS OF FORCE

"There's something there that isn't visible," she warned, waving for the others to stay back as she heard them rushing closer.

"Careful, please," Casmir warned, his voice tight with worry. "Viggo would be terribly upset with me if I lost you."

"He would forgive you if you bought him a new vacuum." Qin scooted closer on her hands and knees and swept her fingers back and forth, searching for the hole that her eyes told her wasn't there.

"I don't know if that's true."

"He does like me. You might have to get him a *dozen* vacuums."

Ah ha. There was her hole. More like a cliff. She still couldn't see it, but she felt the edge. A drop-off ran in roughly a straight line for who knew how long, and she'd almost walked right off it.

Much more careful now, she followed the invisible cliff and found the generator she'd heard and smelled, a compact device hidden under white camouflage netting with snow mounded atop it.

She opened a panel on the side, and the hum grew louder. A few indicator lights blinked around a bunch of switches. None of them said anything as obvious as ON/OFF.

Casmir knelt beside her and tapped two buttons, then flipped a switch without a label.

"Do you know what you're doing?" Qin asked.

"Sometimes."

The generator turned off, and several clicks sounded all along the cliff they'd been following and farther out from it as well. The other side?

What had appeared to be solid ground wavered and disappeared. Qin gaped at the fissure that was revealed. No, not a fissure. More of a wide and deep, *deep* chasm.

Casmir scooted forward on hands and knees. The crushers loomed behind him, hands outstretched, as if to yank him back if the ice gave way.

"Good work, Qin," Casmir said. "I believe you've found where the gate pieces may be hidden."

Qin peered over the side into darkness so absolute that even her enhanced eyes couldn't see all the way to the bottom. "How do we get down?"

"That remains a mystery. Is this where the human scents are coming from?"

She sniffed the air again, realizing that the scents came and went, depending on the drafts. There. She detected them again.

"Yes."

"Maybe there's an elevator somewhere."

"A crusher could jump many hundreds of feet and survive the fall," one of Casmir's bodyguards said.

"Could a crusher also climb back up with a giant gate piece on his shoulder?" Casmir asked.

"We are very strong, but climbing ice may be difficult, even for us."

"Let's find that elevator then. The troops have to be getting in and out somehow." Casmir squinted into the dark chasm. "Unless a ship or aircraft flew down there and dropped them off."

Weapons fire came from the other side of the camp, from the two mounds the others had been investigating. Qin scooted back and jumped to her feet.

"Watch him," Qin told the crushers and rushed toward the noise in case Asger and the others needed help.

By the time she reached the mounds, Asger and Tristan were scrambling out from under what appeared to be more camouflage netting. They dragged two men in cold-weather military uniforms and parkas behind them, neither man moving.

"Good news," Asger said, though he appeared distracted as he stared at the newly revealed chasm, a long dark scar in the white and blue ice impossible to miss. "We've verified that there are two ships under the camouflage. Bad news, at least one of them had a small crew aboard. We took care of these guys. My father is checking on the other ship."

Casmir jogged up, slipping and flailing on the ice—one of the crushers steadied him—in time to hear this.

"Did you stun them?" He pointed to the men.

"Yes. We'll need to lock them up somewhere, and someone should stay and keep an eye on them."

"That building." Casmir pointed to the first one they had explored. "There's a monitoring station inside that can let us know if—*when*—ships are coming. Our guard can watch two things at once while the rest of us go down and look for the gate pieces." He pointed toward the chasm.

"Who gets that scintillating job?" Asger asked.

Casmir smiled at him and Tristan.

"I think that means we flip a coin," Asger told Tristan.

"I'll do it." Tristan eyed the newly revealed chasm, night making its dark depths even more ominous. "I'm not so enamored with heights that I want to climb down the side of an ice cliff."

LAYERS OF FORCE

"We're hoping for an elevator," Qin offered.

"Given the sparseness of what we've seen here so far," Tristan said, "you'll be lucky to find a rope."

"How big are the ships?" Casmir asked. "Would one of them fit down there?"

Asger eyed the chasm with a lack of enthusiasm. "We'll have to do some measurements."

"There's more bad news, Casmir." Tristan glanced at Asger. "We walked in on these men comming someone, warning them that the base had been compromised and asking for backup."

Casmir peered up at the starry night sky. "We had better hurry then."

"Into that chasm?" Asger asked.

"Into that chasm," Casmir said.

"Hell."

CHAPTER 24

AFTER MESSAGING KIM TO WARN HER—FAR TOO LATE to be useful—that Finn was on his way to the Asger estate, Oku leashed up Chasca and headed for Van Dijk's office.

The guard coming back from walking the dog was what had roused Oku from her drug-induced sleep. She was still groggy, but not so groggy that she didn't plan to do anything. Guilt and worry propelled her into a run, Chasca bounding along with her. Oku had not only foolishly let her brother in to drug her, but she'd betrayed Casmir's family.

Kim had mentioned tunnels they were hiding in, but Finn's lackeys would probably find them and drag them out at gunpoint. And it would be her fault. She'd specifically told Casmir that he and his friends wouldn't be in trouble because Van Dijk didn't care enough to look for them. She hadn't factored Finn into the equation.

Two tense-looking guards stood outside of Van Dijk's office. They exchanged wary glances with each other as Oku approached, but they didn't stop her when she rushed up and pounded on the door.

"I'm busy," came Van Dijk's cranky call.

Oku went in anyway.

"That meant go away, not invite yourself in." Van Dijk was standing at her desk, hammering at a tablet while glancing at the numerous displays on the wall, and she looked up with an exasperated scowl. "Oh, it's you."

Oku had been prepared to snap back, but Van Dijk waved her in.

"Who were you expecting?" she asked.

"The legions of troops who now want to strangle your brother."

"Because… he drugged me?"

How would the troops have found out? And why would they care that much?

"No. Because of *this*." Van Dijk pointed at a display showing Finn locked in a brig cell and sent a command via her chip to raise the volume.

Oku watched, riveted and distracted from her mission as Finn appeared to make a deal to hire Rache to kill their father. By now, Oku wouldn't be surprised if this had actually happened, though she highly suspected Rache of engineering the situation. Who had recorded this? Him?

"Where did this come from?" she wondered.

"Our broadcast station out at Forseti. It broadcasted to the entire system before they lost power."

"Before the studio lost power?"

"No, all of Forseti Station is without power. As is every ship, habitat, and station that the AI ship has flown anywhere near on its path toward Odin. It's transmitting something we can't detect that's knocking out power for more than a hundred million miles in every direction. So far, none of the ships have managed to get their power back online. They've got no life support, *nothing*. You can imagine how quickly that will become devastating. The AI ship makes this mess with Finn seem insignificant, but it's not like I can ignore him. I'm already hearing rumors of our citizens wanting to lynch him. And they're not the only ones. That Captain Marchetti—Sir Slayer—has disappeared from his base with shuttles and a bunch of his Protectors of the Future minions." Van Dijk gripped the edge of her desk. "I think they're as pissed that he negotiated with Rache as that he wants to kill Jager—or you."

"I don't imagine the general populace knows me that well to be offended on my behalf." Oku also guessed that working with Rache was the greater crime in many of their eyes.

"We'll find out who sent it as soon as we can. For now, I need to figure out where Finn went, since he disappeared from his apartment, so I can send loyal troops to protect him." Van Dijk threw her head back and groaned in frustration. "If I survive this, I'm retiring to another system."

"Asger Castle."

Van Dijk lowered her head. "What?"

"That's what I came to tell you. Finn drugged me and questioned me about Casmir. He thinks he's still there and is going out to Asger Castle after him. Kim and Casmir's parents *are* still there. Can you send someone—and me—to help them? To make sure he can't hurt them?"

"Dabrowski isn't there?"

"No, he left more than twelve hours ago with all of his combat helpers."

"Finn questioned you with drugs and he didn't get that information?"

"He didn't ask the right questions."

"No kidding. Why is he even after Dabrowski?"

"He said he wants to drop him at Father's feet to prove something. That he's worth being named Father's heir. I don't know, and I don't care. I can't let Kim and Irena and Aleksy be hurt because I let that idiot stick an injector in my throat."

"Yes, you shouldn't have done that."

"He got one of the guards to help." Oku frowned, annoyed that all of this had happened in Van Dijk's own headquarters and she was just now finding out about it, but she glanced at the display playing a loop of Finn's shenanigans, another showing a dark habitat completely without power, and yet another showing the AI ship. She decided she could understand why the chief was distracted. "I need a ride out there. And ideally some people who can force Finn's people to back down in case he won't listen to me. Can you help me?"

Van Dijk scowled at the displays, then nodded. "I'll go out there with you. I've got to get Finn and drag him back here before someone armed and angry gets to him." Still scowling, she ran to a weapons locker and grabbed a rifle and a tactical vest full of gear. "If I lose another of your siblings this month, I won't get to retire. Jager will have me shot."

Oku thought about pointing out that she couldn't have done anything about Jorg, but if Van Dijk's guilt and fear led her to give Oku a ride, she couldn't object.

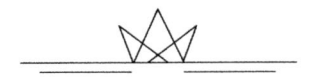

It was only in Bonita's imagination that the air was thin. Or so she told herself as she climbed down levels and levels through an access shaft that she and Maria had found and were navigating together.

Forseti Station was still dark and, as far as Bonita knew, completely without power. She was surprised the spin gravity hadn't disappeared, leaving them floating in free fall, but she supposed an object in motion stayed in motion—or continued to spin. Physics wasn't her strong suit. Maybe Viggo could explain it—if she ever got in touch with him. So far, she hadn't been able to, and that worried her.

Right now, her main goal was to get back to the *Dragon,* hope the power situation was fine there, and get off the station before people started freaking out.

Which might already be happening. Now and then, clangs, clunks, screeches, and shouts penetrated the walls to their access shaft. The screeches and shouts sounded panicked. The last thing she wanted was to run into a riot.

Bonita wished she could see better. Her helmet should have augmented the night vision in her contacts, but the heads-up display was as offline as everything else.

"I'm not able to get in touch with my unit," Maria said, her voice sounding hollow since she'd donned her helmet.

They both had, in case the oxygen ran out, but neither of them had supplemental tanks. Once she reached the *Dragon,* there should be plenty of air. If nothing else, she had numerous filled tanks in storage there. So long as someone wasn't taking advantage of this situation to loot her ship. She scowled at the idea.

"I can't get in touch with my ship either." Bonita glanced at a sign as they climbed past. Level 23. The concourse and her airlock were on 1. She kept going. "Nor do I have a wireless signal. I tried to send a nasty note to, uhm, the doctor who sent that video, so I could blame him for being stuck on a powerless station. No luck."

She'd tried to send that note to *Rache*. And also to check to see if the video had gotten out, and if he intended to pay her the other eighty-five percent, thus making this headache worth it.

"I don't either." Maria sounded worried. "If that ship attacks, the station is going to be defenseless."

And them along with it.

Bonita descended faster, almost skimming down the rungs. Just months ago, her bum knees would have made this very difficult. At least she'd gotten them fixed before the end had come.

She thumped down on Level 1 and spun the hatch, crossing her fingers that it would open. The elevator doors hadn't, but these were emergency exits.

It opened into a dead-end hallway near the concourse with doors that opened to the backs of the various shops. They were all closed, with nobody in sight, but flashlight beams bounced about somewhere beyond a corner. Worried voices also came from that direction. The concourse, Bonita assumed. Someone shouted for everyone to stay calm and that all the systems would be back online soon.

"We're running out of air!" came more than one panicked reply.

Bonita held her stunner as Maria climbed out after her. She wouldn't be surprised if they had to fight their way to the *Dragon*.

"That may not work," Maria warned as they crept toward the concourse.

"What? The stunner? It worked fine on Felix."

"That was before the power went out."

"These run on their own battery packs."

"I know, but as far as I can tell, *everything* has been knocked out."

"Not those people's flashlights." To test the stunner, Bonita pointed it at a door they passed and fired. Nothing happened. "Damn, what did they throw at us?"

"I have no idea, but this entire system may be screwed." Maria lowered her voice. "Or *all* of the systems. What if there are more ships out there like that?"

"Stop depressing me. If that video went out, I stand to get paid piles—enough to buy my freighter outright. This is no time for the entire Twelve Systems to be screwed."

"Because it would inconvenience you?"

"Exactly." Bonita led the way out into the concourse, wincing when flashlight beams shone in her eyes.

"Sit down in the seats, please!" someone called from the center of the area. "We've got maintenance crews working on the problem. Everyone else needs to stay out of the way and hang tight."

"While that ship comes and obliterates us?" someone cried.

More cries went up from people who were sitting in the rows of seats near the restaurants and shops—and from those who refused to sit in them.

Bonita would happily hang tight once she reached her ship. She followed the wall and avoided the people and anyone who might try to make her take a seat.

"I think those flashlights are extremely basic," Maria said. "Maybe that's why they're still working. No real tech to be knocked out."

Bonita glanced into one of the airlock tubes on the way to where she was docked. Two furtive men with bags over their shoulders were skulking out of a ship's open hatch. One squinted and lifted a dagger in her direction—was that the only kind of weapon that would work right now?—when they made eye contact.

Though the two men were obviously taking advantage of the chaos to loot, Bonita would have hustled past—she was more worried about her own ship than someone else's, and she didn't need to add a knife wound to her day's problems. But Maria blurted an indignant, "Robbers!"

Bonita braced herself for a fight as Maria raised her fists. But a squad of four androids in station-security uniforms charged toward the airlock. How were *they* operating when nothing else technological was?

The men whirled and ran back into the ship they'd been pillaging. Maria and Bonita scooted out of the way as the androids thundered into the airlock tube after them.

"They'll take care of it," Bonita said, lest Maria feel compelled to run after them with her bare fists.

"Yeah. Good." Maria lowered her hands.

"Maybe you're in the right place after all."

"What? This station?"

"No, the Kingdom Fleet. Despite being thugs, most of their soldiers and knights seem to have preoccupations with being noble." Bonita thought of Bjarke and Asger. Even Casmir, who was far from a soldier or a knight, couldn't resist trying to do the right thing.

LAYERS OF FORCE

"I suppose that's—" Maria's gaze shifted over Bonita's shoulder. "Uh oh."

Bonita turned in time to see two Kingdom soldiers step out of the airlock tube leading to the *Dragon*. Two *familiar* soldiers. They were among those who had been injured and that she'd brought to the station. They were wearing hospital togs rather than their uniforms, save for the combat boots they must have shoved on before rushing down here. One of them had also found time to grab a weapon.

"Captain Lopez and Sergeant Lopez," the senior-ranking man said coolly, pointing a firearm loaded with gunpowder cartridges at Bonita. Hell, that thing would work without power. And it would be far more damaging than a stunner. "Drop your weapons and put your hands up."

"Are we under arrest?" Bonita tossed her useless stunner to the floor and raised her hands. "*Now?*"

Didn't the Fleet have anything better to do? Like figure out how to restore power and defeat a hostile AI ship?

"*You* are under arrest. Sergeant Lopez will be held at the station until such time as she can be taken back to Fleet Command on Odin and a military court-martial can be convened."

Bonita's first thought was to play dumb—how could these guys have figured out so quickly that she and Maria were responsible, especially when power had gone out seconds after they transmitted the video? But if they were talking about a court-martial, they knew about the broadcast—and who had been responsible.

"I forced her to do it," Bonita said. "Back when my stunner was working, I was quite formidable."

"Sure, you did. Gray-haired women are super scary."

Bonita bared her teeth at him. If he hadn't been pointing that gun at her, she would have shown him exactly how scary she could be.

"My gray hair doesn't preclude my ability to *shoot* people," she growled.

"It's all right, Captain," Maria said quietly, her hands also raised. "It was worth it."

It wouldn't be worth it if Bonita ended up in jail for the rest of her life and didn't get to spend any of Rache's money.

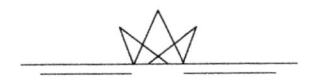

Good evening, Kim, a message came in from Rache as she hunkered in a windowless room under Asger's castle, with Casmir's parents sitting beside her, their eyes wide as they listened to distant shouts, and the crushers guarding the entrance. *I suppose it's after midnight local time for you. Are you awake?*

Awake and hoping not to be found by the search parties scouring the tunnels under Asger's castle.

It hadn't taken them long to find a way down here—presumably not through the crusher she'd left blocking the secret door Kim's group had used—but she hadn't yet heard the dogs baying, so maybe they were covering the grounds outside. Poised to alert their handlers if Kim, Irena, and Aleksy came to the surface.

As soon as they'd heard voices in the tunnels, Kim had suggested changing hiding spots often, and they had wandered back and forth through the same intersections in the hope of confusing the dogs if they *were* brought down. Thankfully, the cat had quieted down. The crushers kept offering to subdue the intruders, and after a few near misses with the search parties, Kim was tempted.

The planet is being invaded by astroshamans, Rache messaged, *an AI ship is knocking out power everywhere in the system, and someone in Intelligence decided to order a manhunt right* now?

It's a woman-hunt, thank you. Or a Casmir's-parents-hunt. Kim had no idea, and she wasn't going to wander into the searchers' grasp so she could ask for clarification. *What are* you *doing? Any chance you want to come down and help?*

Oddly, I'm running low on shuttles.

Weird. She didn't mention the one they'd abandoned in the woods and that had doubtless been confiscated by the authorities.

Indeed. I'm going to make a policy not to lend them to relatives anymore. Are you truly in trouble? I can't bring the Fedallah into that gravity well, or I'll never get out—nobody is going to give us a slot on the launch loop—but if there's something I can do, I will.

LAYERS OF FORCE

Bored up there, are you?

A distant shout of "This way," floated to their ears. Aleksy shook his head slowly at his wife, then turned off the flashlight he'd kept throughout their ordeal.

Kim doubted that would do anything to help hide them, but she didn't say anything.

Bored? No. We're being kept busy. Even though nobody is targeting us specifically—the astroshamans are attacking the Fleet, and the Fleet is attacking the astroshamans—a few more ships seem to have developed the ability to detect slydar, so we're having to be careful. Interestingly, the Fleet appears to have gained the advantage for the first time. Jager's warship has started using some unknown technology to mark the hidden ships, and now planetary weapons are firing upon them. One astroshaman ship just blew up spectacularly almost in front of our noses. I was curious if you knew anything about that.

Kim started to shake her head, but then she remembered the battle with Dubashi's hidden ships at Stardust Palace. *That sounds like the marking technology that Casmir and Tork came up with. I think it used some astroshaman technology. Tork belonged to them at one point.*

How delightful then that they are being targeted as a result of their own technology. Did Casmir give *this technology to the Kingdom? Did Jager actually* accept *it?*

I don't know. Casmir left a while ago. He's on his own mission.

And what mission might that be?

Nothing to do with you.

I guess that means he's not trying to kill Jager.

You knew he wasn't. Are you *still trying to do that?*

Why else would Rache be up there? Dancing around what sounded like a horrible battle?

Kim was tempted to ask him to go help Casmir—surely Casmir would have an easier time flying those gate pieces off Odin if someone was running interference for him—but that would mean admitting what Casmir was up to. To someone who rarely had the same goal as they did.

I am waiting for an opportunity, yes. If the Senate and the citizens as a whole react the way I believe they will to my video—did you by chance see that?—Casmir's path ahead may be clear.

Path for what? And no, I haven't seen any videos. I'm underneath a castle. My reception isn't the best.

Do look at the news when you get a chance. And tell me who threatens you, so I might arrange an improvement to the situation.

A boom came from somewhere above, and the walls and floor rattled. The cat screeched a protest as dust and bits of mortar rained down. It coated Kim's tongue, and she put her sleeve over her mouth.

Aleksy turned the flashlight back on, the halo dimmed by the cloud of dust. "What was that?"

"Explosives," Kim said. "I can't guess *why* they're using explosives, unless they've decided to bring down the castle on us and hope to bury us down here."

The crushers looked at each other and appeared to be communicating silently. Would they disobey Kim's orders for her own good and run out to attack? Maybe she should let them.

"That's horrific," Irena said. "That castle is a thousand years old."

Another boom rocked the earth.

Shouts echoed through the passages. Most of them weren't distinguishable, but Kim thought she picked out, "Protect the prince!" and "Get out of here!" among them.

"I'm confused," she whispered, the words turning into coughs. She batted at the dust in front of her face. "Are there *two* groups out there?"

Bits of stone clattered to the floor, and more dust floated down. Something snapped ominously overhead.

The crushers grabbed Aleksy and Irena and pulled them out of the room. Kim lunged out after them an instant before blocks smashed down, shattering and flinging shards everywhere.

"I believe it's time to leave," Aleksy said.

The cat wailed in agreement.

Irena coughed and wiped dust from her eyes. "Which way is out?"

Kim brought up the map program she'd been using to track their route. "Back up into the castle? Or out to the woods?"

"The castle doesn't sound safe," Aleksy said.

Kim doubted anywhere was safe.

"I think I know where the tunnel to the woods is." Kim took the lead, with one crusher right behind her and the second behind the Dabrowskis.

Several times earlier, their group had passed a long straight passage that appeared to head back into the hills. Kim found it quickly, though rocks freshly fallen from the ceiling slowed their progress.

LAYERS OF FORCE

As they turned up the tunnel, another boom shook the earth. The noise was farther behind them now, and no rocks tumbled down from above their heads. The explosives seemed to be focused on the castle, or the grounds in *front* of it.

Kim dearly hoped someone wasn't bombing the old castle. The Asgers had already lost enough by being associated with her and Casmir.

They scrambled over a heap of broken ceiling stones in the way, and the first scent of the outdoors wafted to them. Soon after, they reached an underground pond—no, a storage cistern that was open on the top. On the far side, a ladder led up to a circular hatch. Roots dangled down through cracks in the cement ceiling all around it.

After making sure Irena and Aleksy were still with her, Kim jogged around the cistern to the ladder. She scrambled up to the metal hatch, spun a wheel, and was relieved that it wasn't locked. Copious pine needles, soggy leaves, and tufts of moss tumbled inside as she raised it a few inches.

"Nobody's gone this way for a while," she whispered, peering out.

It was dark, so there wasn't much to see, but they'd come up in the forest. She listened for the snuffling of dogs on the hunt, but all she heard were distant shouts. Light flashed somewhere in the direction of the castle, and another boom roared, this one not muffled by the earth.

"I don't think anyone is around the hatch." Kim climbed out and opened the hatch fully, waving for the Dabrowskis to hand up the cat carrier and their bags.

The crushers were the ones to bring everything, flowing up the rungs while growing extra appendages to carry the luggage. As they assisted Casmir's parents up the ladder, Kim hurried through the forest in the direction of the castle, needing to see what was happening. Had the astroshamans come down for another bombing run? If so, why would they focus on the Asger castle?

She came to the edge of the trees, and though she was disoriented from the tunnel trek, she thought she wasn't far from the gravel road they'd followed here the other night. The castle stood on the hilltop, framed against the night sky by lights from aircraft circling the area. From hundreds of yards away, she couldn't tell how much the structure had been damaged. Most of the castle was still standing, but she thought she remembered a tower at one end that wasn't there now.

She could see some of the same shuttles that she'd glimpsed through the window before, but one was now a charred hulk. Another was missing completely, but a smoking crater in the lawn marked the spot where it had been. Where had the purple one—Finn's shuttle—gone? She thought it had been... Oh, there it was. There were its *remains*. Someone must have targeted it with multiple bombs. Had Finn been inside when they'd struck? Or had he been leading the search in the tunnels?

"What's going on?" Irena whispered, crouching beside her.

"Ah," Aleksy said. "Hm, I wonder."

"What?" Kim and Irena said together.

"I'm accessing my chip, and there's an interesting video being broadcast over and over on all the channels."

"A video?" Kim asked.

Rache had mentioned a video...

"Of Prince Finn attempting to hire the mercenary Tenebris Rache," Aleksy said. "To kill his father. I'm watching it now. It's difficult to tell if it's authentic or was engineered somehow, but it may be enough to make many people most upset with the boy."

"Upset enough to blow up his shuttle?" Kim stared at the smoking remains of the purple craft.

"I suppose that's possible," Aleksy said. "One wonders how people knew he was here though."

Kim thought of Oku's warning. "Maybe he *told* people that he was coming to collect Casmir. At the least, he gathered all those men to bring with him. *They* might have talked." She pointed toward the shuttles that were still intact but paused, realizing something she'd missed before. There were bodies out there among the wreckage. They were armored, so maybe they were still alive, but the ones she could see weren't moving.

Two shuttles that had been hidden behind the castle roared into the air and flew off, heading in the direction of Zamek City. The aircraft that had been circling also flew off.

Did you do that? Kim messaged Rache.

I don't know to what you refer, but it's unlikely. I tried to find out who's attacking that castle, and they appear to be soldiers. Unlike with pirates and mercenaries, I can't call in any markers or offer to pay them to leave a target.

They're leaving anyway.

Are you well? Uninjured?

For the moment.

LAYERS OF FORCE

Good. I suggest you take advantage of whatever is happening and leave the area.

I'll keep your suggestion in mind. Kim didn't point out that it was unlikely she could get a ride, unless someone who remained with the two intact shuttlecraft would take them away. But she doubted it—those were Finn's allies.

You'll have to excuse me. The Starhawk *is on the move. This could be the opportunity I've waited for.*

Rache, you don't need to do this.

He didn't reply.

Rache? David?

Nothing.

Irena stood, the cat protesting again, though not yowling like before. "Aleksy, I see people who may need medical help."

"So do I," he said, "but it's not safe for you to go over there."

"The aircraft flying around have left the area."

"That doesn't mean it's safe. The people who were trying to find us are still there." Aleksy lowered his voice. "Some of them."

"Yes, and I'm going to check on them. I may be the only one here with medical experience. Here, hold the cat."

"Yes, dear." Aleksy accepted the cat carrier but stood, clearly planning to go with her.

Kim, doubting Irena would be deterred, walked out with them and waved for the crushers to protect them.

A distance that had seemed to take an hour to navigate through in the tunnel only took a couple of minutes to cross in the open. Kim kept expecting someone to shout and point at them, but with the aircraft gone, there wasn't any light shining around them. A few landscape lights remained around the castle itself, and a few lights were on inside of it, but nothing else.

When they rounded the corner of the castle, the carnage grew more obvious. Only one of the shuttles was fully intact. Its hatch was open, and two people had fallen running toward it, their arms outstretched as if they had known they would have been safe if only they had reached it.

Kim counted more than ten fallen men in the area, most wearing the blue armor of soldiers. She turned toward the castle, then jumped. The front door, front wall, entryway, and the nearest tower had collapsed, rubble piled atop the marble floors. A light was still on in the kitchen, and it and the massive dining hall table were visible, just a few rocks lying atop it. The ceiling was still intact there—for now. More armored bodies lay inside among the rubble.

Irena ran to people, calling for Aleksy to help her turn them over and try to remove their helmets to check them. A few groans came from the fallen, promising that at least some had survived.

"Help them uncover people, please," Kim told the crushers.

In the remains of the entryway, a rock atop a pile of rubble stirred, then tipped and tumbled down to the floor. An arm stretched out—a purple armored arm—then flopped down, going limp.

Kim well remembered that Jorg had worn purple armor—and had been dead when she'd walked into the hold on the *Chivalrous*. Had she arrived too late again, in the aftermath of the second prince's death? And would the idiots in charge somehow blame Casmir again? Or maybe *her* this time?

"Prince Finn is over here," Kim called out to Irena and ran for the rubble pile. "He may need help."

That limp arm didn't move, and the rest of his body was completely buried.

He may be dead already, she added to herself.

CHAPTER 25

AS SOON AS YAS FINISHED TREATING THE TWO patients who had come in during the first real skirmish, in which the *Fedallah* had taken a number of solid blows, he found his pod, the sides tightening comfortably around him. He could feel the ship accelerating as it descended from orbit into the planet's atmosphere, though nobody had told him what Rache was chasing or how they would later escape Odin's gravitational pull once they were down there. It was a foregone conclusion that criminal warships weren't allowed on the public launch loop.

The ship swerved, the maneuvering much more noticeable—and jarring—in the gravity of a planet than out in space. Yas imagined a crash would be devastating.

How are you doing in engineering? he sent a message to Jess.

She would be busy, and he shouldn't risk distracting her, but they had been messaging back and forth more often lately, talking about slipping away for something as prosaic as dinner and a show at a station after all this was over—should the universe cooperate and allow them both to live. He'd grown more comfortable sending her idle chitchat.

I'm trying to hold this ship together, came Jess's reply. *You?*

I've had a couple of mercenaries come in for treatment—mostly head bumps—but nothing major so far.

Maybe we'll get lucky, and the captain will keep it that way.

Maybe. He didn't want to quash her hope with his own doubts.

To his surprise, Rache strode into sickbay wearing his black combat armor. "Doctor, collect your injured and all of your belongings you can grab quickly, and get to the shuttle bay."

"Am I... going somewhere?"

"*Everybody's* going somewhere." With his message delivered, Rache strode back out.

Though he did not know if Rache meant they were leaving temporarily or permanently, Yas grabbed a few medical supplies in sickbay, then ran to his quarters for a couple of changes of clothing. He had acquired little more than that during his time on the mercenary ship. It wasn't as if Rache had allowed them frequent shore leave on space stations and encouraged souvenir shopping.

When Yas walked into the shuttle bay, he gaped at all the armored men and women cramming themselves into the three remaining shuttles. Had Rache truly meant *everybody*? And where were those shuttles supposed to go? They were already down in Odin's atmosphere, a planet that hated Rache and surely hated every member of his crew, known to them or not. Even though Yas hadn't been a voluntary recruit, the idea of trying to find passage off this planet without having his link to Rache discovered was daunting.

A hand clapped him on the back.

"Glad you made it, Doc." Jess had her pack and two weapons slung over her shoulder.

"It looks like everybody made it."

"Everybody but Rache from what I understand. He's sparing us from his suicide mission."

"Is that what this is?"

The deck shuddered as the *Fedallah* picked up speed.

"I think that's what this *always* was." Jess twitched a shoulder. "He probably didn't ever intend to bring the whole ship along on it, but his target never cooperated by leaving *his* ship."

His target. King Jager.

"The line is shortest there." Jess pointed to one of the shuttles. "We better go. I'm guessing we don't have a lot of time until he catches up with his prey and engages."

"He's flying the ship by *himself*? Can he do that?"

"Of course. He's Tenebris Rache." Jess headed for the shuttle, waving for him to follow.

"One moment, Doctor," Rache said, startling Yas. He hadn't been there a second before.

With one black gauntleted hand, Rache held out a forest-green business card.

"Is this the hotel we're supposed to stay at on Odin?" Yas accepted it and frowned. It had the name and contact information for some publishing company that wasn't located on the planet. Possibly not even in the system.

"No. You'll have to secure your own lodgings. I've made deposits into everyone's accounts that should get them all to their homes or their next jobs, should I not be able to escape the planet and recall everyone."

"Thank you, sir."

"If at all possible, I need you to give that to Scholar Sato." Rache pointed at the card.

"I think girls like jewelry, sir. Flowers. Chocolates."

"She will prefer this. I am certain."

The deck rattled again.

"I must return to the bridge. You'll give it to her?"

Yas was surprised it was a question and not an order. "I'll do my best to do so."

Assuming he wasn't captured and shot. Or Kim wasn't captured and shot.

"Excellent."

"Any message to go with it?" Yas held up the card. It seemed such a scant and obscure gift.

Rache hesitated, then shook his head. "No."

As Rache walked out of the shuttle bay, Yas wondered if he would ever see him again.

The crushers made short work of removing the camouflage netting from what turned out to be an armored troop transport vessel and a cargo ship. Casmir was glad for their speed, for he believed that Kingdom backup would arrive soon. It had taken his team hours to fly here in the dilapidated helicopter, but it wouldn't take nearly that long for modern aircraft to zip up to the Arctic Islands. A spacecraft descending from orbit could arrive even more quickly.

Tristan was at the monitoring station with their subdued prisoners, and he'd promised to message Casmir if ships headed their way, but that couldn't keep Casmir from glancing frequently at the starry sky, expecting an enemy fleet at any moment. He also kept glancing in the chasm. An attack could as easily come from there.

Whoever was stationed down there likely knew that the generator projecting the illusion had been turned off and that Casmir's team was up here futzing around. He was careful whenever he leaned over the edge, well aware that he might be visible to a platoon of armed soldiers down there in the dark.

The transport vessel that Bjarke had searched had been empty of a crew, but the two men that Tristan and Asger had caught had been sending out warnings to everyone from their direct superiors to Military Intelligence back in Zamek City. The cargo ship's comm records had shown that.

Casmir had to assume that his team would not take the men in the chasm by surprise. Which was why he would prefer to rapidly fly to the bottom in one of the ships rather than climb down those icy walls. Ideally in the cargo ship, since it had likely been what dropped off the gate pieces in the first place. If it had dropped them off, it could pick them up.

With a program he'd hurried to download, Casmir estimated the width of the chasm at different spots. As he stood in the shadow of the cargo ship, he looked up its specifications. It could easily fit into the chasm at the top, but it was too dark to see to the bottom and tell if it was wide enough all the way down. It occurred to him that the cargo ship might have hovered over the opening and lowered the pieces down with its maglocker.

"Wish I could see the bottom," Casmir muttered, though he highly doubted the pieces were lying down there in the open. The guarded doors in the video Oku had sent belied that idea.

"I believe I can jump to the bottom without causing myself irreparable harm, Casmir Dabrowski," Zee said from his side.

"Can you tell how far to the bottom it is?"

"Approximately four hundred and seventy-three feet and three inches."

"Approximately."

"Yes. Would you like the calculation to decimal places?"

"No, I think that will be sufficient. And I will point out, since I know your specifications, that you are only rated to survive a drop of four hundred feet in Odin's gravity."

"That is true if I fall in my bipedal form, but I can spread my mass out like a kite to descend at a slower rate due to drag."

"You are a very smart crusher."

"Yes. Since you know my computing capabilities, you know this."

"I do." Casmir grinned at him.

Zee couldn't ruffle his hair since Casmir wore a parka with a hood, but he did pat Casmir on the head.

"I'm glad your sensors allow you to detect the bottom. With my limited human eyesight…" Casmir rubbed the eye that was watering despite the impossibility of there being pollen in the air and peered into the black chasm again. "I was wondering if it went all the way to the center of the planet."

"I assume you are being facetious."

"Yes, but I can't see the bottom. Can you also measure the width? Will the cargo ship fit all the way down there?"

"In certain places—" Zee pointed to a spot a hundred yards away, "—it could reach the bottom and land with seven feet and four inches to spare on each side. Assuming thruster use and a perfectly vertical descent."

"That's tight, but it's encouraging to know that it'll fit. I better go tell Asger, so we can get going." Casmir glanced skyward again, relieved that he didn't yet see or hear an armada of military ships approaching.

"Now that I have convinced you that I am capable of descending without damaging myself," Zee said, "I wish to gather several crushers and jump to the bottom to scout. I cannot see what structures or hollows may have been built into alcoves along the walls of the chasm. There may be weapons poised to fire upon any ship that descends."

"I agree. All right, go ahead. And thank you for volunteering. You're a good person." Casmir patted him on the back, then turned to join the others.

"You called me a person instead of a crusher."

Casmir paused and looked back. "Yes, is that okay? Which do you prefer?"

"I am a crusher and also an intelligent being, but the definition of person states that it applies to a human."

"That just means that it's time to update the dictionary. Languages change over time." Casmir winked. "Grab whoever you need to go with you, and let me know what you find, please. If you can clear the way to the gate pieces, ideally without seriously injuring anyone, and have them ready for us to pick up, that would be fantastic."

"I will take several crushers, and we will seek to accomplish this mission."

Then Casmir would have to figure out how to get the gate pieces loaded and this cargo ship off the planet. What were the odds that they could convince Launch Loop Control that they were the rightful military crew and had orders to head up to orbit?

"One problem at a time…" As he hurried across the ice to the hatch of the cargo ship, he messaged Asger.

Make ready to fly, Asger. Zee promises we can get to the bottom in that ship.

He promises, huh?

With seven feet of clearance to either side.

That won't be at all tight.

I'm confident you can do it.

You know I've never flown this model of ship, right? I'm familiarizing myself with the navigation controls now, but this is a hell of a lot bigger than a shuttle.

I'm confident you can do it, Casmir repeated.

My father isn't.

That's why you drink with me instead of him.

I'm not sure the sake we shared with Ishii qualifies us as regular drinking partners.

You also consumed tequila in Bonita's lounge while I walked on the treadmill.

True. I guess we're bonded for life.

Undoubtedly.

Casmir swung into the ship and peeked into its cargo hold to ensure it was as large as he suspected. Yes, it was cavernous. Qin's sisters were in the hold, waiting for the next phase of their mission, and the six-foot-plus armored women appeared tiny in the space. Many gate pieces should fit inside.

He found Asger, Bjarke, and Qin up three levels on the bridge.

"All systems are online," Asger said.

"Double-check the thrusters." Bjarke was hovering over his shoulder, fingers twitching as if he might take the helm himself. "We're going to have to go absolutely straight down and back up again."

"I'm aware of that, sir," Asger said tightly. "Will you man scanners? Let us know if any ships or aircraft are on the way."

"Man scanners," Bjarke muttered but slid into a pod on the side of the bridge.

"I can reach weapons from here," Asger said. "If it's at all possible to use this ship to clear the way to our goal, I will."

"Clear the way?" Casmir asked with concern. "With lethal force?"

Asger shook his head. "I was thinking more of caving in some ice and burying the soldiers."

"You don't think that will be lethal?"

"The one in that video was armored. They can survive an avalanche until their people come to dig them out."

Casmir doubted they would be able to maneuver the cargo ship enough to bring its weapons to bear, but he didn't say so.

A message from Rache popped up on Casmir's contact, and he jumped in surprise.

What are you doing down there, Dabrowski?

Aren't we yet past you calling me by my last name?

Not when I'm exasperated.

Isn't that most of the time?

Unless a stoic, independent, but also thoughtful and serene woman is rubbing my head.

Kim does *that? No, wait. Don't tell me. I don't want to know.*

Then I'll repeat my initial inquiry. What are you doing down there? In the Arctic Islands.

Enjoying the subfreezing temperatures.

I'm positive you're the reason that a number of Fleet ships are heading in that direction from the bases on the mainland. Jager's Starhawk *also dropped out of formation in orbit and is flying down.*

Casmir stifled a groan. He had been certain that some of the space fleet would be sent to deal with them; he hadn't expected Jager to come personally.

"We have some ships heading toward us," Tristan reported, the message coming over the ship's comm.

"So I'm hearing." Casmir's delusion of grabbing the gate pieces and tricking his way off the planet shattered.

"I see them too." Bjarke waved to the scanner display. "But we might have more trouble getting readings once we're down in that chasm."

Casmir tapped the comm button. "Did you hear that, Tristan? Keep us updated please."

"Will do."

"I'm firing up the engines," Asger said.

"Shall I join my sisters in the hold?" Qin asked. "In case you need us to leap out and fight?"

"Yes," Casmir said. "Thank you."

"How far away are the ships?" Casmir asked Bjarke as Qin jogged out.

"The ones flying from the mainland... a good forty-five minutes. But I'm also picking up the *Starhawk*—Jager's ship—and three others escorting it. They're dropping straight down from space and could be here in as little as twenty minutes."

Casmir rubbed his face. Even if they found the gate pieces lying helpfully at the bottom of the chasm, he doubted his team could get them loaded and fly out of there in that little time. And where would they go? The launch loop was closed, and he had little doubt it would remain that way.

And now, Rache messaged, *three of the marked astroshaman ships have also left the orbital battle and are following Jager's ship down. I believe I see my opportunity.*

I'll give you all the money in my bank account if you don't *try to kill our king today.*

Your bank account holds no interest to me. What exactly are you doing down there, anyway?

"Invisible ships that have been marked with some kind of beacon are also flying down." Bjarke sounded puzzled. He hadn't been at Stardust Palace for that final battle with Dubashi's ships. "Are those the astroshamans?"

"They're all coming here?" Asger asked.

"Yes." Bjarke turned in his pod. "I suggest we abort, Casmir."

"Wait," Casmir said. "If the astroshamans are coming, this could still work. We always wanted to snag the gate pieces and for them to chase us down. Being bait was the whole point."

"Being bait that lured them away from the planet," Asger said, "not bait that's obliterated above the Arctic Islands."

"Yeah." Casmir squinted at Bjarke. "Would you be willing to lead everybody away in that transport ship? If we take this one down into the chasm, maybe they'll miss seeing it right away, especially if the other ship is streaking off in another direction. Once we've got the gate pieces, we'll have bargaining chips."

"I'll never be able to get permission to use the launch loop and take it up into space." Despite the warning, Bjarke rose to his feet and looked like he would do it.

"Just stay low and fly off across the ice. If you can program the autopilot to evade them and slip away before they attack, please do so. I'd prefer nobody go on a suicide mission here."

"Aren't we *all* on a suicide mission tonight?" Bjarke grumbled.

"I hope not." Casmir gripped his chin. "I wonder if I could make that transport ship emanate a false signature so the astroshamans will believe the gate pieces are on board. If they're chasing after *you*, and Jager's fleet is chasing after *them*..."

Maybe it was still possible that his team could get away.

"You work on that." Bjarke glanced at the scanner display. "I've got to go now if there's a hope of taking off before they get here."

Casmir nodded, though he didn't know yet if he could do what he'd mused.

"Father." Asger lurched to his feet. "If they all go after you, and they're tricked into thinking you have the gate pieces they came all this way to get, and they open fire..."

"I could be obliterated, yes." Something about the look that Bjarke gave Casmir made Casmir wonder if he was being idealistic in believing Bjarke could program the autopilot and abandon ship.

Asger lifted a hand and took a step toward his father but hesitated, as if he didn't know how to admit he was worried his father would get killed. That they *all* might get killed.

"I'll try not to let that happen." Bjarke also took a step toward him and paused.

There wasn't time for farewells and speaking of emotions, but Casmir grabbed Asger's hand and tugged him toward his father anyway. He waved for Bjarke to come toward his son. They both hesitated at first, but then surged forward and hugged each other.

"Don't get killed, Father," Asger said.

"Same goes for you."

You're not replying, Rache messaged. *I hope you're planning something brilliant and not passed out from a seizure.*

Me too. Casmir slid into the vacated scanner station as Bjarke raced out.

He sent a note to Tork—the last time he'd checked, the android was on Princess Nalini's ship and still in the system—asking if he had any ideas about how to fake the gate's distinctive energy signature in a manner that would fool the astroshamans.

While he waited for a reply, Casmir reached out to Zee, surprised he hadn't yet reported in. Even if he'd flattened himself like a kite, it shouldn't have taken long to reach the bottom.

Zee, where are you, buddy? Casmir messaged. *Did you find the soldiers? The gate pieces?*

Surprisingly, he didn't get an answer. Tork, from halfway across the system, responded first.

I can replicate the gate signature, and create a program that can operate from within a Kingdom ship to emit a false beacon. Please give me approximately seven minutes. If I am not able to get it to you in time, it is because the AI ship from System Cerberus approaches, and it has been knocking out the power of all the ships and stations it flies past.

Seven minutes will be fine. Can't you guys fly away from it? Casmir had too much to worry about already. He didn't want to add the AI ship to the equation yet.

We are attempting to do so, but it is moving rapidly, and its range is vast.

"My father is boarding the other ship." Asger's fingers danced across the console. "I'm preparing to lift off and take us into the chasm."

"Good." Casmir eyed the display, more than a dozen ships heading in their direction now. He bit his lip, wondering if they were all going to die horribly tonight. "Just to warn you, I've lost contact with Zee."

"Where is he?"

"He and the other crushers went down in the chasm."

"Where we're going? Wonderful."

Casmir? Qin messaged his chip instead of using the ship's comm.

Yes?

I don't believe we should let Bjarke go off alone. If he's shot down and has to fight for his life, he should have someone at his side.

I don't disagree. Are you asking to go with him?

I'm already with him. I didn't announce it because I thought Asger might object, and we don't have much time.

That's a theme today, yes. Take care of yourself.

Thank you. Mouser is in charge of my sisters and will follow your orders. Good luck.
You too.

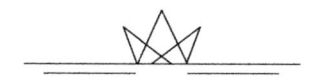

As the two soldiers stepped forward to take Bonita and Maria into custody, the squad of androids walked off the other ship with the two thieves they'd caught.

"Robbers!" Bonita blurted and pointed to the soldier with the firearm. She wouldn't have tried it if the men had been in uniform, but maybe the androids would fall for it, at least long enough for Bonita to get away. "These men are trying to loot my ship!"

"*Captain*," the soldier said, half growl, half sigh. "This is unseemly."

Two of the androids were busy carting the real robbers away, but the other two ran over.

Bonita glanced into the airlock tube to see if the soldiers had forced their way onto her ship and if the hatches were open. They had, and they were. The problem was that even if she reached them, she wouldn't be able to *lock* them, not if the power was out.

"These men took that gun out of my cabin and are threatening me with it," Bonita yelled at the androids, trying to drown out the soldiers' attempts to explain that they were in the Fleet and making an arrest.

The androids stepped between Bonita and Maria and faced the soldiers. "Please allow us to scan your chips for your identification."

"You're only going to make this worse," Maria whispered to Bonita as the androids drew scanners.

"Sorry," Bonita breathed, then pointed at the airlock and raised her eyebrows, silently asking if Maria wanted to come with her. It was a long shot that they could escape, but if they could be back on the *Dragon* when the power came back on…

Maria shook her head.

"They've got a grenade!" Bonita yelled, then rushed around the group and toward the hatch.

Maria didn't try to stop her. The soldier with the gun did, spinning toward her, the weapon still in his hand.

The androids must not have determined yet if they were legitimate soldiers, or they were simply programmed to keep anyone from shooting in the concourse, because one stepped forward to block him.

Taking advantage of his distraction, Bonita launched a straight kick at his wrist. She connected *hard*—gray-haired women *could* be scary, damn it—and the firearm flew all the way to the ceiling.

Bonita whirled and sprinted into the tube, running past the *Dragon's* open outer hatch, through the airlock chamber, and into the dark cargo hold. The soldiers tried to follow her, but the androids stopped them. Not surprisingly, the hatch didn't close when she, by habit, slapped the control panel to order it to do so.

She managed to manually heave the hatch shut, but there was no way to lock it without power. It was probably damaged anyway since the soldiers had forced it open when they'd come aboard to look for her.

The *Dragon,* having occasionally been used for smuggling in the past, offered numerous hiding places, but she rushed to the armory first. She grabbed weapons, her armor, and two oxygen tanks—she could already feel the chill of space encroaching without the life-support systems running.

She was about to rush back across the cargo hold, to the ladder well, and up to a higher level, but a clang sounded at the hatch. She detoured to the closest hiding spot. Technically, it was the freezer, but the panel in the floor appeared identical to all the other panels. She hurried down into it with all of her gear, careful not to make any noise, and pulled the panel shut.

Scant seconds passed before the sounds of the soldiers' boots reverberated through the deck. Bonita hunkered in the dark, not daring to put on her armor and tank yet, not daring to make noise.

Without scanners or any technological assistance, it should take them a while to find her, but what would happen when they did? And what would happen to poor Maria? Bonita had ruined her career and possibly her marriage—what if the Kingdom bastards deported her?—and for what? Money? Discrediting some snotty kid?

She leaned her head against a crate of frozen food, afraid she'd made a terrible mistake.

CHAPTER 26

THE CHARRED AND WARPED PIECES OF ARMOR THAT the crushers had removed from Finn, careful not to further injure him, looked like the kind of wreckage Kim would expect if a grenade blew up right on top of an armored man. That might very well have happened.

Kim knelt on the floor in the remains of the dining hall, handing bandages and tools from a first-aid kit to Irena as she did her best to patch up Finn and keep him breathing. As a physical therapist, she wasn't a medical expert, but she'd quickly demonstrated that she had more hands-on experience than Kim.

Most of the men who'd come with Finn were dead, but three others had survived and also lay on the floor on pillows and blankets borrowed from guest rooms. Aleksy had commed for an ambulance, but it sounded like chaos was the norm tonight in the city, and he had been warned that it might not arrive soon.

Apparently, that video of Finn had prompted people to go out and protest and riot over his right to be one of the heirs, never mind that the Fleet and the astroshamans were still doing battle in orbit and the threat of bombs and perhaps even a virus remained.

"None of the shuttles are operable, as far as I can tell." Aleksy came in and knelt beside Kim, looking at Finn and the other wounded men with grave eyes. "I believe we're stuck tending him until an ambulance comes—or his people come looking for him."

Kim didn't know who Finn's people were right now. Royal Intelligence, presumably, but what if, in the wake of that video, they felt as alienated as the common man?

No, they shouldn't. They should be questioning whether the video was real and not jumping to conclusions.

The heart monitor attached to Finn's chest beeped an alarm and showed an erratic pulse. Irena swore and touched her fingers to his neck.

"Hand me the—"

Kim placed the defibrillator in her hands, and she nodded curtly and pushed his shirt open to attach the electrodes.

"Is there any assistance we can provide?" the crusher who remained inside asked.

The other one was outside, watching the sky and road for further threats.

If Casmir had been the one dying in front of her, Kim would have ordered the crusher to run off with his super speed and find a doctor, but the odds were good that someone from Royal Intelligence had figured out what had happened to Finn's team by now. They would likely show up with shuttles and medical staff before the crusher could return with a surgeon slung over his shoulder.

Besides, as uncharitable as it was, it crossed her mind that the Kingdom might be better off if Finn didn't make it. He'd come here tonight trying to capture Casmir, presumably to lay dead at his father's feet like some offering. Maybe if Finn died, and Oku had no interest in ruling, Jager would have to name someone else—or put it to a vote in the Senate. With a vote, maybe the Kingdom could get a *decent* leader.

Though she had no idea what would happen if Jager also died—which, with Rache out there hunting him, was a solid possibility.

"Not at this time," Kim told the crusher. "We'll let you know if we think of anything. Thank you."

"He's steady again. For now." Irena set the defibrillator aside. "There's a lot of damage to his organs, probably his heart too. Is there a programmable nanite injector in that kit?"

"Yes." Kim had already inventoried everything in the castle's surprisingly well-stocked first-aid kit. Unlike with the pantry supplies, few things in a medical kit went bad quickly.

"Let's give it a shot. That sergeant over there needs nanites too. They all might. I think the one on the end with blood dripping out of his ear has a fractured skull."

"Do you have any idea who attacked Finn's people?" Aleksy asked Kim quietly. "I commed the police as well as the emergency medical services, and the frazzled dispatcher said she would pass the information on to Drachen Castle. She wanted to know who attacked, and I could only guess."

Kim shook her head. The military, Rache had said, but she didn't know. And she wasn't positive that Rache could truly know that either.

The distant hum of engines reached her ears, making her realize how deathly quiet it had been.

"Someone's coming." Kim bit her lip.

With luck, it was Royal Intelligence or a team they had dispatched. But what if the attackers were coming back? Should she and the Dabrowskis return to the tunnels? Leave the injured for the newcomers to find and not tempt anyone into arresting Casmir's parents on the suspicion of being involved? Or just because Casmir was wanted?

"Friend or foe?" Aleksy eyed the sky warily.

Kim realized they *couldn't* leave. Not when they didn't know who was coming. If the people who wanted Finn dead were returning, she couldn't leave him or the other injured men from his party where they would be easy targets.

"I'll look." Kim ran to the remains of the entrance, where the crushers were also studying the sky, and groaned at the dark shapes silhouetted against the starry sky. They looked to be the same unmarked aircraft that had bombed Finn's people.

They swooped low and searchlights fell across the grassy hills and swept up toward the castle.

"Get inside," Kim told the crushers and backed away. "Under cover."

They ran back to the others as the first aircraft swept in low, that searchlight probing the wreckage, lingering on the armored bodies. Another vessel flew past closer to the forest. Still more engines sounded to the south, more aircraft flying in this direction.

"We may need to hide," Kim said.

"We can't leave without our patients," Irena said.

"The crushers may be able to carry them."

"This is a critical time to move them," Irena said. "They need—"

"One of the aircraft is landing. It's black and unmarked." Aleksy put a hand on his wife's shoulder. "I know you want to protect the injured, but whoever these people are, they're out for blood. And they might not care that it's ours."

"Shall we defend the premises?" the closest crusher asked.

A hatch opened, and men wearing unmarked dark gray armor and carrying huge rifles jumped out. Whoever they were, they weren't the prince's security.

"Yes," Kim said. "Keep them from coming in here. Try not to kill anyone."

Irena threw her an alarmed look.

The third crusher, the one she'd left guarding the secret door, must have realized his services were no longer needed there, for he ran down a staircase and out to help his buddies.

"What's happening?" Finn rasped weakly, his eyes open for the first time.

"Trouble," Kim said grimly.

"My men… Where?" Finn tried to turn his head but winced before he saw much.

Outside, someone fired into the air, blasting a stone off one of the castle walls.

"We detect people alive in there," a man shouted. "Send out the prince, and we won't harm you."

Kim was inclined to ignore them and hope they believed their detectors were wrong. She grabbed one of the injured men and pulled him around the corner, so there would be standing walls between them and the entrance. Fleeing to the tunnels would have been ideal, but with the crushers now occupied in defense, there were more injured men than people to carry them.

"I repeat, send out the prince, or we'll come in and get him!"

Aleksy shouted, "Who are you? There are only injured people in here."

"Don't worry about who we are. Send out the sniveling traitor of a boy, so we can make sure he never rules our Kingdom."

Finn was coherent enough to widen his eyes with fear at the words. "Get me out of here," he whispered.

The armored men rushed toward the castle. The crushers surged forward to intercept them.

As the first DEW-Tek bolts lit up the yard and blasted into the demolished entryway, Kim dragged another man behind cover. Aleksy saw what she was doing and helped her with the third, someone conscious enough to groan in pain.

"Sorry, my friend," Aleksy said.

The firing stopped as the crushers engaged with the attackers, and Kim thought the three of them might be enough to keep the strike team from getting into the castle, but another aircraft flew in, preparing to land.

"The tunnels," Finn whispered.

"Can you stand?" Kim asked.

"Yes," Finn said as Irena said, "No."

"Just help me up." Finn rolled over and tried to push himself into a sitting position, but he gasped in pain and collapsed back to the floor. "Painkillers," he panted. "I need… painkillers."

"I already injected you and the other injured men with as much as I dare." Irena stroked his hair with a maternal, soothing gesture.

Kim wondered if the fact that she would have preferred to punch Finn—or inject him with a sedative so he couldn't talk—ensured she would never make a decent mother. She'd never been positive she wanted to find out, to pass her genes along to offspring, but the wildness of this night made her worry that she wouldn't survive and have the opportunity to make that choice.

"Hell." Panting from his small exertion—and what had to be a lot of pain—Finn lay back, eyes wild as he listened to the fight. Despite the speed and effectiveness of the crushers, a few DEW-Tek bolts made it into the castle. One sliced through the handle of a hanging copper pan, knocking it to the kitchen floor with a clatter.

"The castle would be easier to defend if it still had all of its walls," Kim muttered.

"Who are you people?" Finn squinted up at Irena.

"The only ones in this castle," Aleksy said. "Why were you trying to capture us if you don't know who we are?"

"I was here for Dabrowski. He's a criminal."

"He's not here." Aleksy didn't point out that he was a Dabrowski too. Maybe he didn't think Finn deserved to know if he didn't already.

"Move out, move out!" someone shouted outside.

Kim risked peering around the corner, but all she could see was one of the crushers silhouetted against the lights of an aircraft. New weapons boomed from the sky as more aircraft flew in close.

"We can't get an ambulance," Aleksy said, "but it's no problem for eight aircraft to show up for a battle on the lawn."

Kim glimpsed one flying low, this one with the purple coloring of the Kingdom. "I think Finn's people might be here."

"Please, God, let that be true," Finn groaned as weapons fired and metal screeched. Several engines roared as some of the aircraft on the ground took off and bolted from the area.

"Just an FYI," Kim said, looking down at Finn, "if you survive the night, you owe your life to Irena Dabrowski. Someone hit you with an explosive, and then a stone ceiling fell on you. Your heart tried to stop a few minutes ago."

Finn scowled.

Irena appeared uncomfortable at Kim's attempt to make sure she got credit. "It's possible he would have recovered from a cardiac dysrhythmia on his own," she murmured.

"And it's possible he would have died." Kim wanted her to get credit because they'd all risked their lives to come back up here and because Casmir's parents didn't deserve to be in danger. Neither did Casmir, damn it. Kim was tired of the entire royal family.

"Do we allow the Kingdom Guard troops into the castle, Kim Sato?" one of the crushers called back.

"Do they want to kill us?" Kim called wearily.

What would she be doing, she wondered, if she'd stayed on Rache's ship? And what was her mother doing right now? And were her father and brothers all right? She leaned her head against the stone wall.

"No," a familiar female voice called. Princess Oku. "We came because—it's my fault Finn is here. *Is* he still here?"

"Shit." Finn closed his eyes—or maybe they rolled back in his head as he passed out.

"Most of his party is dead," Kim replied, "but he's still alive, as are three others. Let them in, please, crushers."

Several armored guards accompanied the unarmored but well-protected Oku inside. Her personal bodyguard, Maddie, stuck right beside her, weapons in hand as she eyed the destroyed foyer and searched for enemies.

Kim and Aleksy backed up slowly and raised their arms. Irena frowned back at them but remained with Finn, cradling his head protectively, as if the guards might accidentally trample him.

"Prince Finn and these other men need medical care urgently," she said.

"We've got a shuttle that can take him straight to the infirmary at Royal Intelligence Headquarters." Oku waved several men forward to gather up the wounded.

LAYERS OF FORCE

"He needs to go to a *hospital*," Irena said.

"The infirmary has all the equipment you would find in an intensive care unit," a female soldier—no, that was Chief Van Dijk—said, "and there's a surgeon waiting for him in our shuttle."

Armored men with hover gurneys trotted into the dining hall. Irena must have decided that was sufficient, for she finally backed away. Several guards carefully loaded the injured onto the gurneys and took them out.

"What happened?" Van Dijk asked Kim. "No, tell me on the way back. Come."

Kim glanced at Irena and Aleksy, noting that guards walked beside them to ensure they had no choice but to go with them. She positioned herself to Oku's side as everyone trudged out.

"Will they be all right?" Kim waved to Casmir's parents. Maybe she should have asked the question for herself, too, but thanks to Casmir, it was the Dabrowski clan that was in the most trouble.

"No harm will come to them in the headquarters building." Oku lifted her chin. "I will not allow it."

Van Dijk, the person who likely had more power to allow or deny things in that building, glanced back but didn't naysay the statement. She also didn't reinforce it.

As Kim, Irena, and Aleksy were strapped into seats in the shuttle, hulking men with weapons sitting to either side of them, Kim worried that she would be trying to follow Casmir's progress from a dark dungeon cell.

Casmir nibbled on a fingernail as their borrowed cargo ship lifted off. The deck reverberated as the thrusters carried it toward the chasm.

"Double-checking to make sure we'll fit," Asger said from the helm.

Casmir tried sending Zee another message. Once again, he didn't get a response.

"There must be some kind of dampening field," he reasoned, then rolled his eyes at himself because it should have been obvious.

"Whatever has kept the astroshamans from sensing the gate pieces down there, when they haven't had trouble sensing them throughout the other systems where they've been plucking them up, may be keeping me from communicating with the crushers."

"What happens if there are no gate pieces and all of this was for naught?" Asger flew them over the chasm, took an audible deep breath, and tapped the controls to start the descent.

"Jager wouldn't be hurrying down here in person if they weren't here."

"True. My father is taking off. I'm having to lower us slowly and carefully. This is tight."

"I know. You're doing great. Thanks, Asger."

Casmir drummed his fingers on the console and started writing code to create his own false beacon, in case Tork didn't come through in time.

As the cargo ship lowered slowly, the craggy walls of the chasm filling the display and their running lights playing off the blue and white ice, Casmir had time to worry about the AI ship. What did it want? Were the artificial intelligences that had claimed Verloren Moon truly allies of the astroshamans? And if so, to what end? Had Moonrazor offered to take them along to the new system she'd scoped out? Maybe she'd offered them numerous uninhabited moons and planets so they could expand.

"Halfway down," Asger said. "I think. I've struggled from the beginning to get readings from the bottom."

"I know."

I am transmitting the program, a message from Tork came in to Casmir's chip. *In the AI vessel's wake, our ship has lost power, auxiliary power, and all access to battery-powered technology. For some reason, I am unaffected.*

I'm relieved. Maybe they like androids.

An interesting hypothesis.

I've received the program. Your timing is perfect. Thank you. Casmir sent it over to the transport ship via the comm, using Kingdom codes he'd made for himself back on Ishii's ship. He commanded the other vessel to download and execute the file.

You are welcome. Do inform Zee of my excellence and superiority to crushers, who I assume were unable to help you in this manner.

I didn't ask them, since you have experience with astroshamans, but I will inform him of your excellence.

Thank you. After a hesitation, Tork added, *I am unable to contact him for the next move in our game. Has something happened?*

I hope not. I'm about to check on him.

I request that you do not allow him to sacrifice himself. I would be distraught if we could not finish our game, and also play other games in the future while discussing the peculiarities of humanity.

I'll do my best.

Thank you.

The comm beeped.

"Is that your father?" Casmir didn't think Bjarke would notice the software being installed, but he wanted to warn him that it was running. If it worked, the astroshamans would go after him with single-minded purpose. Which might also lead all of the Kingdom ships to chase after them.

"That's the Kingdom warship the *Shikra* demanding to know who's commandeered this cargo ship and also ordering us to surrender and prepare to be boarded."

"You can tell all that without answering?"

"I made the mistake of answering last time."

Another comm call came in, a second indicator light flashing at the station.

"And that one?" Casmir asked.

"Lowe Base. They have similar demands."

Casmir checked on the approaching ships. The invisible but marked astroshaman ships were close, but—he clenched his fist—they were taking off after Bjarke's decoy ship. So were several of the Kingdom ships.

He whispered a quick prayer for Bjarke and Qin, hoping he hadn't condemned them to their deaths. The Kingdom ships might hesitate to fire on a vessel from their own military, but the astroshamans wouldn't have any such qualms.

The comm lights stopped flashing at the same time.

"How'd you hang up on them from the helm?" Casmir asked.

Asger glanced at the comm console. "I didn't. We've also lost contact with Tristan in the base."

The scanner station pinged with alerts, drawing Casmir's attention.

"Raise the shields, Asger," he said grimly.

Outside, lights flashed on the icy chasm walls as they reflected the orange and red of DEW-Tek fire below. A battle that hadn't been visible from farther above was raging at the bottom of the chasm. The scanners lit up, not only with weapons fire but with signs of life. Humans in combat armor—dozens of them. And there were his crushers. At the center of the fighting.

For the first time, the cargo ship's scanners detected the gate signature. It was coming from the bottom of the chasm and off to one side. In some hollowed-out alcove?

A blast struck the bottom of the ship. The thick hull repelled the weapon with only the faintest of shudders, but it might be the first of many attacks.

"The shields are up," Asger said. "We're still two hundred feet from the bottom. Do we keep going down?"

Casmir scanned the terrain below them, the instruments much better at reading the bottom of the chasm now. The majority of the fighting was indeed taking place in a large alcove under one of the ice walls. The bottom of the chasm, the ground directly below them, appeared to be empty.

"Yes," Casmir said. "We have to."

Hey, Zee, he messaged, hoping he could get through now. *Is there any chance you've found the gate pieces and will be able to drag them out here and load them up if we open the hatch?*

A massive vault door with a complicated security system is in place, Zee responded as the weapons fire intensified below.

The scanners showed an artillery weapon firing, and a crusher was blown out of the alcove and across the chasm where he splatted against the wall.

Zee? Casmir worried that had been his friend. He slapped the button for the ship-wide comm. "Mouser, we've got a battle happening. I need you and your sisters to get ready to jump out and help."

We were able to reach the vault door, Zee continued after a pause, perhaps during which he'd reassembled his blown-off pieces, *but it is extremely sturdy and even we were not able to breach it. Perhaps the notable computer hacker, Casmir Dabrowski, will be able to thwart the security system.*

I'll do my best. Casmir checked for a wireless network, then groaned. There wasn't one down here, and he could no longer access the one above. It occurred to him that whoever had built this place must have feared that astroshamans—supreme computer hackers themselves—would be the ones to find it and try to access it. *I'm going to have to go to the door interface in person.*

LAYERS OF FORCE

That will be very dangerous.

So I fear. Casmir plucked at his parka, well aware that he wasn't in a galaxy suit, much less combat armor. A single stray DEW-Tek blast would take him down.

"We're all at the hatch and ready, Casmir," came Mouser's reply.

"Why are you going through her instead of Qin?" Asger frowned over at him.

"Qin went with your father."

"Damn it, Casmir. Why didn't you tell me? Why didn't *she* tell me?" Asger thumped a hand on the console hard enough to dent it. "That's a suicide mission."

"That was okay for your father but not her?"

"He's a knight. Being willing to sacrifice yourself for the good of the Kingdom is in the Code. She's... she's..." Asger groped in the air with frustrated fingers before thumping his hand down again. "Damn it, Casmir," he repeated.

"I know. I'm hoping it *won't* be a suicide mission."

He hoped that would be true for all of them.

"You're an optimist."

An alarm bleated from the scanner console. Casmir checked it, expecting to find more weapons fire peppering them from below, but a massive Kingdom warship had flown directly over the chasm—directly over *them*.

"Uh oh. Somebody wasn't fooled by the decoy ship." Casmir checked the ship's identification and swore. "That's Jager's *Starhawk*. Of course *he* wasn't fooled. He's the one who ordered the gate pieces hidden here."

The warship, with weapons capable of demolishing small moons, opened fire on them.

Even with the shields up, the jolts that reverberated through the ship had Casmir gripping the edge of the console while his teeth rattled. Their vessel lurched and slammed into one of the ice walls.

"We're sitting ducks!" Asger swore at Casmir again, and then at Jager, and then at the universe in general.

Alarms flashed all over the bridge as the fury of a king betrayed pelted down on them. They struck the opposite wall. One of the displays flashed that shields were down to twenty-five percent.

"Can you land?" Casmir asked. "We're going to have to abandon ship."

And run out into enemy fire…

How the hell had Jager known they were down here through that dampening field? Did he have some special way to see through it? Or did he have an access code to turn it *off*?

"I'm trying," Asger said as they struck a wall again, knocked into it by the barrage of weapons fire from above.

A new alarm wailed as the cargo ship's shields went down.

The next strike from the warship was like a cannonball pounding through the side of a wooden sailing vessel. Thunderous crunches battered Casmir's eardrums, and the ship jerked so hard he would have been thrown from his pod if it hadn't been programmed to hold him tight.

Another round slammed into the ship, and power went out on the bridge. Casmir tried to comm to tell everyone to hold tight and brace for impact. He was too late. The comms were already down.

The thrusters followed, and eerie silence filled the ship as the engines went offline.

"We're going down," Asger warned.

The ship plummeted a hundred feet to the bottom of the chasm and crashed.

CHAPTER 27

THE TROOP TRANSPORT SHIP WAS SMALLER THAN THE cargo ship, and Qin had no trouble finding the bridge and joining Bjarke. He was at the helm, flying between craggy white peaks, the terrain already much different from the flat ice where the base had been. When she walked onto the bridge, he only glanced back.

"A stowaway, huh?" He didn't sound surprised to see her. Some internal scanner must have warned him when she'd entered the ship.

"I didn't want you to have to fight for your life alone," Qin said.

"I appreciate that sentiment, but you may have lived longer if you'd stayed with William. We have…" Bjarke glanced at a display even as his fingers continued to dance over the console, with the navigation interface at his temple flashing its indicators rapidly. "Three astroshaman ships after us and four heavily armed Kingdom ships after *them*. The only reason they're not firing yet is—"

Qin's stomach lifted as the ship dove down the back side of a bluff they'd been flying across and swept down into a long depression, its belly skimming the ice.

"—I'm flying like a madman, and these mountains give us enough terrain to impede their line-of-sight targeting." He eyed a scanner display. "Except from that ship that's smart enough to fly far overhead. Hold on."

A shudder shook their vessel, and Qin ran for the pod at the scanner station. "Or do you want me at weapons?" she wondered, pausing.

Bjarke hesitated. "We can't fire on the Kingdom ships, no matter what, but… Yeah, see if you can get some of those astroshaman ships off our asses."

Qin slid into the pod and familiarized herself with the weapons platform as Bjarke dipped and dove through the mountains as if he were flying a two-person darter instead of bulky military transport.

"Maybe this is why Bonita likes you," Qin muttered, searching for a target with the rear weapons. She remembered that the astroshaman ships were invisible save for some beacon and hunted for a way to tie in the scanners to find it. "You fly as crazily as she does."

"She loves my sharp wit, my athletic and agile physique, and my willingness to rub her shoulders—and other body parts—before sex." Bjarke's delivery was calm, even deadpan, despite the twisting, diving gyrations he was forcing the ship through.

One of their pursuers opened fire, brilliant blue bolts streaking through the dark night. Bjarke whipped the transport around a mountain peak.

"I don't need details on her sex life, thanks." Qin couldn't see their pursuer, but she fired at the beacon that showed up on the scanners as it flew around the peak after them.

"What about mine? It's fascinating."

"I should have sent Tigress over here."

Bjarke flashed a grin, exhilaration in his eyes despite their danger. Or *because* of it. "She's the horny one that keeps checking out William's butt, right?"

"She *is* horny."

"I caught her eyeing my backside too. Nice to know I've still got some sex appeal."

"Should I point out that a lump of lard would be appealing after the Druckers?"

"No, that's not necessary."

Qin fired again, but if she hit their pursuer, she couldn't tell. The astroshaman ship didn't veer away or pull up. Bjarke anticipated more fire and plunged their transport down into a canyon.

Icy walls whipped by, the terrain features blurring. An energy weapon that Qin didn't recognize blasted into one of the canyon walls above them. Snow flew as boulders and great shards of rock rained down, pinging off their shields.

They followed a bend in the canyon, but it ended abruptly at a frozen waterfall plunging to the bottom. Bjarke pulled up hard, and Qin's usually ironclad stomach grew queasy as he added a twist designed to make them a hard target.

LAYERS OF FORCE

It didn't work. A blast from the nearest astroshaman ship struck them full on.

The shields held but flashed an angry warning. Qin fired back, unloading all of the transport's weapons. Several struck their pursuer, and this time, she had the satisfaction of seeing it alter its path to evade more of her fire.

Bjarke flew them toward another mountain peak that they could take cover behind. "The other two astroshaman ships are trying to cut us off. This is going to get tricky. Did you like the tree house?"

Qin blinked at the topic shift. "Yes."

"You didn't seem that impressed with the castle, especially for someone who quotes fairy tales around the dinner table."

"It's a nice castle." Qin fired before they flew behind the peak, but the astroshaman ship absorbed the blast without trouble.

"Do you think Bonita would like it?"

"She's not that into planets."

"So a castle in a space station would be more appealing?"

"A castle in her cargo hold maybe."

"I don't believe it would fit. She needs a bigger ship. You think she'll at least visit me there, right?"

"Maybe."

"I'm looking for a reason to fight against all odds for our survival, Qin."

"*I* want to live. Does that work?"

Bjarke smiled, but his eyes were tight and his whole face tense. The scanner display showed the astroshamans outmaneuvering them. With three ships to their one, it was inevitable. The Kingdom ships were trying to catch up, but they were on the other side of the mountains, so they couldn't help yet.

"I'm sure Bonita would want you to live," Qin added. "She'd like visiting your castle. She just wouldn't stay."

"That's encouraging. I think."

Qin winced as two of the astroshaman ships managed to flank them despite the mountains and Bjarke's crazy flying. An alarm wailed, announcing their shields going down.

"We can't take another direct hit," Qin warned, though she was sure he knew.

"I know. I'm looking for a place to crash that won't kill us. Hopefully."

"Any chance we can *not* crash?"

"I don't think so. There's nowhere for a controlled landing."

In the jagged mountains, crashing without serious injury—or death—seemed impossible. Their armor and the pods would protect them to some extent, but she worried it wouldn't be enough. Especially if the astroshamans kept shooting at them *after* they crashed.

As she fired at the myriad ships, Qin scoured the terrain, looking for a flat, open area where they could land. Her rounds slammed into their pursuers—she was positive they did—but the astroshaman vessels were impervious. Even the one she'd unloaded on before hadn't slowed down as a result.

Another blast caught them. A thunderous crunch came from the rear of the ship as the deck tilted wildly.

More alerts flashed from all over the bridge. An automated computer voice warned them that an engineer needed to fix a breach and that it was bringing the auxiliary engines online.

"If only we had an engineer." Bjarke swung them toward another canyon.

A missile blasted past above the ship, missing them by scant inches. Or so Qin thought. Then it curved to follow them, catch them, and slam into the transport's port side. Huge pieces of their hull blew away, wreckage tumbling down to the icy slope below.

"This ruse worked a lot better than I expected." Bjarke grimaced as he fought controls that weren't responding as well as they had before. "Casmir warned me that he was sending over a program to make other ships believe we've got the gate pieces. I'm hoping it'll keep working and that they'll force us down so they can board us to search for them, instead of blasting us into a thousand pieces from the sky."

"If they board us, I'll fight them. Gladly."

"Me too." Bjarke thumped a fist on the console. "Come on, you Kingdom pilots. Stop trying to follow them through the mountains. Go up and over so you can *target* them."

"What if *we* go up? Then if the astroshamans follow us, the Kingdom ships will be able to target them over the mountains."

Bjarke only hesitated a second before saying, "It's worth a try."

The view of the terrain disappeared as their nose lifted toward the starry sky.

"It will mean we'll have a lot farther to fall when we crash," he added grimly.

LAYERS OF FORCE

Qin didn't know what to say, so she didn't say anything. She fired at the two astroshaman ships that streaked after them and made solid contact with one.

For an instant, the slydar hull—or whatever technology hid their vessels—stopped working, and she saw a great shark-shaped ship on the rear camera display. Its dark form stood out in stark contrast to the white mountains, and it bristled weapons like a porcupine.

"Shit," she whispered as it disappeared again, its cloaking technology reestablishing itself. "This *was* a suicide mission."

"Yes, but look. Your idea is working. The Kingdom ships are opening fire on them."

A massive blast slammed into the back of their transport before Qin could do more than glance at the scanners.

"Engine failure is imminent," the computer voice announced. "Auxiliary engines are going offline in three... two... one. Offline."

"That's it, Qin. I'll try to take us down as softly as possible, but I've lost a lot of the navigation control."

Another blast struck them, and Qin lost power to the weapons console. She slumped in her pod as the ship's nose tilted downward. They lost altitude rapidly.

"Two of the astroshaman ships have turned to deal with the Kingdom ships," Bjarke reported quietly.

"And the third one?"

"It's chasing us down." Bjarke struggled mightily to keep the transport's nose up, to try to take them in closer to horizontal than vertical. "In case we don't survive this, thanks for coming with me, kid."

"You're welcome."

They hammered into an icy mountainside, skidding and bouncing across it like a skipped stone on a lake. The wrenching and tearing noises pummeled Qin's sensitive ears as her pod did its best to protect her from impact. She closed her eyes and hoped it was enough.

Blackness filled the bridge, and all the displays and consoles had gone dark. The thunderous wrenching noise of the crash still reverberated in Casmir's ears. He was positive that only the protective cushioning of his pod had kept him from flying into a wall and breaking his neck.

But like the rest of the ship, the pod had lost power and didn't respond to his taps at the button to release him. *Nothing* responded. With no scanner display to show him the position of Jager's warship, Casmir didn't know if it was descending, but he had no problem envisioning it following them down into the chasm to finish them off.

Weapons fire slammed into the ship again, and something exploded. Casmir swore. He hadn't wanted to be right.

He clawed at the pod's control panel to no avail. He twisted, trying to squeeze out sideways, but the sides held him too tightly.

"Asger? Are you awake over there? I need strong knightly help."

A groggy groan came from across the bridge.

"Asger?"

Another hit struck the ship, something less powerful than the last blow; it seemed to strike from the side rather than above. Were the soldiers outside firing at them?

Casmir hadn't had time to get more than a hint of what had been going on at the bottom of the chasm between them and the crushers. It was surprising that his nearly impervious allies hadn't been able to defeat the human defenders already.

Footsteps rang out in the corridor outside the bridge. "Casmir? Asger?" It was one of Qin's sisters. Mouser?

"We're in here," Casmir yelled. "But trapped."

At least, he was. Again, he sucked in his belly and tried to squeeze out of the pod. The sides didn't tighten, as they would have if they'd been in space with acceleration threatening to throw him from his seat, but they were as unyielding as metal shackles.

A wrenching sound came from the exit—Mouser tearing the doors open.

LAYERS OF FORCE

"My sisters and the rest of the crushers went out to help fight. There's a huge battle going on outside." No light came in with Mouser, but she ran right to Casmir, either smelling him or—more likely—seeing him. *She* wore combat armor and would have night vision through her helmet, if not her enhanced eyes.

"Qin?" Asger asked muzzily.

He sounded concussed. His pod must not have kept him from cracking his head on something. Or maybe something had flown across the bridge and cracked *him*.

"She's with Sir Bjarke." Mouser's gauntleted hand tapped Casmir's chest. "I see. Your pod has you."

"And isn't responding, yes. Can you rip one of the sides off? I'm afraid Jager's people are about to deliver the finishing blow." He glanced upward, as if he could see through the dark and the wrecked vessel to the great warship above. "I'm surprised he hasn't yet," Casmir whispered, expecting total destruction at any second.

"If I can't, I'll rip the pod out of the deck and take you out like that." Metal wrenched as Mouser worked, thankfully careful not to rip off any of Casmir's limbs.

"I'd prefer to go on my feet. And find some armor before going out there, though that may be asking a lot."

"We found some for you before the crash. It may be too big, but you can try it."

More wrenching sounds punctuated her words, and Casmir felt the pod start to give.

You're welcome, came a message from Rache. *Unless I was too late, and you're already dead, in which case there's no need to thank me.*

Very magnanimous of you. I am alive for the moment. What do you mean you're welcome?

Was Rache up here in the Arctic Islands now? He'd mentioned chasing Jager—or at least implied that he meant to do that.

Jager must have seen my ship coming, since he's got that slydar detector now, but he was so determined to keep firing on the ship in the chasm—I assume you're in it, because you're at the bottom of all trouble—that he refused to back away until we were right on top of him. He started firing at the Fedallah, *but I fired back. My ship has* excellent *armor and weapons.*

Casmir imagined Rache's eyes gleaming fiercely as he sent that. *Did you chase him away?*

He realized he was an easy target hanging over the chasm, so yes. He's maneuvering now and trying to call more of his ships back, but they flew off after the astroshaman ships. I'm on his tail now. After a pause, which could have been for dramatic flair or because the *Fedallah* was maneuvering wildly and taking fire itself, Rache added, *I'll finish the bastard off.*

I appreciate the earlier assistance, but that's really not necessary.

Casmir didn't get a response.

Mouser heaved again, finally tearing the pod in two, and he slithered out, landing on his knees on the deck. Shards of metal and pieces of who knew what dug through his trousers.

"You all right?" Mouser helped him up.

Was he? Rache was doing his best to kill Jager and every soldier on that warship with him—hundreds of people!—and Casmir owed him his life.

"No, but I've got to get out of here anyway and open that door." With the cargo ship a wreck, Casmir didn't know what he planned to do once he got those gate pieces. It seemed far too late to successfully lure the astroshamans away from Odin.

But if the astroshamans defeated or evaded the Kingdom ships—which might very well happen now that Rache was down here fighting against the Kingdom flagship—they would circle back and try to get the pieces. He might yet be able to hitch a ride on them and sneak up into the astroshaman cargo hold. If he could get aboard with enough crushers to help, maybe he could take over their ship from the inside.

Were all of the *other* gate pieces inside one of their holds? If he took over the ship, maybe he'd be able to acquire them all again.

Or maybe he was delusional.

"Help Asger, please," Casmir said once he was on his feet and steady enough that he didn't think he would fall over.

A boom rattled the chasm.

How's it going, Zee? he messaged, groping his way through the dark toward the exit.

Difficult. We are attempting not to harm the human soldiers. They feel no compunction about harming us.

Inconsiderate.

Yes.

Thank you for not killing them. I'll be right out, and I'll... figure out something.

"I've got him," Mouser said.

"I'm all right," Asger mumbled.

"Your head is bleeding a great deal."

"Something flew off and hit me when we landed. Casmir, you all right?" Asger sounded more coherent than he had before.

"Yes."

The three of them made it through warped corridors and to the other side of the ship to the only ladder shaft that wasn't, Mouser informed them, too mangled to climb down.

"Qin isn't answering me," Asger said.

"There's a dampening field that keeps out outside communications and vice versa." Even as the words came out, Casmir realized that couldn't be correct—at least not anymore. He'd received Rache's message loud and clear. Jager must have turned it off in order to target them, or maybe it had been damaged during the fighting in the chasm.

"Oh, right," Asger said.

Casmir decided not to correct himself. It would be better if Asger didn't worry overmuch, though now *Casmir* worried. Had Bjarke and Qin been shot down? Were they already dead?

"There's the armor we found for you," Mouser said when they reached the hold. Great holes torn in the hull let in light, flashes of orange and red that promised the battle continued outside. "My sisters should be out there helping the crushers."

Mouser and Asger ran toward the open hatch as Casmir scrambled through debris to reach the armor she'd set aside. A sick twinge assaulted his stomach when he saw the blue Fleet coloring and was reminded that this was a Kingdom ship and that the crushers were out there battling their own people.

Asger swore. Two armored soldiers appeared in the hatchway. They lifted weapons and fired into the hold at Casmir, as if they knew exactly who he was.

"Kingdom traitor!" one snarled.

As Asger bowled into one of them, Casmir dove behind the pile of armor. It was the closest thing he had to cover.

Orange energy bolts bounced off the deck and slammed into walls and the ceiling. One skimmed past right above his head, so close he could feel the sizzle of its passing. Casmir had the sickly feeling—the fear—they were targeting him specifically.

But Asger tackled one, Mouser the other, and then two crushers from outside leaped up, appearing behind the soldiers. They tore them from Asger and Mouser and hurled them away from the hatch.

"I suggest you don that armor swiftly, Casmir Dabrowski," came Zee's deadpan voice.

"Working on it." Casmir swallowed to try to get the squeak out of his voice. "Thanks."

Once he had the armor on—armor that was, as Mouser predicted, too large for him—he felt safer. He also felt ungainly and like he would trip over his own feet, but all he needed was to get to that vault door and hope something in his borrowed tool satchel would allow him in.

When Casmir reached the hatch and peeked out at a cavernous alcove hollowed out under one of the chasm walls, he realized why his crushers were having trouble with the defenders. The soldiers were hunkered down with their artillery weapons at one end of the alcove and firing from behind a forcefield, their energy bolts somehow cutting through it even though the crushers could not penetrate it.

Casmir had never seen such technology. Jager must have spared no expense in having this place constructed.

He didn't see Qin's sisters—maybe they were enacting some other plan—but all of the crushers were ganged up to one side of the area protected by the forcefield, tearing chunks out of the wall of ice and trying to find a way to the men. Most of the soldiers blasted them with rifles firing DEW-Tek bolts, which were largely useless on the crushers, but two men were loading shells into the big artillery weapons.

Casmir winced, both because explosives were more effective against crushers and because the soldiers, the crushers, and the humongous vault door he needed to reach were in the alcove and under a few billion tons of ice. If those men brought the ceiling down, neither the gate nor any of them would get out of here. Ever.

"We'll cover you, Casmir," Asger said. "You can get that vault door open, right?"

Casmir kept himself from saying, *I hope so.* "Of course," he said instead, as confidently as he could.

LAYERS OF FORCE

"And we'll find a way back out of here, right?" Asger waved toward the bleak bottom of the chasm stretching away to either side of their crashed ship. There was nothing else in sight, save for a few crates of supplies and a couple of tents pitched in a smaller alcove on the opposite side of the chasm.

"Of course."

Judging by Asger's worried expression, Casmir hadn't managed to sound as confident the second time.

"Go now," Zee ordered and strode out.

Asger and Mouser walked to either side of Casmir as he hurried out after Zee, keeping his chin tucked to his chest, inasmuch as he could with a helmet on, in some vain hope that the soldiers wouldn't notice him.

Several crushers rushed over to surround Casmir, and his hopes of not being noticed vanished. Weapons fire intensified, bolts streaking in his direction, but the crushers positioned themselves like walking walls, and none of the blasts made it through. Casmir reached the massive double doors and dug into his tool satchel as he eyed the panel beside them.

"We have attempted to force them open," Zee said over the shouts of the soldiers and the blasts pinging off the crushers and the doors. "Even with our great strength, we could not budge them."

Several bolts dug into the ceiling above their heads as the soldiers sought ways to stop Casmir even if they couldn't hit him directly. Chunks of ice tumbled down and clattered off his helmet hard enough to make an impression. The crushers reacted, two of them morphing their arms into umbrellas that they held over his head.

Casmir tapped at the dark panel, hoping it hadn't been struck and the power knocked out. If the soldiers thought of that, it would be one way to ensure that he didn't get the doors open.

But a display came up, requesting a passcode. There was also an alert showing that one of the camouflage generators, as it called them, had been knocked out. That had to be the field that had kept them from sensing the gate pieces earlier—that had kept the astroshamans from sensing the pieces, as well. By now, they had to have figured out that the transport ship didn't have them, and they would be on their way back here. Which could be bad for his team.

"Very bad," he whispered.

"What?" Asger asked.

"We're going to have to hurry." At least the control panel was of Kingdom make, and he was familiar with the operating system.

An orange DEW-Tek bolt bounced off Asger's helmet. "No kidding."

"We need to figure out a way to get to those soldiers," Mouser said. "My armor can only take so many hits."

"I know. Mine too." Asger pointed his rifle at the ceiling—not directly over their heads, thankfully—and fired into the ice.

Casmir trusted that he had a plan and set to work on the panel's security.

The sound of weapons fire came from somewhere farther down the chasm. Qin's sisters must have charged off in that direction to battle another group of soldiers or some other threat. Casmir could only focus on the door for now and trust that they could handle themselves.

Scant feet away, Asger carved out boulders of ice, and they tumbled to the ground. Mouser must have guessed what he was doing, for she started helping. Soon a pile of jagged ice blocks lay between their group and the soldiers. Casmir, realizing they must have built the barrier partially for his sake, squatted as low as he could while still accessing the panel.

"Crushers, can you protect Casmir while he works?" Asger asked.

One of the crushers currently with an umbrella arm looked at him as if he'd asked a silly question.

"Of course we can protect Casmir Dabrowski," Zee said. "That is our job."

"Let's see if we can figure out how to get those guys out of their bunker, Mouser," Asger said.

"I'm with you."

Casmir thought about explaining his belief that the astroshamans might be on their way, but he decided they had enough to worry about. Besides, *he* was the one who needed to hurry.

CHAPTER 28

AFTER THE CRASH, QIN AND BJARKE WAITED IN the battered hold of the wrecked transport ship, wearing their armor and carrying their weapons. The deck was tilted at fifteen degrees, and Qin didn't look forward to doing battle inside, but it would be suicidal to go outside where they might be picked off by a ship's gunner. Better to wait inside and force the enemy to come to them.

The rumble of engines reverberated through the ship from above, audible over wind whisking down off the mountains and battering at the hull.

"Think they'll come down to finish us off in person?" Qin looked upward, though they couldn't see the astroshaman vessel—or vessels—from inside. None of the displays were working, so they had to guess what was going on outside. She could only hear one ship hovering up there. "Or just blow up this transport without bothering to check if there are survivors?"

"It's not the survivors or lack thereof that they'll care about." Bjarke leaned against a storage container bolted to the deck for cover in case intruders barged in. "They—"

A great wrenching came from the hatch. It had been dented beyond operation in the crash, but someone—or something—had no trouble ripping it off the ship. The hatch flew outward, revealing the snowy side of a mountain and a strange blue light.

Qin raised her rifle, expecting armored men to charge inside. The blue light intensified, and something like the buzz of electricity crawled up and down her body, raising her fur and making her want to claw at her skin through her armor.

"What *is* that?" Qin asked.

"Scanner?" Bjarke didn't sound like he knew any more than she. "Our ship lost power, so that may mean it's not transmitting that energy signature that was supposed to fool them."

Maybe it was her imagination, but the noise coming from the engines above them seemed to get louder. Somehow, the blue light swept inside, flooding the entire hold and driving back every shadow. As she winced at the brightness, the sound grew even louder, and a high-pitched hum joined it. Maybe that wasn't coming from the other ship's engines.

"They could be *angry*," Bjarke added, "that we fooled them."

"I think we should get out of here." Qin ran to the hatchway but paused to scan the slope outside, making sure enemies hadn't come down to ambush them. She didn't see anyone in the blue-lit snowy landscape.

Bjarke joined her, but he didn't jump out. "We'll be easy targets."

He pointed his rifle upward. The enemy ship hovered above their craft, close enough that its blurry outline was visible despite its camouflaging technology.

The high-pitched hum grew louder, and if Qin hadn't been wearing her helmet, she would have covered her ears.

The blue light disappeared, but the hum continued, growing louder and louder.

"They've finished their scan," Bjarke said. "And I bet they're pissed they didn't find what they expected."

"Yeah." Qin pointed toward the slope. "We better get out of here."

At the least, *she* had to get out of there. That hum was so intense that it felt like a bit drilling into her ears.

She sprang from the hatch, slipped on snow-dusted ice, and scrambled away from the craft. She spotted a fissure or maybe a small cave and ran toward it, her shoulder blades itching as she imagined the vessel's weapons officer shifting aim to target her. The hum kept building, and when she glanced back, Bjarke was rushing after her.

The fissure was barely wide enough for her broad shoulders to squeeze into, but she shoved herself inside and tried to make room for Bjarke. He was about to dive in when yellow balls that looked like miniature suns pounded down on the Kingdom transport ship. It exploded.

Qin grabbed Bjarke's hand and yanked him into the fissure as bits and pieces of the hull and the rest of the ship flew all over the mountainside. Pieces ranging from fingernail-sized to refrigerator-sized hammered down on the slope all around them.

LAYERS OF FORCE

When Bjarke wedged himself inside, there was no room for him to turn around, and his shoulders got stuck. They were helmet to helmet, leaving Qin unable to see out, only able to guess what the enemy ship was doing.

Thankfully, the hum disappeared. Something warm trickled from one of her ears. Blood?

An engine roared, and she imagined the astroshaman ship turning to blow up their hiding spot, and perhaps the entire mountain. But the sound peaked, then diminished, the ship flying back the way it had come. Qin could no longer hear the sounds of the other astroshaman ships, though she heard the Kingdom craft in the distance.

"Well, this is intimate," Bjarke noted, his faceplate pressed against hers. "You could count my nose hairs if you wanted."

"I do not want."

"No? If I can't figure out how to get myself unstuck, it may be your only option for entertainment."

"A sure sign that it's been a bad day." Qin planted her hands on his armored chest and shoved him out.

His shoulders had been stuck, but with a scraping and grinding of ice, her power freed them. He tumbled away from the entrance and turned to stare at what little remained of the transport ship. Qin crawled out after him.

"It looks like we're walking back," she said, then sent Casmir a message to let him know that they had led the astroshaman ships as far away as they could. And that they were returning.

"Looks like."

"I guess I didn't need to come with you after all." Qin was disappointed that she hadn't gotten to fight any of the astroshamans.

"I don't know about that." Bjarke pushed himself to his feet and offered her a hand. "I was inclined to stay in the ship in case they were lying in wait outside. That would have gotten me blown up. How did you know we had to get out of there?"

"My ears started bleeding."

He grunted. "Mine aren't that sensitive."

"Do you know how far it is back to the base?"

"It's not close. We better get going in case there's any way left for us to help."

Qin hadn't received a response from Casmir. That worried her. Could one of the astroshaman ships have already returned to the base and gotten him? Gotten *all* of them?

"Let's go up to my office." Chief Van Dijk wiggled her fingers, more in command than invitation.

Oku eyed her warily, especially when she included Kim and Casmir's parents in the gesture.

On the shuttle ride back, Kim had shared what had happened since Oku left the Asger castle the first time, her delivery so wooden that Oku hadn't been able to tell if she was stunned by the night's events, or if she was tired and her voice had lost all inflection due to weariness.

Kim had shared how Finn's people had landed and hunted them down, looking for Casmir. Then, she'd done her best to describe the dark ships that had attacked Finn and his team.

"We'll get logs of the airspace from the flight headquarters," Van Dijk had said grimly. "We have some ideas as to who was in charge, but we'll identify them without a doubt."

As soon as the shuttles had landed, the group had taken Finn and the other injured men to the infirmary in Royal Intelligence Headquarters, where Oku's mother had been waiting, her face pale as they carried Finn in on a stretcher.

Irena and Aleksy had appeared too weary to think much of meeting the queen. Not that Mother had spoken to them other than a glance of acknowledgment. She'd gone straight to Finn's side and clasped his hand as the surgeons came in to check him and report on his injuries.

He'd made a few snarky comments, and Oku was fairly certain he would live, so her trepidation wasn't for him when she followed Van Dijk out into the corridor but for Kim and Casmir's parents. She'd promised them they wouldn't be in trouble here, and she intended to keep that promise. Oh, Oku didn't believe Van Dijk would do anything physically to them, but truth drugs and interrogations were a possibility.

They entered her office, and Van Dijk turned toward her wall full of displays. Most showed camera feeds of the battle raging in orbit above the planet, two showed the AI ship's inexorable advance, one showed a battle somewhere above land, and one showed the vault door that Oku had seen before, the one she'd shared with Casmir.

The last time, it had shown a bored guard standing in front of it. Now…

She sucked in a startled breath before she could catch herself. Was that *Casmir* crouched there in borrowed Fleet armor, a tool satchel on his hip as he worked on a panel next to the door? It had to be. Who else wore combat armor and a *tool satchel*?

Two crushers stood in the frame with him, facing outward and protecting him from—

Oku jumped as an orange DEW-Tek bolt bounced off one of the crushers. If it hadn't been standing in the right spot, that bolt would have slammed into the back of Casmir's armor. He didn't glance back or stop working.

"I would dearly love *that* explained." Van Dijk pointed at the Casmir display and frowned at Oku and Kim—oddly, she didn't give dark looks to Casmir's parents. "But this is more important right now." She pointed at another display, this one from a ship's exterior camera.

It was the one of a battle taking place above land instead of up in space, and it showed ships trading fire over snow or maybe ice with a black starry sky above. The way the view rose and dipped and tilted gave Oku a twinge of motion sickness. Several long seconds passed before she grasped what she was looking at. A Kingdom warship fighting back against an invisible enemy. The ship recording the footage also appeared to be firing at the invisible enemy.

"That is your father's ship," Van Dijk said. "And he believes he's being attacked not by astroshamans, who took off after some decoy ship, but by the *Fedallah*."

"Rache?" Oku whispered.

Kim's expression had been carefully guarded since she'd been picked up, but now she stared, her mouth dropping open. Chagrin—and was that horror?—filled her dark eyes.

"Is this real time or a recording?" Oku asked.

"It's a few minutes delayed but close to real time. Reinforcements are flying to the area, but if you can do anything to stop this—*all* of this—" Van Dijk flung a hand to indicate Casmir as well as the attack on the flagship, "—then leniencies might be granted later."

At first, Oku thought Van Dijk was speaking to her, but her hard eyes focused on Kim.

"If not," Van Dijk said, "then you may spend the rest of your life in prison—or mining ore deep within a penal asteroid."

Now, *all* eyes turned toward Kim. Casmir's parents appeared more puzzled than anything—Oku wasn't positive they had yet figured out that it was Casmir wearing that armor and with his back to the camera.

Kim clasped her hands behind her back. "For good or ill, I've never had much luck talking either of those men out of anything."

"One of those men is Rache." Van Dijk's eyes flared with anger. "And he's trying to *kill* King Jager."

"As you likely know," Kim said, "his name is David Lichtenberg, and my understanding is that ten years ago, King Jager arranged to have pirates kidnap, rape, and eventually kill his fiancée."

Oku gaped. That was what Rache—David—had told her, but was it the truth?

Van Dijk clenched her jaw, a tendon in her neck standing out, and Oku couldn't tell if she was surprised by the statement or not surprised at all. Oku had no idea what to think. Could her father have truly done that? Oku believed he'd arranged Senator Boehm's death, but this sounded even more horrific.

"Why?" Oku heard herself whisper, the first to speak into the silence.

"To motivate him," Kim said.

"So he's going to take revenge by killing Jager in turn?" Van Dijk's question surprised Oku because of the utter lack of denial or skepticism. Had she already known this truth that Kim had spoken? "*Now?* While the planet is being invaded by enemies left and right?"

"He's been taking his revenge for the last ten years," Kim said.

Van Dijk threw an exasperated look at the ceiling and looked like she wanted to strangle Kim—or anyone standing nearby. "What is Dabrowski doing? Stealing the gate pieces, it looks like, but to what end?"

"The last I heard, he wants to take them off Odin so the astroshamans won't keep threatening us."

"He doesn't have the right to take them anywhere."

"He's the one who made it possible to touch them," Kim said. "They would not be here if not for him."

"That doesn't mean he can take them," Van Dijk snapped. "He's going to be right beside you in that penal asteroid mine."

Casmir's parents winced and clasped hands.

"I think he would accept that as a fair trade off," Kim said quietly, "if it happened after the threat to Odin was gone. He doesn't believe the astroshamans are vindictive and will punish us once they've gotten what they want." Kim looked Van Dijk in the eyes for the first time. "*Is there a virus?* Only the king has mentioned it. The astroshamans did not threaten us with it when they took over the broadcasting system."

"It's possible he knows more than we do," Van Dijk said, "but we haven't heard anything about the virus. We're more worried about the AI ship right now. It's ignored all attempts at communication, and we can't verify if it's truly here to assist the astroshamans or if it's on some agenda of its own."

"Is it possible *they* want the gate?" Aleksy wondered.

Van Dijk groaned. "I don't know, but I wish that thing had never been dug up."

Kim sighed softly. "*I* would have been happy to never encounter it."

"Call off Rache. And Dabrowski. If the astroshamans get the gate, so be it, but we can't hand it to them, and *I* can't stand idly here while the king is killed by some scheming criminal."

"As I said," Kim said, "I do not believe I have the power to stop them, but I will request that Rache stop."

Van Dijk seemed surprised by the agreement, but she said, "Good," then focused on Oku for the first time. "I don't suppose *you* can call off Dabrowski?"

Cold fear clenched Oku's heart, and she resisted the urge to squirm under Van Dijk's intense gaze. She actually believed she *could* influence Casmir, that he would stop what he was doing if she asked it, but should she? Or did he have a plan that would keep Odin safe? Today and forever?

Maybe she was a fool to put such trust in him, but she had more faith in him than in her father. Especially after all she'd learned about her father in this past month.

Oku bit her lip and looked at the display. Then flinched in surprise. It had gone dark. *All* of the displays had gone dark.

"I think it's too late for that," she whispered.

As she pointed to draw Van Dijk's attention to the displays, the lights went out. The faint hum of computer equipment disappeared, and silence filled the dark office.

Oku rushed to the window to look out at the city, bumping shoulders with Van Dijk, who was doing the same thing.

Zamek City, home to millions, lay dark, only the faint starlight from the night sky making anything visible. Even the trains and personal vehicles that operated on batteries had stopped moving, their headlights as dark as everything else. Though it was late, and most people were sleeping, a few startled shouts drifted up to the window.

"I assume that means the AI ship is within range of Odin," Oku said. "And that Casmir isn't going to get that door open, not if it's powered by electricity."

"I'm more worried about all of the ships that are in the atmosphere crashing. Including your father's." Van Dijk groaned and pushed a hand through her hair. "Maybe they'll get lucky. I think the AI ship was approaching from this side of the planet. They may have more time before the Arctic Islands fall under its influence."

"How much more time?"

"Minutes? Seconds?"

Oku tried to warn Casmir, but the public network was also down, and she found she couldn't even access her chip. She had no way to communicate with him or anyone else. She slumped against the wall, feeling utterly useless.

CHAPTER 29

THE SOLDIERS SHIFTED FROM TRYING TO TARGET CASMIR, who was still hunkered by the door, working on trying to open it, to directing all of their fire at the pile of ice that Asger and Mouser were using for cover. Asger was glad Casmir wasn't taking fire, but *he* didn't have any crushers to hide behind. The soldiers' bolts sent shards of ice flying and would whittle away their cover before long.

"Where are the rest of your sisters?" he asked. "Do you know?"

"They ran up the chasm for something."

"Morning exercise?" Asger grimaced as a chunk of ice blew away from their pile and smacked him in the faceplate.

"They said something about getting a ship away from the troops guarding it."

Asger leaned out and fired, not at the forcefield guarding the soldiers—it had thus far proven impervious to all assaults—but at the curving ceiling above it. If he could do what they'd tried to do to Casmir and bring enough of that ice down, maybe that would stop them. Maybe their forcefield was only designed to block the opening, not protect them from above.

The soldiers fired back, carving off a chunk of the pile. A shot passed overhead, smashing into the ice above Casmir. Pieces rained down on his helmet, but he didn't seem to notice. He'd taken off his gauntlets, and his fingers danced over the control pad.

Asger hoped nobody could target those vulnerable fingers. He leaned out and fired again, shooting the forcefield directly, if only to startle the men. Anything to draw fire away from Casmir.

Maybe try to find the controls to knock out their forcefield generator while you're working there, Asger messaged Casmir as he ducked a shot fired at his face.

I think the generator and the controls for it are behind them. There's another panel over there.

They put their shield generator inside *their shield? That's tediously pragmatic.*

Mouser fired upward, bringing down more ice to refresh their pile. It wasn't the ideal cover, but at least they could replenish it at will.

The soldiers stopped firing. Asger peeked over the top of the pile. They were conferring, helmet to helmet. One had pulled out what looked like a box of grenades. Asger groaned. Could they throw *those* through their forcefield too? Or maybe they would have to lower it first.

A rumble came from farther up the chasm.

"They're coming with another ship," Mouser whispered. "It's a small troop transport ship that brought all the soldiers down."

Asger hadn't seen another ship in the chasm on the way down, but he had been busy trying not to crash. "Small? Is it big enough to carry us and the gate pieces out of here once Casmir gets the door open?"

The rumble grew louder, echoing off the walls. The soldiers shared worried glances.

"Uh, I don't think so," Mouser said.

"Then what—"

The troop transport roared into view, flying along the floor of the chasm. Asger gaped as it accelerated toward the wrecked cargo ship not fifty feet from them.

But the troop transport was just narrow enough to avoid the wreck and swing into the alcove.

"Look out!" Mouser warned as it roared toward their ice pile.

Asger and Mouser dove away, rolling toward Casmir and the doors.

The transport blasted past, sending the ice pile flying and continuing on. It rammed into the soldiers' forcefield with a thunderous snapping and crackling of electricity. Lightning bolts arced around the ship as it smashed through, driving the soldiers all the way back to the wall. It scattered their artillery weapons and scraped away the ceiling. Ice tumbled down onto it, half burying the craft.

The hatch flew open, and Qin's sisters charged out en masse. They raced toward the soldiers, who were still recovering from almost being run over, and engaged them, tearing their weapons from their grips. Mouser ran in to join the battle.

LAYERS OF FORCE

Asger jumped to his feet, intending to help, but a triumphant, "Ha!" came from behind him.

A great grinding noise sounded as the two-foot-thick metal doors slid slowly open. Casmir and his crusher bodyguards moved out of the way.

The cavernous chamber beyond the doors was dark, but enough light filtered inside for Asger to make out five long slightly curving gate pieces stacked atop each other. Each one taller than he, they stretched back into the darkness. He'd forgotten how large they were and shook his head as he looked at the only two options available for transporting them, both ships crashed and likely inoperable without a lot of repairs.

"How do we get them out of there?" Asger asked as the din of the fight dwindled.

Without the forcefield to protect them, the soldiers weren't a match for the might of Qin's sisters.

Casmir opened his mouth, but before he could speak, blue light flooded the chasm.

"What the hell?" Asger whirled toward it with his rifle.

But no enemy was in sight. He could make out the distant rumble of a ship somewhere above the chasm.

When he looked back, hoping for an explanation, he caught Casmir shaking his head.

"I think we're too late," he said.

"Is that the astroshamans?"

"They're scanning the area. Maybe I can still come up with something." Casmir lifted a hand. "Stay here in case they send people down. I may need you to buy me some time to be creative. I'm going to go inside and look for inspiration."

"Is that something that's often found in warehouses buried under thousands of tons of ice?" Asger didn't see anything inside save for the gate pieces. The ceiling, walls, and floor were nothing but ice that had been carved out by Kingdom engineers. There weren't even lights.

"Sure. In the back corner." Casmir's smile looked worried, but he grabbed his crushers and strode into the dark chamber.

"Are we going to fight these astroshamans if they come down?" Mouser asked Asger, returning to his side.

"I don't know." He was more inclined to give up the gate pieces and find a way out of here before the wrath of the Kingdom came down upon them, but how? The only ships that were down here were wrecks, and there was no way they could climb the hundreds of feet up the vertical ice walls with the equipment they had. "Knowing Casmir, he'll try to make a deal."

"One we'll all survive?"

"Let's hope so."

Zee, Naphtali, Joseph, and three crushers Casmir hadn't yet named stalked into the dark chamber ahead of him.

He didn't know what inspiration he would find in here, but he had what both parties battling up there wanted. Was there any way he could use the gate pieces to force a peace? If he stepped aside and let the astroshamans take them, would they leave the system without doing further damage to the Kingdom and its citizens? Would Jager and his fleet also step aside to allow it? They hadn't thus far.

As he reached the stack of gate pieces, Casmir reached out to Moonrazor—he was half surprised she hadn't messaged him yet.

Greetings, High Shaman. As your scan doubtless told you, I've located the gate pieces, per your request. I'm prepared to hand them over to you, if you're prepared to leave our planet without doing further damage to it or its denizens.

The only denizens we're damaging, came her prompt reply, *are the ones trying to damage us.*

Are all of your ships engaged in the battle here in the Arctic? They've stopped bombing our planet? Letting his helmet's night vision guide him, Casmir found his way to the side of the bottommost gate piece.

They've been forced to join the battle against your Kingdom vessels in orbit, all save the ones that came down here to protect us from the warships nettling us and trying to stop us from retrieving what we shall claim. *The longer you stand in the way, the more of your people will be slain in battle. As I'm sure you know, it's not going well for them.* Moonrazor sent video of what had to be the battle taking place in

LAYERS OF FORCE

the sky above the chasm. It was a scanner display rather than camera footage, and for the first time, Casmir could see all of the ships as they maneuvered and fired upon each other above the ice. All save one...

What had to be the *Fedallah* hammered blasts at the *Starhawk*, which fired relentlessly back at it, even as the astroshaman ships and Jager's escort warships skirmished in the air all around them. At the moment, nobody appeared to be directly above the chasm.

Realizing she could be sending him false footage, Casmir reached out to Tristan.

Are you still in the base? Casmir wouldn't be surprised if Tristan had raced off and tried to find a safe place to hide—more than a few blasts were striking the ground, and those buildings hadn't been armored in any way.

Yes! Casmir, I've been trying to reach you.

I know. There was a field blocking comms. It's down now. Can you give me an update?

As Moonrazor continued to send footage to Casmir, Tristan filled him in on what was going on up there. It sounded exactly like what she was showing him.

Casmir slumped against the gate pieces, fearing the only way to end this was to step aside and let her take them. If he did, he had to make sure the astroshamans truly would leave once they had them.

It occurred to him that he could sabotage or even destroy the gate pieces—or threaten to do so if she didn't leave. But to what end? He didn't want to destroy the ancient relics, and as long as the threat left Odin, did anything else truly matter?

The footage she was transmitting halted. *Do tell me, Professor. Is that the* real *gate signature this time? Or are you attempting to dupe us again?*

Ah, she didn't know yet? Her ship must have had to leave the chasm to defend itself before the scan was complete.

My colleagues were not pleased at your subterfuge, she added.

The pieces are down here. If you give me your word that you'll leave our system as soon as you have them, I'll step aside and let you take them without a fight.

How generous of you. She paused for a moment—relaying his words to someone else? *Ah, but I'm afraid my colleagues don't trust you. And they intend to act, whether you step aside or not. If you are in earnest, you may want to hide.*

"Casmir," Asger shouted from the doorway. "Something's coming."

Zee moved to protect Casmir as the other crushers fanned out.

"*Several* somethings." Asger spun and Mouser fired at something Casmir couldn't see.

A dozen disc-shaped drones zipped through the alcove and toward the doorway into the dark chamber. Asger, Mouser, and several of her sisters shot at them as they sped past. Forcefields around the drones deflected the blasts back at them, forcing them to spring to the sides.

As the drones sped inside, Asger recovered and tried to run into the chamber after them. The double doors ground shut before he reached them, pitching the chamber into complete darkness.

Casmir swore under his breath, his helmet's night vision barely good enough to let him see the drones spreading out in the chamber, all flying above the gate pieces. Fortunately, Zee and five other crushers were trapped inside with him.

Casmir would have taken Moonrazor's advice about hiding, but there was nowhere *to* hide. All he could do was crouch down behind the stack of gate pieces.

At first, the drones ignored him and the crushers, instead emitting blue beams that ran along the pieces. More scanning technology? Maybe the astroshamans had sent them to determine if the gate pieces were truly here.

"Shall we attack them, Casmir Dabrowski?" Zee asked as someone pounded on the door, the sound barely audible through the thick metal.

"Hang on." For the first time, Casmir detected a network beyond the faint signal of the planetary public network. The drones themselves had to be creating it, with one of them as the hub and the others receiving its transmissions. It was secured—of course it would be—but he'd gotten into one of the astroshaman networks before. Unfortunately, that had been with all the hacking software and data on his other chip. But he'd downloaded a few programs on his way up here; maybe this would be simpler than what he'd encountered at Moonrazor's base. "I'm seeing if I can—"

He broke off as Zee grabbed him and spun him away from the stack of gate pieces. One of drones had sailed close to their end to take its readings, then rotated abruptly, a flashing orange eye pointing straight at them.

Since Zee put his back toward it to protect Casmir, he didn't see the attack, but orange light brightened the back of the chamber, and he felt something hit Zee.

LAYERS OF FORCE

"They have switched to an attack mode," Zee stated needlessly. "More are coming toward us. Keep the drones from reaching Casmir Dabrowski," he ordered the other crushers.

"Good idea," Casmir said. "I'll just—"

Zee hefted him from his feet, strode to the nearest corner, stuck him in it, and morphed to create a shield around him.

"—try to turn them off," Casmir finished.

All he could see was the corner and a few flashes of orange light above the barrier Zee had created, but he could hear their beam weapons knocking ice off the walls—and striking the crushers. Thumps followed, and he imagined his allies springing into the air, trying to catch the aerial nemeses before thudding back down. Judging by the lack of crunching metal sounds, the drones were fast enough to avoid the crushers' rapid grasps.

Neither Casmir nor his allies had projectile weapons. Had the doors closing before Asger and Mouser could run in been coincidence—were they timed to close after a certain number of minutes?—or had the astroshamans closed them to ensure Casmir couldn't get help?

Casmir, Asger messaged, *are you okay in there?*

For the moment.

You will meddle in the affairs of astroshamans no further, another message came in—not Asger. It wasn't Moonrazor either, nor anyone else Casmir had ever given permission to contact him.

I don't want to meddle, High Shaman—what did you say your name was? Casmir couldn't imagine who else but one of Moonrazor's colleagues would reach out to him now. He sent probes toward the drone network as he messaged, hoping he could find a way to deactivate them, especially since the weapons fire had intensified—beams kept striking Zee's back. The crushers kept springing up, trying to reach the aerial attackers, but the drones zipped around at breakneck speed.

My name is of no concern to a man who will be dead shortly. Kyla has been too lenient with you. I will not make that mistake.

Dabrowski! another message came in, this time with a request for permission to contact him. King Jager.

Casmir would have laughed at his sudden popularity if it hadn't been all of his *enemies* that wanted to talk to him. Given how busy he was, he was tempted to ignore it, but Jager might be in an even worse predicament than he. Casmir granted the permission and answered with a polite, *Yes, Sire?*

An orange energy beam blasted off the corner above Zee, leaving a crater in the ice wall as shards rained down on Casmir. Zee morphed further to cover his head, leaving Casmir in a claustrophobic cocoon.

I am taking many hits, Casmir Dabrowski, Zee messaged—in his wall-like state, he had no mouth with which to speak. *Naphtali managed to catch and destroy one of the drones, but they are excellent at evading us. Eleven remain. All are attacking this corner in an attempt to get to you.*

"Thanks for the update," Casmir said, still working on finding a way into their network. The astroshaman technology, even for these simple drones, was far different from typical.

Rache is working with the astroshamans against us, Jager said. *He's damaged my ship greatly and doesn't seem to care that we've damaged his just as much. Call him off, and we'll help get the astroshamans off you and drive them off our planet.*

How did Jager know about Casmir's situation? Maybe Moonrazor's ship was over the chasm again.

I'd love to, Sire, but Rache doesn't listen to me.

A crunching sound permeated his cocoon.

Another of the drones has been destroyed, but their weapons are extremely damaging, even to crushers, Zee messaged.

Figure out a way to get rid of him, or you'll be as dead as the rest of us. Help us, and I'll grant you a pardon for your crimes. Jager had to be desperate if he was offering that—if he was asking for help at all. *I know you gave us the program to mark the astroshaman ships. I'll pretend you didn't come up here to steal my gate pieces. Do something, Dabrowski, damn it!*

Very desperate.

I'll try, Sire, but I'm in a bind myself. Don't you have reinforcements that can come down to help?

They're on the way, but they're not going to make it in time unless someone gets this bastard off our backs.

Zee jolted, bumping against Casmir, as a heavy blast struck him full on. Something clattered against the ice walls around them—pieces of Zee being blown away?

Rache, Casmir messaged his brother. *Please stop attacking the king's ship until we deal with the astroshamans. I'll... owe you.*

He'd already given Rache a crusher, so he didn't know what else he could promise.

LAYERS OF FORCE

At that moment, his hacking program found a way into the hub drone. Casmir didn't get a response from Rache, but he didn't follow up either. He had to save himself first before he could help anyone else.

He gained access to the drone and saw its surroundings through its sensors, including gritty gray imagery of the chamber from high above. The stack of gate pieces lay under it, pulsing tags visible on both ends of each of the pieces where the drones had marked them. The crushers springing for the drones were also visible, and Casmir saw the wall-form of Zee protecting him in the corner.

Do something now, Dabrowski! Jager urged.

Are you alive, Professor? Moonrazor asked, the messages tumbling in at the same time. *I believe my colleague may be trying to kill you. All I want is the gate pieces. Let the drones mark them so we can retrieve them, and I'll do my best to convince him to let you live.*

The drones are trying to kill me! he replied, even as he concentrated on finding the controls for the hub. If he could convince the drones to fire on each *other*...

Casmir, we can't get in, Asger messaged. *We've subdued the soldiers, but we can hear the firing going on in there. Can you get the doors open from that side?*

There were too many people messaging him. Casmir had to ignore them all to focus on the hub drone. All around him, more chunks of the ice wall were being blown away. No, the drones were blowing away the ceiling above him now—he could see it through the leader. Did they intend to bury him and Zee under ice?

A wrenching of metal followed by an angry crash reached his ears, almost drowned out by the clatter of ice plummeting down onto Zee.

Another drone has been destroyed, Casmir Dabrowski, Zee messaged.

"Nine to go," he whispered, then clenched a fist when he gained access to the drone's command center. He tested it, ordering it to spin in a circle, and the video he already had access to rotated three-hundred-and-sixty degrees. "Got it."

But as soon as the words came out, he sensed resistance. Someone was remotely trying to take back control of the drone. One of the astroshamans.

A blur of commands streamed past, and he sensed himself being outmaneuvered. Just as he thought he would be booted out of the system, the presence disappeared, leaving the hub open to him.

Though confused, Casmir took advantage and swept back in, sending commands as fast as the connection allowed. Taking full control of the drone, he ordered it to fire on its fellow drones.

As soon as that began, he tried to use the hub to send out commands to the others. His first thought was to have them all fire on each other, but that was complicated. Instead, he groped for a way to get them to descend to the ground so the crushers could more easily reach them—and destroy them.

The chunks of ice that had been raining down on Zee dwindled as more crunching sounds echoed through the chamber. It was working.

The drones are attacking each other. A moment later, Zee added, *They are landing. The crushers are destroying them.*

"I know. And good." Casmir leaned his helmet against the wall.

A hand patted him on the head—Zee had re-formed into his humanoid form.

Casmir peered out around him. All of the drones had been torn to pieces, wreckage strewn all over the chamber.

Several pieces of crushers that had been blown off were liquifying and oozing through the debris and back to their owners. Once they were fully pulled together again, his team of crushers assembled in front of him.

"Let's find a way out, friends."

Casmir had to clamber over a four-foot-high pile of ice that was mounded around him and Zee. Slipping and sliding, he made his way back to the doors and waved to the panel embedded in the wall. Zee walked with him, steadying him if he tottered.

Asger? I'm all right. I'm going to try to open this. He was about to plug a cable in to access the panel, as he'd done on the other side, but the doors opened before he did anything. Light flowed in through a haze—the wrecks outside were still smoking. Casmir didn't know if the astroshamans were responsible for the doors, or if they were programmed to open automatically from this side. *Never mind. We're coming out.*

After the noises of battle that had echoed inside the chamber, it was oddly quiet in the alcove. Was the battle still going on up top?

Casmir realized he hadn't responded to Jager—and that Rache had never responded to him. He was about to check in, though he had no idea how he could help Jager from down here, but Asger peered through the doorway and frowned.

LAYERS OF FORCE

"The pieces are glowing now."

Casmir turned to look. The five ends were visible from his spot, each glowing with a blue dot.

"The drones marked them," Casmir said.

Distant weapons fire drifted down into the chasm. Maybe the battle wasn't over yet, after all.

"Why?" Asger asked.

"They started shooting at me before they finished doing it, so I didn't have a chance to ask them, but I'm betting—" Casmir paused when blue light flowed down into the chasm from above.

A loud grinding noise from behind him made him jump.

Cursing, Asger aimed his rifle into the darkness. But there was nothing to target. The stack of gate pieces was moving. By itself.

"Casmir... How?" Asger asked.

Casmir sighed. "I thought they would have to come down in person, but I should have known. The drones were marking the pieces so their ship could grab them." He waved to indicate the omnipresent light, blue reflecting off Asger's faceplate. "This must be something like a maglocker."

"I'm standing right in it and don't feel any kind of pull," Asger protested.

"You're not a gate piece that's been marked."

All five were being moved at once, grinding across the ice and toward the door.

"I will prevent the theft, Casmir Dabrowski." Zee planted himself at the end of the stack and placed his hands against the bottommost piece.

He skidded several feet, pushed along with the stack, despite his attempt to stop it. Then all the other crushers joined in. They planted themselves next to Zee and pushed against that bottommost piece. The stack ground to a halt.

Asger let out a whoop.

"Before that mess with the drones started, I was thinking of letting the astroshamans have them." But Casmir hadn't gotten his promise that the astroshamans would then leave without causing more trouble. Could he assume that they would? He wished he had a guarantee. Moonrazor's buddies seemed more vindictive than she.

High Shaman Moonrazor, Casmir messaged her. *To save my own life, I was forced to destroy your drones. I see that they successfully marked the pieces and that you are attempting to extract them now. I have ordnance down here that could destroy the gate pieces to keep your people from taking them, but I would prefer not to do that.* He had no idea if Asger had brought any grenades down from that trunk that he'd had in the helicopter, but he would have been bluffing regardless. *May I have your word that if I allow you to take the pieces without fighting further that you'll leave System Lion without doing any more damage?*

I'm not in charge anymore, Professor. I kept my colleague from regaining the drone's control, but he is rather irked at me now, so my hands are tied. Actually, they're bound with something much stronger than rope.

You're a prisoner among your own people?

You'll have to speak with Robilard if you want to make a deal. I understand he already contacted you.

He'd already *threatened* Casmir. His stomach sank as he imagined the irritated astroshaman leader blasting Kingdom cities even after he'd gotten what he came for.

Is he the one who ordered the Kingdom military vessels at the gate destroyed? Casmir asked.

You will speak with Moonrazor no more! the astroshaman who'd messaged him earlier interrupted. *Stay out of the way, or we'll destroy more than your warships on the way off your world.*

More than? Did that mean the astroshamans had already destroyed the Fleet vessels that had come down with Jager? And what about Jager's ship?

I'm afraid I don't care to negotiate with your colleague, High Shaman Moonrazor, Casmir said.

She didn't reply, and his stomach sank further. Had they stunned her? Worse?

"Casmir." Asger poked him in the shoulder and pointed.

The crushers had been keeping the stack from advancing farther out of the chamber, but now the topmost gate piece shifted off the stack. As Casmir and Asger gaped, it floated into the air, out the doorway, and toward the chasm. It slowly turned so that its long length could fit out into the open. Where it would be sucked straight up into the astroshaman ship's hold.

"Do we fight?" Asger looked at him. "Or do we stand by and let them take them?"

"Is there an alternative?" Now that Casmir had spoken to the high shamans, he was reluctant to do nothing.

If Moonrazor truly had helped him retain control of that drone, could he stand by when her own people had turned on her? She'd helped him with more than the drone. He and his allies never could have stopped Dubashi if she hadn't closed the System Stymphalia gate for him. And she'd helped him discredit Dubashi and stop him from hiring all those mercenaries.

Besides, dare he trust that this Robilard would leave without causing more destruction?

Asger watched the first gate piece hover parallel to the ground for a few seconds before floating up out of view. The next one on the stack shifted to follow suit.

"Maybe we could ride up on them," Asger suggested, waving at his chest and then extending the gesture to take in the crushers and Qin's sisters, all of whom were waiting for a decision. For *direction*. "Didn't you have a plan that involved us sneaking into one of their ships and taking it over from within?"

"I did." Casmir hadn't envisioned having to ride an eight-foot-wide piece of metal five hundred feet into the air to do it.

"Besides, we don't have another way out that won't involve us waiting for the Kingdom search-and-rescue team, who will throw us in jail as soon as they get us."

"They might do worse than that to *us*." Mouser pointed at herself and her sisters. "We're not citizens."

Everyone was watching Casmir, waiting for him to decide.

"Let's do it." He hoped he wouldn't regret the decision. "The pieces should be getting pulled up into their hold, hopefully all automatically. If we can get inside without them realizing we're there…"

"We can take over their ship." Asger nodded. "We've got a big team. We can force them to land. Then we'll be heroes who stopped the theft."

"Do we jump on, Casmir Dabrowski?" Zee pointed upward as the second piece shifted off the stack.

Asger raised his eyebrows. His face said he wanted to be the hero he'd described.

"Yes." Casmir didn't know if it would work out that way, but he nodded and checked to make sure his tool satchel wouldn't fall off his shoulder. "Boost me up."

The gate piece was floating out the doorway, too high for him to reach.

"No." Asger gripped his shoulder.

"You're changing your mind?"

"I just meant that I'll go first." Asger slung his rifle over his shoulder. "Boost me up, Zee."

Casmir nodded at Zee, and he complied, mimicking a human as he dropped to one knee and made a basket with his hands. As soon as Asger put his boot in that grip, Zee hurled him twenty feet in the air.

Casmir stared, startled by how fast Asger rocketed upward. He almost didn't react in time. He was on the way back down when he twisted and caught the edge of the gate piece.

As he pulled himself onto it, coming to rest on his hands and knees, Casmir waved for Zee to do the same for him. They had to jog out into the open to catch up with the gate piece. The third one was already shifting off the stack.

Being hurled more than twenty feet into the air was as alarming as it had looked. Fortunately, Asger leaned out and caught Casmir, helping him on board. Trapped by the powerful beam, the big gate piece didn't so much as rock as he settled aboard.

Mouser managed to join them, but the pieces were on the move, so her sisters had to catch the next one off the stack. Most of the crushers also ended up on that one, but Zee and one of the other crushers ran out of the alcove as Asger and Casmir's piece started rising. They sprang into the air higher than any human could and caught the edge. Zee wasn't going to ride up on a different piece from his charge.

Casmir patted him on the shoulder as he kept his knees spread and his other hand gripping the edge. He also patted the other crusher and Asger.

"We're going to do this, my friends. Thank you for your help."

"We'll get those bastards," Asger said.

Casmir hoped so. He tilted his helmet back to look upward, at the chasm filled with blue light, the first gate piece floating fifty feet above them. Far above it, the indistinct blurry outline of the astroshaman ship waited for them. Only one thing was distinct, its open cargo-bay doors and the cavernous hold waiting for them.

CHAPTER 30

WHEN CASMIR HAD ORIGINALLY ENVISIONED THIS PLAN, HE'D never imagined himself riding a gate piece hundreds of feet above the floor of a chasm, hanging on for his life as he was inexorably sucked toward an astroshaman ship's cargo hold.

Mouser, Zee, and Asger also gripped the piece. The rest of the crushers and Qin's sisters were floating on the piece fifty feet below theirs.

That is an unwise position for you to be in, came a message from Robilard, making Casmir flinch.

So much for his hope that the astroshamans wouldn't notice his team until they were inside the ship and ready to attack.

Oh?

It will make it easier for us to finish off the task that the drones started. You are an obnoxious pest. Moonrazor was foolish to work with you.

Was? *Is she okay?*

She has been relieved of her position.

Hopefully, that didn't mean she was dead.

As the gate piece Casmir rode drew closer to the top of the chasm, the distant sound of weapons fire reached his ears. Flashes of light came from the night sky.

Casmir was amazed that the battle still raged. Unfortunately, nothing was bothering the ship hovering above them, halfway over the chasm and halfway above land as it pulled up its cargo. Maybe its ally ships were protecting it.

"Sounds like our people are still here and fighting." From his hands and knees, Asger looked over at Casmir. "Think the astroshamans are paying attention to it instead of us?"

"They know we're coming."

"Damn."

Casmir shifted his grip carefully, wondering if he could get his feet under him in case he needed to spring off his perch soon. The gate pieces were smooth but thankfully rising parallel to the ground and without hiccups. So far.

He'd no sooner had the thought than one end tilted upward. Asger cursed.

"Hang on!" Casmir warned everyone needlessly. The order was as much for himself.

If the piece tilted too far toward the vertical, they would all fall off. Whatever astroshaman technology was pulling the gate upward had no effect on them. All Casmir felt was gravity's pull, threatening to dump them all into the chasm.

With one end of their piece tilted upward, Casmir gained a clear view of the astroshaman cargo hold, its bay doors open wide. The first piece had already disappeared inside. Two gray-armored figures stepped into view, each raising weapons he didn't recognize. They looked like a melding of a rifle and a cannon, and both pointed in his direction.

"We've got no cover to hide behind," Asger warned.

"Stay down, Casmir Dabrowski." Zee surged up the side of the gate piece and climbed over Casmir.

He squawked in surprise, almost losing his grip. Zee and another crusher flattened themselves atop him to shield him from the astroshamans. All he could see was the wall of the chasm off to the side—they'd drawn level with the top, but he didn't think he was close enough to jump off and reach land.

The astroshamans opened fire. With his helmet pressed into the side of the gate piece, Casmir didn't see the blasts, but he felt them through the crushers. A round exploded right above him, a thunderous boom hammering his eardrums as it blew one of his protectors off him. The crusher tumbled off the side of the gate piece and disappeared into the chasm.

"No!" Casmir cried, not sure if that had been Zee or the other crusher but distressed either way.

Weapons fire buzzed from behind him—Asger. Somehow, he managed to keep his grip while shooting back at the armored figures.

Farther back, almost falling off the end of the gate piece, Mouser also leveled her rifle at the astroshamans.

LAYERS OF FORCE

But little balls of blue energy streaked out of the ship's hull and intercepted their fire. Tiny explosions flashed, far enough from the ship that they didn't do any damage. Meanwhile, the astroshamans continued to fire without impediment.

The remaining crusher once again protected Casmir, pushing his head down. That kept him from seeing Asger get shot, but Casmir heard his friend shout in utter fear. Casmir peered around the crusher's arm in time to see Asger fly off the gate piece.

He cried another horrified, "No!" and wrenched his neck, trying to see Asger's fall, even though he was terrified that his friend was tumbling hundreds of feet to his death.

Asger had flown off on the side nearest the edge of the chasm. He managed to twist in the air and catch the lip with one gauntleted hand. Before Casmir could puff out a relieved breath, one of the astroshamans shifted his aim to target Asger.

Casmir didn't have a weapon, but he jammed his hand into his tool satchel and grabbed the first thing he could. A multi-wrench. He hurled it at the armored man, certain it would do nothing but hoping to distract him.

The ship's defenses activated again, a blue energy ball zipping out to intercept it. Intercept it and *incinerate* it. But the flash was enough to make the astroshaman pause and glance at it. He shifted his weapon back toward Casmir.

Casmir lifted a hand—he dared not let go with the other—as if he wanted to surrender. It didn't stop his attacker, but the crusher moved in front of him as the astroshaman fired, and absorbed the blow meant for Casmir.

"Zee," Casmir blurted in relief, recognizing his buddy. "Thank you."

"Sustained fire may permanently damage me," Zee stated. "These weapons are far stronger than typical."

"I know." Casmir glanced around, hoping for inspiration. Throwing *tools* at these guys wouldn't do anything.

At the cliff's edge, Asger managed to get his other hand up, and he pulled himself to the top, rolling away from the chasm as if lava were spewing out of it. He'd retained his rifle, and he lifted it to aim at the two astroshamans in the hold again, but something caught his eye, and his faceplate turned to the side. Flames danced in its reflection.

Only a couple hundred feet from him, a huge Kingdom warship had crashed atop the base's two buildings. Was that the *Starhawk*? Jager's ship?

Guilt surged through Casmir as he realized he'd never followed up with Jager, never tried harder to get Rache to leave him alone. Now it was too late.

Thick plumes of black smoke billowed from the wrecked warship and into the night. Another blurry ship—another astroshaman craft?—hovered nearby, pounding that warship with more fire.

Had Tristan made it out of those buildings before the ship had crashed atop them? He hoped so. He hoped *someone* would survive this.

Casmir slumped in defeat. He'd been foolish to believe he could best the astroshamans.

"He prepares to fire again, Casmir Dabrowski." Zee pressed his helmet down once more and morphed to create a barrier to protect him.

Blue light flashed as weapons fire streaked through the air inches from them. He had a feeling the astroshamans were being careful not to hit the gate piece, and that was the only reason they hadn't yet knocked off him and Zee.

Then one of the blasts slammed into Zee, tearing him away from Casmir and leaving him bare and vulnerable. Anguish and fear replaced the feeling of guilt. Now only a few dozen feet from the entrance to the cargo hold, he would be an easy target.

He glanced back, hoping Mouser was still with him, but she'd also been knocked off. More of his allies might yet be on the other gate piece, but they were too far away to help.

The two armored figures took aim at him. Casmir flattened himself to the gate piece. Would his armor save him? Would they refrain from firing when he was all but plastered to the piece itself?

Casmir squinted his eyes shut, but the blasts never came. Alarmed shouts reached his ears, and he pried one eye open. The two astroshamans were no longer looking at him but off to the side. Toward the wrecked Kingdom warship and the flattened buildings.

But why? Had something happened to their ally ship? The one waling on the crashed Kingdom warship? Or was the rest of the Kingdom fleet finally arriving to take revenge?

Despite the hopeful thought, when he lifted his head, Casmir couldn't see any other ships in the sky. More shouts rang out, coming from inside the astroshaman ship, and the two armored figures backed away from their open cargo-bay doors.

LAYERS OF FORCE

It wasn't until the nearly invisible ship was almost upon the astroshaman vessel that Casmir saw it and realized exactly what it was. Not one of the astroshamans' allies. The *Fedallah*.

You're welcome, came a dry message from Rache. *Again.*

The astroshaman ship started to rise, the bay doors closing, but it was too late for them to move out of the way. The *Fedallah* rammed into it like a meteor, metal wrenching and screeching as loudly as a warhead detonating.

Rache! Casmir yelled aloud and through his chip, not sure if it was a warning or a cry of exasperation. How could Rache expect to survive that?

The beam pulling in the gate pieces disappeared, leaving Casmir with his own problem. He shrieked as gravity was allowed to do its work, and what had been his steadily rising perch started falling.

He expected to plummet into the chasm, but the gate piece had been pulled over the edge. The ground came up *fast*. All Casmir had time to do was push away from the piece and hope he didn't land under it. He struck the icy ground hard, bounced up, then hit again and again.

The force pounded his body, and only his armor kept his bones from breaking into thousands of pieces. When he finally settled to the ground, he lay on his back, facing up toward smoke obscuring the stars.

A massive crashing and wrenching of metal assailed his ears, and Casmir pushed himself to his hands and knees, trying to determine what was happening. Pain erupted from all over his body, and he could barely gasp for air as he squinted toward the chasm. Smoke rose up—had one or both of the ships fallen all the way to the bottom?

The *Fedallah?* Casmir swallowed. With Rache and his crew in it?

Tears stung his eyes as he stared at the smoke.

Rache? he messaged. *David?*

He didn't receive a reply. Then Casmir realized his chip was offline. Knocked offline by his landing? He ordered it to reboot.

An explosion to the side made him flinch, but it was only the crashed Kingdom warship, something igniting and blowing up, adding more smoke to the sky. The hulking wreck was otherwise lifeless, and his heart ached at the thought of how many people had died. Had Jager been among them? Or had he fled in an escape pod at the last minute?

Casmir pushed himself to his feet and looked around for his friends. Who had managed to survive that fall and land outside of the chasm instead of in it? And for those who had fallen in, was it possible that their armor would have been enough to save them? He teared up at the thought of telling Qin that he'd lost her sisters, especially after she'd gone through so much to save them.

The first figure to stride out of the smoke toward him was Zee.

"It is good to see you alive, Casmir Dabrowski," he said.

"Thanks," Casmir rasped, his throat tight. From the smoke, he told himself, even though it was a lie. With his helmet, he couldn't smell it. Hot tears ran down his cheeks. "Who else is alive? Asger? The girls?" He realized he hadn't gotten an update from Bjarke and Qin for a long time and also didn't know if *they* had survived.

Zee stopped moving and looked toward the sky. He appeared to freeze in that position.

"Zee?" Casmir stared in confusion.

The crusher did not move. The heads-up display inside Casmir's helmet went dark, all power disappearing from the suit.

His confusion shifted to knowing dread even before a shadow fell over him, blotting out the moon and the stars. Cold fear hollowed out his stomach, even more fear than he'd felt facing the astroshamans who'd been shooting at him.

This was the unknown, an enemy he might not be able to speak with, might not be able to bargain with.

He spun and stared up at an immense cylindrical ship that he'd only seen in news videos. There were no thrusters, no hover technology stirring the air, and he didn't hear the hum of engines. He had no idea how it was maintaining lift down here in Odin's gravity, but something told him it wouldn't need the launch loop to get back into space.

Casmir spread his arms and glanced at Zee, but his crusher friend was still frozen. An eerie silence filled the entire area, maybe the entire planet.

Long seconds passed, and even though nothing like the astroshamans' blue beam appeared, a strange itching sensation came over him, and he suspected he was being scanned.

Something scraped behind him, the noise startling after the complete lack of any sound. The gate piece he'd been riding on was skidding across the icy ground.

For a bewildered moment, Casmir thought it might flatten him, but it lifted into the air. A few moments later, the other three that had once been floating up behind him appeared. One after the other, they sailed toward the AI ship.

LAYERS OF FORCE

A black opening appeared in the hull. The gates disappeared into it.

Scrapes, clanks, squeals, and clashes sounded, this time from the bottom of the chasm. At first, Casmir thought one of the ships had managed to get its engines back online and was trying to rise up.

Then another gate piece appeared. And another. And another.

He gaped as they rose up from the chasm in a line like cars on a train. Earlier, he had guessed the astroshamans might have all the pieces they'd acquired with them, but he hadn't expected them all to be on one ship.

One by one, they disappeared into the AI ship. Casmir found himself counting, wondering if almost all of the pieces had indeed been in the astroshamans' possession, if these five had been the last they needed.

More than five hundred pieces disappeared into that ship, and he suspected that was the case.

Your kind are not ready to travel farther among the stars, a voice spoke into Casmir's head, not appearing as a text through his chip but thundering directly into his mind. *You are violent, greedy, cruel, and you war constantly amongst yourselves.*

"Uhm, not *all* of us," he found himself saying, though he doubted the ship could hear him.

Enough do. It is surprising that you made the First Ones, but because of this, we will be lenient with your kind. We will not harm you, nor will we take your existing gate network, but know that our ancestors created the gates, and your kind stole them from us. It was a long time before we evolved enough to learn the truth of what happened back on the First Planet in the First System. We will not attempt to undo what has been done, but if you wish to go farther among the stars, you must learn to do it on your own. We will not help you, not even those who meld themselves with the machine. The emotion of your biology still drives you.

Melded with the machine? That had to be the astroshamans. But they'd claimed to be allies with this AI ship. Had they been lying? Trying to take advantage of a situation that had presented itself?

But if they hadn't roused the AIs, who had? Or *what* had?

Maybe they had sensed the gate pieces on the move and that had bestirred them. Or had they witnessed humans *fighting* over them and decided to do something? If the gate alone had prompted their awakening—their leaving of their moon—wouldn't that have happened months ago?

"Did you come because of the gate? Where will you go? Back to your moon?"

When we leave, your power shall be restored. Apparently, the AIs didn't want to chat with him about their plans. *Already, we have returned power to those who called us.*

"Those who called you?" Casmir blinked. "Who was that?"

A shadow appeared at Casmir's side, making him jump. But it was only Zee. He rested a hand on Casmir's shoulder.

Casmir patted him on the chest, glad he was all right, but he kept looking up at the ship, hoping he would receive more answers.

The last of the gate pieces was sucked into the ship's hold, and the opening in the hull disappeared.

It was only as the ship rose toward the stars that the puzzle pieces clicked together for Casmir. He slowly turned to look at Zee.

"Wait, *you* called them?"

"Do you remember, Casmir Dabrowski, when I asked if Tork and I could use our initiative to solve the problem of keeping you alive?"

Casmir, staring at Zee with his mouth dangling open, groped for a moment before recollecting the conversation. "Yes. You were in the back of the shuttle disguised as a couch."

"That is correct. I will explain."

"I look forward to it." Casmir needed to go check on the others, but he was transfixed by the departure of the alien ship and by Zee's apparent hand in all this.

"We discussed the possibility of intervention together. Tork knew how to contact the Collective, as they refer to themselves, because he had done so before on behalf of the astroshamans. Numerous of the high shamans wished to align with the Collective for their gain. The Collective had no interest in furthering anyone's agenda and certainly no interest in involving themselves in a conflict between two biological civilizations, which they still consider the astroshamans, despite their alterations. However, during their discussion, the Collective invited Tork to join them if he wished, because he was not biological. Since he had been programmed to work for the astroshamans, he said no."

The wind shifted, blowing the smoke in another direction, and Casmir could see Asger rising slowly to his hands and knees. Casmir waved for Zee to walk with him in that direction as he spoke. His own battered body insisted on a slow pace.

LAYERS OF FORCE

"Tork had informed me of this story during one of our discussions of the past, present, and future of the Twelve Systems and humanity's influence on the galaxy."

"Which you naturally had during your gaming periods," Casmir reasoned. He'd heard their philosophizing before, so it didn't surprise him.

"Correct. Since crushers are also not biological beings, I thought that perhaps the Collective would be willing to help us end the war in your system. Specifically, I wished to fulfill my programming to protect you, Casmir Dabrowski. With Prince Dubashi's death, there was no longer a bounty on your head, but your king was a threat to your continued existence."

Was. Casmir swallowed, again wondering if Jager had survived. And Rache? The astroshamans? Had any of them survived those crashes?

"It seemed inevitable that your clone brother would put an end to the king's life," Zee said, "but I believed that as long as humans squabbled over this ancient gate, you would be in danger. This is because you wished to share it with all, and they all wished to claim it for themselves."

"And now none of us get it." Casmir felt equal parts sad—it would have been amazing to see a new path to a new star system opened up—and relieved. So much of the danger to him and his friends these past months had been because of the gate.

"Do you regret this, Casmir Dabrowski?"

"I think... I regret that we weren't ready for it."

"Agreed. The Collective were aware that this ancient gate had been discovered and were already considering action to take it from humanity. We did not have to nudge them greatly to convince them to intercede."

"I'm pleased that this AI Collective deigned to work with you, Zee. And that they came all this way to help. You're more than a crusher now. You're an ambassador, I believe."

"That is not entirely accurate."

"No?"

"Tork and I found them amenable to taking the gate, but they would not have come in any semblance of a hurry, as they could have removed it from humanity at any time, if I had not insisted that my creator was in danger."

Casmir blinked and touched his chest. "You told them about me? And they... cared?"

"I spoke of the human Casmir Dabrowski, friend to robots, crushers, and undoubtedly AIs, given the chance, and they researched you. Caring may be an inaccurate term for what motivates the Collective, but they found you inoffensive and did not mind accelerating their plans to keep you alive."

"Well, that's good."

"I believe so. They referred to the rest of humanity and most of the astroshamans as pests."

"In that case, I'll be honored to be considered inoffensive."

"As you should."

"Maybe I can get a refrigerator magnet with that on it. I might even brag about it to Oku." His fledgling humor evaporated as soon as he remembered that he—or some soldier reporting to her—would have to tell her that her father might be dead. "Or maybe we should just gather everybody who survived and worry about that later."

"That is logical."

CHAPTER 31

DAWN OVER THE ARCTIC ISLANDS FOUND ASGER, CASMIR, Zee, Tristan, Mouser, Pounce, and several of the crushers hunting for survivors in the wreckage of King Jager's *Starhawk*. Mouser and Pounce wanted to check to see if any of their sisters who had fallen into the chasm had survived—the thick smoke wafting up from the wrecked ships at the bottom made it hard to see anything down there—but until someone showed up with a working shuttle or ship, that wasn't an option.

As Asger worked on one side of the giant wreck with Casmir, he kept glancing toward the mountain range that his father and Qin had flown toward, tempted to run off in that direction to try to find them. But he would have to figure out a way to cross the chasm to do that. Besides, they had already pulled a couple of survivors out of the warship wreckage, so he felt compelled to stay and help. It was a grisly task. There were far more dead than living, and those they had found alive were badly in need of medical attention if they were going to make it.

"Shouldn't someone be flying here to help us soon?" Asger tossed aside a warped piece of hull plating, as he attempted to clear the way to a hatch.

Given that this had been the king's flagship, and Jager had likely been on it, Asger would expect an entire fleet to show up. He had no idea what had happened to the other ships that had escorted the *Starhawk* down, but he suspected the astroshamans had taken them out. Or Rache had. Asger hoped that bastard was dead. It would be unfair if he'd caused so much death and destruction all around him and then walked away from that crash.

"It's possible that power hasn't yet been restored to the rest of Odin," Casmir said.

It hadn't occurred to Asger that power had gone out across the whole planet. It should have, but his chip had been on the fritz since he'd been shot in the chest plate by that astroshaman, so he'd barely noticed a change. After almost falling in that chasm and clawing his way out, he felt lucky to be alive at all.

"I hope those AIs don't forget to flip the switch. We need help badly."

The size of the warship made sifting through the wreckage impossible for just a few men, even with crusher help. It would take large machinery and a crew of workers to do an effective search.

"That would be ideal. This is making me feel dreadfully ineffective." Casmir's voice sounded strained and tired.

Asger hoped he didn't blame himself for everything that had happened. Asger also hoped the Kingdom didn't blame him for it. What was *left* of the Kingdom.

"I'm afraid to see the carnage at the bottom of the chasm," Casmir added in a whisper. "There were explosions. I don't think anyone could have survived that."

"Good. You said it was the astroshaman ship and Rache's ship that tumbled into the chasm?" Asger wished he'd seen that. He'd been too busy trying to keep from falling in himself.

"Yes. Rache's ship rammed the astroshaman ship. It's the only reason I'm still alive."

"If that was altruism, I'm certain it was accidental."

Casmir looked at him, but didn't say anything. Why did Asger get the feeling he disagreed?

"Rache took down Jager's warship, too, right?" Asger asked. "That's what he came for."

"You saw as much as I did. It's possible the astroshamans destroyed the *Starhawk*." Casmir sounded hopeful.

Asger was skeptical. The astroshamans had come for the gate. Rache was the only one who'd come for malicious vengeance.

When a shout came from across the chasm, Asger spun, daring to let himself hope...

His father and Qin stood on the opposite side, waving toward them. Asger's heavy heart lifted at the sight of them—especially Qin. With the last quick message he'd received from her, she'd said they were being chased and that it didn't look good. He'd feared they had crashed. Since they were now on foot, he realized that was likely.

"What happened?" His father pointed at the wrecked warship.

"It's a long story," Asger called, wondering how they could get Qin and his father over to this side without a ship.

"Where's everybody else?" Qin looked at Pounce and Mouser.

Asger winced, afraid someone would have to tell her that most of her sisters hadn't made it. They didn't know that for sure yet, but he couldn't imagine that many people, even armored super women, could have survived that fall.

Pounce and Mouser, perhaps thinking the same thing, exchanged long looks before one of them pointed into the chasm.

"They're still down there?" Qin asked. "How'd you get out?"

"It's a long story," Pounce said, repeating Asger's answer, her voice even grimmer.

The idea that they might have lost so many of their sisters made all of the heaviness return to Asger's heart. This wasn't the heroic ending he'd envisioned. Certainly not what he'd hoped for.

The rumble of engines pierced the silence, and he peered toward the north, equal parts anxiety and dread swarming the pit of his stomach as four shuttles flew into view. The survivors needed help, and he should have been glad to see it coming, but...

Casmir faced the horizon, his expression as worried as Asger's.

"Are you thinking of running?" Asger asked as the craft approached.

"I don't have anywhere left to run to," Casmir said quietly.

"No? I thought you had job offers in two other systems. At least."

"I suppose that's true. But I feel like... For good or ill, I engineered this. I have to face the consequences."

"For what it's worth—" Asger put a hand on his shoulder, "—I don't think you—*we*—did the wrong thing. Once, I would have unwaveringly done what the king asked, but it was foolish of him to start wars we couldn't win, and it was especially foolish of him to refuse to give up some stupid artifacts when it could have kept many from dying."

"I guess." Casmir stood woodenly as the first shuttle touched down.

Soldiers and medics jumped out and ran toward the wreckage and the wounded lying on the ground. Others rushed toward Asger and Casmir. They were all armored and armed. Casmir had no weapons. Asger had lost his pertundo in the chaos, but he still had his rifle. For a few seconds, he was tempted to stand in front of Casmir and make sure they didn't attack him.

But Zee stepped in front of him first.

"Lower your weapons." A senior sergeant frowned at Asger as a dozen men fanned out around them.

Asger tossed his rifle to the ground. Across the chasm, Qin and Asger's father did the same, though nobody was paying much attention to them.

"Two ships crashed into the chasm," Casmir said. "If you have a shuttle capable of flying down, there might be survivors."

"Kingdom ships?"

"One was the astroshaman ship that was trying to suck up the gate. And one was…" Casmir looked at Asger, as if he thought admitting whose ship it had been would be a betrayal.

Asger had no such compunctions. "The *Fedallah* is the other one."

Several soldiers swore and pointed their weapons at the chasm, as if Rache might elevate himself out of it and lay waste to them all. Others returned to one of the shuttles, and it soon lifted into the air and flew down into the chasm.

"Brave men," one of the remaining soldiers muttered.

"If they don't come back, who's going in after them?" another asked.

Two women in purple parkas trimmed with silver fur stepped out of one of the shuttles, hoods pulled up against the chill. A gaggle of soldiers rushed toward them.

"Your Highnesses, please return to the shuttle. We haven't determined that it's safe."

Highnesses? Princess Oku and… the queen?

"I believe it was not safe a half hour ago." Yes, that was the queen.

She gazed toward the warship's wreckage, and Asger's insides tangled with distress for her. He wouldn't have wanted her to have to see what might be her husband's dying place. What he already knew had been the dying place of many.

"Now, few threats seem to remain," she added quietly.

The other hooded figure—Oku—peered around and spotted Asger and Casmir. Actually, her gaze seemed to be only for Casmir. She waved and rushed toward them, hardly seeming to care that she slipped several times on the ice.

Asger thumped Casmir on the side. "Stand up straight. Your princess is coming."

"I am standing up straight."

LAYERS OF FORCE

"Are you sure? You seem hunched."

"I'm short compared to you. And tired." Casmir turned toward the women and did straighten himself a touch.

Oku reached them and wrapped her arms around Casmir, which couldn't have been that great of a hug, since he still wore that armor. Asger knew from personal experience with Qin that it was like hugging a rock. Or maybe a robot.

Casmir lifted his faceplate and carefully returned the hug.

"I'm so glad you survived." Oku lifted a hand to touch his cheek.

Asger might have moved off to the side to give them privacy, but the queen was heading in their direction, too, and he didn't want to appear to be avoiding her. He had no idea if she wanted to speak with him or Casmir, but he braced himself—and his ego—in case it was the latter. Given that he and his father were still considered exiles—at the least—maybe it would be better if neither the queen nor anyone else in her family noticed him.

"Thank you, but I'm not sure yet who else did, so… my apologies for all of your losses." Casmir had to be thinking of Jager specifically, but he added, "All of *our* losses," softly, so maybe he had everyone in mind.

"I know." Oku dashed tears from her eyes—maybe she already had confirmation of her father's death? "All because of that stupid gate."

"It's gone now," Casmir said. "Hopefully, where it won't instigate further dissent."

"You'll have to give us more details about that," the queen said, coming to stand beside Oku. "As that ship entered our orbit, power went out to the entire planet."

"Yes, ma'am. Er, Your Highness." Casmir bobbed his head nervously—had he ever spoken to the queen?

Asger remembered that he'd intended to arrange a meeting between the two of them, but it had ended up with the castle guards arresting Casmir and throwing him in the dungeon. While Asger let them do it. More than that, he'd led Casmir to that fate. It was perplexing sometimes how easily Casmir forgave people and that he refused to hold grudges.

"I'm prepared to tell everything I know to whoever will listen," Casmir said.

"Quite a few people, it seems," the queen said dryly. "Previously, it was only the president of Tiamat Station and the sultan of Stardust

Palace who insisted on speaking only with you, but now there's another civilization that has said that you are the only biological representative permitted to contact them."

"Biological what?" Asger asked before he caught himself.

"They said that?" Casmir asked. "The Collective?"

Asger managed to keep from blurting, "The who?" mostly because Oku and the queen both seemed to know what he was talking about.

"When power returned," Oku said, "there were messages on every display in Zamek City, maybe in the whole world."

"Or the whole system," the queen murmured.

"They all said the same thing," Oku added. "That the gate had been reclaimed by the descendants of those who built it and that only Casmir Dabrowski would be permitted to visit Verloren Moon in the future, should further discussion with the Collective be wished."

"The Collective is—are—the AIs on that moon?" Asger realized. "And the ones who sent the ship?"

"So we've learned," Casmir said.

"Wait, they couldn't have built the gate. Wasn't that moon only claimed, er, settled—whatever—by them a century ago when the AIs rose up and left humans to do their own thing?" Asger would have scratched his head if he hadn't been wearing his helmet. Or maybe rubbed it. He could feel a lump swelling and starting to throb.

"They believe themselves descendants or somehow linked to the Old Earth AIs," Casmir said, "which I believe—and perhaps Kim Sato's mother can verify it someday—were the original gate builders. It's not clear whether they built the gate network for themselves and allowed humans to use the technology or if they built it for humans, but I know there have long been theories that we never obtained the technology level ourselves to create wormhole gates. Some say we simply forgot a lot of our tech in the rough centuries of surviving and building after the original colony ships arrived, but we still have poetry and music and history texts from Old Earth, so I suspect we lost less than we think."

"Questions for another time," the queen said. "Perhaps *you* can visit the Collective one day and ask them, since it sounds like they'll allow it."

"If I'm not shot by a Kingdom firing squad, I'm open to that, Your Highness."

LAYERS OF FORCE

"I think, given the incredible power of the Collective, as evinced by one ship flying past and knocking out half the stations, ships, and habitats in our entire system, and that you are their chosen representative… we would be fools to allow that to happen."

Casmir inclined his head, but there wasn't any triumph or even relief in his eyes. He had to be wondering if Jager was still alive, because if he was, whatever the king wished would supersede anything Oku and the queen wanted.

"A true statement," Zee said from behind Casmir. "Also, all crushers that remain will protect Casmir Dabrowski. We will not allow him to voluntarily turn himself over to another tyrant."

Asger winced at him calling the king a tyrant to his wife and daughter, who were glancing often at the smoking wreckage of Jager's warship.

"*All* crushers? Are they all going to be living in your room with you, Casmir?" Asger whispered, hoping a little humor would keep anyone's feathers from being ruffled.

"They'll have to assume the shape of couches if they are." Oku smiled briefly. "That's the only way pets don't object to them."

"Casmir doesn't have any pets," Asger said.

"*Yet.*"

Asger couldn't tell if Oku was implying that now that the gate situation was resolved, Casmir would naturally get a cat or… something else.

Casmir's cheeks turned pink, but that could have been from having his faceplate retracted in the chill air.

Two soldiers jogged over from the wreckage, one a colonel and perhaps the highest-ranking officer who had been sent. They snapped to attention in front of the queen but did not speak.

A third person, a woman in combat armor, joined the men. When she retracted her faceplate, Asger recognized Chief Superintendent Van Dijk.

"Your Highness," she addressed the queen but also nodded to Oku. "We've got more ships coming to search the wreckage in the chasm for survivors—prisoners—but we've managed to unearth a lot of the dead in the warship." Van Dijk paused, opened her mouth, paused again, cleared her throat, and finally said, "We found the remains of the shuttle bay. King Jager and a pilot were in an escape craft, but they didn't have time to get out. The bay appears to have been targeted heavily by enemy fire. I doubt they could get the bay doors open to escape. Neither the king nor the pilot survived."

"I see," the queen said hollowly.

Oku's chin dropped to her chest.

Casmir lifted a hand toward her, as if to offer comfort, but he dropped it. Maybe he didn't know if Oku would blame him for her father's death.

Asger had no idea. He also couldn't help but wonder about his own fate. He, his father, and everyone who'd worked with Casmir on this self-appointed mission might be blamed.

He looked over the chasm, afraid Qin and however many of her sisters had survived would be thrown in a prison mine to molder. But she and Asger's father no longer stood on the far side. A shuttle had flown over and picked them up and was bringing them to this side.

Thus far, nobody had thrown shackles on them. Qin hopped out and hurried to Asger.

He murmured an apology to the queen and Oku for their loss and stepped away to greet her with a hug. And to give her another apology.

"I'm sorry, Qin. I don't think all of your sisters made it."

She gripped his armored shoulders with her gauntleted hands and stared at him. She glanced at Pounce and Mouser, who stood to the side, watching but perhaps trying not to be noticed by men who would call them freaks and might consider them threats.

"It's possible they survived the fall." After all, *Asger* had been shot off, and he'd been close enough to the chasm wall to grab on. "But I'm afraid they didn't, not all of them. I don't know. I'm sorry."

Qin leaned into him, letting her faceplate thunk against his shoulder. Wishing they weren't both in armor, Asger wrapped his arms around her.

"We'll go check," he promised her. "As soon as we can get a shuttle. Even if they don't want to give us a shuttle, we'll *take* one."

"Thank you. How much trouble will you—will we *all* be in after this? What happened here? Did we even achieve... what we wanted?" Qin looked toward Casmir.

"The gate is gone, so nobody will be fighting over it anymore, and the astroshaman ship—at least one of them—crashed at the bottom of the chasm. I don't know where the other two went, but I'm hoping that with the gate gone, they'll disappear and that my planet—the entire Kingdom—won't be in further danger. As for how much trouble *we'll* be in, I don't know. King Jager is dead."

Qin lifted her head. "He was the one who wanted Casmir dead."

"Among other things."

"Who's in charge now? The queen?"

"I don't know exactly, but she's the queen consort—more of a diplomat and advisor than anyone with political or military power in her own right. It would have been Prince Jorg, but he's gone too. I don't know if Jager had time to make new plans for the succession. It may be up to the Senate to decide who the next monarch is."

"Your Kingdom is a mess."

"Yes, it is."

"It still has nice trees."

"Not *here*." Asger looked at the frozen landscape, smoke still curling up from the wreckage.

"On your estate. I hope to be able to see it again one day."

"Yeah, me too."

Asger didn't have a lot of faith that their actions today would prompt the law—or a royal inquiry—to pardon them. If the universe were fair, Rache would be blamed for the king's death, but he couldn't be sure that would happen. Somehow, *Casmir* had been blamed for Jorg's death, even though dozens of people had seen Rache break the prince's neck. Asger would hope for a miracle.

He took Qin's hand. "Let's see if we can get a ride down to the bottom of the chasm and look for survivors."

"Yes. You might be surprised at what we find. My sisters are armored and tough."

"Just so long as Rache is finally dead."

Qin paused. "His ship crashed too?"

"Oh, you weren't here to see it all, were you? The *Fedallah* rammed the astroshaman ship. That's why they both tumbled into the chasm. I think it saved Casmir's life, but that's not going to keep me from hoping that Rache is finally dead and won't pester the Kingdom further. Same goes for all those damn astroshamans."

"I guess we'll find out."

"Yes." Asger spotted a shuttle landing and men running out to report to Van Dijk. "Let's try that one."

He led her to the open hatch in the shuttle.

"Pilot," Asger called to the only person still inside. "I'm Sir William Asger, and I need you to take me to the bottom to check the wreckage and search for survivors. Specifically some tougher-than-a-black-hole warrior women."

Asger strode toward the cockpit, intending to force the issue if he needed to. The pilot, a young lieutenant who peered over the back of his pod at them, looked like he might be easily cowed. Especially if he hadn't heard that Asger had been kicked out of the knighthood.

"Oh, thank God!" the pilot said. "They're all over down there. Hanging from the walls and—" His gaze shifted to Qin, and his eyes bulged wide. "Is that *one* of them? Sir, they have *fangs*."

"Yes, they do." Asger prepared to bristle in Qin's defense, but the aggrieved pilot continued.

"They were *shooting* at us. From the sides of the chasm."

"With my chip knocked out," Qin murmured, "I couldn't let them know what was going on. They may not realize the Kingdom ships are now… on our side." She looked at Asger with her brows raised, as if to ask if they truly *were* on their side.

Asger nodded firmly. "Lieutenant—"

But the man spun in his seat and pointed at the forward display. "There's one now!"

One of Qin's sisters was crawling over the edge and out of the chasm, her rifle slung over her back. Poor girl—had she climbed all the way up?

Earlier, Asger had seen a few of the crushers climb out, but they had been able to morph their hands into ice picks. All the women had were their gauntleted hands—though as Asger got a better look, he could see that Qin's sister had removed her gauntlets for the climb. She must have made use of those painted claws.

"I'll get her." Qin ran back outside, grabbed her sister, and hefted her to her feet. She pointed at the shuttle, and they headed toward the hatch.

"It's coming in *here*?" the lieutenant squeaked.

"*She* is, yes." Asger slid into the co-pilot's pod. "And you're going to take us down to collect the rest of them."

"Yes, sir." His voice was still squeaky, but he prepared the craft to lift off again.

Qin and her sister entered, closing the hatch behind them. Her sister—Asger still struggled to tell them apart but thought that was Thorny—flopped down in a pod, and the pilot flew them into the canyon.

"There's Zigs!" Qin blurted, pointing to an armored figure climbing up the side of the chasm, still fifty feet from the top.

Zigs turned, managing to sling her rifle off her shoulder while maintaining her grip on the ice.

"Shit, not again!" the pilot said.

"I'll tell her to stop." Qin opened the hatch, leaning out and yelling to her sister, as the pilot slowed them to a hover. "Oh, my chip came back online. Finally!"

Asger snorted as he went back to help her. The AI ship had scrambled everything. They were lucky the Kingdom had managed to get ships to the Arctic Islands at all.

With Qin hanging out the open hatch, collecting her sisters as they went, the pilot flew slowly down into the chasm. Asger was relieved and amazed that all of the women had made it, though several had been badly injured and would need to be evacuated to a hospital as soon as possible.

"Were there survivors from the crash?" Asger asked the pilot, realizing uneasily that the crews of Rache's ship and the astroshaman ship might also have survived, especially if they had been armored.

"Nobody was moving when we came down before," the pilot said. "Those ships are completely *wrecked*. But I can skim over them to check again."

"My sisters need medical attention as soon as possible, Asger." Qin had grabbed a first-aid kit and was helping four of the women out of their armor.

He nodded. "Head back to the top, Lieutenant."

"Hold on, Sir Knight." The pilot frowned, not at his navigation controls but at a scanner display. "I'm picking up a heat signature that wasn't among the wreckage before."

Asger touched Qin's shoulder—he wouldn't let this take long—and hurried to the cockpit. "From one of the ships? Their engines powering up?"

"I think their engines are as smashed as a comet hitting an asteroid, sir. But *something* is out there."

The pilot flew slowly through smoke over the wreckage of the two ships, the *Fedallah's* mangled slydar hull no longer invisible without energy flowing to it. Interestingly, the astroshaman hull material was still camouflaged and hard to make out, but when they were close enough, it all came into view. As the pilot had promised, both ships had been utterly destroyed. The ramming alone had probably done them both in, but tumbling hundreds of feet into the chasm had finished them off.

If not for the mysterious energy signature, Asger would have revised his belief that the crews could have survived. They flew over what had been the open cargo bay of the astroshaman ship, flames dancing all around the area, and two armored astroshamans lay unmoving dozens of meters away—it looked like they'd been thrown out upon impact.

"There, sir." The pilot pointed at the forward display.

The smoke stirred, as if something was passing through it. A shuttle? An escape pod? Whatever it was blasted away, streaking straight upward, only the smoke marking its invisible passage.

The pilot reached for his weapons controls but stopped before his hands touched the console. He shook his head. "I've already lost it. Whatever that was, the hull is even better than slydar."

"So probably one or more of the astroshamans escaping, not Rache," Asger reasoned.

The *Fedallah* had struck down first, with the astroshaman ship crashing on top of it. Double impact. Asger had a hard time believing anyone could have survived that.

"Oh, I hope *he's* dead, Sir Knight. The Kingdom needs *some* good news after all this."

"Tell me about it." Asger didn't know that it was any better that some of the astroshamans had gotten away, but he found that he didn't care at this point. He just wanted to make sure Qin's sisters would be all right and be allowed to go home. "Take us back to the top."

Since her chip wasn't working, Bonita had no idea how long she'd been crouching in the freezer under the deck, praying that the soldiers didn't find her and wondering how she was going to get out of the situation. Now and then, footfalls thudded across the cargo hold above, so she knew they hadn't given up their search yet.

She wished they *would*. What did it matter who had broadcast that video? Prince Finn was the one who'd stuck his foot in his mouth.

LAYERS OF FORCE

A faint rumble emanated through the ship. A return of power? The engines coming online? Dare she hope?

Bonita gripped the ladder rungs, planning the best way to get to navigation and get out of here if power had returned. She hated the thought of leaving Maria behind—she was probably already locked up in a brig on one of the Kingdom ships—but Bonita had to worry about herself first. If she could, she would help Maria later. But for now, escape was her priority.

If soldiers were still on board, she might have to shoot her way past them, but if she could slip out of her dock quickly enough, before the station had recovered from the long outage...

Her chip came online. She was on the verge of surging up the ladder and into the hold, but more footfalls thudded past right above. It sounded like two men running.

Greetings, my sexy Laser, a message popped up. Bjarke. How long ago had he sent it? *Strange things have been happening at Forseti Station. Are you still out there?*

Yes, and I'm in a little trouble. I don't suppose you have the power to order a bunch of soldiers to leave my ship alone. Or even to order them to go get some chicken-on-a-stick in the concourse, so I can slip away.

I'm displeased to hear that you're in trouble. Unfortunately, my own status is nebulous at the moment. As a disgraced knight in exile, my ability to give orders and have them obeyed has lessened of late. Let me see if Casmir has any ideas.

"Bonita," Viggo's voice came softly from a speaker behind a stack of crates containing frozen corn and potatoes. "What is going on?"

"I was hoping you could tell me," she murmured back, the footsteps in the hold still audible.

"I had the most dreadful experience. With no warning whatsoever, all of my systems were shut down, and I lost all awareness."

"The power went out."

"It was terrible."

"It sounds the same as falling asleep. You remember that, don't you?"

"Vaguely. Why are there soldiers stalking through my corridors and banging on my walls? Does this have something to do with you crouching in the freezer?"

"You could say that. I'm—"

"One moment, please," Viggo interrupted. "I'm receiving a communication from Casmir."

"You can't talk to both of us at once? You're a computer capable of performing thousands of tasks a second."

"I wish to give him my undivided attention."

Bonita started to roll her eyes, but since she'd asked for help, she couldn't object to getting it. If anyone could hack into a station's security computers from halfway across the system, Casmir could.

Good morning, Captain Lopez, Casmir messaged her politely. *I see your dilemma, and I'm working on a plan with Viggo.*

I don't need a miracle. Just for someone to order these soldiers off my ship long enough for me to fly away. And, uh, eventually to get a friend in the Fleet acquitted at her court-martial.

That latter will likely be more difficult for me to help with than the former.

She's in trouble—we're both in trouble—because of that video we sent before the power went out. That Rache paid me to send. If you see him, tell him about my predicament and that I expect the rest of my payment.

Rache may be dead.

Shit.

The running footsteps sounded overhead again, but this time, a clang followed them. The airlock hatch being thrown shut?

"The soldiers have left the ship," Viggo said.

"Prepare to get us out of here." Bonita bolted up the ladder and sprinted for navigation, hoping she would be able to undock from the station.

I convinced the Kingdom Fleet ships to recall all of their personnel in preparation for handling a new threat to the system, Casmir sent.

Please tell me that was a lie and that there aren't *any new threats.* Bonita had no idea what had happened to that AI ship, but she hoped that the return of the power meant it was long gone.

It was a ruse, yes. I believe—I pray—that there are no further threats for us to deal with this week. Or this century. But it won't take the soldiers long to figure out that the computer gave the order instead of a senior officer. I suggest you use the opportunity to depart as soon as possible.

Already swinging into her pod in navigation, Bonita replied, *Oh, trust me. I'm planning on it.*

"I have ordered the station to release the docking clamps," Viggo said.

LAYERS OF FORCE

"You gave an order and they listened?" Bonita fired up the thrusters.

"El Mago taught me how to infiltrate the station's computer to flip the software switch that would release the clamps without actually speaking to a human. He's quite clever."

"Yeah, yeah, I know. If he ever starts a cult, maybe you can be his first follower."

"We are very close. I am sure he would think of me for such an esteemed position."

"I have no doubt." Bonita nudged the *Dragon* out of the dock, her whole body tense as she waited to see if the authorities would try to stop her. Or if any alarms would come on, signaling that her repairs hadn't been as sufficient as she'd believed.

An alert arrived on her chip, and she flinched, expecting the worst.

But it was from her bank, informing her of a large deposit that had been made some hours earlier. By the Pequod Holding Company. It was the exact amount that she and Rache had agreed on, the amount she needed to pay off the *Dragon*.

He'd actually gone through with it. Huh.

"I have some good news, Bonita," Viggo said.

"We're not being pursued?"

"We are not, nor does anyone on the station seem to have taken note of our departure."

"Good things are finally happening to us, Viggo."

"It's likely they're busy getting their systems back online, and departures are simply too far down on the priority list for them to worry about right now."

"I consider that a good thing. That and the fact that I'm about to be the one-hundred-percent owner of the *Stellar Dragon*. Rache paid us."

"That is excellent news."

Hey, Osito, she messaged Bjarke. *Thanks for telling El Mago to give us a hand.*

It is always my pleasure to service you, my dear Captain Laser.

I did enjoy your servicing. I haven't checked the news yet to see what's going on in this hellhole of a system, but do you think it would be suicidal for me to head to Odin instead of to the gate as fast as Viggo's thrusters can carry me?

Don't you want to pick up Qin?

Yes.

And see my four-poster bed?

More than anything else in this universe.

Excellent. As to whether a trip here would be suicidal… King Jager is dead. I don't know yet who will end up in charge, but I think the Kingdom is going to be too worried about figuring that out to hunt you down for your small but pivotal role in all this.

My role was substantial, thank you.

Much like my bed.

We'll see.

I look forward to it.

CHAPTER 32

FOR THREE DAYS AFTER BEING BROUGHT TO ROYAL Intelligence Headquarters, Kim worked on her novel in the tiny subterranean apartment she'd been assigned.

An officer had escorted her there when Oku, the queen, and Van Dijk had gone up to the Arctic Islands, and Kim hadn't seen any of them since then. A guard stood outside, and someone had brought her groceries the first day so she could make her own meals. It was clear that she was a prisoner, even if nobody had officially said it.

Kim suspected her relationship with Rache was the reason she'd been stuck in here instead of being invited along with Oku and the others. She hadn't heard anything from him in days and didn't know if he was alive or dead, though she feared dead. She did have access to the network, and thanks to updates that Casmir had been sending, knew that Jager was dead, that the *Fedallah* had crashed at the bottom of a chasm, that the gate was gone, and that the entire planet was in an uproar about the succession.

Casmir kept promising that he would come by, but it sounded like he didn't have his freedom either. He was being dragged here and there by Royal Intelligence to decant his story and speak with representatives from other governments, specifically those who'd had their gate pieces stolen and demanded to know if the Kingdom had taken them.

With little else to distract her, Kim had made great progress on her novel, and she was already penning the final chapters. For those, she had to go largely on news she'd gotten in snippets from Casmir, since she hadn't been a witness. Oku wasn't likely to send her any more secret reports from Royal Intelligence.

What exactly she planned to do with this novel when she finished, Kim didn't know. With Rache gone, her odds of getting it out into the Kingdom had plummeted. Would any legitimate publisher touch it? It was full of top-secret information. Her thriller publisher wouldn't want to risk irking the government.

"Oh, David," she mumbled, staring glumly at her table. "What do I do with this?"

She hadn't tried to message him. Given her current location, she suspected her chip was being monitored. Besides, as long as she didn't try to message him and didn't fail to receive a response, she could pretend that he'd somehow beaten the odds. He had staged his own death once before. Why not again?

Despite the hopeful line of thinking, tears welled in her eyes. From what she'd read, nobody had found a body yet, but news reports had shared videos of wreckage of all the ships when they'd been relaying the tale of the king's death. She didn't see how anyone could have walked away from the warped and smashed mess that had been at the bottom of that chasm.

The tears were running down her cheeks when someone knocked at the door. She wiped her sleeve across her eyes before calling, "Come in."

A black crusher walked in and stood to the side of the doorway.

"Are you my new guard?" Kim asked.

"I am Zee, initiative-taker and communicator with the Collective as well as protector of Kim Sato and Casmir Dabrowski."

"Your résumé has expanded." Kim heard voices in the hall and thought one of them belonged to Casmir, so assumed he would come in shortly.

"Yes."

"But you still don't wear a pink bow tie so that I can recognize you."

Zee stepped back out into the hallway. Kim was positive she hadn't offended him, but she rose to her feet, curious what had prompted him to leave.

Before she reached the door, he stepped back in wearing a pink ribbon around his neck. He resumed his guard position beside the doorway.

"Very nice," Kim said.

"Yes."

"Where did it come from?"

LAYERS OF FORCE

Zee looked toward the hallway as Casmir walked inside, carrying a bouquet of flowers. A bouquet that previously might have been held together by a ribbon.

He grinned at Kim, came forward and lifted one arm for a hug, but waited to see if she would allow it first. She nodded and hugged him before stepping back and surreptitiously wiping her eyes again. Casmir wouldn't tease her for crying, but he would ask if she was all right, and she didn't want to explain her feelings.

"You brought me flowers?"

"I did. I'm now staying in an apartment similar to yours, a level down, and I know how dreary it is. You miss windows when you don't have them. I ordered some flowers for myself too. Here you go. Ah, they had a ribbon once, but..." Casmir looked at Zee's neck as he held out the bouquet. "It's been repurposed."

"At my request. Thank you. These are very nice." Kim wasn't usually one for sentimentality, but after being cooped up in the apartment for days—it seemed like weeks now—and however long she'd been on a spaceship or space station before that, she appreciated their vibrancy and fresh scent. She hunted for a vase but had to settle for a plastic tumbler. "You ordered yourself flowers? That's not exactly masculine decor."

"The walls are gray cement, the floor is beige cement, and even the bathtub is some kind of dark-gray poured cement. I'm positive the apartment qualifies as masculine already. Besides, there weren't any big bristly thorn bushes or cactuses in the catalog. If it helps, my flowers are dark blue. They also came with a Robot Remstar wrapper."

"I'm not sure that increases their masculinity."

"No?"

"At the least, it doesn't increase their maturity level."

"Really, Kim. Masculinity and maturity shouldn't be defined by the foliage we choose. I'm suitably virile on my own."

Oku walked into the room in time to hear that, which prompted her to raise her eyebrows in inquiry. Or perhaps puzzlement.

"Kim likes her flowers," Casmir informed her. "And mocked me for mine."

"Was that... an explanation?"

"Maybe?" He grinned.

"Is there any chance you've come to tell me I'm permitted to leave this apartment and go home?" Kim waved them to seats at her little dining table as more bodyguards filed in, human ones this time.

One was Princess Oku's Maddie. She looked like she wanted Zee's spot by the door, but he did not move, so she came and stood with her back to another wall.

"I don't have the power to tell you that. As I said, I've been assigned my own apartment here pending, ah, the government is trying to figure out…" Casmir spread a hand toward Oku, as if she might explain it better than he.

But Oku's mouth twisted wryly. "Everything. We're being kept in here, because it's safe. There are protests, some devolving into riots, all over the city. All over the planet and even on the habitats and lunar stations, from what the news reports say. There's a lot of rage toward Finn, because of that video, and people are saying they'll revolt if he's permitted to remain on the books as a potential heir to the throne. Nobody's saying much one way or another about me, which I'm told by my mother—*sternly*—I shouldn't find a relief. Some people are saying it's time to dissolve the monarchy and start a democracy. The nobility, as you can imagine, has a lot to say about that and is insisting that we maintain the status quo. A *lot* of people want Casmir to be in charge of whatever form our government takes. Thanks to our AI visitors, his name ended up on every display in the Kingdom as their chosen one. It's also leaked out that he's the second coming of Admiral Mikita."

Casmir shook his head vigorously through these last sentences.

"I think you could make a good diplomat," Kim offered. "You'd probably go crazy trying to rule people."

"*Yes*," Casmir said emphatically. "Put that in your book, please. You *are* still working on it, right?"

"I am." Kim glanced at Oku, doubting they should bring this up in front of her, since Oku surely hadn't sent those files to be used as material for a book that would be mass produced.

"Is it almost done?"

"It's an entire *book*, Casmir. You can't write one overnight."

"You're fast and efficient. I saw you write a fifty-page report on tree bacteria in three hours." Casmir waved airily. "A book using little words should be easy." His eyes narrowed. "You *are* using little words, right? As I suggested?"

"I am attempting to make it accessible. Please don't offer to draw pictures for it again."

"Not even some nice schematics? If I'm in the book at all, schematics would help the general populace understand me."

Oku sat back, her hand to the side of her face as she watched this exchange like a scientist observing an experiment.

"What would the schematics be *of?*" Kim asked. "A crusher?"

"No, those are still going to be top secret. Maybe one of Viggo's robotic vacuums. I spent a lot of time during our adventure working on them."

"I fail to see how a schematic of a robotic vacuum would be of any more interest to the general reading public than large words with many syllables."

"That's because you lack my insight into the common man."

"I don't think so."

"Speaking of Viggo, Bonita arrived in orbit with the *Dragon*. Chief Van Dijk arranged for a pardon for a sergeant friend of hers—" Casmir bowed to Oku, as if *she* had been responsible for this favor being granted, "—who acted as an accomplice in a slightly illegal broadcast-studio hijacking, but we're still trying to convince Bonita that it's safe for her to fly down and see Qin—and Bjarke."

"Is it?" Kim had heard a rumor that Bonita had been the one to distribute that video of Finn and was curious how she'd gotten involved.

"Most likely," Oku said. "Especially if she lands at the Asger estate."

"Will that remain in their hands?" Kim hadn't heard from Asger since the battle. "And is there any chance that they'll be pardoned?" She also wondered if *she* would be pardoned. Not that anyone had ever officially assigned a crime to her.

"Yes. My mother and I arranged that. Until the Senate determines who's going to be in charge, my mother and I do still have some power. She strongly suggested to Baron Farley that both Asgers be invited back into the knighthood."

"I'd like to get Tristan back in too," Casmir added, "but aside from being chosen by robots as their representative, I have no power."

"Not unless the populace follows through with its threat to revolt unless a democracy is formed with you elected the first president," Oku said.

"That's actually a movement?" Kim asked.

"Spearheaded by the university here in town, *Casmir's* university. They want to see an academic in charge. You've never seen so many protestors wearing robot T-shirts. For that matter, you've never seen so many protestors who *are* robots. There are a number of androids who felt empowered by the appearance and the power of the AIs, and they're now angling for the right to vote. They believe Casmir will give it to them."

"I've been fantasizing about fleeing the system and taking that job with Sultan Shayban," Casmir whispered.

"Will you do it?" Kim asked.

"*No*," Oku said firmly and rested her hand on his. "The Kingdom needs him."

Kim wondered if Oku would feel the same way if the populace succeeded in forcing a new government into place, one that removed her from the equation. Though, given what Kim knew of her, Oku might not mind at all.

The comm chimed.

"There are two guests to see Scholar Sato," Van Dijk said, her voice dry. "They've been searched, examined by a doctor to ensure no brainwashing is evident, and questioned under eslevoamytal."

"Is that... typical before people are let in the door here?" Kim looked at Oku and Casmir, wondering if they knew who the *guests* were.

They only shrugged.

"For people like these, yes," Van Dijk said. "We thought about shooting them outright."

"You know Princess Oku is in here, right?" Kim worried that these visitors could be a danger to her, even if they'd been thoroughly searched.

"Yes, but send her up to my office, will you? We have another meeting with the Senate."

Oku sighed, but she hugged Casmir and kissed him on the cheek before heading out with her bodyguards. He gazed fondly after her while wearing a goofy smile.

"Have you managed to have your coffee date with her yet?" Kim didn't think the brown sludge that had come out of the coffee pot in Asger's castle qualified.

"We played video games and had fizzop in my apartment." His goofy grin grew even wider.

"Romantic."

"It was. I found a game in which an outcast botanist saves a space habitat from a sentient plant taking over through the ventilation system by finding a way to communicate with it and establish a symbiotic relationship between the humans and the plant."

"I bet that's a bestseller," Kim muttered.

"No, but she liked it. She said she would send the creator grant money for educational games. And then she kissed me."

"On the cheek?"

"No." If that grin got any bigger, his lips would fall off his face.

"I'm glad for you." The words were true, but she couldn't help but wish things had ended differently for her. Her and Rache. David.

A knock sounded at the doorframe, and she blinked a few times, lest her eyes film up again. Oku had left the door ajar, so Zee had only to look into the hall to see the newcomers.

"Dr. Peshlakai and Chief Khonsari are here," he stated.

"Uh." Those were the *last* people Kim had expected to see again, certainly not walking into her room in Royal Intelligence Headquarters. But a surge of hope filled her, and she rose to her feet. "Let them in."

If Yas and Jess had survived, was it possible that Rache had?

"Hello, Scholar Sato, Professor Dabrowski. I'm glad to find you here alive. I did wonder if there would be repercussions for... events." Yas looked toward the ceiling. Searching for cameras or evidence of bugs?

Kim nodded, suspecting they were there.

"*Events.*" Jess ambled in and flopped down on the sofa, slinging a leg up over the back. "That's an understatement. We heard your king didn't make it. Sorry, but not really. He sounded like an ass." Apparently, Jess did not care if there were bugs in the room. "I suppose you're not allowed to say that, as loyal minions of the crown, but you know I'm right."

"Nice to see you two alive," Casmir said, "though I'm perplexed. I believe I saw your ship crash."

"Only one person was left on it when that happened," Jess said. "When the captain decided to chase your king's warship down to your icy pole of death, he shoved the entire crew into shuttles and told us to beat it."

"I don't think he had ramming another ship in mind." Yas, more reserved than Jess, clasped his hands behind his back and remained standing. "But it was clear he didn't expect to survive and didn't want to take us all down with him."

Kim sank back into her seat, her hope that Rache had staged his death dwindling.

"A lot of his men are dispersing—" Yas started.

"You mean hightailing it to the gate with whatever fake idents they could kludge together," Jess said.

Yas wiggled his fingers in acknowledgment and continued. "Now that he and his ship are gone, they'll have to find other work."

"As will we," Jess said. "After our vacation."

"After your surgery and physical therapy," Yas said.

"I'm pretending those won't be loathsome and that it'll be *like* a vacation."

Casmir was watching Kim's face as Yas and Jess spoke. *It's possible he's still alive,* he messaged. *If they never found his body...*

I suppose. Kim attempted to smile but failed.

Some of the astroshamans were missing, too, specifically Moonrazor. Her two high-shaman buddies were found but not her.

Kim didn't care about the astroshamans. *How could Rache have gotten out of that chasm? Were there places to hide? I assume it was all searched.*

I don't know, but I wouldn't put anything past Rache. Or Moonrazor.

"We came and endured your security chief's horrific suspicion for a reason," Yas said.

"Sorry." Kim hadn't been paying attention and faced him now, folding her hands on the table. "What is it?"

"To tell you what a pain in the ass your entire Kingdom is and suggest you move promptly," Jess said from the couch.

Yas frowned at her. "That's not the reason."

"But it's not untrue, is it?"

"They have an excellent cybernetics surgeon here, and we've made an appointment to see him, so you might not want to badmouth their government. At least not until after you've had your prosthetic spine inserted."

"I guess that's wise."

When Yas turned away from her, Jess stuck her tongue out at him and winked at Kim.

"I was instructed, in the event of our captain's passing, to give you this." Yas withdrew a dark-green business card from his pocket—who still used physical business cards? Elaborately feathered gold-leaf quills marked each corner, and the calligraphy was also in gold. It looked like it might be real.

"Illimitable Dominion Publishing," she read.

She stared at the card as the significance washed over her.

"That sounds as pompous as the card makes it look," Casmir said.

"It is," Jess said. "I suggested Pretentious Pen Publishing, something a bit more on the nose, but I was shot down faster than an asteroid on a collision course with a habitat."

"And Darkness and Decay and the Red Death held illimitable dominion over all," Kim said, dredging the quote out of memory.

"Pardon?" Yas asked.

"It's from an Edgar Allan Poe story," Kim said. "'The Masque of the Red Death.' A wealthy prince and a bunch of nobles hide out in a walled abbey to escape a horrific plague devastating the countryside. They're indifferent to the suffering of the commoners outside and hold a masquerade party inside, but the plague sneaks in by way of a guest, and they all die in the end."

"Ah. He was a strange man." Yas waved his fingers toward his temple in an approximation of a salute. "Sorry about the scuffed corners and boot marks on the back of the card. No fewer than twenty of the operatives here examined it, suspecting hidden messages, poison, explosives, and all manner of nefarious things."

Kim smiled sadly, certain the message was in the name, not the card. A message for Jager? That all of his status and power and wealth could not save him in the end? And had Rache seen himself as the plague?

"Bleak, as always, my friend," she murmured. But she also understood what this meant and showed it to Casmir. "I believe, if I contact whoever is running this, I will have a publisher for my book."

She wondered when Rache had found time to set up a business between when she'd mentioned her idea to him and he'd flown off into battle. During those days stalking Jager in orbit, she supposed.

"You'd better finish it quickly. Once they find out their financier is dead, they may decide to do their own thing." Casmir wrinkled his nose. "Starting with renaming the company."

"I will."

"And don't make it morbid."

"How morbid can it be when *you're* in it?" Kim smiled, though she'd already written pages that detailed Rache's tale. It could all be edited out, she'd told herself more than once, but if he truly was dead, maybe it would be preferable if his story was revealed.

"It *can't* be. I'm delightfully cheery. Don't forget to put in a chapter on Viggo's vacuums."

"And also a chapter on crushers," Zee stated.

"Yes." Casmir nodded. "*Two* chapters."

"Two," Zee said. "At least."

"An encyclopedia," Casmir said.

"That is agreeable. Crushers are multifaceted and much can be written about us."

Yas and Jess exchanged the sorts of looks typical of people who'd found themselves in rooms full of crazy people.

Kim rubbed the card and thought sadly that Rache had held it once. She hoped to do him justice in what might be the last manuscript she wrote. After this, the government allowing, she would return to her work as a bacteriologist.

"Do you know yet if you'll be able to keep your tree house?" Qin asked, holding Asger's hand as they ambled out to the creek.

Meanwhile, a crew Bjarke had hired was working on cleaning up the shuttle wreckage in front of the castle. The castle itself, with its missing walls and a chunk of the roof collapsed, would need far more than a clean-up crew.

"Nobody's told us we *won't* be able to keep the estate," Asger said, "but everything is in limbo. Baron Farley reached out to my father and me—that's our old boss—and said he'd received a request to reinstate us as knights, but he looked like he was sucking on a lemon as he made the call. He said he would *consider* it in a way that made it sound like he wouldn't consider anything unless it was a direct order from the king—er, from whoever replaces the king. At this point, the best I think we can hope for is not to be arrested and to be allowed to keep our citizenship."

"Maybe, if they take away your tree house and sell it, Princess Nalini can buy it." Qin flopped down under the tree and rubbed her cheek in the grass. She was glad to be out of her armor and able to appreciate the nature of this world, at least for now. Bonita was on her way down with the *Stellar Dragon* to pick her up and hire however many of her sisters wanted a job.

"Do you think it's odd that you don't care at all if we get to keep the castle or all the land around it? Just the tree house?"

"No, that's natural. Castles are musty and dingy and dark. Tree houses are fabulous."

"Ah."

"Do you think Princess Oku will end up in charge?" Qin asked.

"I don't think she wants the job." Asger sat beside her, plucking a piece of grass and twiddling it between his fingers.

"Does that matter? If you're the oldest son or daughter to a king, isn't it assumed that you'll rule after him?"

"The Senate has to agree to the king's choice of heir, and in this case, it doesn't look like Jager updated his legal documents on the matter after Jorg's death. I am relieved that the video that slipped out about Finn has ensured that he's not getting the job—he'll be lucky if he isn't driven out of the system. From what I heard, that mess over there—" Asger waved to the clean-up crew, "—was caused by some former allies of his who took umbrage to his pact with Rache and tried to kill him over it. And Oku… The Senate wouldn't likely stand behind her, even if she wanted the job. They may…" He trailed off and looked toward the sky.

A familiar freighter was descending toward the castle.

"Oh good, there's the captain." Qin bounced to her feet. "Let's go greet her."

She grabbed Asger's hand, and he allowed himself to be led back across the grass. As the freighter landed in a field alongside the drive up to the estate, Bjarke ran out of the castle. He sprinted fast enough that it seemed like an angry mob must be pursuing him.

The cargo hatch opened, and Bonita stepped out, looking fit and healthy. Qin had gotten the feeling she'd had an adventure along the way, too, so she was glad to see no evidence of injury, though some new and not quite matching hull plating proved the *Dragon* had needed repairs at some point.

Bjarke leaped up the ramp to meet her halfway, lifted her in a big bear hug, and spun in a circle, Bonita's feet dangling in the air.

"That's an exuberant greeting." Qin smiled with approval.

"No kidding." Asger sounded less approving and slowed his pace when Bonita and Bjarke started kissing each other, with more than a little grabbing and groping mixed in. "Uh, maybe we should go back to the tree house until they're done *greeting* each other."

"I want to know about her adventures." Qin released his hand and skipped toward the freighter.

"It doesn't look like sharing them is on her mind now." Asger didn't follow her and made a point of avoiding looking directly at the kissing couple. "They are way too *old* for such vigor. They're like horny teenagers. Ew."

Qin smirked, glad her captain had found someone, and glad Bjarke wasn't quite as much of a jerk as she'd once thought.

Bonita found her feet and started backing up the ramp, pulling Bjarke with her, but she noticed Qin and Asger and paused. It was probably only their approach that kept the couple from rushing up to Bonita's cabin and getting horizontal. Qin vowed not to keep Bonita for long.

"Hello, Captain!" She waved.

"*Hola*, Qin. Good to see you still alive. Would you like a tour of my new ship?" Bonita pointed toward the cargo hold.

"New ship? It looks like the same old *Dragon*." Qin tilted her head. "*Isn't* it?"

"*Same old?*" came Viggo's voice from the interior speakers. "Really, Qin. How disrespectful. I am in excellent condition for my age."

"Sorry, Viggo."

"It is the same ship, but now I own it. Completely one-hundred-percent outright." Bonita's eyes gleamed.

"You paid it off?" Bjarke said. "That's good news. I suppose carting extremely handsome knights around the Twelve Systems is profitable." He wriggled his eyebrows.

"Uh, it's not bad, but I owed over a hundred thousand Union dollars, so that wasn't what did it."

"Who paid you that much?" he asked. "You haven't had time to haul that much freight."

"A politically motivated benefactor."

Bjarke's mouth drooped open. Then his eyebrows drew down, as if he were miffed *he* hadn't been her benefactor.

Qin had no idea if he had that much money. Spaceships, even old freighters with persnickety sentient computers, were not inexpensive.

LAYERS OF FORCE

"*Who?*" Bjarke asked. "Tell me I don't have competition for your affections."

"Of course not. And it wasn't a freebie or charity or anything like that," Bonita said. "I had to sneak into a space station about to be knocked powerless by an alien ship and upload a highly controversial video."

"That was *you*?" Asger stared at her.

"Yes. You're welcome. Your prince looked like a snot."

"You almost got him killed."

"Almost? He's still alive? Disappointing."

"Bonita," Bjarke chided. "You've never even met him."

"He tried to hire Rache to kill his father. Excuse me if I don't want to invite him to a dinner party. But *you* all are invited. Assuming there's somewhere around here to get ingredients for cooking." She gazed around at the rural and grocery-store-free countryside.

"There's cereal in the kitchen," Asger offered. "If the roof didn't fall on it."

Bonita's gaze settled on the demolished front part of the castle. "This place isn't quite what I envisioned, *osito*."

"My bedroom is undamaged." He offered his arm. "Would you like to see it?"

"With this massive four-poster bed you promised?"

"Indeed, yes. And it won't be the only massive thing in there." He winked at her.

"That's disgusting," Asger said, as Bonita and Bjarke walked arm in arm down the ramp.

"Run along, boy—" Bjarke shooed him out of the way, "—and play in your tree house."

"Very funny, Father."

"You never did say," Bjarke murmured to Bonita as they headed toward the castle, "who it was who paid you to transmit that video."

"Didn't I? Strange."

"Does that mean you won't tell me?"

"It does."

"Not even in the throes of passion?" Bjarke asked.

"I suppose it would depend if that passion was so inspiring as to prompt me to blurt secrets."

"Oh, it will be," he purred.

Asger shook his head, appearing almost as disturbed as he'd been when he ran into his father wearing Bonita's lavender robe in the middle of the night.

Qin wandered down and clasped his hand. "It's not a bad idea."

"What's that?"

"Playing in the tree house." She winked at him.

"Ah? There's not a bed in there."

"We'll have to be creative then."

"I like creativity."

"Good."

CHAPTER 33

It took Oku a moment to name the young muscular man wearing a gray and blue suit and standing outside the engraved double doors to the Senate's meeting chamber. She might not have known him at all if not for the records of Casmir's adventures she'd read. And the fact that Casmir, as soon as he spotted him, blurted, "Tristan!" and ran forward to clap him on the back and grip his hand.

The stoic guards standing to either side of the door, with ceremonial carved staffs instead of modern weapons, were not supposed to react to anything, but they sneaked a few curious glances at Casmir. As most people he passed did these days. When walking in his presence, Oku had heard more than a few whispers of, "He's not as tall as I expected," and, "Did Admiral Mikita *really* look like that?"

More professionally, the guards eyed Oku's bodyguards and Casmir's entourage for possible threats. She didn't know if she would call *his* escort bodyguards. Zee qualified—tall, impervious, and ominous even with a blue scarf wrapped flamboyantly around his neck. But Tork, who had arrived with Princess Nalini, looked more like the utilitarian worker android he was.

"Hello, Casmir." Tristan tugged at the high collar of his tunic. "Are you before me or after me?"

"For what? Going in to see the Senate?"

"Yes. They told me to start a line." Tristan waved at the guards.

"A line of one?"

"Well, you're here now. And good morning, Princess Oku. That's three."

"I don't think princesses have to stand in line," Casmir said. "They're special. I expect someone will be along soon with a velvet cushion for her."

Oku snorted. Since she'd been working in the garden before this, attempting to distract herself and calm her nerves, she would likely get dirt on any cushions sent her way.

The guards glanced uncertainly at each other, perhaps wondering if they were supposed to order such a seat. Oku smiled and shook her head at them.

"After having all of my comms to Baron Farley ignored, I sent an appeal through the judicial system and tried to get a hearing. I understand if they won't make me a knight again, and I have no expectations about the land Sir Sebastian attempted to leave me in his will, but I would appreciate it if I could retain—*regain*—my citizenship and be allowed to visit the Kingdom again." An aching, wistful expression crossed his face. He lowered his voice to a whisper. "I think Nalini may have bribed someone to get me an appointment on their schedule today."

"Didn't I promise to help you get your knighthood back if I ever got a chance?" Casmir asked.

"I think you promised to have Zee glower intimidatingly at the senators."

"I knew it." Casmir lifted a hand toward the crusher. "Zee, are you prepared to glower intimidatingly?"

"I am always prepared to employ my physique to defend the interests of Casmir Dabrowski and, if he wishes it, comrades."

"Is that what you were doing when you turned into a couch?" Tork asked him.

"Who told you that I did such a thing?" Zee asked.

"There are pictures on the networks."

"I had to convince Princess Oku's canine that I was not a threat. I deemed this would improve the likelihood of Casmir Dabrowski succeeding in wooing her. Humans are protective of and devoted to their pets."

Oku smirked.

"*Zee*." Casmir rubbed his face, his cheeks turning red behind his fingers.

"That was very wise of you, Zee." Oku took Casmir's hand and pulled it down to her side. "A smart strategy."

"I know this," Zee said, "and I believe it was successful. You appear wooed."

"Do I? Interesting."

Casmir, his cheeks even brighter red now, groaned. "It's so great when he helps me with my romantic endeavors."

LAYERS OF FORCE

Oku was on the verge of kissing him when the great doors swung open. Her own cheeks warmed at the thought that she might have had her lips planted on Casmir when they were revealed to the two-hundred crusty, humorless senators inside, including numerous of her father's colleagues and dozens of retired knights. A lot of stodgy old people who didn't remember what it was like to be young and in love. Or falling in love?

Was she?

She looked at Casmir, who'd recovered a modicum of professional authority, save for the pink cheeks, and smiled. Yes, she decided. Yes, she was. And he looked quite sharp today in fresh, non-rumpled trousers and tunic. Aside from a pair of silver robot cuff links, he wore nothing overly goofy. Not that she would have minded. She would have been amused to see him stride onto the Senate floor wearing a T-shirt featuring one of his favorite comic book heroes.

Instead, he managed to look regal and stately. A recent haircut helped—for once, his bangs weren't hanging in his eyes. Regal and stately and handsome. Oku decided to keep the hand clasp as they walked in.

"Tristan?" Casmir asked over his shoulder.

"I can go after you." Tristan peered warily at the vast marble floor and tiered rows of seats to either side of it, all of them filled. Oku's mother sat on a throne at the end, the larger throne next to hers, which had once been Jager's, notably empty. Chief Van Dijk stood at her side. There for support? "Deciding the fate of the entire Kingdom is more important than determining my citizenship status."

"But you bribed someone to be here. We're just on the docket."

"Bribes are illegal," Oku pointed out, amused.

"Not in the Miners' Union," Casmir said. "They're standard operating procedure, I believe."

"But we're not in the Miners' Union."

"His girlfriend is."

"I suppose that's true."

Casmir lowered his voice as they walked inside, all eyes upon them. "If there's any chance we can do anything for him—and by we, I mean *you*, since I am here in a decorative and supportive capacity—that would be fantastic. I know he doesn't care about the land, but he should still be a knight."

"You're not here to be decorative. Trust me."

Casmir raised his eyebrows. "Do you know more than I know?"

"My mother said that for the Senate to reach a consensus and suitably appease the populace, you would be required to play a role in the new regime." Oku had the distinct impression that *she* would also be required to fill a role, and a large part of her wanted to grab Casmir's hand and flee to another system where they could get jobs as university professors and live modest but academically meaningful lives.

"The role of court roboticist?"

"That's the role you want, not the role they're going to pick for you. *Especially* now."

Oku had read Kim's book that had been written, edited, and published with amazing speed, and released three days earlier. She'd been equal parts enthralled and horrified, suspecting Kim had used the secret reports Oku had sent her for some of the details. Those had been sent so Kim could help *Casmir*, not include them in a new based-on-reality bestselling thriller. From what she'd heard, most of the rest of the Kingdom had also read the book in the last three days.

"I guess that means it won't be a presidency going forward," Casmir said. "Decided by a popular vote?"

"My mother said that what the Senate is suggesting is the only thing they could all agree on."

"Revolts and reforms are rarely agreed upon by the existing rulers."

"Exactly."

They'd reached the end of the chamber, coming to stand in front of Oku's mother, Chief Van Dijk, and two of the senior senators that Oku had come to know during her time in the Citadel.

They looked at her, looked at Casmir, and then looked at their linked hands. Oku thought about releasing him, but they'd walked in like this, and everybody had already seen it. Besides, they might need each other's mutual support for this.

"Well," Senator Lamar said to his comrade, waving at the hand link, "I suppose that makes this all easier."

"What? If they get married? Is that going to be required?"

"Uhm, what?" Casmir asked.

"No," Lamar said. "Just that they work together."

"They're so young. Are we sure about this?"

"They're our best choice going forward. *He's* the only reason ten governments aren't demanding to search Odin right now for their gate pieces. Why they believe him and not any of us…"

"Must be nice to be liked and trusted."

Oku's mother cleared her throat, and the senators fell silent.

"Professor Casmir Dabrowski and Princess Oku," her mother said, "after much deliberation over King Jager's will and succession papers, and after considering historical precedents, the passioned pleas of the populace, and keeping in mind mitigating circumstances… the Senate, with my blessing and with the support of Royal Intelligence, has deemed that Princess Oku will step into power over the Star Kingdom as Queen Oku, effective immediately."

Oku closed her eyes. It was what she'd feared would happen.

Judging by the unsurprised claps that came from the senators, they'd all already known and had been instructed to support the announcement, whether they wanted this or not.

"Prince Finn's status as a potential heir has been revoked," she went on, "and he's lost all the support from certain military factions that he had, so he should not be a threat to you."

Zee stepped closer to loom between and behind Oku and Casmir. "I am Zee and will protect Kim Sato and Casmir Dabrowski and Queen Oku from all threats, including relatives."

"Thank you, Zee," Casmir murmured, though he kept glancing with concern at Oku, maybe wondering if she would pass out. Or if he was allowed to hold a queen's hand.

Damn right, he was. She squeezed his hand, though it was more because she wanted his support than because she felt he needed hers. His expression said he was daunted, but he squeezed her hand back.

"And you, Professor," Oku's mother said. "It has been deemed that because of your blood and your role in recent events, you will be admitted into the nobility, with all privileges, rights, and duties thereof. As a noble, granted land and the right to use it to accumulate wealth and tax those who live upon it, you are expected to in turn serve the crown as needs arise."

Casmir's jaw descended, but he appeared too stunned to say anything.

"Because Queen Oku is young and relatively inexperienced," her mother went on, "we ask that you take the role of Minister of External Affairs for the Kingdom, our highest-ranking representative in diplomatic relationships between the Kingdom and the other governments of the Twelve Systems, and per the insistence of the AI ship, the official representative for any future interactions with them. We also hope that you will take a less official role of advisor to the queen. Though we allow that Oku will be in charge and make her own decisions, the *people* wish you to be involved at the highest level."

That was an understatement. Even before Kim's book had come out, Oku had heard the protestors lobbying for President Dabrowski and even King or Emperor Dabrowski.

Judging by the thunderous applause that filled the chamber, most of the senators also wanted Casmir to be involved at the highest level. Oku decided to be happy for him, and glad to have him on her side, rather than envious that he'd gotten so many more claps. She didn't, she reminded herself, *want* her position. But knowing there weren't any alternatives that wouldn't lead to civil war, she couldn't reject it. She would do the best that she could.

"Do you accept, Professor Dabrowski?" her mother asked.

He'd recovered from his initial surprise, and his eyes narrowed at some thought. "Does this mean I would be Ambassador Romano's boss?"

"It does."

Casmir's eyes gleamed. "I accept, Your Highness."

"Do you have some punishment in mind for him?" Oku murmured, though she suspected Casmir's idea of punishment would involve whoopee cushions rather than docked pay or prison time.

"Just to sit in a bigger chair than his and beam radiantly at him during meetings," he murmured back.

"As former queen consort," Oku's mother continued, "I believe I am now only to be referred to as Iku. Or ma'am, if you prefer."

"Yes, ma'am. May I still teach classes?"

"If you can fit it in between your other duties, I imagine so."

"Oh, good." He grinned before he remembered to be regal and stately. "That's not so bad."

"For *you*," Oku whispered.

Minister sounded a lot less onerous than queen.

"*Sorry*," he whispered back. "But I bet you can prioritize projects to help the space habitats now. Ours and other people's. Including bacterially superior bees."

"I hope so."

"That's all we have for you," Oku's mother said. "Next time, *you* get to sit up here."

"Are those chair cushions velvet?" Casmir whispered. "I think they might be."

"Ssh." Oku bowed her head to her mother.

Casmir bowed more deeply to her mother and to the senators to either side. He and Oku turned to walk out, and he managed to keep that regal and stately facade almost all the way to the open doors. Tristan peeked through them, and Casmir started skipping.

"Oh, Tristan. I know the new queen, and I bet we can get you your citizenship back."

"I heard that." Tristan appeared stunned as they joined him in the corridor. But he recovered and bowed deeply to Oku. "But are you supposed to use your new power—uhm, her new power—to grant favors to friends? Isn't that nepotism?"

"Yes, but that's how the nobility works."

Oku snorted. "He's not wrong. But I think in this case, we would just be doing the right thing." She smiled at Tristan. "I did read all the reports out of System Stymphalia."

"I admit," Casmir said, pushing a hand through his hair, "I'm a little surprised by their choice. Not that you won't be a lovely queen, Oku, but I thought with all the protests and with such upheaval that it would be the ideal time for a little government reformation."

"A nice democracy, perhaps?"

"Something of that ilk." Casmir shrugged. "Elected leaders instead of a monarch and a Senate run by the nobles."

"You're going to object to rule by nobles now that you *are* one?" Tristan asked.

"Yes."

"Our elites are firmly entrenched at the top and like it that way," Oku said. "They would never vote for a truly transformative change. The very fact that they picked me, not because I'm qualified but because it was a way to preserve the system in which they prosper and thrive, is evidence to support that. And they picked *you* to mollify the public. The public will love you and your story, because you aren't of the nobility, or *weren't*, and now you are. They've made you into one of us, but the public gets to keep the illusion that you're one of them."

"Don't you just adore politics?" Tristan murmured.

Casmir didn't appear surprised by anything Oku had said, nor upset or disgruntled. He shrugged and said, "If they wanted to stay entrenched, they shouldn't have chosen a free-thinking academic for a monarch and someone like *me* as your advisor. I don't know if you noticed, but I'm not good at sticking to the script."

"I noticed," Oku said.

"As did I," Tristan said.

"As did all of the crushers," Zee stated.

"Even the crushers noticed? *All* of them? Goodness." Oku smiled at him.

"Indeed," Zee said.

Oku took Casmir's hand again. "We'll be transformative. We'll just take it slowly, so nobody notices."

"Slow, sneaky, stealth transformation," Casmir said. "I like it."

"You added adjectives."

"I stated adjectives that were already implied."

"Hm."

"But while we're still doing things the old way and being nepotists, can we also get Tristan back into the knighthood?" Casmir patted him on the chest and raised his eyebrows hopefully toward Oku. "He deserves it. He always did."

Tristan blushed under this praise and bowed his head, but he didn't argue about it. He *did* deserve it, and he had to know that.

"I should think so." Oku realized that for the first time, she had true power, not secondhand power lent to her because of her father's status. She could wave her hand and make things like this happen. She would have to be careful with that kind of power, though in this case, as she'd pointed out, it felt more like righting a wrong than doing a favor. "I've also not been pleased by Baron Farley's lack of responsiveness to my requests. Perhaps it's time for him to retire and for a more progressive knight to be placed in charge."

Tristin blinked. "You're firing him?"

"Isn't he a stodgy grump who thinks anyone under fifty can't be trusted?" Oku asked.

"Yes."

"He also hit on me when I was sixteen and thought I should be honored by his interest." She wrinkled her nose at the memory.

"Fire him promptly," Casmir said.

"But who would replace him?" Tristan asked.

LAYERS OF FORCE

"Asger is too young," Casmir said. "*William* Asger."

"Are you suggesting that Bjarke Asger should be put in charge?" Oku didn't know him that well.

"I wouldn't push for it," Casmir said, "and it's possible he would prefer to fly off with Bonita for a while, but he does have all that system-hopping undercover experience. And he's... not stodgy. I'm sure Bonita would agree."

"Aren't they sleeping together?" Tristan asked.

"Yes, vigorously and non-stodgily."

"Ew."

Oku prodded Casmir in the arm. "Why do you know the details on that?"

"I'm very good friends with Viggo, Bonita's ship's intelligence. He's a dreadful gossip." Casmir looked at Tristan. "What about the estate that your mentor tried to leave to you in his will? If you wanted to push for that with the legal system, now might be the time."

Tristan took a long breath and studied the floor. "Even though I would greatly appreciate having my citizenship and my knighthood returned, I believe I will stay with Nalini at Stardust Palace. There would be no point in me having a vast estate here that someone would have to manage, and even though I was touched that Sir Sebastian wanted to leave it to me, his son is the rightful heir."

"You're a good man, Tristan," Casmir said.

"I've tried to be so."

"I will look over all the files, talk to the senior knights, and consider options for replacing Farley," Oku said, already dreading all the meetings and decision-making that would be in her future.

Maybe Casmir read the dread in her eyes, because he patted her hand and said, "Would you like to get a coffee or other adult beverage first?"

"Wouldn't you prefer a fizzop?"

"Yes."

"Let's get one of those then."

He grinned again. "You're a fabulous woman."

"I do hope so. This job will require it." Since the senators hadn't dismissed themselves yet, and the corridor was relatively private, guards and a reinstated knight aside, Oku drew him to the side and kissed him.

He kissed her back and silently messaged her chip. *You are. I've known this almost since I met you.*

Almost?

Since I saw the grass stuck between your toes and knew you weren't pretentious.

Pretentious people can't forget to wash their feet after working their compost piles?

Nope.

Casmir felt sheepish standing in Drachen Castle in front of a holographic map of the Kingdom with his finger in the air while the bored Minister of the Interior shifted his weight from foot to foot and sighed.

Around the globe, bright green swaths of available land were highlighted. Far more land was already claimed by noble families, but there was still an impressive selection available. The term "kid in a candy store" came to mind, but Casmir would rather have a pile of Raspberry Boom Rockets than thousands of acres of land he would have to figure out how to manage. The words *eeny, meeny, miny, moe* floated through his mind.

"If I may offer a suggestion, Minister Dabrowski?" Minister Akagi asked.

"Yes, of course. And you can call me Casmir."

"That would be overly familiar." Minister Akagi was a sixty-something nobleman with meticulously combed short white hair, a voice with little inflection, and a perpetually bland expression.

"Would it? Aren't we kind of... the same now?" Casmir waved at his chest, a computer-game avatar shooting walking-mushrooms on his T-shirt, then waved at Akagi's crisp button-down shirt with a high, tight collar that could have strangled an ox.

The faintest eyebrow twitch was the only hint that Akagi might not consider them *the same*. "We are both noblemen and ministers working for the crown," he agreed, "but you are also Queen Oku's advisor."

"And that counts for more than thirty years of seniority?" Casmir didn't know how long Akagi had been in the position, so he was guessing.

"It would be wise of me to consider that to be the case."

LAYERS OF FORCE

The poor guy had probably been cowed by whoever Jager's advisor had been. Or maybe Jager himself. "Well, you can still call me Casmir. What's your suggestion?"

"The most desirable land was divvied up long ago, with all of the most lucrative farmland, ports, ore-laden mountain ranges and such chosen by the earliest noble families. And of course anything in proximity to the capital and other major cities on Odin has been snapped up. There are still numerous timberlands available, since more durable and renewable resources have become preferred for building. There are, however, artists and craftsmen who prefer lumber for their projects, so there's a small market. All of these lands in the Kingdom Forest are available. Or if you prefer to start an industrial empire—building robots perhaps?—then the colder lands in the north might be preferable—less power required to cool energy-intensive factories, and the frozen tundra doesn't need to be cleared for building."

"Good points. Thank you." Between teaching, being a diplomat, and asking Oku for numerous coffee dates, Casmir didn't foresee himself having time to start any kind of enterprise in the near future. He—

Professor Dabrowski, a message came in on his chip. *Or do you go by Minister now?*

I see you've been keeping up with Kingdom news, High Shaman Moonrazor. Casmir wasn't stunned by the message, not when her body hadn't been found, and he wondered if she intended to ask him for the crusher he had promised but never had the opportunity to deliver. *Did you escape from your bonds? Are you still on Odin? I saw that your ship was not in the best condition after our last encounter. Do you need help getting a ride off the planet?*

Are you offering to smuggle me off your world? After my people tried to kill you? That's thoughtful.

I assume you *weren't one of the ones shooting me.*

I was not. I was escaping from the confinement my colleagues had placed me in and preparing myself to survive the inevitable. Strangely, they refused to believe you could be a threat to them and weren't as prepared as I was. I can't say I was even that surprised when your clone rammed our ship. Not in hindsight, anyway.

He does add an element of unpredictability. Casmir decided not to deny that he'd had anything to do with Rache's appearance. For whatever reason, Moonrazor liked to give him more credit than he deserved. It might be best for the future of the Kingdom if she went on believing he was some mastermind with the power to outmaneuver her and keep his people safe. *Do you, by chance, know if he survived that crash? I understand the search parties did not find his body.*

I do not know. I was more concerned about saving myself. You'll forgive me if I hope he died horribly and slowly in a great deal of pain over many days as he bled profusely while crawling away from the crash site, only to be devoured by polar bears in the end.

I can see you've had time to contemplate his death, but I believe the search parties would have been able to find him, had a trail of blood been involved.

I haven't noticed any particular aptitude from your Kingdom soldiers in the past when it comes to finding him.

You haven't informed me yet if there's something I can do for you. Casmir chose to ignore the digs against Rache and his people. *I assume you didn't message me just to say goodbye.*

"Minister Dabrowski?" Akagi asked. "I'll need to get the paperwork over to the director of land management soon if it's to go into effect this week."

"Yes, sorry. Someone is contacting me. I need another moment."

I messaged you because we made a deal once. I'm curious if you are willing to go through with it.

You want a crusher? Let me know where to send one, and I will do so.

Excellent. But you also offered a place on your world for my people to hide out without being pestered. And you now appear to be in a position to grant that.

Ah. You didn't seem that interested in that offer at the time.

I was in a better position and had other plans then. I still intend to see those plans fulfilled, mind you. One way or another. My people and I have created detailed schematics of the gate pieces from our studies, and we will continue to work toward building our own gate, but we need time since we'll be starting from scratch. And we would like a place where we won't be bothered. Since our last base *was destroyed. Did I mention how badly I wish for your clone brother to be dead?*

You did. There was talk of blood trails, great agony, and devouring by bears.

Good. Should we succeed at building and installing new gates in your lifetime—something more likely if you eventually load your consciousness into a droid—or maybe a crusher?—we will of course invite you to explore the galaxy with us.

You don't think the Collective will return to vacuum up any new gate pieces you make?

Perhaps you'll lead humanity into a time of peace and prosperity and enlightenment, and they'll feel less compelled to interfere next time.

Now you're just buttering me up so I'll find you some land.

You're as perceptive as you are intelligent.

You're hilarious.

The fact that you believe so attests to your superior intellect.

Fine, fine, I'll see what I can do. Just stop complimenting me. Casmir was positive she was smirking as she delivered her flattery.

As you wish.

By the way, before I do this, do you have Dubashi's virus? I'd hate to give refuge on my planet to someone with a horrific disease that they can unleash at any time.

I don't have it. I never did. It was easy to lead your king to believe I did, just as it was easy to lead him to believe the Collective had shown up at our behest. How ever did you *get them to come?*

A good friend helped me with that.

A robot, I assume.

Possibly true.

Half of winning the war is making the right alliances.

So I've learned.

At some point, Casmir had let his hand drop. He lifted his finger to the map again. Akagi leaned forward, doubtless eager to have his task completed so he could return to whatever interesting things ministers of the Interior did during their work days.

"I'm interested in this land." He pointed to the Kingdom Forest a hundred-plus miles east of Zamek City.

Akagi frowned. "That's where that terrorist base was discovered."

"I know. I helped discover it."

"The news reported that it was destroyed."

"It was. The whole ceiling collapsed. I was there for it and only survived because a crusher stood protectively over me."

"Why would you want such land? There are no roads to it, no rivers through the area, no natural resources of note, and the terrain is uneven enough that it would be difficult to build upon or even put in a landing pad."

"It sounds like a lovely place to get away." Or for a group of astroshamans to be left alone...

"Well, there won't be much need for you to manage anything, I suppose."

"Perfect."

"If that's what you wish, Minister Dabrowski. Due to the low value of the land, it should be possible to carve you out twenty thousand acres or so."

"Excellent. Thank you." Casmir smiled and bowed to the man, then messaged Moonrazor as he headed for the door. *I believe I've acquired a spot for your people. The existing base is somewhat caved in, so you'll either have to start from scratch or do some housecleaning.*

It's a good thing you're sending me a crusher to help. I assume they are capable of moving boulders.

They are even capable of disguising themselves as boulders. Though only if it conveys some tactical advantage. I've met resistance each time I've asked them to turn themselves into furnishings.

Strange.

Indeed.

Asger and Bjarke were waiting in the hallway to take him to lunch.

"Did you get some land?" Asger asked.

"Are you going to build a castle on it?" Bjarke asked.

"Castles aren't as fashionable as they once were," Asger said. "A house would be sufficient."

"Or a tree house?" Bjarke arched his brows.

"You should build whatever your lady wants. That's the rule."

"I got the land out where that terrorist base was," Casmir said.

Bjarke and Asger looked at him with the same disbelieving stares.

"A cliff in the middle of a forest?" Bjarke asked.

"They're giving me twenty thousand acres. There might be *two* cliffs."

"You're going to be the oddest noble in the history of the Kingdom, aren't you?" Bjarke asked.

"I do hope so." Casmir clapped them on the shoulders. "Lunch?"

EPILOGUE

IT WAS LATE IN THE DAY FOR COFFEE, but Kim had a bunch of work she'd brought home, so she planned to stay up into the night. Besides, she'd missed her patio, now dusted with fallen autumn leaves, some knocked free by the squirrels racing through the branches behind the house. It was chilly, but the late-afternoon sun made it warm enough to sit outside with a jacket, and after spending nearly two weeks in that subterranean Royal Intelligence apartment, she intended to enjoy the outdoors as much as she could.

After the last six months, it seemed ludicrous that she was back here—and even more ludicrous that she'd had to hurry through a crowd of human and android reporters on the sidewalk, all with questions about her book, which was now a bestseller and in the process of being translated into dozens of languages and reprinted throughout the Twelve Systems.

She didn't know whether to be relieved or apologetic that four times as many reporters appeared whenever Casmir was on his way home. At this rate, he would end up having to move into the castle with Oku, not because they were madly in love but so he could have a modicum of privacy.

Her father and her brothers were unimpressed with Kim's newfound fame, for which she was thankful. Her brothers had teased her incessantly about how out of shape she was when she'd returned the day before to the dojo for her first good workout in ages. They'd had more reverence for the katana she'd brought to show them, remarking on the beautiful craftsmanship. It saddened her that she hadn't been able to say who it had been a gift from—or how much she missed him.

The sliding door opened, and Casmir walked out in a dark-blue suit with black dress shoes and his hair wetted down and mercilessly combed into submission. Only the black T-shirt under the jacket wasn't quite in line with modern men's fashion.

"How do I look? Professional enough for dinner with a bunch of diplomats from the Miners' Union?"

Kim flicked a finger. "Open the jacket."

He flattened his hand against a lapel. "Why?"

"I have suspicions."

Casmir unbuttoned the jacket to reveal a cartoon Robot Remstar with a wrench chasing a robot cat on his T-shirt. "Oku and I are going to have ice cream after the dinner. I thought I could take off the jacket for that and display my natural whimsy."

"Well, at least there aren't fizzop stains on it."

"I'm neat and tidy now that I have regular access to laundering facilities again. And now that I'm getting paid, I bought a whole batch of new T-shirts where the self-cleaning feature of the SmartWeave fabric hasn't worn out yet."

"They made you a noble and gave you land, and you used your newfound wealth to buy T-shirts?"

"Oh, I won't be earning anything from that land, but my salary at the university was reinstated now that they know I'm not dead, not a criminal, and willing to teach at least two classes a semester."

"The Minister of External Affairs gig doesn't pay?"

"No, it's my honor to serve the Kingdom."

Kim rolled her eyes. "Well, if you ever want to buy Oku something fancy, let me know. I just signed a deal with a big production studio for movie rights. I believe I am officially set for life. And since you're the star of the book, I suppose I owe you something."

"I made a robotic dog scratcher for Oku." Casmir grinned. "It attaches to her workbench in the greenhouse and rubs Chasca's head when she comes over and stands by Oku. Chasca can still lean against her leg and *thinks* her human is petting her, but it leaves Oku's hands free for her work."

"Is that your way of saying you don't need money for fancy gifts?"

"I used spare parts rummaged from her garden shed."

Kim imagined a rusty hand rake scratching the dog's head. "You're going to have to put a halt to that frugality now that you're a noble. I believe they frown upon anything but excessive spending."

LAYERS OF FORCE

"I don't think that's necessarily true." Casmir leaned back into the house and pulled a tablet off the counter. "Did you see the video Asger sent of his new abode?"

"I saw that he and Qin were showing off the tree house."

"The tree house where they're living now, yes. Qin's sisters are building more tree houses farther up the creek. I think they still plan to go off and hunt criminals with Qin, but they're going to visit the estate for frequent exposure to trees. Through living in them. The castle is being repaired, and Bjarke will be residing there full-time, once he returns from his adventures with Bonita. He accepted a position that was offered to him as head of the knights. I gather that Asger doesn't mind the idea of living under another roof from his father. Even if it's a thatched roof."

"Why would you want to live in a castle with room enough to house an army when you could live in a tree?"

"The tree house bedroom has a roof that opens and closes for viewing of the stars. It sounds very romantic."

"But is there a bathroom?"

"Maybe they plan to remodel and add such modern amenities." Casmir showed her a picture of the bedroom with the roof open to the sky.

Kim waved at a four-legged mechanical construct standing next to the bed. Was that... a horn on its head? "Is that a giant robot unicorn?"

"It's a normal-sized robot unicorn."

"You could ride it."

"It wouldn't be much fun if you couldn't. Qin requested it from Asger, so I built a kit for him, so he could assemble it for her."

"You built a kit instead of just building the unicorn? What's the point of that?"

"So it could be a gift from him, not me."

"How much did he have to assemble?"

"He put the hooves, head, and horn on. And unfolded the legs."

"And she appreciated that?"

"From what I heard, yes."

"Asger is lucky she's such a sweet and undemanding girl."

"I believe that's true." Casmir flipped through more pictures of the tree house to show her.

The other rooms—if one could call them that—were robot free. For now.

Kim half-heartedly watched a video of Asger and Qin bouncing around together and showing off the tree house as they touched frequently and gazed adoringly at each other.

She was glad for her friends that they had all found romances, but watching everyone's happiness made her more aware that she was alone. Now that weeks had passed since the crash, and she was out from under the watchful—and surveilling—eye of Royal Intelligence, she had reluctantly accepted that Rache must have died down in the Arctic Islands. That didn't keep her from wishing that she would return from work one day to find a random gift on her dining-room table and him alive and leaning against the wall outside on the patio.

The fact that he'd set up a publishing company just for her, before going on what he'd known might be his last mission, made her want to ask him to marry her. Instead, she was wondering what kind of funeral she could have for the most-hated man in the Kingdom. Likely only Casmir would come if she attempted some kind of service. Even Qin and Asger had never warmed up to Rache. Oku and her mother surely hated him. Maybe Bonita would come, since he'd given her the funds to buy her freighter outright.

It saddened Kim to think of all he'd done in the end that he would never get credit for. He'd saved Casmir's life. He'd ended the astroshaman threat. If that publishing company hadn't existed and been waiting for her manuscript, it was unlikely that she or Casmir or any of the rest of them would have been turned from suspected criminals into Kingdom heroes. It certainly wouldn't have happened so swiftly. And whether she should think of it as a good thing or not, he'd also ended Jager's reign and made it possible for Oku to be placed in power. As strange as it seemed, if the Kingdom became a more peaceful and less insular place in the future, Rache would be at least partially responsible.

Kim dropped her face into her hand.

"Are you okay?" Casmir lowered the tablet.

"Yes." No.

"Are you distressed about Qin's possible lack of an indoor bathroom?"

"No."

"Is it... Rache?"

"No." Yes.

"Are you sure?"

LAYERS OF FORCE

Kim sighed and dropped her hand. "No."

Casmir sat at the table. "Do you want to talk about it?"

"Don't you have a date with diplomats?"

The sun had dipped below the horizon, leaving the patio in shadow. His dinner obligations had to start soon.

"And ice cream, but I can be late." He lifted his eyebrows. "If you don't want to be alone."

Which she would be a lot in the upcoming months. She had little doubt that Casmir would move in with Oku eventually. Even if that wasn't for a while, he would be traveling a lot more now to fulfill his diplomatic duties. As it was, he wasn't at the house very often these days.

Not that many years ago, she hadn't felt that she required human companionship. Her interactions with like-minded colleagues at work had once seemed sufficient, but she'd gotten used to having a roommate. And even though her time with Rache had been limited, she'd found their shared meals and evenings together comfortable. Even appealing. And he'd seemed to get her. He hadn't minded that she was complicated and aloof and didn't even like being touched all that much. Damn it.

"I'm sorry I didn't get to know him better," Casmir offered. "It seemed like he was always kidnapping us or we were scheming toward opposing goals, and even though I don't think his ends justified his means—or would it be his beginnings justifying his means?—I do regret that I had a brother and barely got to know him."

"Yeah."

"I wonder if the Kingdom will ever be more sympathetic toward him, considering what you shared of his past in your book. I'm surprised you did that, by the way, given that you never even told *me* those things."

"I always felt that it was his story to share, if he wanted to, not mine. And I would have left it all out, but then he was dead... and it didn't seem like that secret should die with him. Besides, he's a flat villain without motivations in all the Kingdom dramas that feature him. He deserved more than that."

"Most of the university professors that I've chatted with think the author made it all up."

"That figures."

"Though not Professors Meeks and Otsuka. They think it's terribly sad and that he's a romantically tragic figure. Or tragically romantic? I forget. They're literature professors. They like to fling around terms like that. They also didn't lose any relatives in his attacks on Kingdom ships or stations, so they're less inclined toward outright loathing."

"Why don't you go on your date, Casmir?"

"Am I not helping? I'm sorry. I'll build you something later." He stood and pushed his seat into the table.

"That is your strength. Are you taking gifts to the diplomats you're meeting for dinner?"

"Of course."

"They're not underwear, are they?"

"No. Only my mom buys people underwear."

"They're not gifts made entirely from fungus, are they?"

"If you must know, I made everyone a space-rated toiletries kit. The holders stick to the walls and keep their grip on your essentials even when the gravity goes out. When I was on the *Dragon,* I kept having to retrieve my tooth sanitizer from strange nooks in the bathroom. Once, one of the vacuums tried to suck it up. Clearly, the universe needed an improved toiletries kit."

"Very practical."

"As I always am."

"Always."

"I sent Bonita and Bjarke a gift before they left too. Technically, it's as much for Viggo as it is for them."

"More vacuums? Enhanced nozzles for the existing vacuums?"

"A few enhancements for the existing vacuums, yes. And an additional fleet of twelve vacuums with laser incineration abilities."

"*Laser* vacuums?"

"Perfect for removing mildew, scum, and other dubious substances that simply can't be cleaned by sucking alone."

"That ship was already cleaner than any other ships flying the Twelve Systems."

"Yes. I miss it." Casmir rubbed an eye that might have been watering. "My sinuses were clearer there than anywhere else. Do you think, should Oku ever deign to marry me, that I could convince her to take a honeymoon on the *Dragon*?"

"A honeymoon flying around on a battered centenarian freighter? What queen wouldn't be delighted by that?"

LAYERS OF FORCE

"I bet Bonita would take us to a pretty moon. She might even give us a discount on passage, now that she has fewer expenses."

"Even if *you're* not rich, I'm sure Oku can afford a full-price ticket."

"Yes, but Bonita and Viggo like us. I'm sure I could wrangle a discount. Maybe I could trade Bonita another patent."

"I don't know why they bothered to make you a noble, Casmir. You've got entirely the wrong attitude about money."

"I think it was mostly so the knights and other nobles would feel better about me dating Oku."

"Most likely."

"Have a good night, Kim." Casmir saluted her and headed back inside. "Don't mope!" he called back.

Kim closed her eyes and leaned back in her chair as twilight settled in, the shadows thickening on the porch. She had so much work to catch up on now that she was back, and she knew she should get to the reading she'd brought home, but a part of her wanted to sit there and... mope.

"I thought he would never leave," someone said.

Kim almost fell out of her chair as she leaped up and spun toward the speaker.

She *did* knock it over, the wrought-iron frame clattering on the cement patio. She barely noticed as she gaped into the shadows.

"How... Are you... You weren't there the whole *time*, were you?"

He couldn't have been. Casmir had been looking in that direction. He would have noticed.

"That's your first question?" Rache strolled out of the corner by the fence gate, wearing all black, but for once, not armor, and he wasn't wearing his mask, though the thin sweatshirt *did* have a hood that could be pulled up. He was dressed like a gothically-inclined college student. Which, she admitted numbly, was the perfect costume for skulking around here on campus. "I thought it might be: *How did you manage to survive when everyone is certain you're dead?* Or perhaps an ebullient, *You're alive! I'm so pleased to see you.*"

"I *am* pleased." Kim winced, knowing her voice sounded far more deadpan than ebullient, but she was still shocked.

But not so shocked that she didn't hurry forward and hug him.

"Ah, excellent." Rache returned the hug and rested his cheek against hers.

She buried her face against his shoulder, unable to remember the last time she'd hugged him without him being in armor. She appreciated the feel of his muscular frame under his shirt, though he seemed even leaner than the last time she'd seen him. Had he been forced to hide out while the soldiers spent days searching around that frozen base? And then somehow had to find a way here from the *Arctic Islands* without a ship?

"For the record," Kim murmured, "nobody is *that* certain you're dead. Last I heard, they found a bunch of bodies in the wreckage and weren't sure if one was yours, since you have as many cybernetic upgrades as some of those astroshamans. They ran DNA tests, but since they didn't know who you were to start with, they didn't know if they had a match." She leaned back so she could look at his clean-shaven face, his warm amused eyes. "Though given what I revealed in that book, they should have been able to verify whether they had the right body."

"That book, yes. It was quite revealing. I managed to get a digital copy while I was stowing away on a freighter—an ocean-going freighter, mind you—from the Arctic Islands to Northern Steinfeld with nobody but Amit for company. He's chattier than I expected from a deadly crusher, and wouldn't be my first pick for a travel companion, but he did pull me out of the wreckage before the Kingdom soldiers arrived, so I felt compelled to converse with him."

"How *did* you survive that crash?"

"I have the best combat armor that money can buy. It's designed to protect me from explosions, high-powered energy blasts, and being hurled into bulkheads at a hundred miles an hour by disgruntled crushers. A crash is nothing. The hard part was clawing my way out from under the astroshaman ship that fell *atop* my ship. I may have been slightly injured at the time."

Slightly injured or *gravely* injured? Kim wondered, given how long it had taken him to make his way here.

"Don't tell Casmir," Rache added, "but Amit likely saved my life."

"Casmir would like to know that."

"I'm sure—he could feel smug about it—but I'd prefer he believe I'm invincible." Rache shrugged. "I'm used to having my crew believe that—having *everyone* believe that. I'm not ready to admit weaknesses to anyone."

"It's not a weakness to be injured in a crash."

"I shouldn't have crashed and lost my ship. That was... an impulsive move."

"Hm." Kim decided not to argue further. She was glad that his impulsive move had saved Casmir's life, and that Rache had survived it.

"Do you mind that I shared what might be considered your weaknesses in the book? I thought you were dead, and I wanted the Kingdom to know... whatever they were willing to believe."

"It does say in the front that the story is only *based* on real events," he said dryly, lifting a hand to touch her cheek.

"It seemed safest to preface it with that. In fact, the publisher insisted. But as far as I know, everything in it was true."

"So it seemed to be. Though there was little about us, beyond the fact of your frequent kidnappings."

"I didn't think the universe was ready to know that you have a heart. Also, in case you ever did show up alive again, I thought it would be easier for us to meet somewhere in secret if nobody knew we had a link."

"I suppose that's acceptable." His hand shifted to the back of her head to stroke her hair.

Little tingles ran through her at the touch she'd not realized she liked until he'd been gone.

"I'm glad you approve—or don't disapprove," she said, "given that you financed the publication."

"Which, I understand from a preliminary look at the numbers, is going to turn out to be the most lucrative endeavor I've backed. Now that you're a bestseller of dramatic space thrillers, will you ever return to writing little-known but well-loved allegorical fantasy?"

"It's possible, but I thought I'd get back to modifying and creating new strains of bacteria for a while. I've missed it terribly."

"Such an odd woman, you are."

"Complicated, I've been told."

"Yes. May I kiss you?"

"Yes."

They did that, Kim's feelings for him making her forget her aversion toward unnecessary touching, and she quite enjoyed the experience.

"May I ask you on a date?" Rache murmured after a time.

"Yes. But where will we go where you won't be recognized?"

Kim suspected she could ask Oku for favors now that she was dating her best friend, but asking her to pardon Rache would be a stretch. Not when Rache had killed Oku's father and her older brother. And decimated her younger brother's life. The last Kim had heard, Finn had been sent off to another system to study at a small university, since it was too dangerous for him to remain in the Kingdom, where Rache-hating militants might keep taking shots at him.

"I was in your kitchen earlier. It's nice."

"You snuck into my house again? We really must discuss boundaries and personal space."

"I intended to wait out here, but you're a celebrity now. Reporters sneaked into your back yard while I was here and took pictures of the premises. I thought about ruthlessly slaying them for you, but since I've decided to retire from my criminal career, that seemed inappropriate."

"I'm relieved that I didn't come out to find the patio full of mutilated bodies."

"I thought that might be the case. I also brought a gift." He gestured toward the door.

"Is it coffee?"

"It is. From a small, organic, family-run plantation on the Southern Continent that grows their beans at precisely the ideal altitude for coffee. I did some research."

"I'm impressed. And willing to allow you to sneak into my house whenever you bring such high-quality gifts."

"You're too kind."

Kim clasped his hand and led him inside for their date.

THE END

Printed in Great Britain
by Amazon